CIRCLE
OF BONES

CIRCLE
B OF ONES

A CARIBBEAN THRILLER

CHRISTINE
KLING

f THOMAS & MERCER

Text copyright © 2013 Christine Kling

Published by Thomas & Mercer

PO Box 400818
Las Vegas, NV 89140

ISBN-13: 9781611097856
ISBN-10: 1611097851
Library of Congress Control Number: 2012948063

This one is for my mother,

the ghost I talk to most.

The tale is different if even a single breath
Escapes to tell it

from "The Shipwreck"
by W.S. Merwin *(1956)*

Where secrecy or mystery begins,
vice or roguery is not far off.

Samuel Johnson *(1709–1784)*

Map of Central Caribbean Islands
of Guadeloupe and Dominica

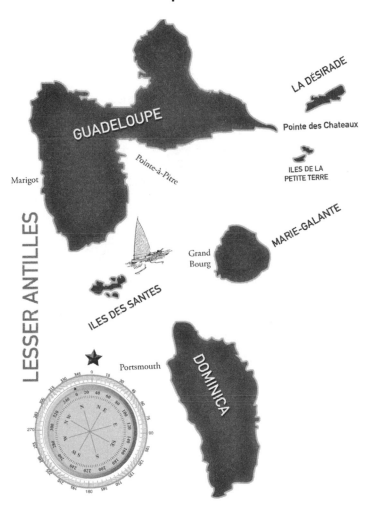

LA DÉSIRADE

GUADELOUPE

Pointe des Chateaux

Pointe-à-Pitre

ILES DE LA
PETITE TERRE

Marigot

MARIE-GALANTE

Grand
Bourg

LESSER ANTILLES

ILES DES SANTES

Portsmouth

DOMINICA

PROLOGUE

Cherbourg, France

November 19, 2008

The man lingered in the shadows at the mouth of the dark alley across the street. From her seat inside the window, Riley blew at the steam rising off her café au lait and watched him through the gray veil of rain that poured off the café's awning. He rocked, shifting his weight from one foot to the other. Rain dribbled from the baseball cap jutting out from under the hood of his black slicker. She couldn't see his face, but she looked down anyway. She knew it in her gut. He was watching her.

Her chest got that dizzy, hollow feeling as her heart rate climbed. She concentrated on slowing her breathing as she had been trained to do. She tried to sip her coffee with nonchalance but grimaced at the taste of it. Either the French had forgotten how to make coffee, or her mouth was dry from nerves. She'd thought she was over all this.

When she glanced up again, the man had disappeared. Riley brushed the hair back from her eyes and pressed her nose to the window. She checked the street in both directions, her breath fogging the glass. There was no sign of him. Closing her eyes, she rested her hot forehead against the cool glass. She was getting as bad as Cole. Perhaps paranoia was contagious, she thought, and that made her sit back in her chair and shake her head.

God, how she missed him. After all these months, she thought of him a dozen times each day. Anything could bring him to mind. Even the steady morning rain outside the café window reminded her of the falling ash. Down in the islands, it had covered every-thing—been impossible to wash away. It had blanketed her boat's decks, clogged her nostrils, turned her sails gray.

But that was more than six months ago. Now she was back in France, in Normandy, watching as another shower battered the awning in front of the café where she sipped from a soup-sized bowl of café au lait, thinking of all the dead—and tasting ash.

Tossing some euros onto the table, she abandoned her coffee and pushed back her chair. She pulled on her yellow foul weather jacket, but when she stepped out from under the awning, the rain had stopped. She shoved her hood back and glanced up at the gray sky. A last fat raindrop caught her in the eye. As she brushed the back of her hand across her wet cheek, she squared her shoulders and quickened her pace down the sidewalk. Not today. No tears.

From behind, someone grabbed her arm. Her fists flew up as she spun around, yanking her arm free from the grip of that hard hand. The man in the black slicker and ball cap stood behind her. He grunted and held a cardboard sign in front of his chest. Words scrawled in black marker stated that he was both deaf and dumb, a veteran of *la guerre l'Indochine*.

She lowered her hands and examined him, the adrenaline again making her breathe too fast. His face was partially covered by wraparound sunglasses. Was he blind as well? Scraggly whiskers framed his yellow teeth, and beneath his slicker, she saw layers of torn and dirty clothes. He bent down and picked up a crutch; his left leg was wrapped in bandages. Long strands of wet gray hair trailed out from under his cap. Riley inhaled a whiff of day-old garbage, and she saw the look of disgust on her own face reflected in his large mirrored lenses. He reached out a grimy hand, offering her one of several small brown paper bags of roasted chestnuts.

He *had* been watching her—but only because she was a tourist, a likely mark.

She swallowed the sour taste in her throat and dug into her bag. He was a soldier. Or had been. Like her. She placed a ten-euro note in his palm, and his fingers closed around hers.

All the nerve endings in her fingers lit up as his hot flesh squeezed her hand tight. Her heart ricocheted in her chest as she tried to pull free. What was going on with her? The Marine Corps had trained her not to react, to be a stone-faced sentry, and she'd been damn good at it.

Then he pulled her fingers open and started to place the brown bag in her hand. She yanked her hand free. Waving off the bag, she backed away. Not certain if he could see her, she mumbled, "*Non, non.*"

She turned and started walking.

The man hobbled after her grunting and shaking the brown paper so hard, she heard the sound of the nuts clicking together. She would have to take the bag to make him leave her alone.

She stopped. "*Merci,*" she said as she stuffed the paper bag into the pocket of her rain jacket, careful not to touch him again. Then, she turned again and marched down the street, not knowing where she was going, but only that she had to get away.

When she'd put enough distance between herself and the old man, she stopped and leaned against the wet stones of a small church. What was that about? Her reaction hadn't been fright—but what was it?

Thinking about the past was making her jittery. But that was why she was here. Riley pulled out the small map the hotel concierge had given her. She found her way to the yacht basin, circled the marina to the outer jetty.

It was important to arrive first. She didn't know what she'd say to him, but she wanted to have a chance to see the meeting place and to think.

From the sea, the *Surcouf* memorial was designed to look like a submarine's periscope. The large bronze plaque on the face of the monument had weathered so green from battling years of sea spray, it was difficult to read. Riley ran her fingers over the names of the dead. *Speak to me.* She listened for their voices on the gusting North Atlantic wind but heard nothing aside from the *whoosh* of the waves breaking on the jetty and the cries of the gulls swooping behind a fishing boat chugging out to sea. Just because her brother, Michael, spoke to her on occasion, it didn't mean all the dead would.

So many names. There were one hundred and thirty of them. LAMOREAUX—CLAIRMONT—MICHAUT—GOHIN, and on and on, including the three British Royal Navy men: MCKAY—MULLINS—WOOLSEY. Column after column like the stark white crosses in a military cemetery. But each name had once been a living, breathing man—a son, a brother, a father.

The blustery wind whipped her cotton skirt against her legs, and she tried in vain to keep the stray wisps of hair from blowing into her mouth as she read aloud:

Aux morts
du
Sous-marin Surcouf
Le Surcouf construit et lancé a Cherbourg le 18 octobre, 1929
Disparu en mer le 18 fevrier, 1942 sous le
commandement du Capitaine Alain Lamoreaux

The big boat had fled France before the Nazi occupation, assisted Allied convoys in the Atlantic, and finally, left Bermuda bound for Panama just weeks after Pearl Harbor. But she never arrived.

Disparu. But what disappears *can* sometimes be found. Cole and Theo had proved that. And she'd played a part in it, too. Riley remembered watching the clear, green water and the odd, colorless fish on the small video screen, feeling that gun pressed to her ribs in the eerie stillness of *Shadow Chaser*'s wheelhouse. They'd crowded around the monitor while Theo steered the remotely operated vehicle carrying its camera into the coral-encrusted hold.

Closing her eyes, she tried to banish the images that replayed in her memory like some kind of Mobius filmstrip. She felt her face crumpling, but she fought it off, because damn it all, it still hurt too much to see that last image of Cole Thatcher, his mouth grinning impossibly around his scuba regulator, his eyes seeming to look right into hers through the face mask, lens, camera, cable.

Like the screen they had been watching that day, she tried to make her mind go blank. Now you see him, now you don't. *Disparu en mer.*

She swallowed hard. No tears.

What disappears cannot always be found. Ashes to ashes.

After everything that had happened these past six months, only a few words had drawn her back here to France. She came because this was the birthplace of the submarine that had once been Cole's love, his passion. Riley came to the memorial because she was tired of looking back over her shoulder all the time. She checked her watch for the hundredth time. But most of all, she thought as she gazed back down the pier, she had come to this sea-swept jetty because it was the perfect place for a reunion.

CHAPTER ONE

Royal Naval Dockyard
Ireland Island, Bermuda

February 12, 1942

Lieutenant Gerald Woolsey shuffled down the quay, his head bent into the chill wind, his thick arms hugging the wooden crate to his chest as if in a passionate embrace. He had no desire to find out what might happen if he dropped the thing—he was no expert with explosives. Likely wind up nothing more than a red stain, and while that was happening to the rest of his countrymen with a gruesome regularity, he was determined to survive this war. His kind generally did.

He stopped and hiked the crate up, lifting the weight of it with his thigh, trying to improve his grip on the rough wood planks.

He was counting on the fact that the French sentries aboard the submarine had been doing a lousy job ever since he and the other two Brits, McKay and Mullins, had come aboard. His fellow Brits were a telegraphist and signalman, and Woolsey was the BNLO, British navy liaison officer, assigned to serve aboard the Free French sub because God knows, you couldn't exactly trust the Frogs with the Allied naval codebooks these days, not even these

7

Free French sailors who claimed allegiance to de Gaulle instead of Admiral Darlan. Free French or not, this crew didn't like the English one bit. But then, the feeling was mutual.

Most of the time, when he boarded the sub, the sentry, if there was one, merely gave him that Gallic look of disdain they all managed so well.

As he closed in on the massive boat, Woolsey thought again that she looked a good bit better from afar than she did on closer inspection. Her tall conning tower and topsides were painted the same color as the low, threatening sky, but her bulbous forward gun turret and aft hangar made her appear almost comical—as if she sported some sort of sausage with a tumor. The French had named her *Surcouf*—after an eighteenth-century privateer, Robert Surcouf. There were those who referred to her as the "Pride of the French Navy," but they tended to be either Frogs or politicians. They didn't know that at 361 feet and 3,250 tons, she was the biggest white elephant on the sea.

When they'd assigned him to this boat, his superiors had assured him *Surcouf* was the first of a new class of radically different submarines, an underwater cruiser with her twin eight-inch guns in that waterproof turret, antiaircraft cannons, machine guns, twelve torpedo tubes, and a hangar with her own reconnaissance seaplane. But the truth was, she'd been plagued with bloody French design flaws from the first—even before he came aboard. Everything from her electric motors with faulty armatures to the batteries, spilling sulfuric acid and nearly poisoning all the crew, to the hydroplanes that struggled to keep her from rolling when she dove—all had kept this sub returning to shipyards from Portsmouth to Halifax. Though first launched in 1929, she had yet to fire her guns in battle, and the Allies were bloody tired of paying the tab to keep her afloat. Given the number of ships lost to the U-boats the last couple of months, who'd notice one more?

As he approached the dark hull, Woolsey nodded to the sentry who, for the first time he could remember, was standing at the base of the gangplank. He tried to will the hands that gripped the crate to look relaxed, yet still hold tight. *Just a box of radio equipment,* he had told the captain before he left that morning on the launch to Hamilton to go to pick it up. A radio with new frequencies the Germans weren't onto yet. He'd tried to sound as if he knew what he was talking about, all the while being vague enough not to arouse suspicion.

"So long as you are back aboard by this afternoon," Captain Lamoreaux had told him. They were to sail for Panama on the tide that evening. So he'd promised to shake a leg to make it back to the boat in time. Woolsey smiled at the thought. The captain wanted to make certain he returned to the boat. The fool.

The sentry's jersey was wrinkled and stained with what looked like coffee, and the red pompom on his cap hung loose by a thread. A cigarette dangled from a corner of the man's mouth. He glanced at the crate Woolsey carried, but he made no move either to question him or to offer assistance.

What was the point of keeping a sentry if the bloke was too lazy to even have a look at a crate of equipment coming aboard? Blithering idiots, the French. They deserved what was coming.

Once on board, Woolsey made his way through the hangar and down one deck to the signal room. He was surprised to discover both the companionways and the radio room were empty. He encountered only one man, who opened a door a crack, then clanged the door shut. The giant sub seemed strangely quiet apart from the constant hum of her generators and fans, and Woolsey wondered briefly what was going on. Whatever was afoot, Woolsey planned to be gone before he'd have to worry about it. He stepped over the coaming into the cramped compartment, set the crate on the floor, and slid the metal door closed behind him.

He leaned against the door for a moment. God, he'd be glad to get away from this stink. Sweat, those damned French cigarettes, and the ever-present smell of diesel fuel combined in a pervasive stench he could no longer wash out of his clothes.

Taking his sailor's rigging knife from his pocket, he knelt on the deck next to the crate and pried up first one of the wooden slats, then another. The device looked just as lethal as they had told him it would—all tubes and wires on the side of a black box. Carefully, he lifted out the timing pencil detonator and crushed the copper end under the heel of his boot as instructed. This, they'd told him, would release the cupric acid that would then eat through the wire holding back the striker.

"You'll want to get out of there fast as you can," the chap had said when he showed him how to arm it. "We design them to go off in twenty-four hours, but explosives are funny, ya know? They sometimes have a mind of their own."

Woolsey hadn't said so aloud, but he didn't see how blowing oneself to bloody bits could be considered funny.

Twenty-four hours. He consulted his wristwatch. It was half past four. Assuming they did sail in two hours as the captain had promised, that would still leave plenty of time for the massive sub to get well away from the island and other prying eyes. She would be out where they measured the depth in miles instead of fathoms when she disappeared.

Without him. Woolsey had no intention of being aboard when *Surcouf* took off on her final voyage.

He tucked everything back in place, not wanting to touch it now any more than he had to. Once he replaced the staves, the crate looked untouched. He stood and folded the blade back into his knife, noticing his palms were wet with sweat. The only one among the French crew who ever ventured in here now was Henri Michaut, their signalman and interpreter, a wiry, scrappy little chap from Normandy. Mullins had nicknamed the man Kewpie because he had a strawberry birthmark on his right cheek in the shape of a heart. Woolsey left a note for Michaut and the two Brits warning them not to touch the crate, that it was fragile radio equipment.

He glanced at the clock on the bulkhead and resisted the urge to grab his gear and race off the boat. If he did, they might not leave port, they might stay to search for him. He needed to get the locked and lead-sealed mailbag from the strongbox at his feet and then head up to the bridge to show the captain the decoded message from London detailing his reassignment. He had prepared it himself the evening before. He'd leave the codebooks behind. They could go down with the boat. But the man who had passed him the mailbag from the Canadian frigate two days out of Bermuda had told him the documents inside that bag had to get to the United States as soon as possible. He would deliver them to New Haven, personally, as promised.

He had just started to dial the combination to the strongbox when he heard footsteps and shouting outside in the companionway. The door flew open, and Ensign Gohin, a huge Olympic-weight-lifter type, filled the doorway and waved a pistol in the air.

"Allons, depeche-toi, Anglais."

"What the bloody hell?"

Henri Michaut squeezed his little ferret-like face into the doorframe. He spoke the best English of any of the crew. Whenever he was excited, the birthmark on his cheek darkened, and at the moment, it almost pulsed with color. "Lieutenant Woolsey, you must come with us."

"What the devil's going on, Michaut?"

Gohin began babbling in French. He grabbed Woolsey's arm, jamming the gun against his ribs.

"Lieutenant, please," Michaut said. "Do as he says."

The beefy ensign yanked Woolsey out the door and marched him down the narrow passage, barking what Woolsey gathered were insults aimed at his English parentage. One huge hand gripped his shoulder, the other held the gun hard against his side.

Through the deck, Woolsey felt the throb of the sub's twin Sulzer diesels revving up. It was too early, damn it. The captain had said evening—they couldn't be leaving yet.

He struggled against the ensign's iron grip and was rewarded with a stunning blow to the side of his head. Blood filled his right eye, nearly blinding him as he staggered against the bulkhead. Gohin pulled him forward.

Michaut said something to the bigger man. Woolsey sensed the young signalman was arguing on his behalf. When Ensign Gohin replied, it was with words all seamen understood.

He told him to go to hell.

At the sub's massive cargo hold, Gohin stopped and handed Michaut the captain's key ring. Michaut unlocked the padlock and chain that secured the watertight door, and Woolsey caught the frightened look in the young man's eyes. Once Gohin turned the wheel and released the seal, the door swung inward. Woolsey planted his feet and struggled to wrench his arm away from the big man. His mind was focused on the device he'd left hidden in the signal room. This could not be happening to him.

"Stop! I've got orders to get off this ship! Back in the signal room. Wait! You've got to get me off this ship. I'm not to sail!"

The opening to the cargo hold yawned like the mouth of a black adder, and the air wafting out smelled of their goddamn rotting cheese.

"Allez!" Gohin shoved him hard into the darkness.

"No!" Woolsey cried out, but he was falling into the black as the steel door slammed shut.

CHAPTER TWO

The island of Guadeloupe

March 25, 2008

Cole Thatcher steered his Boston Whaler dinghy through what passed for surf on the leeward side of the island, cutting his engine and lifting the outboard just before the bow nosed onto the black volcanic sand. He slid over the side and grabbed the line on the bow, then dragged the boat up the beach away from the tug of the waves.

The small, isolated cove was familiar to him. He had been diving a search grid in the area for over two months now. After he peeled off his wet suit and booties, he stood still, leaning his leg against the bow of the boat, feeling the warmth of the late morning sun erase the cold from his naked body. The Caribbean waters were warm enough at the surface, but at the depths where he'd been diving, the chill reached right through the neoprene suit to his bones.

He closed his eyes. From habit, his hand clutched at the gold coin hanging from a chain round his neck, his thumb rubbing over the raised image. It was crazy diving alone, and he knew it, but he'd had to let the rest of the crew go. It was down to just him and Theo, and though his first mate was born down here in the Caribbean, he barely knew how to swim.

Things weren't exactly turning out the way he'd dreamed they would. As a kid, Cole loved watching reruns of those old TV shows like *Adventures in Paradise* and *Sea Hunt*. He thought he'd grow up to be just like Mike Nelson, but here he was feeling more like Gilligan. This three-hour cruise had turned into months of fruitless searching, and after signing their checks over a year ago, his investors were beginning to demand results.

All the supposed experts in World War II maritime archeology claimed the French submarine *Surcouf* lay somewhere on the seafloor outside Panama, where she sank after a collision with the freighter *Thompson Lykes* on February 18, 1942.

But Cole knew otherwise. He just had to prove it. And he was certain after all these months, he had to be close. But *they* knew it, too.

Not the academics or his investors. He'd fled the world of academia. But his doctorate and the time he'd spent working on the Ocracoke Shipwreck Survey had brought in most of the investors when he started his company, Full Fathom Five Maritime Exploration. His credentials convinced them he was legit and not some paranoid, crackpot treasure hunter. He'd assured them the old man's journals were the equivalent of a treasure map that would lead them straight to the wreck.

But today, he'd hit a dry hole. Again. Just as he had every day here in Guadeloupe for the last two months.

His investors weren't the only ones waiting for news of the sub's discovery though. Cole knew there were poachers out there. The cutthroat scumbags waited, just over the horizon, letting guys like him do all the research and discovery work, and then they'd swoop in at the last minute, guns blazing, to steal the find out from under him. Modern-day pirates. It was the rumors of gold that drew them out of their dark little hidey-holes. He'd dodged a pair of them up in North Carolina, but they were still out there somewhere—he could feel them closing in like a school of sharks—and he wasn't about to let them near his wreck.

And if it wasn't the poachers? Then God help him. Pirates he could deal with, but he wasn't ready to deal with *them* yet. He didn't even know who *they* were—but he was certain they knew of him. OK, it wasn't as if he'd seen black helicopters following him around—he wasn't *that* crazy—but he'd caught glimpses of them even if nobody else believed him. The strangers whose gazes lingered just a little too long in his direction. *They* were watching him—had been ever since his father's death. Of course, back then if they'd thought the old man's diaries contained any real intel, the volumes never would have made it to his hands.

He'd heard about what it was like the day they'd found his father's body, how the local Brit constabulary had kept the press and the old man's friends at the end of the lane while a fleet of unmarked black sedans had driven in and stayed for hours. He supposed the only reason the cleaners hadn't taken the journals along with the rest of his father's notes was because they seemed innocuous enough, personal memoirs and unintelligible rants kept only for the benefit of a distant American son the old man never really knew.

They should have known better.

After several minutes, the tropical sun had done its work, and his naked skin began to feel the tingling heat of dried salt. Stretching his arms wide, he opened his eyes and followed the trickle of water that crossed the black sand from deep in the shade of the trees. A small stream flowed down the steep ravine into a pool just back from the beach. The water originated as rainfall up on the cloud-shrouded sides of the volcano, La Soufrière, and by the time it fell into the deep pool here, it was still cold as the depths where he'd been diving. But the water was fresh, and that was why he'd taken to stopping here for a cool, revitalizing rinse after every dive.

Broad-leafed taro plants and lacy palm fronds sprouted from the black rocks that ringed the pool. Tall, old-growth trees shaded the glen, and the water gurgled over a small waterfall on the far side, ruffling the surface of the dark pool. On the leeward coasts of the Caribbean islands, the vegetation grew lush deep in the valleys where the streams flowed, while drier cactus and bush struggled for a foothold high on the sides of the windswept cliffs.

Cole waded in until the icy water was at his knees. He paused, then lifted the gold chain over his head and squinted as he examined the coin for the thousandth time.

"What is the key?" he asked aloud. He turned the coin over, then rubbed his thumb over the surface. With a long sigh, he placed the medallion on a smooth rock that bordered the pool. He lowered his body into the water and shivered. The depth was no more than four feet, so he slid his legs out toward the center and dipped his head back until the cold water covered his face. The noise from the waterfall sounded different underwater, louder and more immediate. Floating on his back, he watched the branches high up in the canopy where little banana quit birds flitted among the still leaves. He closed his eyes, listening to the water roaring ever louder, wondering if he had enough of his father in him to see this thing through.

Cole bobbed his head back to the surface and rested his bare feet on the soft mud bottom. He shook the water out of his ears. That was no longer just the waterfall he'd been hearing. He stood up, the water streaming off his skin, and he looked over the black sand beach to the sea. A gray inflatable dinghy had rounded the point from the north, and it was already halfway across the cove heading for the beach at top speed.

"Damn!" Cole ducked down into a squat, hoping they had not spotted him.

The noise of the outboard engine wound down and then stopped. He knew the boat was gliding in for a landing. Barely lifting his head, he took another look. The dinghy slid to a stop on the sand, and a man leaped out. A second, bigger man sat on a pontoon as the first guy dragged the rubber boat up the sand. They were wearing full-body wet suits complete with black hoods. Both were carrying spear guns.

Cole dropped back into the water, then looked around at the volcanic rock jutting out from the sides of the ravine. Beyond, he could see little but the green of the brush. He heard their muffled voices now. They saw his boat. They would know he was close by. There was nothing for it but to run.

He had both feet out of the water before he remembered the chain and coin. He stopped so abruptly, he lost his footing on the algae-covered rock and fell back into the water. The sound of the splash seemed to echo off the canyon walls. He stood, ran his hand over his face, rubbing the water from his eyes, and in one smooth movement, he scooped the chain up, slid it over his head, and leaped out of the pool.

The sharp rock cut into the soles of his feet, and the ferns and vines whipped at his bare legs. He couldn't allow any of that to slow him down. He ran up a narrow animal path, but that route stopped at a huge boulder. He headed straight up the crumbling dirt wall, then dodged around the scattered prickly fruit of a soursop tree. In places, the side of the ravine was nearly vertical, but he grabbed at roots and branches to pull himself up. Crabbing his way across ledges and over rock outcroppings, he tried to keep under the tree canopy, seeking some sort of camouflage. His scrambling feet let loose a deluge of tumbling stones and dirt that would act like an arrow to point out his route to the men following him. His only hope, he thought as he heard their voices in the glen below, was that he had a good head start.

The higher he went, the more arid the climate grew, and the ferns turned to thorny century plants, easy enough to avoid but providing little cover. He'd never felt more exposed. The dry, sandy soil was easier on his shredded feet, but oddly enough, after the first few steps, he felt no pain.

He couldn't look back. That would slow him down too much. But he could not stop thinking about the men below him with their metal spears and the fact that his most tender parts were out in the open, right above their heads, literally daring them to take a shot.

"Shit!" He'd reached over a large rock to get a good handhold, and his hand had come down on a bed of cactus unseen behind the stone. He held his palm up and saw it was covered in a pale blond fur of tiny needles.

"There!" he heard a shout below him.

Using the side of his hand, cradling the injured palm, he pulled himself up over a dirt ledge and rolled. He sprang to his feet and saw he had come to a flat and narrow plateau on the top of a razor-back. He assumed he would start the climb down the other side, but when he ran to the far edge, he found a precipice falling straight down to the dark sea. The water stretched unruffled to the distant horizon marred only by the white sail of a single boat.

Cole took several steps back from the edge, and from behind him came the huffing and chuffing of at least one pursuer. The breathing sounded close. The cliff dropped straight down, was even undercut by centuries of storms. The water below was inky blue, not the pale turquoise of the shallows.

He made his decision and started running back the way he had come. The black-hooded man widened his eyes when he crested the ridge and saw a naked man running straight at him, flailing his arms in the air, and whooping like a Hollywood Indian. The hooded man scrambled to his feet and began to lift his spear gun at the very moment Cole reversed direction.

Cole Thatcher saw a metal spear fly past his right shoulder just as he took a running leap off the cliff and into the air.

CHAPTER THREE

At sea off Guadeloupe

March 25, 2008

Seated on the cabin top, in the shade of the mainsail, Riley cradled the sextant in her left hand, recorded the numbers off the dial into her logbook, then leaned back out of the shadow. She lifted her face to the sun and closed her eyes. The corners of her mouth drew up in a small smile.

Sighing, she sat up straight and glanced down at the instrument. It was secured to a small tether she wore around her neck. She considered celestial navigation a painful necessity. Like her father's nursing home insurance, it was something you hoped never to use, but if you needed it, you'd be glad you had it. Sure, she had GPS, but on days like this one, when the wind was light and the water was flat in the lee of the island, she dragged out the sextant to get in a little practice. She'd learned that in the service. Drill, drill, drill.

She checked her watch, and then ducked under the sail to squint up at the sun again. Her boat was drifting off the southwest coast of the island of Guadeloupe, and she was waiting for the morning sun to rise high enough—and for her boat to sail far enough south—so she could get a more accurate shot with her sextant. She swiveled her head around the horizon, checking for boat traffic. Earlier that morning, she had sailed past an empty Boston Whaler flying the red-and-white diver-down flag, but other than one sportfishing boat anchored close to the island, she now had the sea to herself.

Her father, Richard Riley, was the one who had taught her celestial navigation back when he had been posted to the US Embassy in Barbados. She was ten and her brother, Michael, a year and a half older. The Bajan kids there had been cruel, teasing her older brother about his small stature and the thick lenses that magnified his blue eyes like the bulging eyes of a grouper. Their father, who always talked of his youth sailing out at the Cape, had bought a Bequia boat there, the first of a long line of boats named *Bonefish*. She and Mikey ran home every day, both to enjoy the lively little boat and to escape the taunts of the street. In time, her father taught her to sail the boat alone—and to use the sextant.

"Those were the good years, eh, bro?" she said aloud and winked at the light breeze passing under the mainsail. "Captain Maggie and first mate Mikey, the twin terrors of the Caribbean."

That was one of the best things about sailing single-handed—there was nobody around to hear her when she spoke to her dead brother's ghost.

God, she was glad to be out here. Alone. Away from the stench of exhaust that flooded in their DC townhouse windows and the pissy smell of her father's Depends. His doctors said dementia wasn't deadly, and he could last another ten years, though it had gotten to the point where he didn't recognize her most of the time. A better daughter perhaps would have stayed and wiped his ass every day whether he recognized her or not. She couldn't. Not after what had happened to her brother. If her father hadn't forced Michael to go to Yale, her older brother would be alive today. Every time she looked at her father, the pain of losing Michael hit her all over again. Besides, Mrs. Wright was taking good care of him, and he wouldn't miss a daughter he didn't even recognize.

From inside the boat's cabin, her computer chimed to signal an incoming e-mail. "Shit," she said aloud, then reminded herself of her resolution to stop swearing. The civilian world didn't look favorably at a woman who could swear like a sailor—even if she was one.

With her satellite hookup, she'd been able to send and receive e-mail throughout most of the islands. It wasn't cheap, but her work depended on it. A mug with the remains of her morning coffee stood next to her MacBook laptop, obscuring her view of the computer screen. She assumed the e-mail was from the Mercury Security Group, her employers back in DC. They were sending her to design a system of cameras and alarms for a perfume factory on the island of Dominica. She had an appointment there next week.

And if she didn't finish with this celestial practice and get moving, she wouldn't make it to Pointe-à-Pitre tonight. She'd fall behind on her itinerary and miss her Monday appointment, or worse yet, miss her "date" tomorrow night—the one several years overdue. As important as the work was, the real reason she was headed to Guadeloupe's capital city was to meet up with the Ivy League son of a bitch who had walked out of her life down in Lima. Call it crazy, or call it closure. She wasn't sure, but she had agreed to meet him. When the e-mail had come from out of the blue after more than two years of silence, she had not hesitated. She wanted some answers.

Riley lay back on the cabin top and looked up at her clean white sail curving against a sky so blue, the beauty of it made her dizzy.

She didn't feel like talking to anyone or even reading her e-mail at the moment. Life was simpler out here. The overnight sail across the channel from Antigua had been spectacular, with a moon just past full lighting the island of Montserrat, the dome of that island's very active Soufrière Hills Volcano trailing wisps of white smoke in the strong trade winds, and *Bonefish* charging along at seven knots under a reefed main and jib. She sighed, closed her burning eyes, and felt the heat of the morning sun wrap around her like a soft blanket.

* * *

Flames consumed the bodies that danced and writhed in front of her while the foul smoke filled her nostrils and burned her lungs. Hot, so hot. She could hear their cries, see their mouths, great yawning holes of black as the burning skin of their faces curled off the bone and the ashes floated to the ground. She flung her arms out, reaching, yet she could not touch their flames. She tried to run forward to help them, but it was as though she was on a treadmill floor. She could make no progress. Running flat out, screaming through her parched throat, she never moved one inch closer to the dying men.

Riley felt something touch her shoulder, and her eyes snapped open. She gasped and jerked up into a sitting position. She shook her head, trying to clear away the nausea and calm her hammering heart.

She had reached one man that day. Danny Hutchinson. Her fellow prankster, the guy she'd watched *Blazing Saddles* with more than a dozen times, laughing so hard she'd almost peed in her pants. Hutch had looked like a human torch when she ran into the entry of the burning house, but he was still alive. She threw her damp towel over his head and hoisted him over her shoulder in a fireman's carry.

Now, she touched the same shoulder, running her fingertips over the tender ridges of the scar. When she'd lowered Hutch to the grass in front of the house, his eyes stared without blinking. The fire had burned through her shirt, melting both his flesh and hers.

That was Lima, Peru. She had been posted for nearly a year as an MSG—Marine Security Guard—at the US Embassy, where she had fallen for the handsome ex-pat Yalie only to learn later that he was a spook and their affair was strictly forbidden. By the time he told her his real identity, though, no rules could have kept them apart. She had never opened her heart and her life to a man like that before.

After the bombing at the Marine House, she'd spent weeks at Bethesda in the burn unit waiting for the call that never came. She'd played it all over and over in her head. When they discharged her from both the hospital and the Corps, she told herself that she had been a fool to think he'd loved her. He had used her, and to what extent she still wasn't sure. It had been over two years since the bombing, and tomorrow she intended to get the answers she hoped would make these dreams go away.

She checked the horizon for boat traffic. Nothing. She'd dozed off for—she checked her watch—shit! Nearly an hour. Her fingers went to the spot just past her scars where she had felt or dreamed her brother's touch. He was always careful not to hurt her.

"Thanks, Mikey."

It had been weeks since she'd last dreamed of the fire. The sailing had been so good for that—much better than her life back in DC—but no matter how many miles she put between herself and that life, the flames followed her.

Riley raised her arms over her head and stretched her aching muscles. Thank goodness Mikey was always there to look after her.

She lifted the sextant and placed the 6x scope to her eye again. The sea was unusually flat. Facing southwest, she swung the instrument around, looking for the sun. Just when she found the glowing orb and started to slide the arc to bring it down to the horizon, she was startled by something waving from the surface of the sea.

Blinking, she lowered the instrument and squinted against the brilliant sunlight dappling the surface. No doubt about it, there was a guy in the water out there about a quarter mile off, waving his arms at her. She glanced over her shoulder at the island. She was close in but still at least three miles off shore. What the devil was he doing swimming out here?

CHAPTER FOUR

New Haven

April 16, 1992

"Skull and Bones, accept or reject?"

Diggory Priest nearly spilled his café latte all over his copy of *Thus Spoke Zarathustra*. A hand gripped his shoulder as the deep voice spoke behind him. He attempted to squash the flinch he always felt when a stranger touched him. Though he had been expecting them, he hadn't even heard them enter his room. He didn't want to look rattled—didn't know if he should turn and look at them, or continue facing forward, staring at the stars and stripes on the Bush/Quayle poster he'd hung on the wall above the desk.

"Accept," he said.

The word had barely cleared his lips when a paper packet landed on his textbook, and then, although he could not see them, he *felt* they were gone.

Dig reached for the packet and closed his eyes for a moment. He'd waited three years for this. He exhaled, then opened his eyes. The folded paper was heavy, red, and wrapped with a black silk ribbon. He ran his fingers over the smooth black silk. It felt rich.

When he turned it over, he saw the seal pressed into black wax: a skull, two crossed bones, and the number 322.

He touched the insignia. Most of them got here by birthright, but his father had denied him that, denied even that he was his son. And now he had proven to the old pater that he didn't need him. He'd earned this all on his own.

The words inside were written in black ink, the letters formed like those on an ancient parchment.

This evening, at the hour of VIII, go forth wearing neither metal, nor sulfur, nor glass. Look neither to the right nor to the left. Pass through the sacred Pillars of Hercules and approach the Temple. Knock thrice upon the sacred portals. Remember well, but keep silent, concerning what you have read here.

The streetlights were on, but few stars had appeared when Diggory turned off Chapel and onto High Street. He looked up at the ominous stone pillars on each side of the gate that led to the Old Campus and the Tomb. The dark clouds massing in the sky behind Harkness Tower were still tinged with an eerie sanguine glow, and a cool wind had come up from the river. In spite of the dust and leaves dancing in the gusts, the evening was pleasant. Unusual for that hour, there was not a soul to be seen on the street.

The blue blazer had seemed the right choice back in his rooms, but now on this spring evening, he was sweating. Perhaps he was overdressed. They would notice. They would notice everything about him on this night.

Diggory approached the steps leading to the massive wooden doors, wondering if he was being watched. He pounded three times with his fist.

The door opened a crack, but it was too dark inside to make out who was there. He wasn't sure if he was supposed to say anything, so he raised the red paper invitation to the crack.

A deep voice spoke from inside. "Neophyte Priest?"

He started to answer, but a thick arm reached out and pulled him through the half-opened door. Someone jammed a black cloth hood over his head before he had a chance to see anything in the darkened room. Each of his arms was seized from behind, and he stifled the urge to squirm out of their iron grip. It was hot inside the room, hotter yet under the hood, and he heard heavy breathing from all directions. He couldn't guess how many of them were there.

The crowd propelled him forward, pulling at him from both sides, trying to make him lose his balance. When his feet got crossed, they held him up and dragged him through various rooms of the house. Other hands were grabbing at his arms and his shoulders, pressing into his ribs, and when his hands brushed against their bodies, he felt slick, sweaty skin. He gritted his teeth and squeezed his eyes shut, trying to maintain control, trying not to demand they stop touching him.

At last, they stood still. It grew silent around him.

Then from far ahead in another room, he heard a deep voice call out, "Who is it?"

All around him a wave of voices shouted, "Neophyte Priest!"

They shoved him forward, and the arms supporting him vanished. He nearly stumbled. Someone yanked off the hood.

Diggory blinked to clear the sweat from his eyes. He was standing in front of a table in a darkened room lit only by candles and a fire in an enormous fireplace. On the table was a parchment scroll, and behind it stood a man in a robe wearing a grotesque Halloween mask of the face from the Edvard Munch painting *The Scream*.

As Priest turned his head to take in the room, he saw others dressed in skeleton costumes with jeering masks. To his right was a man seated in a throne-like chair and dressed as the pope. On the far side of the room was another in the costume of a Spanish knight. Behind him, standing in the doorway through which he had come, were four huge fellows dressed only in jock straps, high-top sneakers, and their skeleton masks. The sweat on their skin glinted in the candlelight. In all, there must have been twenty of them in the room, and every one of them wore a mask. Except him.

Diggory bowed his head, feigning deference. He saw on the floor between himself and the table was an inlay of mosaic tiles depicting the infamous 322.

Out of the silence, their voices erupted. "Read it. Read it. Read it!" they shouted.

He took a step forward and looked down at the parchment on the table. Before his eyes could focus on the writing in the dim light, they began shouting again.

"He can't. He can't. He can't!"

Then a short character dressed as a devil ran into the room cackling like a deranged monkey. He danced around Diggory, beating him with the forked tail of his costume. At first, Diggory raised his arms to fend off the blows. The others were shouting and waving noisemakers, which sparked in the near darkness when they spun them round and round. The noise was just as painful as the whipping, but he lowered his arms and stood straight, his eyes focused on the man behind the table, the man in the robe. Diggory knew this part of the ritual. They called him Uncle Toby.

The eyes staring out through the mask were so dark they looked black in the candlelight. The holes in the plastic were large enough he could see pouches of pinkish skin sagging beneath the eye sockets. While the noise swirled around them, their gazes remained locked, even when the older man's right eye flashed white as the eyeball wandered off looking at someone on the far side of the room. The left eye continued to stare fixedly into Diggory's eyes, questioning him, watching to see if he was worthy.

The robed man reached behind himself, then raised a cup shaped like a human skull with the cranium sawed off. A dark-red liquid sloshed onto the table.

He looked from the cup to the older man's face, and while the wandering eye still showed only white, the man's good eye shone with the challenge. He did not speak a word aloud, but Diggory thought he could hear the old man's thoughts.

Bastard, he seemed to say. *Who let you in among the chosen ones?*

Diggory took the cup from the man's hands. He wasn't about to let some old man stop him now. Not after all he had been through to get into this place. Better not to think, just get it over with. He tipped the cup up and drained it in one swift move, the flat metallic taste causing his throat to close. The cup clattered to the table, and he forced the liquid back down his throat.

He stared back at the black eye. *There, old man, you see? A barbarian, no more. I'm one of you now.*

The skin around both the good eye and the wandering eye crinkled with condescension. *Never. Fool. You don't belong here.*

One of the brawny, near-naked men grabbed his arms from behind, dragged him across the room, and shoved him to the floor in front of the pope. A slippered foot rested on a stone skull. He understood what they wanted him to do, but the thought of it caused his stomach to roil. He lowered his head. With lips that barely brushed the silk, he kissed the foot.

This would be the last time, he thought. His day was coming. Someday, they would all be kneeling in front of him. Especially that old fool Uncle Toby.

His handlers jerked him to his feet again and propelled him over to the Spanish knight, whom he realized was meant to be Don

Quixote. Again, they pushed him to his knees. The Don raised a heavy sword above Diggory's head and brought it down fast as though he were about to take off his head. Diggory didn't flinch. He couldn't.

The sword came to rest on his right shoulder. Then the knight swung it over to his left shoulder.

"I dub thee Thor, Knight of the Order of Skull and Cross Bones."

CHAPTER FIVE

At sea off Guadeloupe

March 25, 2008

"Are you all right?" Riley called out after she cut the engine. Her boat ghosted to a stop.

"Yeah. Sure am glad to see you, though. Don't know how much longer I would have lasted."

The man's face was deeply tanned, and even though his brown hair was slicked back against his skull, she could see the streaks of sun-bleached blond. His legs moved like shadowy blue scissors beneath the sparkling surface, and he was breathing hard from the exertion of swimming.

Riley unsnapped the shackle on the gate at the stern and motioned the man around to the boarding ladder. "You can climb aboard back here. Just duck under the dinghy." Her inflatable hung in davits above the water.

As he swam to the stern, she scanned the water for another boat, her senses on high alert. She'd read that piracy was rare in these waters, but all her years of training made her suspicious. There was not another boat in sight.

He pulled himself onto the swim step aft. He was stark naked except for a gold coin on a chain around his neck. Where the chain crossed his collarbone, two words were tattooed onto the brown skin, written in a script she couldn't read from that distance.

It wasn't as though she had never seen a naked man before; in seven years in the service, the sight of buck naked men had grown too common around whichever Marine House she was calling home. She averted her eyes, more out of courtesy than modesty— but not before noticing he had no tan lines on his stocky, muscular body.

"Wait there," she said.

She was standing by the boat's companionway, and she backed her way down the ladder, her eyes flicking right to check the dive knife she kept in a scabbard lashed to the bulkhead.

She tossed him a large beach towel.

"Here."

"Thanks," he said, and he flashed her a wide grin. "Sorry I didn't dress for the occasion."

He was standing out there drying off, in no hurry to cover himself.

"You saved my life, you know. I mean it. Thank you."

She didn't say anything to that. Didn't know what to say. He was exaggerating. She'd seen those muscular thighs. The boat wasn't that far off the island. Swimming to shore in flat water like this would be no problem for a man in his shape.

"I'm glad you're all right," she said as she busied herself straightening up the main salon. Not that it needed straightening, but she had a naked man in her cockpit. She reached for her mug on the table and drained the last of her now cold coffee. She certainly wasn't feeling sleepy anymore.

After grabbing some water bottles out of the fridge, she climbed back into the cockpit. She was glad to see he was wearing the towel wrapped around his waist now. She narrowed her eyes trying to read the tattoo. The curling script spelled *Carpe Diem.*

When she glanced up at his face, his sea-green eyes were alight, daring her to ask about the tattoo.

She handed him the water instead and watched his Adam's apple bob as he drained half the bottle. What sort of person would get a tattoo of the phrase "seize the day" in Latin?

When he tilted his head back to drink from the water bottle a second time, she leaned in and examined the coin he wore. The words on it were French: *Liberté, Égalité, Fraternité.*

"So, how'd you wind up out here swimming in your birthday suit?"

He smacked his lips in pleasure, handed her the empty bottle, and shook his head. His brown hair curled on his neck well below his ears. "Stupid."

She waited for him to add more. If he thought he could get away with that short an explanation, he was mistaken. She waited him out.

"I was in a runabout," he said at last. "Fishing. Was gonna run down to the Îles des Saintes. I was, you know, enjoying the clothing-optional lifestyle when I stepped to the rail to take a leak, and…" He shrugged.

"So, what happened to your boat?"

"Beats me. Last I saw her, she was headed thataway." He pointed west. "Rental boat." Shrugging, he said, "I guess it may wind up in Yucatan."

She thought she heard something Southern, a little redneck-like in his speech. "And your name?"

He paused for an almost imperceptible beat before answering her. "Robert—Bob Surcouf." He held out his left hand for her to shake.

"Something wrong with your other hand?"

He cradled it against his body and did not offer to show it to her. With a shrug, he said, "I must've cut it on a barnacle climbing aboard." He smiled at her then, revealing a pair of deep dimples.

She smiled back but didn't say anything at first. She had cleaned her boat's bottom back at Nelson's Dockyard, Antigua. She knew there wasn't a single barnacle growing anywhere on the *Bonefish*. Dimples or no, she needed to keep her distance from this guy. There was too much about his story that didn't add up.

"Well, welcome aboard, Bob," she said at last, reaching out to shake in one of those backhanded handshakes. "I'm Maggie Riley. Most people just call me Riley."

He couldn't sit still. She saw the bloody footprints as he shuffled his feet across the white paint of her cockpit floor.

"Pleased to meet you, Miz Riley. You singlehanding?"

He *was* fishing—wanted to know if there was anyone else aboard. She considered lying but decided against it. She nodded, then reached down and turned the key to start the engine. There was only one of him, and she was confident she could handle him if she needed to. After all, he certainly wasn't carrying any concealed weapons.

CHAPTER SIX

The Atlantic south of Bermuda

February 12, 1942

Woolsey lay sprawled out on the cold steel deck in utter darkness. The pain in his head and shoulder where he had slammed down onto the deck seemed almost to glow in the black hold. He wasn't sure if he'd lost consciousness, or for how long, but it was several minutes before he could clear his head enough to think through the pain. The noise of his own breathing was so loud inside his head, it nearly drowned out the throb of the diesel engines. Then he sensed the change in the vibration of the steel plate that pressed against his cheek. No more idling. The screws were turning. *Surcouf* was heading out to sea. He felt the sour taste of panic climbing up his throat.

No. Not him. He would survive. Gohin's words kept repeating, like a chant inside his head. *À l'enfer avec toi.* No. He wasn't one of them.

If he didn't figure a way out of this hole, and soon, they'd *all* be blown to hell.

Woolsey pushed himself up into a sitting position, and he realized he was sucking in mouthfuls of the foul air. He crawled forward until he found steel, and banging his fists on the bulkhead, he began to shout.

"Hey! Let me out of here! Stop this boat!" He beat on the steel until his throat burned and the bones in his hands ached. He fell back on the steel deck with a sob. It was useless.

He'd hated the goddamn *Surcouf* since the first day he had come aboard. She looked like a bloody coffin, and the few times they'd taken her below the surface, he had suffered inexplicable panic attacks, sure he was going to drown. He felt the panic welling up in him now. The cold sweat dampened his armpits; his breathing grew shallow.

Closing his eyes, he attempted to slow his breathing. He had to get himself under control. His fingers explored the rising knot on the side of his head where Gohin had frapped him with the pistol. The hair on the side of his head was matted and sticky with warm blood. Damn scalp wounds bled like mad. The smell of the blood was almost stronger than the stink of the cheese.

Through the bulkhead he heard the muffled sound of a voice on the speaker. Even if there had been a speaker inside the hold, he would not have understood a word. Stupid bloody French. When the distant voice stopped issuing orders, the hold seemed quiet in spite of the rumbling engines.

The darkness was so complete he felt the vertigo of not knowing which direction was up or where the walls were. At least, he hoped it was just the darkness and not a concussion. Control, man, think! He'd been in bad spots before this—thought he was going to die and hadn't. He couldn't just lie down and wait for the boom.

He'd heard about this compartment but never been inside since he had come aboard. It was a cargo hold of sorts, designed originally to hold up to forty prisoners of war. *Surcouf* could sink some good-sized ships with those guns of hers, and she was designed to pick up the survivors afterward, shut them all in here. They hadn't been firing any guns this trip—or for years before, for that matter. The cook stored some foodstuffs in here, but as far as Woolsey knew, Captain Lamoreaux was the only one who had a key. The Frenchie had always been a bit touchy about it when he'd asked. Woolsey had figured the captain was using it as a sort of private wine cellar for his better stock—better than the plonk the rest of the crew got out of the tanks. That was a detail he'd once found amusing—only a French sub would have tanks designed to carry wine.

He ran his fingers in an arc across the deck on either side of him. He felt nothing but the fine grit of dirt on the cold steel. He rolled onto his hands and knees and began to crawl forward, reaching out and patting his fingertips against the steel plate ahead of him like a blind man tapping his cane. He inched forward, expecting at any moment to come up against something, but he kept moving. He tried to sense where the bulkheads were, but he had no concept of the size of the compartment, nor whether there was anything in it. Odd because his personal radar usually worked better than that. The thought flashed in his head that there were no sides to this darkness, that he had fallen into some infinite black hole. He shuddered, shook his head, and told himself to stop thinking such foolishness. He kept on creeping forward.

After what seemed like a ridiculously long time, his knuckles brushed against rough wood planks. His fingers crawled over the surface and he found it to be a box, roughly two feet square. Between the slats, he felt the cool, smooth surface of glass. And there was another box, and another after that. Wine. Cases of it. The captain's private reserve.

The wooden cases were stacked one on top of another three high. He came to one spot where a single case was out of alignment, and he tried to slide it back out of his way. The thing would not budge. Heavy buggers. He went around it.

He followed the cases of wine, fairly certain he was moving aft, until, at last, he reached a bulkhead. Steadying himself with one hand on the wall, he stood. Then he slid one foot forward several inches, followed by his other foot. The hold could only have four sides, and of course, there was a door. He would find a way out of here. He had to.

He slid his foot forward again, and his shoe came to a stop against something solid. It didn't have the firmness of the cases of wine. Cheese, he thought. The stink had to be coming from somewhere. It was probably sacks of the stuff, the round ripe cheeses the Frenchies had to have on the table at every meal. He prodded at it with the toe of his shoe, but it did not move. He bent his knees and squatted down into a crouch, swinging his outstretched fingers in the cold dark air, feeling for the object in his path.

There was something about the darkness in front of him. It was denser, somehow. His radar seemed to be clicking back on. Though he could not see anything, he sensed more than saw there was something large there on the deck. He slid his leg forward and kicked at it, a little harder this time.

"Bugger off."

The deep, menacing voice startled him, and when he yanked his leg back, he lost his balance and toppled onto his backside.

CHAPTER SEVEN

Aboard the Bonefish

March 25, 2008

"Thanks for picking me up. I really wasn't sure I was gonna make it to shore." Cole looked back at the island, his left hand at his throat, his thumb caressing the coin.

He had been almost a mile offshore already and still swimming hard by the time *their* dinghy rounded the point. They had searched the coastline for almost an hour, but they never turned around, looked behind, never figured he'd head out to deep water.

He turned to face the woman. She looked to be in her early thirties, maybe five foot five, with a body that showed she worked out often. But there was something different about her, too, a cool air of competence.

"Where you headed?" he asked her.

"The capital, Pointe-à-Pitre." She pointed at the small GPS chart plotter affixed above her compass. "It's a little over thirty miles. I can drop you off in town once I clear customs and immigration."

"I sure would appreciate that, Miz Maggie." After all the years he'd spent on the Outer Banks, he could imitate their Southern speech and manners. Given that he hadn't a stitch of clothing, there was little else he could use as a disguise. "And after you clear in, where you headed?"

She engaged the autopilot, set her course, and then climbed back down the companionway. He could see her wariness. She didn't trust him. Smart woman.

"The Saintes, probably, for a day or two," she said. "It's where most cruising boats go. And please, it's just Riley."

He nodded, then looked back at the island. There was no sign of the boat or the men. For now.

"Don't know many women who go by their last names. Especially when they got such a nice name as Miz Maggie Magee."

The woman had disappeared into her cabin, and she didn't respond. In her absence, he checked out her boat. He didn't know much about *sailing*, but he knew boats well enough. She kept a tidy ship. A handheld VHF radio sat in a bracket within reach of the helm, she had jack lines for securing her safety harness, and a pod of navigational instruments surrounded the helm. Up on the foredeck, a canister containing an inflatable life raft was bolted to the deck. From the water, as her boat approached, he had noticed the radar, wind generator, and the insignia on the mainsail: a large letter *C* with the number forty.

She reappeared in the companionway with a first-aid kit and was about to hand him the box when she paused, set the box down, and took out the bandages and a tube of antibiotic cream. She tossed them to him.

"For your hands and feet," she said.

"Thanks." He knew what she was thinking. She didn't want to give him the box because it contained sharp implements. She was very savvy for a civilian. Surely, they wouldn't have thought ahead and sent a woman? No, they were good, but not that good. Besides, his instinct told him she was not one of *them*.

When he rested his ankle across his knee, he saw the sole of his foot was crisscrossed with white, puckered lacerations. Most of the bleeding had stopped, but his feet still left faint pink footprints on her white decks. It stung like hell when he massaged the cream into the cuts. He began to wrap his foot with the white gauze bandage. Walking was going to be a bitch for a while.

She was standing on the companionway ladder, her elbows resting on either side of the hatch, watching him.

"What kind of boat is this?"

"A Caliber 40."

"It looks like a lot of boat for one person to handle."

"Yeah."

"Must be nice just sailing around the Caribbean without a care in the world."

"Yeah, must be."

She turned to look across the water toward the point they were approaching. She crossed to the far side of the cockpit and began pulling on one rope and easing out another. The sail at the front of the boat unrolled like a window shade, and the boat leaned over a little. They picked up speed.

"Sailboats don't go very fast, do they?"

"Nope."

"Four hours, you said?"

"Yup."

"Guess you'd never outrun anybody on a boat like this."

She turned and looked him straight on, no blinking, no fear. "You don't like the speed we're making," she said, "you could swim instead. I'd be happy to drop you off right here."

"Seems you really don't want to talk to me, do you?"

"Nope."

* * *

He woke with a start. He had not intended to fall asleep, but when he stretched out on the foredeck with the sun warming his face and the trade wind breeze riffling his hair, he had started again trying to figure out where he had gone wrong in his calculations. He thought he had deciphered the text correctly, but if so, he should have found the wreck by now. Something wasn't right, he'd thought. And that was the last thing he remembered.

He sat up and looked past the bow. He massaged the muscles at the back of his neck and rotated his head around in a circle.

The tall buildings of the capital city of Guadeloupe lay a few miles ahead, spread out against the backdrop of the lush green highlands of Basse Terre on one side, the rambling cane fields of Grande Terre on the other. If one looked at the chart of this island, its shape resembled a butterfly, and Pointe-à-Pitre, a combination of bustling commercial port structures and crumbling colonial architecture, lay on the body where the wings joined. He had thought the place was a dingy, dirty backwater at first, but in the months he and his mate Theo had spent around the island, he'd grown to like the city with its combination of French and Creole cultures. Off to the east stood the pink-and-white hotels and condos on the beach at Le Gosier, the resort the European tourists flocked to by the thousands. Few Americans visited the island of Guadeloupe at all, and Cole had decided that was one of the place's principal charms.

When he glanced aft, he saw the woman, Riley, was sitting behind the wheel holding the binoculars in front of her face. Her short-cropped auburn hair accentuated her long, graceful neck, and the white T-shirt she wore fit tight enough to show the swell of her breasts above the flat belly. Her hips were slender, almost boyish, and the skin of her upper arms was carved around her taut biceps. She was a fine-looking woman to be out here all alone. After watching the way she handled herself and her boat, though, he suspected she was pretty damn good at protecting herself.

In the shadow of the binoculars, he saw her lips moving. She was talking to herself, and he decided he liked that. Maybe she wasn't quite the hard-ass she was pretending to be.

Off in the distance behind her, he saw a large white sportfisherman pushing a big wave and churning toward them at nearly twenty knots. The man who stood on the side deck looked familiar, even at this distance. He hoped he was wrong, but there weren't many people as funny-looking as this dude. Cole hobbled back to the cockpit on his bandaged feet and slid onto one of the cockpit cushions. He picked up the binoculars from the seat where she had just set them down, and he focused on the big fishing boat. It *was* him. Things were starting to make sense. Did they know he was aboard the woman's boat? No way. Damn!

CHAPTER EIGHT

The harbor at Pointe-à-Pitre

March 25, 2008

Riley did not like having this stranger down alone inside her boat, but after they had been motoring for over four hours, when he'd asked to use the head, she couldn't refuse him.

Bonefish was passing the entrance buoy at the start of the long channel leading into the harbor off the capital city when a big Bertram sportfishing boat with gleaming stainless steel rails and the name *Fish n' Chicks* in gold letters on her transom cruised past at twenty knots, throwing a monstrous wake. She'd wondered at first if it was the same boat she'd seen anchored that morning, but the Yank fish boats all looked pretty much the same. The man on the bridge deck had long hair under a baseball cap pulled low on his head. She figured him for a mechanic taking the owner's boat out for a sea trial. Another weird character with a white Afro and dressed all in white stood on the side deck holding tight to a railing, looking like a seasick ghost.

Riley gripped the steering wheel as their wake rocked her little boat, but the ghost didn't even turn to look at them.

She wondered if Bob was still in the head getting rolled right off the toilet.

The sun was angling in under the Bimini top that shaded her cockpit. She slid her sunglasses up the bridge of her nose, trying to make out the channel ahead. Between the binoculars, the GPS, and the paper chart spread out on the cockpit seat, she was still having a time making out the ship channel markers.

She was glad she had moved the dive knife on her last trip below. And she'd slid her rigging knife into her pocket. He seemed harmless enough, but she was not about to drop her guard.

During the last few hours, he had tried several times to start a conversation. Each time, she'd answered him with curt, one-word replies, hoping he'd get the message. Eventually, he'd given up on conversation and walked to the bow, where he'd stretched out on top of the cabin and seemed to fall asleep.

Until fifteen minutes ago when he'd sat up, moved aft, looked all around with her binoculars, and then asked to go below. She wished she knew what his story was. Was he on the lam, or was he some kind of freak down there trying on her underwear?

Riley glanced away from her chart and tried to focus on the dimly lit cabin. It was too strange having another person on the boat again. She'd left DC in October with her best friend, Hazel, as crew. They had a fine trip going down the Chesapeake to Norfolk and through the Intracoastal Waterway to Beaufort, North Carolina. Though the two of them could not be more different, both were State Department brats, and Hazel was the closest thing to a sister Riley had.

So, on the trip south, she'd talked to Hazel about Lima. About her affair at the embassy with the man who was so right, yet so wrong for her in so many ways, and then about the bomb. She told her about how she'd seen Mr. Wrong for the last time on the day of the bombing, and he had just walked away into the smoke. About how later, through the endless interviews and debriefings, she waited to hear from him. Total silence. Compared to that pain, the burns were nothing.

Afterward, she left the Corps, using her father's illness as an excuse, and swore off men for good.

It felt good to talk about it after years of holding it inside. But looking back now, it bothered her that it had been so easy to leave out parts of what happened. Was she lying to her best friend by not telling her everything? But then, not even Riley knew the *whole* truth. She hoped to find that out here in Guadeloupe, tomorrow.

In Beaufort, Hazel said her tearful good-bye, and Riley took off for a straight shot to Puerto Rico. Ten days later, she pulled into Boqueron, pleased with her first solo ocean passage, and she'd been alone ever since. She liked solo sailing, she told herself, so why, when Mr. Wrong e-mailed her out of the blue, as though years of silence were nothing, had she agreed to meet him in Pointe-à-Pitre?

She was thinking about Lima and leaning over the side, out from under her Bimini, to look up at the bridge of a passing freighter when a loud voice spoke right next to her ear.

"Nice boat you've got here, Maggie Magee!"

She banged her head on the stainless tubes of the Bimini frame, and she nearly knocked Bob off his feet.

She rubbed her hand on the back of her head. "Stop calling me that."

"Little jumpy, aren't we?"

She didn't say anything, and she hoped he didn't notice her discomfort. Her other hand had brushed against the sarong she'd given him, and she was trying very hard not to think about what she'd felt beneath it.

"Pretty comfortable down below—for a sailboat."

She continued to ignore him, which was difficult since he'd picked up her binoculars—*again*—and trained them on the Bertram. She squinted at the boat in the distance, wondering what his interest was all about.

He lowered the glasses. "I see you're reading one of those books."

OK, it seemed like a safe topic. She'd bite. "What books?"

"All that about the Knights Templar and the Illuminati?" He sighed. "You don't believe that stuff, do you?"

"It's fiction. Just a fun read."

"Dead right." He sat down on one of the bench seats that ran the length of the cockpit. "They're not the ones we've got to worry about. But the Bilderburgers, the Trilateral Commission, the Council on Foreign Relations? You know, the whole Skull and Bones crew?"

She flicked a quick glance down at him. "I've heard of them." So he was one of those, she thought. Conspiracy nut jobs generally weren't dangerous.

"They're the ones really in charge now," he continued. "They're running the shadow government. They've completely screwed up our country, spying on us with satellites, tapping phones, stealing elections, carrying out false flag attacks, getting us into this friggin' war, and torturing people. These billionaires and their banking buddies have made ass wipe out of the Constitution, and they intend to keep it that way. But the closer we get to this election, the more frantic they get. That's what those guys should be writing about."

She looked at his face to see if he was kidding. He had a strong chin, and the muscles of his jaw were set. "And I suppose you believe in the second gunman on the grassy knoll and that MI-6 killed Diana?"

His green eyes looked at her without blinking, and one eyebrow lifted just a fraction. "Don't you?"

She turned her head aside and rolled her eyes. "I'll believe in conspiracy theories when you can show me more than two people who can keep a secret."

"What about Project MK-Ultra?"

She sighed and turned back to look at him. "And what was that?"

He stood, smiled, and pointed his index finger an inch from her nose. "My point, exactly," he said.

She somehow managed to stop herself from reaching over and breaking his finger.

He plopped back down onto the seat. "In the fifties and sixties, the CIA was doing mind control research by giving all kinds of drugs—including LSD—to unwitting citizens. It didn't come out until the midseventies."

She'd heard about that, but she didn't know enough to venture an opinion. What was she doing arguing with this nut case anyway? "OK, so there may be stuff that goes on behind closed doors in government, but there's not a whole lot we can do about it besides voting."

"Yeah, right," he said. "On an electronic voting machine made by a subsidiary of Haliburton?"

She rubbed the sweat from her eyes. "But you and I aren't going to change that."

"See, that's where you're wrong, Magee. If we don't do it, who will?"

She had once said nearly identical words when she'd enlisted in the Marine Corps. She'd been so angry after her brother's death, she'd wanted to reveal all the secrets, right all the wrongs. When had she grown so cynical?

Riley knew the answer to that one. After Lima.

She ventured a quick glance at him. His eyes reminded her of the ocean—of that glowing shade of grayish green when the first sunlight breaks through after a thunderstorm. He looked up and caught her staring. She turned her head away, as though she had heard something behind them.

She knew better than to argue with a conspiracy nut. When she faced forward again, she said, "Listen, Bob, we're about to enter the anchorage, so I'd appreciate it if you'd sit still and keep quiet until the anchor's down."

She had given him a tropical print sarong along with an old, extra-large military-issue T-shirt. His fingers rubbed at the cloth of the olive-drab shirt. "You military?"

She kept her eyes trained on the channel ahead. "Marine Corps."

He nodded as though that somehow explained something. "Never met a woman marine before."

She drew in a deep breath. "*Former* marine. And I told you to sit down and be quiet."

Riley was trying to decide whether he looked adorable or ridiculous in her knee-length sarong when he pivoted around on his butt, leaned his back against the side of the cabin, and put his feet up on the cockpit seat, his legs bent at the knee. She looked away. Peering ahead, out through the windows of the dodger, she could feel his eyes on her. On top of that, after his hours in the sun, he smelled of male sweat and testosterone. From the corner of her eye, she could see he hadn't moved, and she stared straight ahead, determined not to smile.

Behind the freighter, a wide, high-speed catamaran ferryboat was also trying to crowd her out of the channel. These French didn't seem to have very good manners. Like her passenger. He was still grinning at her.

"What do you find so amusing?" she asked without looking his way.

"You."

Her eyes flicked for a second in his direction, then away. He still hadn't changed his position. She said nothing.

"Don't you ever smile, Magee?" he asked.

"I told you to be quiet. And stop calling me that."

He made a big show of pantomiming zipping his lips closed and throwing away the key.

She looked at him, not letting her line of vision stray lower than his chin. "While you're at it," she said, and though it took some effort to keep a straight face, she managed. "When you're wearing a skirt, you might want to keep your legs closed, too."

CHAPTER NINE

Washington, DC

March 18, 2008

Diggory Priest stood at the center of the star on the floor of the Capitol Crypt and checked his watch for the second time. Most of the tour groups had finished for the day. There were a couple of stragglers on the far side of the large room, teenagers giggling in front of a glass case that held a model of an earlier design for the Capitol. The Crypt was located on the first floor of the United States Capitol, directly under the rotunda. Though the room over Priest's head had sometimes hosted the lying in state of dead presidents and other luminaries, he'd been told the Crypt, in spite of its name, had never been used for funerary purposes. Nonetheless, Diggory thought the man he was meeting had quite a sense of humor to have chosen this location. He checked his watch again. He had not ever known him to be late to a meeting, but given the vagaries of political emergencies, he would give him five more minutes.

It was only after the gigglers had disappeared that Diggory heard the tapping of leather shoes crossing the polished stone floor. The man who approached him was wearing an elegant charcoal suit, white shirt, and red tie. The suit looked good on his lean frame, and he carried a buttery soft and worn Italian leather attaché case. He extended a hand as he approached.

"Thank you for agreeing to meet with me on such short notice. I hope I haven't kept you waiting long?"

"Not a problem, sir. It's always a pleasure to see you," Diggory said. He was uncertain of the protocol for names in this particular situation—much depended on the nature of his assignment. Traditionally, members called one another by the names they had taken on the night of their initiation, but this man was so well known from newspapers and television, it was difficult to call him by anything other than his title. Diggory's Bones name was one formerly used by Averell Harriman and Dean Witter Jr., among others. Thor: God of Thunder.

The man standing before him was Beelzebub.

"I haven't got much time, Thor, so let me get straight to the point."

At the sound of that name, Diggory relaxed. "I'm listening, sir."

"We have a sub rosa exigency."

Diggory nodded. They all did it. It was their way of talking down to him by trying to talk over him. Sub rosa. Secret. As if he didn't know. As if he hadn't made it his fucking specialty.

"It's down in the islands. Your neck of the Caribbean." The Agency had sent him on assignments from Barbados to Haiti to Latin America. Places that oozed poverty and hordes of dark-skinned people. Now, men like Beelzebub saw him as their trouble-shooter in the region.

"I'm asking you to handle this for us with the kind of discretion that has become your trademark."

"I'd be happy to."

"Something may surface—bringing up a top-secret past operation. One we thought was long buried and gone. This cannot come to light. Not now, not ever."

"Understood."

"As I'm sure you are aware, these are tenuous times for us. If this information were to go public at this point, with the election barely six months off and the fucking economy imploding—impossible to contemplate the damage. We've got one of our own in office—but they'd use it against him. Hell, both sides would. We've had a man on the scene down there for several weeks, but I'm not satisfied with his results. I asked the circle to name the top man for this sort of thing, and it was unanimous."

"I can be on the first plane out." Top man, perhaps, he thought, but what they were really looking for was their top janitor—still taking orders. Cleaning up their sub rosa exigencies in dirty little corners of the third world.

"Excellent. You'll be going to Pointe-à-Pitre, Guadeloupe. Your contact is Caliban. He will fill you in on the necessary details."

"Yes, sir." He shook Beelzebub's hand.

"Thor." The older man tightened his grip and locked his eyes on Dig's. "You've never had a more important assignment. Our very existence is at stake."

Diggory slipped out the north entrance of the Capitol and headed up New Jersey Avenue to the Hyatt, where he had checked in the night before. As he navigated his way across intersections and up the street, he raised the collar of his coat and thrust his hands deep into his pockets.

Blasted cold. Thankfully, he was now headed south. But this was more than merely looking for a more hospitable climate. This was the opportunity he had been waiting for. He had always known one day they would ask him to clean up a mess so big he would be able to use it to his advantage. The time had come for him to take what was rightfully his. What had Beelzebub said? *Impossible to contemplate the damage.* Or the power that would be his if instead of making it all disappear, Dig made it his own.

In spite of the cold, he smiled. The timing could not be more perfect. The stars were aligning for him. It so happened he also had a bit of unfinished business down in the Caribbean. Business with someone who, last he'd heard, was in Antigua on her boat and headed south. She was key to the whole operation. All things come to he who waits. He had waited long enough.

CHAPTER TEN

Pointe-à-Pitre

March 25, 2008

Once the anchor was down and she'd made certain it was set, Riley hurried to lower the dinghy.

"You sure you won't let me give you a hand?" he asked.

"No, I've got it."

He stuck his lower lip out in a pretend pout, and this time there was no getting around it. He did look adorable. It would have been easy to accept his help, but for her own reasons, she needed to do it alone. It wasn't that she had anything to prove. It was simply part of the discipline. Once she started accepting help, it would be easy to start *expecting* it. Next thing you know, against her better instincts, they'd be involved. That's what had happened down in Lima, and look how that had turned out.

She went below to her cabin, closed the door, pulled off her T-shirt, and changed into a clean white polo shirt for her trip to Customs and Immigration. In the main salon, she slid on some boat shoes, then stopped at the navigation station to collect her paperwork.

When she raised the hinged tabletop and looked inside, it was obvious that her papers, charts, and instruments had been disturbed. On a small boat, everything had to have its place, which suited her.

Son of a bitch. What had he been looking for? She'd known something was not right about *Bob* from the first. His injured hand, his shredded feet. The conspiracy gibberish. She didn't like strangers, especially paranoid, crazy ones, rummaging through her chart table. If she accused him, he'd only deny it. Better not to let on that she knew.

She stuffed the ship's papers into her canvas briefcase. Dimples or no dimples, she was not going to leave this guy alone with access to her boat. She grabbed the boat's padlock on her way topsides.

"Look. I'll go in to Immigration and talk to them. Then, once I've cleared, I'll come get you. I'm going to lock the boat up, but you've got water and shade here. I shouldn't be more than an hour."

"Take me ashore with you, and I'll just take off," he said. "The French will never know. I already cleared in here."

Yeah, she thought. Right. "And if somebody has already seen you on my boat and reports it to the authorities? No thanks. They could impound my boat for trying something like that. You're not on my crew list."

His eyes widened as he looked around the waterfront that fringed the harbor. "You really reckon they're watching us?"

"I'm not going to assume they aren't."

"I thought for sure I'd lost them back there."

"Lost who?" Now she wasn't at all certain whom he meant by *them.*

"The aliens." He grinned. "A couple of guys from Uranus."

The sooner she could get rid of him, the better. He really was one of the tin-foil-hat wack jobs. She shook her head. "I'm not going to risk getting charged with doing something illegal. You sit tight and I'll have you ashore in an hour." Sooner if she could manage it.

He cocked his head and watched her as she closed the companionway doors and secured the hatch with the combination padlock.

"You don't trust me alone on your boat, do you, Miss Maggie Magee?"

She sniffed and raised one eyebrow. "Would you?"

* * *

"He was right here," she said. She was standing in the cockpit of *Bonefish* only forty-five minutes after leaving him alone on her boat.

"*Oui, mademoiselle*. So you told us, but where is he now?" The French immigration officer, Monsieur Beaulieu, stood on her stern boarding platform in his leather shoes. He was looking down his long nose at the stainless rungs on the ladder that led up to the cockpit.

"I can't believe this." Riley sat down hard on the cockpit cushion.

"As I told you, *mademoiselle*, we have no record of a *Robert Surcouf* clearing through immigration."

She looked at the Frenchman standing on the swim step of her boat, his upper lip curled in disgust.

"You are sure you got the name right, *mademoiselle?*"

"Of course I'm sure."

She should have seen this coming. Was the craziness just an act or a cover? She was supposed to be the security expert, and he'd played her. *Bob.* Yeah, right. Bet he either swam ashore or hitched a ride with a passing dinghy. The fact that she'd been distracted by her "date" tomorrow was no excuse. She thought about the clothes she'd given him. She'd miss that old shirt. Glancing around the cockpit one last time, she realized the handheld VHF radio was gone, too. Damn him.

"So, mademoiselle," he said. "We go?"

Monsieur Beaulieu sat on a pontoon in the bow of the dinghy talking into his cell phone and waving his free hand through the air as she ran him back to the inner harbor her chart referred to as La Darse. The brightly painted hulls of local fishing boats were tied along the eastern wall, so she continued to the head of the harbor in front of the Place de la Victoire and the still-bustling fish market. White plastic buckets filled with ice and red squirrel fish were lined up behind the men who displayed the larger kingfish and grouper on their tables. Creole ladies with headscarves and huge shopping baskets were haggling for better prices. Riley smiled at their waving arms and shrill voices, not so different from the man in her dinghy.

Since she and Beaulieu had been speaking in English, he apparently did not realize she spoke fluent French. He was discussing what to charge her with. He snapped the tiny phone closed and sniffed as she turned the boat to come alongside the seawall.

Once Beaulieu had his feet on terra firma, he brushed his hands together as though he had dirtied himself by getting ferried ashore.

"You are certain your mysterious passenger was American?"

Riley stood in her dinghy looking up at him, one hand on the seawall steadying the boat. "Yes, no doubt about it. And he assured me he had already cleared into your country. Why do you ask?"

"The name he gave you. Surcouf. It is French, and I am surprised he would use it."

"Why?"

"There was a very famous French submarine with this name. *Surcouf.* Named after a pirate. This submarine disappeared in the Caribbean in *la seconde guerre mondiale.* Over one hundred and thirty men died."

"I've never heard of it."

"*Exactement.* You are an American." He shrugged. "You know so little about *l'histoire* of the rest of the world."

Great. A fake name, and a French one, no less. God only knew what he was into. And the jerk stole her only handheld VHF radio.

Beaulieu waved his hand toward the immigration building on the waterfront. "You are coming."

It wasn't a question.

"You've got my paperwork, and you know where to find me," she said.

"That is not sufficient, mademoiselle. This man you brought ashore, the man you insist was American, has not passed through immigration. He is an illegal, undocumented alien. You will come with me."

CHAPTER ELEVEN

Marigot Bay, Guadeloupe

March 25, 2008

The Citroën pulled to the side of the road and screeched off again almost before Cole had fully climbed out of the vehicle.

"Thanks a lot," he said to the red taillights as they disappeared around the next curve.

He reached down to brush the dust off the tropical-print sarong. What did he expect when he was out hitchhiking in a dress—and going commando, no less? The driver had made certain assumptions, and he hadn't exactly been happy when Cole turned him down.

He started down the steep dirt road leading to the narrow, rocky beach at the head of the bay. He picked his way between the stones since his bandaged feet had started to hurt again during the ride. He'd plucked the cactus needles out of his hand with tweezers he'd found in the head on Riley's boat, and he flexed his hand as he walked. Nearly good as new.

The last rays of sun lit the treetops high on the mountain above him, but down in the cove, night was descending. A restaurant was perched on the ledge above the dark water, its colored lights illuminating the small grove of coconut palms. When he reached the bottom of the hill, Cole lifted the green T-shirt and grabbed the VHF radio he had clipped to the waist of his sarong.

"*Shadow Chaser, Shadow Chaser,* this is *Shadow Mobile.*"

A few seconds later, the radio crackled to life. "*Shadow Mobile,* where the hell are you?"

"Switch?" he said, and the voice acknowledged. They switched to the VHF radio channel they always used. He didn't want to broadcast his location in case *they* were listening. Once Cole explained how he had arrived, his first mate grudgingly agreed to pump up the spare dinghy and come ashore to pick him up.

Twenty minutes later, he heard the oars splashing as his mate struggled to row the tiny boat in through the cove's small surf. In the deepening dusk, he could make out neither the man's dark skin nor the black rubber dinghy against the dark water of the bay.

"Over here," Cole said, stepping out of the shadows.

The dinghy ground onto the shore, and Theo Spenser stumbled onto the beach, the rope in the bottom of the tiny inflatable dinghy wrapped around one of his long legs. When he managed to disentangle himself and straighten up, he stood almost half a foot taller than Cole.

"Quite a landing, Theo."

"Mon, I hate this boat," Theo said in his proper, island-accented English. He adjusted the wire-rimmed glasses on his face and peered down at Cole. "Is that a skirt you're wearing?"

"I'm starting a new fashion craze."

"The Scots beat you to it."

"That's me. Always a day late and a dollar short." Cole bent over the small rubber dinghy and began to adjust the oarlocks.

"I've heard people call you 'a few cards short of a full deck,' but the day late one is a new addition to the list."

Cole stood up with the dinghy line in his hand. He smiled. "I'm always striving to upgrade."

"What did you do with the Whaler, anyway?"

"It's a long story."

"As usual. And where did you get the radio?" Theo took it from Cole's hand and held it close to his face to examine it.

Cole reached to grab it back, but Theo held it at the end of his long arm.

"It's a rather nice one," Theo said, nodding. "Waterproof."

"Hey, be careful with that. It's borrowed. I'll tell you the story when we get out to the boat." Cole put a hand on his friend's shoulder. "And on the way out, I'll row."

Once off the beach, the swells were gentle rollers, so Cole took the opportunity to row facing forward and admire his boat as they approached. *Shadow Chaser* was sixty-four feet overall, a former shrimper he'd bought in Fernandina and then spent six months converting over to a research-and-salvage vessel. Her navy-blue hull was barely visible against the dark foliage across the bay, but the accommodation lights in the wheelhouse reflected off the water. From her businesslike raked bow, the lines of her hull swept aft with a slight hollow in her sheer to the lovely rounded transom. God, she was a beauty. She still had her big A-frame crane aft and the outriggers in place, so she looked like the workboat she was, not like some Ivy League asshole's yacht. But it was Theo who had really done magic with the money they raised.

The kid was amazing. Cole had been teaching in the Maritime Studies program at East Carolina when he met him on the docks at Ocracoke. Theo had arrived one morning as a crewman on a gleaming white motoryacht. Cole was down in the launch, trying to clean the carburetor on an old Johnson outboard when this tall, gangly black kid came over and asked if he could have a look. From Cole's vantage point, squinting up at the young man, he couldn't make out any features in his face. The sun behind his head made him look as if he had a brilliant celestial aura, and he spoke with an island accent that sounded more like it belonged on the BBC than on a greasy, salt-baked dock on the Outer Banks.

"You know anything about outboards?" Cole asked. "'Cuz I'm just about ready to give up on this one."

When the young man jumped down into the wooden tender, Cole saw his skin and hair were the brownish black of one who'd spent hours in the sun. His hair was close-cropped, his white shirt and shorts were threadbare but clean and pressed, and behind his gold-rimmed glasses were dark, bright eyes full of intelligence. He shook Cole's greasy hand and took the wrench without a word. Ten minutes later, the jets were clean and the motor reassembled, and the exhaust was producing clouds of bluish smoke as the stranger gunned the engine.

Cole shouted, "Nice work. What's your name?"

The young man shut down the engine and wiped the sweat off his forehead with a clean handkerchief. "Theophilus Spenser. Just call me Theo."

"Where you from, Theo?"

"Dominica. It's an island."

"Yeah, I know."

The young man hopped easily up onto the concrete pier and looked down at Cole with a sigh. "Not the Dominican Republic."

Cole laughed. "Yeah, *I know*. My old man spent some time down in the Caribbean. On Dominica and Guadeloupe."

Theo inclined his head in approval. "Very good. All right. Cheerio."

Cole watched as the fellow began to head back toward the yacht that had arrived that morning. Did people really still say that? Cheerio? "Hey, Theo," he called out. "You know diesel engines, too?"

In Ocracoke, the big yacht left, but Theo stayed, and Cole had seen it as his chance to go out on his own, to say, "See ya" to that world of academia that never would accept him anyway. Cole started Full Fathom Five Maritime Explorations, and thanks to the support of their one big, then-anonymous donor and a handful of guys who'd made a bundle in Internet start-ups, he bought his own boat and fitted her out. Theo even designed and built their Remote Operating Vehicle, or ROV, which had an underwater video camera and a mechanical arm. Cole had named it *Enigma*. It was better than the one he'd been using at the university. Together they had turned *Shadow Chaser* into a state-of-the-art vessel for the search and recovery of archeological artifacts. To their investors, that translated as a treasure hunter.

Once aboard *Shadow Chaser*, both men headed for the galley, and Cole filled the coffeepot while Theo walked forward to the pilothouse to check the gauges on the Cummins generator he'd left running. He brought the chart back and spread it out on the Formica dinette table. Cole slipped into his cabin to change into a pair of shorts. He was about to lift the woman's shirt off his head, but when the fabric was across his face, he stopped and inhaled. There it was, that citrus smell somewhere between orange and lime. He'd smelled it in her hair when he'd brushed close to her, and again down in the head on her boat. He smoothed the olive-colored fabric down across his chest. No need to dirty another clean shirt just yet.

Back in the galley, he turned off the stove. When they both had steaming mugs of thick black coffee, they slid onto the red vinyl bench seats of the galley dinette and looked at the chart.

"I'm waiting," Theo said.

"OK. I was diving out here," Cole said, his finger tracing a line off the southwest coast of the island.

Theo didn't say anything.

"I had the handheld GPS, and I was over the coordinates where we'd got that last reading from the magnetometer. I drew a blank, though. Didn't see a thing."

Theo rubbed his chin. "So I suppose there are two possibilities, then. Either the sub broke up into pieces that are now so covered in coral you couldn't see them—or we still haven't broken the code right, and the magnetometer got those readings off some other kind of trash."

"I don't care if it's been more than sixty years, we should be able to see *something* from a sub that in her time was the biggest submarine in the world. Coral wouldn't cover it that fast." Cole shook his head. "We haven't got it right yet. But I know it's here." He wasn't sure if he was referring to the code in the journal or the submarine itself—or both. "Anyway, after I'd exhausted a couple of tanks just chasing fish around, I took the dinghy into this little cove where there's a spring." He finished the story, telling Theo about the men who had arrived, his escape, and how he'd been picked up by the *Bonefish*.

"So what did she look like?"

"What?"

"Don't bloody try to act like you didn't notice. It's not like we've had women crawling all over this vessel the last few months. Christ, man, you were butt naked and all alone on a little sailboat with a woman. Did you do her?"

"Shut up."

"Aw, come on, Cap'n." Theo stood up, put his hands under his shirt, and poked his fingers out to make imaginary breasts. He waggled his eyebrows up and down. "Was she hot?"

"I don't know." Cole rubbed his hands across the chart, smoothing out nonexistent wrinkles in the paper. "I was more worried about the guys who'd been trying *to kill me* an hour earlier."

"Yeah, right," Theo said, sitting back down looking dejected. He took a long drink of his coffee. "So somebody's after you. *Again.*"

Cole held up an index finger and pointed at Theo. "One of these days, my friend, you are going to have to eat those doubting words."

Theo leaned forward, his close-cropped head hovering over the chart. "So, who do you think *they* were this time?"

"The Brewster brothers."

"No, mon." Theo leaned back, screwed his eyes closed for a second, and made a face like a man who had just sucked on a lemon. "Not again. Not those two trogs?"

Cole wasn't thrilled about it either. The Brewsters were half brothers, a couple of Outer Banks lowlifes. Spyder, the older brother, had once told Cole they were "from the same crackhead mama, different white daddies."

"How'd they find us?" Theo asked. "I thought we left them back in the Carolinas."

Cole shrugged. "Word gets around. Especially *that* word— gold. And *Shadow Chaser*'s not exactly inconspicuous. Even a moron could track down a boat that looks like her in the Caribbean."

"I wouldn't give our friend Spyder that much credit." Theo sipped from his coffee mug.

"Spyder, no. His brother, yes. Besides, I'm pretty sure I spotted them on a boat as the woman was bringing us into Pointe-à-Pitre."

"What? Tell me they didn't see you."

"No, I went below to use the head. They've got a Bertram sportfish now, named *Fish n' Chicks*."

Theo chuckled. "Probably stole it and renamed it. That sounds like Spyder."

Cole nodded. "I'm almost certain they were the ones after me this morning. With those wet suit hoods, I didn't really see their faces, but only one of them really chased after me. And later, I was looking out the port when this boat passed us. It sure looked like Pinky out on deck."

"Him, I'd recognize anywhere."

"You've got that right," Cole said. There was a time he'd felt sorry for Pinky, who suffered from a condition called vitiligo. Most of his skin was the light-brown color of walnut shells, but vitiligo had caused odd patches to lose all pigmentation. The result was he sported a white Afro and his skin looked as if somebody had splashed him with a bucket of bleach.

Theo walked to the galley sink and rinsed out his mug. "So, what about the Whaler?"

"Let's head down there and look for it tonight. I can't afford a new one. And all my dive gear was in it, too. If we're lucky, they left it there. Decided they'd rather leave it for us so we can find the wreck—which they intend to steal from us later."

"What I don't get is, if they followed us here, why show themselves now? Why chase you?"

"Theo, you're trying to apply logic and intelligence to the Brewsters. Hello?"

"But he tried to shoot you with a spear gun."

"He didn't hit me, did he? I think he would have if he'd wanted to. My guess is that they've been following us and they got bored and did something stupid that Spyder cooked up. Man thinks he's a rocket scientist, and he probably thinks he can do a better job finding the sub than we can. My guess is he's after the coin."

Theo shook his head. "You and your bloody big mouth."

"Hey, that's *Captain* Big Mouth to you."

CHAPTER TWELVE

Pointe-à-Pitre

March 25, 2008

Diggory Priest leaned back in his café chair, took a sip of the decent Bordeaux they'd served him, and surveyed the large concrete square aglow in the tawny light of the late afternoon sun.

"They'll get the job done. It's just a matter of time."

Diggory turned to look at the older man who had just spoken—whom Dig knew only as Caliban. The man rested one elbow on the back of his chair at their outdoor table at the Café Caraïbe, while the fingers of his other hand were tap-tapping on the glass tabletop. He had a full head of thick silver hair and a tan that spoke of hours either on the deck of a yacht or a golf course. The man reeked of old money. But there was no surprise in that. Not in this business. Diggory looked at the man's profile. He was almost twice Dig's age, yet women still looked at Caliban with as much desire as they did at him.

Diggory had known he was good-looking even before he hit puberty, had known the power of his smile. As a kid, after school, he'd always gone straight to the diner where his mother worked, and the other waitresses fawned over him, calling him pet names and touching him, always touching him.

He swallowed to suppress the shudder. Diggory had learned early on how much women wanted him and how easy it was to manipulate them. Caliban clearly enjoyed the same knowledge. To the rest of the world, both men shared a similar casual arrogance, but Diggory knew that while he worked at it, Caliban was born to it.

"They'd better get it done," Diggory said.

"This business was a mistake, clearly. You need to make sure they understand that. I didn't order them to go after it. Those two did this on their own initiative. That's the problem. Right now they should be in observation mode. The coin matters, but at this point, it will only confirm what we already know. It becomes an enormous problem if the rest of the world knows."

Diggory watched a couple of young girls in miniskirts teetering on high heels as they crossed the uneven pavement in the street. "I hate counting on them. Sounds like they're not merely barbarians, they're Neanderthals. Shallow end of the gene pool."

"I understand that, but we don't want our fingerprints on this." From his shirt pocket, Caliban removed a pack of Dunhill cigarettes and lit one with a silver Zippo lighter. He blew a stream of smoke toward the umbrella hanging over their table. "These fellows don't have a clue. That's what makes them perfect for the job. We risk nothing."

It wasn't how he would have done it, but they were bringing him in now to clean up their mess. He had to tread lightly here. Politics and all.

Diggory took another sip of the wine, swirled it around in his mouth, and swallowed. Yeah, he thought, we risk nothing but more wasted time if these idiots screw up again. The wine had a supple, earthy taste. Not bad for a no-name label.

Caliban continued. "Don't know how the devil old man Thatcher got onto this. It was more than sixty years ago, for God's sake. There've been rumors, but nobody ever got it right. We had one of ours onboard. Went down with the rest of the poor bastards, and in those days anything sunk that deep was irretrievable. Only a handful of people ever knew the truth, and they're all ours."

"Once the technology was there, our people should have gone after it."

Caliban stubbed out his cigarette. "We've had our hands full elsewhere, and this was well buried."

"What about Thatcher's son?" Diggory said. "If he gets there before—"

"If that happens, I'm confident you'll deal with it, Thor."

Diggory had no doubt the man knew both his real name and his reputation. There was a reason they had called him in on this one. They needed him.

"And you'll do a better job of it than what happened with the father."

Dig felt the corner of his mouth begin to turn up. He shouldn't laugh, but really. They went a bit overboard with that one. Sexual strangulation and in a getup like that? Amateurs. Most of those he worked with were old-school professionals with years of service in intelligence work, but some of the new generation had read too many books, watched too many movies. Whomever they'd used on that job in England had had more imagination than experience.

"I don't suppose you're going to tell me what it is on this sub that's got everyone's panties in a wad."

Caliban dragged on his cigarette, looking at Dig through squinted eyes. He blew smoke from the corner of his mouth. "No," he said.

Asshole, Dig thought. He's enjoying this. It's all a power play to him. Then again, it's possible even he doesn't know. "Just so I'm straight on this—if Thatcher does find the damn boat and it follows our worst-case scenario—in other words, if the goods are retrievable, what do they want me to do? Salvage or destroy?"

The silver-haired man crushed his cigarette out and then flicked a finger in the air without glancing inside the café. He reached into his back pocket, withdrew a slender wallet, and by the time the waiter arrived with their bill on a saucer, he dropped a handful of colorful euro bills on the plate. Once the waiter was out of earshot, Caliban leaned close to Dig's ear.

"As far as the rest of the world is concerned, Thor, it never happened. Keep it that way. What is down there, even how it got there, could change everything. De Gaulle was our ally, for God's sakes. This administration is already on rocky ground as it is. This would not only ruin their legacy. Not to be overdramatic, son, but it would *change history.*"

Dig drew back, the corners of his mouth pulled down in disgust. *Son.* Someday, he would make this man regret his choice of words. "I won't go into this blind."

The older man leaned back in his chair and sighed. Then, turning away and gazing across the street, he said, "You don't have any choice, Thor." He reached up and ran his palm over his head, smoothing hair that didn't need smoothing. He sat forward again and said, "I can tell you this. We have managed since the beginning to stay in the shadows. That's the only way an organization like ours can be effective. If these documents were retrieved, they could verify the extent of our influence. That's all I can tell you."

Documents. At least he now knew that much. But it was crumbs, he thought. Dig nodded. When the time came, he would get a look at this, whatever it was, himself. These documents would be his.

Caliban continued. "We don't need somebody, *anybody*, finding this now—or at a future date. So, it doesn't exist. We need you to make sure of that."

Dig nodded again. They needed him. "It doesn't exist. I'll make sure."

The man stood, glanced at the gold watch on his wrist, and placed a hand on Dig's shoulder. Dig held his breath, calming the desire to shake off the hand.

"You've had years of experience dealing with this sort of thing, Thor. Yorick taught you well. I speak for all the others when I say we have every confidence in you."

"As you should."

* * *

Diggory watched the silver-haired man cross the Place de la Victoire and disappear into a narrow street. He stretched out the fingers of his right hand, and then, starting with his pinkie, one finger at a time, he folded them into a clenched fist. He rotated the fist on his wrist. He repeated this over and over, flexing and strengthening the muscles of his right hand, as he stared unseeing at the passersby.

It had been awhile since anyone had mentioned Yorick's name to him. Since his forced retirement, this new lot tried to pretend the old man had never existed. Feared they'd never quite live up to the legend.

After presiding as Uncle Toby at Diggory's initiation and doing his damnedest to drive off the fatherless youth, Yorick had followed Diggory's career. The old man began to appear like a dark shadow, laughing when Dig's waitress mother hugged him at graduation or writing effusive letters of recommendation when Diggory applied for jobs. Later favors had done little to change what Diggory felt every time he thought of his first night in the Tomb. That empty, wandering eye and the other, the one that always judged him and found him wanting. Diggory had played the role of pet mutt, sitting at the great man's knee and soaking up the knowledge. And only he knew that one day this dog would turn on its master. That day was nearly here.

This Caliban was not up to Yorick's standard. Though an elite group, there were still incompetents within their circle. Not many. He hadn't made up his mind about this Caliban. Using the barbarians was a mistake. Yorick never would have tolerated it. But men like Caliban—and Yorick—were on their way out. Whether they knew it or not.

He walked out of the café, then paused at the street, undecided about which way to turn. Though it was only just past six, it was dusk already. Strings of colored lights had been looped across the street the full length of the Place de la Victoire, giving the evening a festive air. Caribbean pop music spilled from the restaurant on the corner.

His rendezvous with the barbarians wasn't until eight. And after that, nothing scheduled until his meeting tomorrow evening. That was the important one. Like the old adage about killing two birds with one stone. Literally.

He could take an early dinner, handle the meeting, and then retire, or he could telephone that little German schoolteacher he had met out at Saint Francois in the discotheque. She had been drinking zombies as if they were water, and each time the bartender served her another drink, she showed him how she could tie a knot in the stem of a maraschino cherry with her tongue. He smiled at the memory. She would be delighted to hear from him after she'd nearly begged him to stay in her room last night.

He pulled out the small cell phone he had purchased for local use and cursed when he saw it had no signal. The damned French couldn't even build a cell phone network that worked. He had used the phone earlier down by the waterfront, so he began to walk in that direction. When he arrived at the Rue Duplessis, the phone was working, and he scrolled through his recent calls.

On the periphery of his vision, he saw movement. He scanned the area with a quick glance. There was a woman, down on the quay, waving her hands and shouting. She was wearing khaki shorts and a white polo shirt that showed off a firm, compact shape with tanned and muscular legs. Her auburn hair was cropped short, and it curled at the back of her long neck. He was thinking there was a certain resemblance, but the hair was different. Then, she threw her arms into the air and walked around in a circle. He saw her face. Diggory smiled like a boy who had just received an early Christmas gift.

CHAPTER THIRTEEN

The Atlantic south of Bermuda

February 12, 1942

Woolsey scrambled into a crouch and peered into the dark. He'd recognized the voice. "McKay, you bastard, you scared the friggin' daylights out of me."

"Piss off."

"What about Mullins?"

"Over here, sir."

"Glad to know you're both all right, then."

"S'not what it sounded like to me." Sean McKay, the telegraphist, was a career navy man serving in his second world war. Built like a cartoon seaman with massive biceps, one of which sported an anchor tattoo, and a neck near as wide as his head, he looked more as if he belonged in an old boiler room than where he was usually found—in the radio room hunched over the telegraph key with his headset on. He filled the tiny compartment, but he had one of the fastest hands in the British navy. He had made it plain from day one that he didn't like the young lieutenant. Woolsey had heard McKay call him "Lord Muck" and "Lieutenant La-ti-da" under his breath due to his RNVR rating from the Royal Naval Volunteer

Reserve. Woolsey had been attending university in America only a few months earlier when he returned home to join up.

"So what happened to the two of you?"

"I was in my bunk, sir," Mullins said. His voice was close to an octave higher than McKay's. They made an odd couple. Mullins, a refined, self-educated lad, was born to working-class parents, but his innate intelligence was getting him ahead. Already, his tastes ran to classical music and opera. Woolsey supposed the boy was a poof, but it was none of his business.

"Catching up on sleep, sir, before the long night watches I reckoned were ahead. They came for me and dragged me out of my berth. Kewpie didn't even let me put my shoes on."

"No injuries, then?"

"No, sir."

Woolsey was about to say something more, but his words were cut off.

"No thanks to you."

Woolsey heard the challenge in McKay's voice, and he didn't know what to do about it. His only hope of leading a man like Sean McKay was through military authority, and it appeared the French were doing their best to break that down.

He tried to ignore the big man. "Walter, did you hear them say anything? Any idea what their plans are?"

McKay wouldn't let the young signalman speak. "All we heard was you out there begging with them Frenchies, then crying in here." McKay imitated Woolsey with a high falsetto voice. "'Let me off. I got orders. Let me outa here.' Couldn't help but notice you didn't say *we* had orders. Planning on leaving us on board, were you, Lieutenant?"

"Whatever you think you heard, that was nonsense. I was only trying to talk my way out of this. Mullins, you understand that, right?"

"Sir? I'm not sure what I heard, sir."

"I was making up a story. Trying to get them to take me to the captain."

"Bollocks," McKay said. "You was savin' your own skin, Lieutenant."

In the dark, Woolsey heard the *shhh* of cloth moving.

When McKay spoke again, his voice was much closer. "Sounded to me like you knew exactly where to lay your hands on those orders. A little bloke like you wouldn't try to take on a guy like Gohin. Too scary lookin' for the likes of you."

Woolsey began to crab his way backward across the deck.

"Lieutenant La-ti-da had those orders, didn't you," McKay said. "You was leaving us."

"For Christ's sake, man, it was a bluff." Woolsey was now scrambling, crawling as fast as he could—away from that deep voice. "I was just saying whatever came into my head. It was nothing."

With a dull thud, his head hit the steel bulkhead behind him. At the same time, a ham-sized hand closed around his ankle and dragged him away from the wall.

"Sean McKay, I am your superior officer. You lay your hands on me and—"

"Shut up, you friggin' arsehole."

Woolsey felt the man's fingers close around his throat. In a choked and raspy voice, he said, "McKay, I'll get us out of here. Figure out something."

"You couldn't organize a piss-up in a brewery." The big man's hands began to tighten, closing off his air supply so Woolsey couldn't make another sound. "Why wait for the Frenchies to throw us to the sharks? I'm doing you a favor, mate. I'm giving you a quick way out." McKay started to laugh.

Even over the ever-present rumble of the engines, they heard the grinding noise followed by a clunk as the wheel turned on the outside door, then light flooded the compartment, blinding them all. Woolsey squeezed his eyes shut against the glare, then gasped for air when McKay released his throat. The big man scrambled back into the shadowy recesses of the hold. Woolsey, still closest to the door, curled up on the floor and tried to cover his head with his arms, protecting himself both from the light and the likelihood that the French soon would rain blows to his body. He waited, but no one touched him. Several different voices were shouting in French, then Woolsey heard a thud as a body hit the floor not far from him, and the hatch door slammed shut.

He understood now why no one had spoken when he was thrown inside. It was bloody quiet after all that row stopped when the hatch closed and they were plunged back into darkness. The advantage would go to the one who had the most knowledge, and he didn't want to speak to give away his location. His breathing sounded so loud, he did his best to hold his breath.

The quiet seemed to stretch on for hours, though it was, in fact, only a minute or two. The silence was finally broken when the recent arrival groaned. Woolsey heard the man's clothes rustle as he got to his feet, then footfalls as he walked to the far side of the compartment, confident as though he could see. Then came the sound of wood cases sliding on the floor and the clink of metal tapping on glass. The man was digging through the cases of wine. What the devil could he be doing?

Then a voice exclaimed, "Ahh! *Voilà*," and there was a click and the thin beam of a torch lit the compartment as well as the man who now held it.

"I thought you three would be here," Captain Lamoreaux said, his face smeared with blood.

CHAPTER FOURTEEN

Pointe-à-Pitre

March 25, 2008

Riley pushed open the door to the customhouse and charged down the steps to the street, leaving the door to slam behind her. How had this day that had started out so great turned into such a complete mess? Under her arm, she carried her portfolio that normally contained her ship's papers, passport, and money. Clutched in her hand was the sheaf of papers marked up with various official stamps; one was a receipt for her confiscated passport, and another demanded her presence at a hearing the following week.

The sun was gone, and the sky over the outer harbor had turned a dark, iridescent blue. To the east, a cluster of ash-colored clouds was rimmed with molten red. She hadn't realized they'd kept her inside the office that long, but the bureaucratic desk jockeys in there couldn't get it through their heads you don't smuggle illegal aliens into a country one at a time. It had probably been so long since they'd had any sort of real international crime on this island they just couldn't wait to charge her with something. The gendarme had looked at her over the top of his half glasses as if he were inspecting bad meat when Beaulieu had asked him to write up the paperwork.

That was when she'd told the gendarme she wanted to report that this *Bob* had stolen her handheld radio, and he'd smirked at her. Smirked! What? Did they think she was making the whole thing up?

When they were kids, her older brother, Michael, was the only one who could ever get away with teasing her or laughing at her. Being back in the Caribbean reminded her of the Barbados years. St. Winifred's was the name of the school. She must have been eight years old and Michael nearly ten. She was a skinny kid but already taller than her older brother and growing so fast her mother had bought her school uniform a size too large. Several boys followed them from school to where they were to catch their bus. They started calling Mikey names like Midget, Fathead, and Fish Face. She was going to ignore them until they called her Faggy Maggy in the Baggy Pants.

She knew even back then to go for the leader. She turned around and walked up calm as could be. She asked the bigger boy his name. He preened and looked to his friends for encouragement, but before he could answer, she slugged him right in the nose. He staggered and fell, but got right back up and charged her, going for a head butt. She dodged him, and he tripped over the leg she extended. Then her brother grabbed her hand, and the two of them ran down the street and onto the bus. They hurried to the backseat and looked out through the exhaust at the red-faced boy on the ground wiping at his bloodied nose.

"Remember that day?" she whispered. She saw Mikey's face in her mind, the glasses sitting crooked on his big ears, the watery blue eyes behind the thick lenses, the thin blond hair spreading out from his crown making him look as if the barber had used a bowl to cut his hair. She always pictured him as she had seen him that last time, standing ramrod straight at his full five foot four in the doorway of their apartment in Paris, the strap of his laptop case crossing his narrow chest bandoleer-style, and that lopsided grin. She grew older, but Mikey was eternally eighteen, just as he had been that fall when he'd left home for Yale.

I'm not going to let them do this to me, Mikey. It's like when we were kids, Brother. It's time to fight back.

If the authorities weren't going to help her get her radio back or do anything about *Bob*, she was going to have to find the man herself. She had that meeting next week for Mercury Security in Dominica. This was the first time they had entrusted her to handle an entire project, from bid through installation, and she wasn't going to mess it up. Taking long strides up the street rimming the edge of the inner harbor, she rounded the corner and nearly ran into the Creole ladies who were packing up their Scotch bonnet peppers at their roadside stand.

"*Pardon*," she said to each woman, popping her P's in the explosive French way and clutching her canvas briefcase.

The tall streetlamps around the inner harbor clicked on and lit the quay with a sickly yellow light. She stopped in her tracks, stunned for a fraction of a second, before she began to run.

"Hey, stop that man!" she yelled. "*Arretez! Allez, quelqu'un!*" A fat man was in her inflatable, attempting to unscrew the clamps that held the outboard to the transom, and though she was yelling at people to stop him in both French and English, not a soul moved to help her. As she ran, she called out to the group of young boys standing on the quay in front of her dinghy, the red ends of their cigarettes glowing in the dying light. She waved her arms, portfolio in one hand, papers in the other, pointing at the man's large behind that now obliterated her view of the engine.

The boys turned and looked at her with narrowed eyes. The man in her boat, meanwhile, gave up on the outboard and stood up. He glanced in her direction, then he grabbed the oars and leaped to the seawall with remarkable agility for a man his size. By the time she reached the quay, he had disappeared into the evening crowd gathering on the Place de la Victoire.

She spun in a circle and flung her arms down at her sides, looking for someone or something to kick. It took all her willpower not to violate her resolution about cursing.

When her temper felt more or less under control, she motioned aside one of the boys in the group and questioned him in French, asking him if he knew the man. She pointed out to him that the cable she had used to secure the outboard and lock the dinghy to the rusted chain on the seawall had been cut. Surely, he had seen the big man cutting the cable and known something was wrong. She asked him why, as a good citizen, he didn't do something to stop the thief.

The youngster shrugged and blew air through his pooched-out lips. He told her it was none of his business, that if she had a problem, she should call a *flic* or gendarme, not bother him.

She turned away from him, throwing her arms into the air to blow off steam so she didn't grab the little twit by the throat and pinch his pouty lips right off. Here she was, trying to be a good Samaritan, and the result was the someone she'd been trying to help—*Bob*—had stolen her radio and caused her to lose her passport. And now, in the middle of the city, under the eyes of half a dozen people, a thief had nearly taken her outboard and had stolen her only set of oars. She turned back and began to lecture the youth on his civic duty, when someone tapped her shoulder and she heard her name.

"Riley?"

CHAPTER FIFTEEN

Pointe-à-Pitre

March 25, 2008

Riley swung around, then blinked. "Diggory?"

For a moment, she hoped it was all a dream. Perhaps she had fallen asleep on the passage across from Antigua, and she would wake aboard *Bonefish* and neither *Bob* nor Beaulieu nor her missing passport—nor any of the day's events including this moment—would be real.

She wasn't ready for this—not here, not now.

"Riley, you look like you could use some help." As she was trying to think through her confusion, unable to stop staring at those electric blue eyes, he turned his back to her and walked the boy back to his group of friends. She saw him remove a fat gold money clip from his pants pocket, the fabric pulling tight across his backside as he did. He handed one bill to each of the six boys, and they all took off running. When he turned back around, he held his arms out and smiled.

God, he looked good, she thought. Tall and slender and dressed as if he'd just stepped out of a photo shoot for some very expensive Scotch. She shook her head. "You must be joking."

"No kiss?" he said, forcing his lips out in a pout. "That's all right. It has been awhile. I know we have our date tomorrow, but I saw you from my table across the square, and I thought you looked as if you could use a hand. You look fabulous—as usual. I like the haircut. It suits you."

She could not believe it was really him. If this were a film, she thought, the soundtrack would be soaring about now. How long had it been? Ha! As if she didn't know down to the day. She hadn't seen him since that last day in Lima when he had walked right past her in the midst of the foul smoke and rubble. Neither of them had said a word.

God, her shoulder ached.

Back at Bethesda, she'd thought she would get a phone call, an e-mail, a note. Certainly, he had been recalled to the capital, too. He had to be out there somewhere in the city answering their unending questions the same way she was. But as time passed, and they grafted layer after layer of skin onto her shoulder, she questioned whether she even wanted to recover.

And now, here he was smiling as though the past years had never happened.

She stepped back and put her hand to her forehead, as though to shade her eyes from the nonexistent sun. "Dig, what did you say to those boys?"

"I heard you asking them about your oars, so I gave them each five euros and told them the first one back here with the goods would get a hundred-euro note. I'd say it won't be more than ten minutes." He pointed to a small kiosk with a couple of sidewalk tables on the harbor end of the Place de la Victoire. "Shall we have a drink while we wait? I want to hear all about what you are doing with this boat." He lifted his chin in the direction of the dinghy and took hold of her arm.

She pulled her elbow out of his grip. "Wait a minute. Stop. After the day I've had today, I can't believe this." She walked away from him, hands on hips, needing the room to breathe.

She'd wanted to meet him on her terms. She wasn't ready yet.

"Riley," he said, speaking her name in the familiar intimate tone he had used hundreds of times before.

She looked back at him. Even after all that had happened between them, she could feel places deep inside her moving. Parts of her traitorous body that had lain happily dormant were now thrumming with the expectation of his touch. But her mind was sending other signals. Danger! Flee! She took a deep breath to fend off the nausea crawling up her throat.

"Dig, I can't do this, not today—maybe never."

"What?"

"Let's turn around, pretend we never saw each other. Start again tomorrow."

He spread his hands, palms up. She glanced at the white skin on those palms, crisscrossed with hundreds of lines. She remembered what it felt like to have those hands sliding down her naked skin, the feathery touch of those long, slender fingers. Those hands could make her do almost anything. Forget about the angular jaw, black curly hair, and the little dent in his chin she had once found so sexy. No, she could have resisted any of that. He had seduced her with those hands.

"Riley, I've never stopped thinking about you. You just left— disappeared. Now that I've found you again, don't push me away. Don't make me into a ghost like your brother. You're having a bad time of it. I can see that. At least let me help you."

Oh, he was good. She had to grant him that. He told women what they wanted to hear. And he knew how to listen. The most talented chameleon she had ever met, but that was all part of the job, of course. As if he couldn't have found her anytime he wanted to. She shook her head and turned her back to him. Yeah, he was lying, something she normally found unforgivable, but part of her didn't give a damn. In fact, very specific parts of her wanted to grab a cab with him and head straight to his hotel room.

"Whatever it is, I'll take care of it," he said, touching the back of her neck, brushing his fingers along her hairline.

She could see he was baffled by her silence, and she felt a brief moment of triumph at his unease.

"I have resources, you know," he said. "Come on, let's share a glass of wine, and you tell me all about what's been happening with you. Surely you have time tonight to share a glass with an old friend?"

He slid his hand over to her shoulder and squeezed. Her scars ached, and she felt sick, as though her belly were full of shards of ice.

"Get your hand off me." Her voice was low, trembling as she struggled to keep in control.

"Oh, come on, love, you don't have to be like this."

Her hand was in motion before she was conscious of her decision, and the crack of her palm striking his cheek startled the evening strollers like the sudden bang of a balloon popping. She kept her eyes focused on his as he lifted his hand to touch the growing red spot on his cheek.

"Don't call me that," she said in a harsh whisper.

He bowed his head once and said, "I apologize. I didn't mean to offend you."

"Offend? Oh please. Love? As if you knew the meaning of the word. I've been waiting more than two years for some kind of communication from you, some explanation of what really happened that day. Dig, people I loved *died* down there. Others were maimed and wounded, and their lives changed forever. Including me." She yanked at the collar of her polo shirt and exposed the patch of mottled skin on her right shoulder.

Dig's eyes flicked to the injury, then away again. "Riley—"

"No. You take a long look, Diggory. And that's after Bethesda's best did their work. After months in the hospital. Wondering what happened to you, but knowing I couldn't reach out to you. Waiting. And did I hear one word from you?" She tried to force a laugh. "Offend me? Every time I think about what happened, I feel like I'm going to vomit. Those flames haven't stopped burning. I've carried this, this—" She stopped, not knowing what to call it, afraid to put it into words. Just like all the other times when she thought about that day, she smelled the greasy smoke of burning flesh, and the stench of it made the bile burn at the back of her throat. She shook her head. "I don't want any more of your lies. What I want is the truth. The truth about what happened down there."

"Do you really?" he asked.

He spoke in those seductive tones, and she clenched both of her fists in an effort not to hit him again.

"There's more you and your kind aren't telling me," she said. "I know it. And if you won't tell me…" she started, then stopped short of saying it.

"What? It was a terrible thing, but it had nothing to do with us."

"Oh really? Why is it I have such a difficult time believing that? I kept my mouth shut, kept you out of it, and every day I grew sicker with myself."

His hands started for her, ever confident that his touch could quiet her.

She raised hers in self-defense and stepped back. "You keep your hands off me, Diggory Priest. You hear me? I'm out of it now."

Riley spun around and ran across the quay to her dinghy. Her outboard engine started on the first pull, and she spun the throttle, gunning the engine, forcing the small boat onto a plane. The hot wind stung her face and blew the tears from her eyes as her boat roared out into the dark harbor.

CHAPTER SIXTEEN

Pointe-à-Pitre

March 25, 2008

Diggory stood on the quay and watched the small dinghy disappear out of the inner basin and into the night. The harborside fish market was now abandoned, the tables empty, the dark awnings flapping in the breeze. Some movement attracted his attention farther down the dock, and he saw a fat brown rat tightrope walk the dock lines securing one of the local fishing boats. The animal disappeared into the hold.

Diggory shuddered, then began walking down the street that formed one side of the inner harbor. He walked down the center of the asphalt, his strides growing longer with each step. By the time he reached the end of the street where it curved left, he broke into a run. He could still hear the high-pitched whine of the straining outboard engine. One hundred yards ahead, the houses gave way to a waterfront restaurant. He rushed through the tables, pushing aside empty chairs and startling diners who watched wide-eyed as he hurried to the terrace. At the railing, he stopped, breathing hard, staring out into the anchorage where the half dozen or so cruising sailboats bobbed in the wind chop.

The sound of the outboard died. He waited. He was not disappointed. A masthead light blinked on. Straining his eyes, through the darkness he made out the white of the hull, the dim yellow of a cabin light. Her boat was a white-hulled sloop anchored close to the red flashing channel marker. It would be easy for them to find.

"*Monsieur, est-ce que vous voulez quelque chose a boire?*"

"*Non, merci,*" he said to the waiter who had appeared at his elbow. Much as he could use a drink, now wasn't the time. He had found her, and this time, he would see it through to the end. Marguerite Riley represented one of his rare missteps, and now, here she was like a gift.

He hadn't been lying when he told her she had improved with age. She was the physical embodiment of Nietzsche's Superwoman: fit, smart, and most of all, well bred. There had been few women he remembered longer than a week or two, few who had been of his class. Riley had been different. He could not ask her to do the things he asked of the whores or the bored foreign service wives he encountered. He knew—from the first moment he saw her in her crisp, creased USMC uniform, brown shirt, blue pants, chest covered with ribbons, firm grip announcing herself as Sergeant Riley—he had to have her and his usual sexual repertoire would never be seductive to a woman like her: the little upper-crust daddy's girl masquerading as the enlisted working class. She was the sort of girl who had acted as though he were invisible back when he was in high school and sitting in a booth waiting for his mother to get off work.

Only a few days later, he'd asked her out and brought her back to his apartment in San Isidro. He'd shuddered at that first embrace when her fingers stroked the naked skin of his shoulders and back. With her, he had come the closest to feeling the pleasure of a caress. She was the polar opposite of the human offal his mother had worked with at the diner.

And now, she said she wanted to know the truth about what happened down in Peru. He squinted his eyes at the dim cabin light bobbing on the water. *Riley, darling, you of all people should know when to leave well enough alone.* And the amusing part was that he had every intention of telling her why, in good time.

Diggory left the restaurant and ambled back toward the harbor on autopilot, lost in memories of Lima. As he passed the immigration office, he surfaced from his reveries, paused, and looked back in the direction of the anchorage. After a moment, he climbed the steps to the government building. He tried the door. It was open.

The reception desk inside stood abandoned. The clicking of his shoes echoed as he crossed the tile floor, and he heard giggling from a back room. He cleared his throat.

About a minute later, a young woman with enormous breasts and a huge gap between her front teeth emerged from the back room pushing at her lopsided bra with the back of her wrist. Her hair was tousled, and her skin flushed when she saw him look at the open buttons of her blouse. She clutched at her neckline and said, "*Bon soir, monsieur.*"

He told her who he was and explained that he needed information.

Whether it was his ID or his charm, he didn't know or care, but the secretary immediately showed him into the office of Monsieur Beaulieu, the French Immigration officer who, the girl said, had been on duty that afternoon. He was the one who had spoken to the American woman.

The man was in his shirtsleeves, his tie pulled loose, his enormous nose reddened from the half-empty bottle of wine and the pair of smudged tumblers standing on his desk. Diggory showed him the same ID he had shown the secretary, and Beaulieu, impressed, invited him to take a seat. The immigration man told him that technically they were closed. That was the reason things were so informal at the moment. Clearly, he wanted to make a good impression on the important American agent.

Diggory didn't care if he was preparing to slam it to the secretary on the desktop in the next hour. He just wanted some information. He spoke to the bureaucrat in flawless French.

"You understand that the questions I am asking you are confidential and of utmost importance to the national security of both of our nations. The young American woman on the sailboat in the harbor. Marguerite Riley. Did she clear in here?"

"Yes, as a matter of fact, I have her passport right here. There was a serious difficulty."

"What happened?"

"She came in to clear, and she told us she had one passenger on her yacht. Picked him up in the water offshore off the coast of Basse Terre this morning." He snickered and made a snorting noise in his large nose. "She said he was totally nude. Well, except for a necklace."

"Describe this necklace."

"She said it was a coin of some sort. Gold."

"And the man's name?"

"He gave her a false name."

"What was the name?"

"Robert Surcouf."

* * *

Diggory closed the door behind him, leaving the immigration officer and his secretary to continue with the disgusting little rendezvous he had interrupted. He stood on the doorstep and watched the lights reflecting on the water of the inner harbor, the French tourists and locals mingling as they hurried on their way to home or dinner or, like Beaulieu, to surreptitious meetings or animal gropings.

There were more than six and a half billion human beings roaming this earth, most of them little better than the vermin that climbed aboard the fishing boats at this time of night. How marvelous that his Riley had crossed paths with the man he now sought. He would enjoy the opportunity to use her again and to finish, finally, the business he had started. Even Yorick would have to appreciate the symmetry of the situation. Life appeared random, that is until something like this fell into his lap. But here was another signal that his time was at hand. While he didn't believe in God or destiny or that any force like fate ruled men's lives, Diggory saw this as proof that men like him, superior in intellect and breeding, often also had plain luck on their side—and the intelligence to know how to take advantage of it.

He patted the front pocket of his shirt, feeling the shape of the passport there, and he felt the hot blood rushing to his core. She was his now.

CHAPTER SEVENTEEN

Aboard the Bonefish

March 25, 2008

Riley didn't stop crying until she reached her boat. She hoisted the dinghy in the davits, unlocked the main hatch, and turned on her anchor light. Routine always saved her. In the service, it had been her job, her duty, and the best way to move beyond what had happened to her brother. When you had a job to do, something you had trained for, you could lose yourself in the work. After she'd left the service, she'd floundered back in DC, chafing under the memories and her attempt to live with her father. She'd always lived frugally and saved during her years on the government's payroll, so she took her life's savings and bought and moved aboard the *Bonefish*. On the boat, she had maintenance, routine, things she had to do to keep herself sane and the boat safe and secure.

On this night, her routine allowed her to get back in control, but her mind wouldn't turn off. Seeing Dig again had brought it all back. He'd called her that last morning in Lima, and she had gone to his apartment. They'd made love, and then with the sunlight streaming in the window bathing their naked bodies in golden light, he had asked her to do a favor for him. Of course, she had said. At that moment, she would have done just about anything to get to spend more time with him.

Stop it, she told herself. She reached up and turned on the overhead light in the main cabin, then slid onto the settee in front of her MacBook laptop computer. She tapped the space bar, and the screen blinked on to reveal her e-mail inbox. She still had not opened the e-mail she'd received from Mercury that morning, but the name Hazel Kittredge was listed beneath the name of her employer, and she clicked on her friend's e-mail instead.

Darling,

How are you and where are you? Please tell me you're shacked up on some luscious Caribbean island with a well-endowed, gorgeous man who owns a rum distillery or some such romantic thing. You're not still doing this all-alone-Super-Woman routine, are you? Call me!

XX,

Hazel

Riley smiled and felt for the first time in over an hour that she might be able to shake off the pall that Diggory Priest had cast over her life. She reached for her cell phone and thought a moment before dialing, wondering where and in what time zone her friend might be.

Like Riley, Hazel had grown up the daughter of a career diplomat, but Hazel's father had never needed to work. Hazel's grandfather had started life as a sharecropper until he'd invented some device that improved car mufflers back in the fifties, and ever since, her family had been *those* Kittredges of Atlanta.

She dialed Hazel's US cell on the off chance she was stateside. Hazel picked up on the second ring.

"Darling! Where are you?" Her friend's soothing alto voice worked better than a Valium.

"Pointe-à-Pitre in Guadeloupe." Riley turned her body on the settee, settled back into the pillows, and stretched her legs out on the velvet upholstery.

"And you're headed down to the Saintes, I hope?"

"Yup. Tomorrow morning."

"I envy you. They make better croissants there than in Paris. You know Daddy has a little place down in Martinique. Maybe I'll fly down and we can catch up."

She sighed. "Hazel, that would be so great."

"Riley, what's the matter? I can hear it in your voice. Something's wrong."

"I ran into an old acquaintance today." She stopped, trying to remember how much she had told Hazel last fall. "Remember that guy I told you about? The one from Lima?"

"The son of a bitch who couldn't even be bothered to call you after the fucking terrorists nearly blew you up? Oh yeah, I remember him."

"He surprised me on the street today. We exchanged a few words, and I sort of lost it and slapped him."

"Good for you!"

"Not really. Not good at all. I thought if I ever saw him again, I'd be able to figure it all out. You know, like my old shrink used to say, 'find closure' and all that. But instead, I smack him and run off crying like some silly female."

"Contrary to your tough-guy self-image, my friend, you are still a female and you're not bulletproof. But silly? Girl, you wouldn't know how to do silly."

"I was such an idiot." On a shelf, behind the settee, dozens of books were held in place by a long bungee cord. She snapped the elastic absentmindedly. "I thought I was over him, over all that drama. I'd agreed to see him because I wanted to know more about what happened down there. I was prepared to be fully in control."

"That's my girl."

"But I couldn't believe how pissed off I got just seeing him." Riley stopped. She didn't know how to explain the feelings she'd had.

"What did you expect?"

"Hazel, I thought Lima was the end of something. It wasn't. In fact, I think now it was just the beginning."

"What are you talking about?"

"I still don't know what *really* happened down there. I haven't told you all of it, Hazel. I can't. I need to know the truth, but I'm afraid, too. There are things that he—that they won't tell me. Things that don't add up."

"Riley, he works for the Agency. Girlfriend, you *never* will be able to add it up. You know how those people are. They think they fucking rule the world."

Riley laughed. "You remind of another guy I picked up today. He was a real nut case."

"You picked up a guy?"

"He was swimming way out at sea," she said. Then, after pausing for effect, she smiled and added, "*Buck naked.*"

"You are having fun!"

"Oh yeah. He says I saved his life."

"So that should make him your slave for life?"

"Not exactly. He disappeared on me—after I'd reported him to Immigration. So now, thanks to him, the French authorities here think I'm smuggling in illegal aliens. They seized my passport."

"Good God, girl! I can't let you out of my sight. You might be a big, strong marine, but you aren't doing so well away from the government tit."

"I'm doing fine." She didn't want to worry her friend, so she tried to sound as though she meant it. "The wanker stole my radio, too. I've got to fix this whole thing on Tuesday. They've scheduled some kind of hearing. I still have plenty of friends at State. I'll get it straightened out."

"You let me know if you want me to call Daddy."

"No. I just have to find my illegal alien. When I plucked him out of the water, he mentioned he'd been headed down to the Saintes. So, that's where I'm going in the morning."

"So, back to the naked guy. Was he cute? Was he a keeper, or was the water too cold to tell?"

Riley laughed again, and it felt so good. She'd needed this call. "The water was quite warm, and not that I noticed, but he had a body worthy of a *Playgirl* centerfold."

"Darling, I want details. Dimensions! Are you going to see him again?"

"First, he was eye candy only. A bit soft in the head—a sort of a hard-bodied hillbilly spouting New World Order conspiracy crap. You know, the old 'the government is out to get you' type. But there was something about him, Hazel, something sweet, almost innocent. Like he still believes in tilting at windmills."

"One sight of all that man flesh and you're making him heroic."

"Not really. It was just something he said." Riley pictured him standing next to her in the cockpit of her boat. He was so different—not tall and elegant like Dig. *Bob* was broad-shouldered and built solid. But, she reminded herself, you've given up on men, remember?

"Hazel, I think he's more the redneck, butt-crack-flashing type. You know, great ass but no class. Has about an eighth-grade education. And yes, I'm going to see him again. I'd better. I plan to haul that sweet ass of his into this court hearing so I can get my passport back."

"Now listen to who's gone all snob on me."

From anyone else, the remark might have stung. Riley came from a family of high achievers—her father had attended Yale, her mother the Sorbonne. After Michael died his freshman year at Yale, she had *enlisted* in the Marines—much to her parents' chagrin—and attended no college at all.

"Hazel, you always think my life should have more drama in it."

"Darling, you and your redneck illegal alien can have lots of little no-neck children. This sounds like a match made in Tennessee." Only Hazel could come up with that one. They'd both been Liz Taylor fans and watched every movie they could find with her in it.

"As in Williams? Now look who's being catty!" Riley said, and she heard her friend groan through the phone. "Besides, Maggie and Brick? I don't think so. In the movie, they didn't have any no-neck monsters. That was the problem, remember?"

"Ahhhh. What am I going to do with you? You and your prickly personality. Girlfriend, you need to get laid."

"I've told you—I'm done with that. I've joined the Semper Fi Immaculate Heart Convent for Wayward Marines. I'm going to devote my life to good works."

"Ha! That'll be the day. Riley, darling, I live in hope that some fellow is going to come along with an ax and chop his way through the forest of thorns you've built around yourself. I mean you don't want to wind up one of those old cat ladies, do you? Tell me you haven't got a cat."

"No cat, Hazel." And with a grin, she added, "Not yet."

CHAPTER EIGHTEEN

Aboard the Shadow Chaser

March 25, 2008

As *Shadow Chaser* motored out of Marigot Bay, the moon lit the sky from behind La Grand Soufrière Volcano. Cole spread out the chart in the wheelhouse and examined the islands called Îles des Saintes, where Riley had said she was headed. There was another bay named Marigot down there. It was confusing in these islands. Like the Grand Soufrière Volcano on Guadeloupe—which was not to be confused with Montserrat's Soufrière Hills or Soufrière St. Vincent. All were active, but at least this one here on Guadeloupe hadn't erupted since 1976. Though no lives were lost on Guadeloupe that year, it had caused more than a billion dollars' worth of damage. Montserrat was the island that had lost two-thirds of her habitable land from the many eruptions since 1995. Over twenty people had died on Montserrat, and the capital had been destroyed. The remaining inhabitants lived with the impending threat of another huge eruption. On clear days, when Cole could see the smoking lava dome to the north, he understood why many of his colleagues referred to the area as the Caribbean Ring of Fire.

Cole left Theo at the helm and slipped into his cabin. From the bottom of the hanging locker, he extracted a sheet metal box with a padlock on it. He set the box on his bunk, spun the combination, and withdrew three worn leather journals. Inside the first two, every page was filled with his father's neat printing. He had read them all many times. The first entry in the first journal was dated three days after Cole's birth. Each entry started with the words "Dear Son."

He'd still been busting his hump at East Carolina U when word came that his father had died at home in Cornwall. There were no details, which didn't surprise him at the time. Communication with his father had always been a bit odd. Cole had been the result of a brief love affair and an even briefer marriage between an American nurse, Kara Greer, and a British businessman, James Thatcher, twenty-five years her senior. Cole's mother had told him that his father was not suited for family life, and she'd sent him back to England. It was not until the journals arrived in a package from Bodwin, England, that he had learned his father's side of the story.

He opened the first of the leather volumes and began to read.

Dear Son,

Just received word from the States of your arrival three days past. You must take after your mother—quite punctual, that is. Any woman who could marshal that lot at her hospital could presumably have even got the Italian trains to run on time. Alas, all her attempts to tidy up my life went awry. Love does not conquer all. She's a scientist, that one. Maybe unconquerable. She's a queen from Amazonia, our Kara is, a warrior princess who has never needed a man for much. Could have been much more than a nurse, not to degrade her profession in any way, but she sees the world in the black-and-white of certainties— truth and falsehood and ne'er shall anything dwell between. That, my boy, is where I think life begins to get interesting. In the 'tween.
—JT

Cole closed the leather cover and sighed. He wondered how it was possible he could have ended up so much like this father he never knew. He had thought when he went to school to study marine science that he was following his mother's first love: science. But when he enrolled in graduate school to study maritime archeology, he had shifted over to his father's world *in the 'tween*—the world of suspicions and rumors, conspiracies and plots. The shadowy world of dreams.

And the day these journals arrived, Cole had learned how far into the *'tween* his father had gone. Theories only remain theories until someone proves them right or wrong. James Thatcher hadn't been given the chance to do that, but he'd sent his words on to his son. And the more Cole read, the more he, too, became a believer, not only in the theory, but in the idea that it was his father's search for the truth that had gotten him killed.

"Hey, Cole, you want me to take her into the cove?" Theo called out from the helm.

"Hang on. I'm coming." He slid the journals back in the box, locked it, and returned it to its place in his cabin.

* * *

Little more than two miles down the coast from Marigot Bay, Cole eased the big vessel in close to shore while Theo stood out on the bow with a handheld spotlight. The younger man panned the light down the beach, but there was no sign of the Whaler.

Cole stuck his head out the wheelhouse door and asked Theo to come take the con.

After the younger man had taken the wheel, Cole went alone onto the foredeck and searched the beach with the spotlight himself. No doubt about it. The Whaler was gone. He shut off the light and sat in the darkness for several minutes, contemplating how he was going to continue diving with nothing but that rubber ducky of a dink. They had no more money. He wasn't even sure what he was going to do when they ran out of fuel. Finally, he stowed the spotlight and returned to the wheelhouse.

Theo sat in the comfortable chair in front of the wooden ship's wheel, his feet propped up on the console above the helm. Over his head, several screens glowed, including a computer GPS chart plotter, radar, and a down-imaging sonar/depth finder, while resting on his lap was a small laptop that could convert into a tablet computer. Theo's fingers danced on the keys with the speed of a court reporter.

"Are you paying any attention at all to the con?"

"It's called multitasking, my good man."

"Take us out, then, Mr. Multitasker."

"Aye, aye, Captain," Theo said without removing his eyes from the tiny screen. "Back to Marigot, then?"

Cole stood in the doorway to the galley, his eyes bouncing from Theo to the chart to the radar. The vessel was turning, and he heard the rpm increase as the bow of *Shadow Chaser* cleared the land. Theo had not touched the wheel or the throttle.

"What the hell?"

Theo grinned. "You like my new toy?"

"You're controlling everything from there?" Cole pointed at the laptop. "How?"

"The magic of wireless, my dear friend. I don't even need something this big. I could do it from a Wi-Fi-enabled cell phone. Back to my question. What course, Captain?"

Cole shook his head. "Damn. You're really something. The Saintes. We're going to Marigot Bay number two at Bourges des Saintes," he said, trying to make his mouth into the right shape to say the French words, but mangling it in the end.

Theo looked up from his computer, his eyes wide behind the glasses. "Really? Why? What about the journals? *Surcouf*? As you said, we're getting close."

"I told you—I saw the Brewsters going into Pointe-à-Pitre. I couldn't take a chance that they'd see me on the streets, find it on me. I *had* to hide it. I left it on her boat."

Theo's feet dropped to the floor. He flipped the laptop shut and slid it across the console. "You did what?"

"And then there's the matter of the radio I borrowed." Cole looked up at Theo's face. "Don't worry. She'll never find the coin."

"But what about us? Are we going to be able to find it?"

"No problem. We'll find her, I'll get aboard her boat and get it back."

Theo threw back his head and started laughing, then he collapsed into the helmsman's seat. He flipped open the laptop and began punching in waypoints, his shoulders still shaking.

"What?" Cole said finally.

"I got my answer. She was *hot*."

CHAPTER NINETEEN

Pointe-à-Pitre

March 25, 2008

"Monsieur?"

Diggory Priest heard the boy's voice before he made out his shape at the bottom of the steps. The child scrambled up to the door of the Immigration offices dragging two aluminum oars. Diggory paid the urchin, and the boy ran off into the night without another word.

From his high vantage point, Diggory leaned on the oars and considered how best to take advantage of the evening's events. Across the Place de la Victoire, he noticed a man hurrying through the crowd, shoving people aside. He was wearing a red windbreaker over his T-shirt and frayed cutoff jeans. The man rushed past an elderly couple who were coaxing a well-coifed tiny dog toward a patch of grass. The red-jacket man failed to see the dog until his leg tangled in the leash. The small ball of fur was whipped into the air, and Diggory heard the high-pitched yelp from fifty yards away. The man turned, swearing in English, then kicked the dog airborne again while disentangling himself. He rushed on, leaving the elderly man shouting curses and the woman bending over the whimpering fluff.

By the time Diggory reached the sidewalk, the barbarian had already disappeared into the Rue Victor Hugo. He recognized him from a photo Caliban had shown him. Diggory allowed the man to get ahead and disappear among the pedestrians, autos, and motorbikes that jostled along the narrow street. The man's destination, Le Mambo, was a small bar up an even darker alley, the place where Diggory was supposed to meet him at eight—in fifteen minutes.

Maggie Riley would have to wait.

Le Mambo had once been a backstreet dive, but a younger French crowd had now discovered it. Dig squeezed past a voluptuous woman standing in the narrow doorway. She was trying to talk into a cell phone without dislodging the largest hoop earrings he had ever seen. Her white-blond hair was molded into dozens of short, sharp spikes. When she paused, she stuck a cigarette between her lips and sucked until the end of the butt grew cherry red and her cleavage swelled.

Once inside, Diggory waited for his eyes to adjust to the minimum light provided by the few red-tinted bulbs that hung from the ceiling on wires. The tables were only half-filled, as it was still quite early for the French. The clientele tended toward the pierced-nose-and-leather crowd, and the music pounding out from the large black speakers was the frenetic Franco-Caribbean pop they called *zouk*.

The man was sitting at the corner of the bar with his back to the door, the red windbreaker appearing almost black under the red lights. He was a mongrel, a mixed breed. His skin, or what Diggory could see of it round his neck, looked more gray than brown, and his dark, frizzy hair was pulled back in a ponytail. Along his face hung several long, thin braids with cowry shells knotted into the plaits.

Diggory leaned the oars against the bar and slid onto the stool around the corner from the windbreaker man. He rested his arms on the bar, his steepled fingers very close to the barbarian's sweating glass of beer.

When the man turned to face him, Diggory was amused to see a silver skull and crossbones hanging by a chain through his left ear.

"D'ya mind?" the man said.

"I beg your pardon?"

"I said, d'ya mind? Stay on your own fuckin' side of the bar."

Dig did not move. "Caliban told me I'd find you here."

"Shit. Why didn't ya say so." The man tipped up his glass and drained his beer. Then he stuck out his hand. "Name's Spyder, with a Y."

Diggory ignored his hand as the bartender approached. He was an effeminate black man with hair shaped like abstract topiary and contact lenses that tinted his eyes an unnatural green.

"He don't speak nuthin' but French," the barbarian said. "I tried."

Diggory ordered a glass of red wine, which he had no intention of touching. Then he turned to the American and spoke in English. "We hired you to do a job."

"Hey, I got this shit under control. We got the guy's dinghy."

"No, you do not have this shit under control, do you?"

The man gave Diggory a puzzled look. "What d'ya mean?"

The bartender set the glass of red wine on the bar. Priest waited until he moved away before continuing. "I noticed you crossing the square from over one hundred feet away. You attract too much attention. This is a quiet business. Covert. Do you know what that means?"

"Are you calling me stupid?" the man asked, his words loud enough to be heard over the music from across the room.

"Lower your voice. Yes, I am calling you stupid. I also asked you a question. You don't know what covert means, do you?"

The cheek on one side of the man's face bulged as his tongue explored the molars behind his brown-colored front teeth.

"Covert means secretive. Hidden," Dig said. "You don't want to broadcast to everyone what you are doing here. You want to blend in." He felt as if he were talking to one of the rodents roaming the streets. He pinched the nylon fabric of the man's windbreaker between his fingers. "Red is not a color for someone who does not want to be noticed. Pushing people out of the way, kicking their dogs—this is not good practice for someone who does not want to be noticed. Are you getting my drift here?"

The barbarian stared at his glass and said, "Yeah."

"I want you to follow orders, now. My orders. Do you understand?"

"Yeah."

"Look at me when I speak to you."

The man ran his fingers across his two-day growth of beard, and Diggory saw that every finger was tipped with a crescent of black dirt under the fingernail. The man swiveled his head around and met Diggory's eyes. His pupils were huge black pools.

"There's a woman," Diggory said. "I want you to follow her."

"But that Caliban guy said he wanted me to grab the doc, maybe get that coin."

Diggory remembered Caliban claiming it was the barbarians' idea to go after Thatcher, and he wondered which party was lying. "And you were so successful at that."

"Hey, I said I got it under control."

Diggory did not say anything for almost a minute. He kept his eyes on the other man's face. At last he said, "Do you understand that you work for me?"

The windbreaker man looked away and signaled for the bartender to bring him another beer. When he spoke, he did not look at Dig. "Yeah, I got it."

"You will do exactly what I tell you to do, and you will stop making these feeble efforts to think for yourself." Diggory gave the man a description of Riley and the location where she was anchored. "The boat might be named *Bonefish*." Diggory remembered her dream of owning a boat and naming it after the vessels she had sailed with her brother.

"I want you to locate the boat tonight, and…" Diggory twisted around and picked up the oars. He handed one to the other man and rested the remaining oar across his knees. The oars were designed to be taken apart for easier stowage. A small button protruded where the two halves of the oars joined, and when Diggory pressed it in with his thumb, he was able to slide the two aluminum tubes apart. "I want you to leave these on her deck without her knowledge." He pulled out a small object that looked like a silver AA battery. He slid it into a tiny ziplock bag, then, using several napkins from the pile on the bar, Diggory stuffed the wrapped device into the oar and connected the tubes once again. He held the second oar out to the barbarian.

The man started to take it, then hesitated. "That ain't a bomb, I hope."

"No, it's not a bomb. I don't want her to know who left the oars. Understand?"

"Yeah, right. Covert."

"Call in twice daily." Diggory slid a slip of paper across the bar.

The man picked up the paper and looked at it as though it were written in an undecipherable code. "Call you? But that dude Caliban said—"

"Yes. Call me. Once in the morning, once at night. Stick with her. Tell me where she is and what she's doing. But do it *covertly*."

"And what about the other—"

Diggory lifted his palm to hush the man. "No questions, no thinking for yourself. You work for me now. Do you understand?"

The man shrugged and shoved the paper into a pocket of the nylon windbreaker. He drained the beer, his Adam's apple bobbing between the taut tendons in his neck. He left without another word and without leaving any money.

Filth, Dig thought. He'd always disliked using nonprofessionals for anything other than information, but it came with the job.

When he was on his way out the door, past the woman with the earrings who was still talking on her cell, Diggory felt his own phone vibrate in his pocket. He stepped away from the doorway and started down the street. Once he was alone, he pulled out the phone and looked down at the glowing screen. He recognized the number as that of the German schoolteacher from the night before. An image of her naked body flashed in his mind. There were reports to write and arrangements to be made for the surveillance. Then he thought about how exceedingly limber and inventive this teacher was, and when he'd told her what he wanted the previous night, she'd viewed it as a challenge. With a flick of his wrist, he opened the phone and pressed it to his ear.

CHAPTER TWENTY

The Atlantic south of Bermuda

February 12, 1942

The captain swung the torch beam around the compartment and fixed it on each man in turn. As the three Brits stared at him in silence, he raised his arm and wiped his face on his sleeve, which only served to smear the blood and make him look worse.

"My men want to go home," he said in heavily accented English, "but my orders are for Panama." The French captain appeared smaller, deflated.

Woolsey felt his mouth open to answer the man, then he realized he had never spoken to the captain without the benefit of Henri Michaut's translation. "You speak English?" he asked.

The captain continued as though Woolsey had not spoken. "Who can blame them? The worst thing about putting into port is that we get mail. With news from home, their families tell them that life in occupied France is not so bad. They have mothers, girlfriends," he shone the light on Mullins, "and boyfriends. So we are now headed for Martinique."

It was obvious he spoke the language damn well. Thinking back, Woolsey wondered how many times he and the other Brits had spoken freely in front of the old man, thinking he didn't understand a word.

"So the Frog crew gave you the boot, eh, Capt'n?" McKay spoke from deep in the depths of the hold.

"What does this mean, the boot?"

"Mutiny, mate."

"Ah, yes, this is the word. They intend to surrender to Admiral Petain in Martinique."

"How long will it take—" Woolsey began.

McKay barked out a laugh. "Fuckin' hooray."

Lamoreaux ignored him. "It is just over one thousand miles to Fort de France. Our electric motors are still giving trouble, so we must stay at the surface. It would be too dangerous to dive. At the surface, the best we can do is ten knots."

Woolsey didn't have to know much about ships to do that math. Two hundred forty miles a day meant it was at least four days to Martinique. They didn't have one.

Lamoreaux was rummaging about in the cases of wine bottles, the torchlight making the shadows dance on the bulkheads.

"Captain, may I have a word?"

"*Ahhh, voila, c'est ici,*" the captain whispered to himself. He produced a sommelier's knife and corkscrew, sat down on a crate, and began to open a bottle. The loud *pop* of the pulled cork brought McKay out of the shadows. The captain handed him the bottle and went to work on another.

Woolsey thought McKay sober was bad enough. "Captain, sir, I'm not sure that's such a good idea. We need to keep our wits about us."

After taking a drink from the bottle in his hand, Lamoreaux looked up at Woolsey and studied him for a moment. "I do not think you understand the situation."

"I know I'm not ready to give up. There's got to be something we can do. Surely some of your men remain loyal to you."

Lamoreaux closed one eye and looked up at the ceiling with the other. He appeared to be running through the list of men in his head. At last, he spoke. "No, not a one." He took a long pull on the bottle.

Woolsey knocked the bottle out of the man's hand, and it broke when it hit the deck a few feet away. The sharp, fruity smell of the wine filled the compartment.

"Lieutenant, that was not wise. There is not so much wine here as you might think. Not for what we need."

What was the man talking about? There were cases and cases of wine. "Captain, you can't sit here and get pissed while your men take over your command. Get hold of yourself, man. There are four of us here. We can overpower the guards next time they come in. This is your boat."

Lamoreaux had reached for another bottle and was in the process of screwing the metal coil into the cork. He paused. "Lieutenant, there is no way that the four of us are going to succeed against one hundred and twenty-five men. Either they are going to feed us to the sharks en route, or they are going to send you three to prison camps and they will hang me for treason for joining de Gaulle. My boat—the *Surcouf,* the pride of the French navy—will go off with the Huns. You don't think that is enough reason to get drunk?"

"Captain, there is something aboard this boat that your men know nothing about."

Lamoreaux set the bottle aside and aimed the torch beam on Woolsey. "You know? What is this?"

"This thing, Captain, involves a third possible fate for us all— and it will sink your precious boat."

"What are you talking about?"

"Captain Lamoreaux, there is a bomb on this boat, and it is going to go off within a matter of hours."

The captain threw back his head and laughed. "Psshht. Lieutenant. For a moment, I thought you really knew something secret about my boat. But this? *Non.* You cannot trick me into trying something with you English."

"This is no trick, I assure you, Captain. I set the thing myself."

CHAPTER TWENTY-ONE

Le Gosier

March 26, 2008

Diggory counted the revolutions of the ceiling fan blades spinning over the center of the room and tried not to think about the naked woman lying next to him, facedown on the bed, her right leg draped across his thighs. He could feel the sweat pooling in the spaces where her skin touched his. When she inhaled, the soft tissue at the back of her throat vibrated, and the snores seemed to rise out of her open mouth like the bubbles of cartoon speech. There would be no sleep for him.

He had arranged to meet the schoolteacher—her name was Ulrika—at the casino, leaving himself enough time to return to his rooms and change into the clothes, slicked-back hair, and glasses of the Peruvian businessman she had met in St. Francois. After a few drinks, they went to the La Cheyanne in Le Gosier, where the gyrating crowds, pulsing lights, and blinking images on the big screens had excited her more than any pharmaceutical could. He didn't enjoy dancing, not in among the throngs of filthy French and Creole young people who crammed themselves into beach discos on the weekends, but he was good enough at it so as not to be noticed as either too good or pitifully bad.

She had suggested they go back to his room, and instead, he gave her a handful of euro notes and had her check in to the Hôtel Arawak under her name. Once in the room, she had torn off her clothes and been more willing than most to do what he asked of her. She had not needed him to touch her like so many women did, and she had been very good at squatting over him on the floor and taking him into her. He watched her as she rocked and bounced, her fingers touching the glistening flesh where she held him, her nipples erect, breasts swinging. She'd called out in German as her muscles squeezed around him, her contractions sending him over the edge, her face contorted, her damp hair stuck to her skin with sweat.

Watching them, knowing that he had the power to turn them into animals only heightened his pleasure. So long as they did not put their hands all over him.

When he could stand it no longer, he lifted the sleeping woman's leg and climbed out of the bed. He crossed the plush carpet to the sliding glass door. Opening the panel on its silent rollers, Diggory stepped out onto the cool tiles of the balcony. The trade wind breeze cooling his sweat-covered skin was ripe with the briny smell of low tide. On the horizon, white lights winked as vessels traversed the waters between Pointe-à-Pitre and the Îles des Saintes.

Ulrika had been a pleasant distraction, but even when he had been inside her, his thoughts had drifted to Riley. In Peru, when he had discovered the attractive marine's pedigree, he had been unable to resist bedding her. This secret knowledge gave a new dimension to his pleasure. But in the end, she became cloying, as they all did. They'd meet for a meal at one of the trendy cafés in the El Barranco section of Miraflores, and while he was cutting his steak, she would reach across the table and touch his arm. She started to talk about love and *their* future together. He'd had to end it before anyone caught on. Granted, things hadn't played out as he'd expected, but the end result was the same. The affair ended, and she had disappeared as a threat to him; yet he knew there was still unfinished business there. He'd always known she would play a part when the time came for him to seize control of the organization.

From inside the room, he heard Ulrika's voice. She called out a name, but not the one he had given her.

"Thor? Someone is calling for Thor?" she called out in her accented English.

He slipped back into the room, and in the dim light that passed through the gauzy curtains, he could see her sitting naked and cross-legged on the bed holding his satellite phone, the small screen aglow.

"What kind of phone is this? What's this thing stuck to it?" She wiggled the voice encryption device that snapped onto the data port of his sat phone.

He grabbed the instrument from her hand and stepped back out onto the balcony, closing the door behind him this time.

"Yes."

"I am surprised at you, Thor. Letting a civilian have access to your secure phone."

"I'll take care of it."

"You do understand the gravity of the situation."

"I do."

"Yes." He paused, and Diggory knew that his silence spoke more than words. "I understand you told them to follow some woman. I want to know what it's about."

So Caliban had contacted the barbarian to check up on him. He wondered if the older man was following orders or merely trying to assert his power by keeping Diggory on a short leash. The late hour led him to believe the latter.

"It is a woman sailor who knows Thatcher. I have reason to believe she will lead them to him if they follow her."

"I see."

"You brought me in to do a job. Either leave me to do it or get someone else."

"Yes. Absolutely. I understand, but you do need to keep me informed."

"As soon as I have something concrete, I'll be in touch. Is there anything else?"

"Thor, I know I don't have to tell you this, but..." Caliban began.

Dig held the phone a distance from his ear, disgusted with the man's pedantic tone.

"We are headed toward this election at home, and though I cannot say any more about what exactly is at stake here, I can stress to you that this project is of the utmost importance to our future."

"I understand," he said. He closed the phone before the other man could answer.

* * *

In the dark room, her body was an undistinguished lump under the sheet and comforter. Her dark-brown hair splayed out across the pillow. The snoring had resumed. He sat on the side of the bed, and she stirred. She murmured to him in German, "Who was that on your phone?"

He said nothing.

She rolled over to face him. "Is something wrong?"

He reached out his hand and traced his fingers along the side of her face, gently tucking a strand of hair behind her ear. "My phone was inside my jacket."

"Yes, but I didn't see anything. I just got out the phone."

Of course she would not be so quick to say she had not seen anything unless she had. She would not have been able to miss the heft of the gun.

"You should not have answered that phone."

"I'm sorry." She ran her tongue around her lips, her intentions bare. "It's just that you were outside, and I thought it might be important. I was a bad girl, but that's what I like about you. You're a bad boy, and you like bad girls, don't you?"

He looked away from her, out the window, and thought about what she did know about him. The gun. The phone. And she'd called him Thor. He looked at the open sliding door. The hour was late. He wondered how much noise she would make.

"I won't do it again," she said and squirmed her body to press her breasts through the sheet against his thigh.

He placed his left hand on the mattress on the far side of her body, then he pulled down the sheet to admire her long neck and the heavy breasts with large pink areolae. He leaned down close, pressing his rib cage against her naked skin and watching her eyes as his fingers traced the line of her jaw then slid up under her chin. "No," he said. "You won't do it again."

She was an athletic woman, and the tendons in her neck were strong. He saw it in her eyes when the pressure registered, when the last vestiges of sleep were ushered out by the arrival of terror. She flailed at his back with her fists, trying to reach his head, but he fended off her blows by pinning her arms with his elbows. Her feet were tangled in the bedclothes, and she arched her back, her eyes growing wider, her face starting to darken. She tried to kick her legs free.

He increased the pressure on the carotid, and her eyes flicked and darted around in their sockets, panic driving out all reason. But the lack of oxygen and the blood that continued to pump into her head slowed her struggles. When her eyelids drooped, he released his grip on her throat. He heard the intake of air and was pleased. He needed to see her eyes to watch for that exquisite moment. Her eyelids fluttered, and the eyes rolled and began to focus as the realization flooded back into her that he was still there.

He felt her chest expand as she made ready to scream, and her eyes locked on his with a hatred so vile he imagined he could feel the heat. Once they were resigned to what was going to happen, they always turned from terror to a venomous enmity. They wanted him to know their last thoughts, and he found a strength in that. With his powerful right hand he squeezed hard, cutting her scream so that she emitted only a feeble squeak before her face darkened again and her eyes began to bulge. This time he reached over with his left hand and held her eyelids open as she lost consciousness and the life drained out of her.

He watched, wondering if there would be a moment when he would see the change in her, when she would see if there was something beyond this world or not. There were so many stories of visions, of a light, a tunnel, of people seeing the other side, and he always watched for that moment when he might learn if it was so. But like all the other times, she merely departed. One second she was there, then came the instant when he knew that even if he released his grip, she would not breathe again. When she was gone, he moved his face close to hers and tried to find the words to explain how different the eyes looked without that inner light. Dull, glassy, inert. The eyes were now all these things, but none of those words got to the essence of what had changed.

Heaven, Hades, angels, Lucifer—all that seemed quite preposterous if you thought about it. The only way people could possibly believe in that was to force themselves to suspend their reason and disbelief—and that he could not do. As Hegel said, "The rational alone is real." Saints, sinners, miracles, the Bible. It was all as fantastic as something made up by Poe or Disney. Ludicrous. And if it didn't exist, then what on earth would drive men to act except their own desires and appetites and self-interest? If the whole structure that defined good and evil was based on falsehoods, then his life made perfect sense. As did her death, he thought as he flexed the fingers of his right hand, remembering the feel of her smooth, warm skin as she struggled.

But in the back of his mind, there was always that little niggling doubt that said, *yes, but what if it all were true?*

He went to work with the precision of a Broadway set dresser. From another pocket of his jacket, he removed a pair of latex gloves and a small microfiber cloth. He cleaned the room, flushed the spent condom, and then stood, one gloved hand on his chin, and stared at the corpse. Her clothes, underwear, bra, and pantyhose were draped over the armchair where she had left them. He looked up at the ceiling fan still turning over the center of the room—then back at the pantyhose, and he nodded. They'd started this with that clumsy business back in England, and it would be amusing to repeat it. Tying the pantyhose around her neck, he gave her one last smile, even though the blank eyes showed no appreciation for his charm.

CHAPTER TWENTY-TWO

Aboard the Bonefish

March 26, 2008

Guadeloupe's Soufrière volcano stood off to starboard, invisible beneath its cloak of snagged trade wind clouds. The lower, gentler slope of the mountain was dotted with red-roofed homes, towns, and farms. Riley hummed to herself as she sailed the *Bonefish* hard on the wind bound for the Îles des Saintes. The wind was from the east-southeast, and she was sailing due south to clear Capesterre Belle-Eau. In truth, the autopilot did most of the steering, leaving her free to play with the lines, adjusting the trim of the sails, trying to eke out an extra half knot from each wind shift. She moved from one side of the cockpit to the other, her yellow oilskins streaming water from the waves that smashed against the small boat's bow and the wind-blown spray that stung her cheeks.

She shook her head like a dog whipping the water off his fur. The hood of her jacket was pulled tight round her face, cinched in by the drawstring under her chin, so it was only her face that got wet. The salt water streamed into her eyes. She didn't care. The stout little boat smashed into another wave, and spray reached nearly to her mast's first crosstrees.

CHRISTINE KLING

She whooped like a rodeo cowboy, ducked under the dodger, and patted the boat's closed main hatch. "Atta girl," she said aloud. Her Caliber 40 was no racing boat, but she was making a solid seven and a half knots punching through the seas, rarely slowing down. This was the kind of adrenalin-pumping sailing Riley loved, with the lee rail almost underwater and the lower edge of the genoa dripping seawater. Off her stern, the quarter wave rose with a whoosh as the *Bonefish* slipped through the water, pushing to reach beyond her own hull speed. She was a sweet boat all right, and Riley had grown to trust her, aware that the boat was tougher than she was. This morning *Bonefish* was overpowered with full jenny in the eighteen to twenty knots of wind, but she was pounding her way through the Caribbean chop without a care. All the hatches and port lights were closed down tight, and Riley was proud of the fact that her boat never leaked a drop in bad weather. The only seawater that made its way below would be what she tracked in once she arrived.

Riley braced herself in a corner of the cockpit and admired the view of the island she was leaving behind. She still hadn't worked out what she was going to do about her passport situation. The night before, she had lain in her bunk staring at the overhead unable to sleep, thinking about Diggory and wondering if she should sail to the Saintes with such thin evidence *Bob* might be there. She knew she was looking for an excuse to stick around and go find Dig in the morning.

Finally, she got out of bed and dug into her chart table for her old scrapbook. In it were family photos, plastic sleeves filled with yellowing newspaper clippings, her discharge papers, and the various ribbons and medals she'd once worn so proudly. She opened the book to the snapshots from Lima. In one, she and Diggory were sitting at an outside café table, smiling for the camera, arms entwined. She looked so happy, so ignorant. Then she slammed the book closed, stuffed it into the bookcase behind the settee, and climbed back into her bunk.

Seeing she had cleared the cape, Riley eased off the wind a bit. The boat speed picked up by another half knot. It wasn't even midmorning, and she was more than halfway there. Her predawn departure had paid off.

She remembered the moment she'd ventured on deck in the dark and found her oars tucked inside her cockpit—the thought that he or some errand boy had been there that close to her while she was sleeping made her feel queasy. She abandoned any thoughts of trying once more to find him. Hazel was right. He would never tell her the truth. If only she'd trusted her instincts instead of her libido, she never would have slept with him in the first place. Now, she would have to find the truth on her own. And to do that, she needed to get her passport back.

Ahead, the small islands rose out of the sea like dark-green gumdrops. At this rate, she should be able to get the anchor down before lunch, go ashore for a fine French midday meal, and then work it off with an afternoon walking the streets—all the while keeping her eyes open for the elusive *Bob*.

She checked the GPS chart plotter at the helm and saw that her speed was sometimes exceeding eight knots. *Bonefish* was flying on her favorite point of sail, rolling as the seas lifted her stern quarter. Riley sighed, sorry that this sail would end too soon, and she would have to get back to the real world of people and officials and finding this jerk who had put her into this situation.

When she began to see the red roofs of the village and the masts of the many boats anchored in the harbor, Riley peeled off her oilskins. The seas had quieted in the lee of the island, and she was sweating inside the waterproof fabric. As she tucked her jacket up under the dodger, she heard her cell phone ring inside the Velcro-sealed pocket. She fished the thing out and recognized the number of her father's townhouse in DC.

"Hello?"

"Maggie? It's Eleanor Wright here."

She closed her eyes for moment, picturing the woman standing next to the wheelchair where her father spent his days propped up in front of the second-story bay window. He liked to watch the neighbors hurrying to work or walking their dogs or pushing strollers on the sidewalk in front of his Foggy Bottom townhouse. "Your father has been asking about you. We haven't heard from you in a while."

She opened her mouth prepared to defend herself, then closed it again and breathed in through her nose. "Communication is difficult down here. How is he?"

"He's having a good day today. Would you like to talk to him?"

It was the last thing she wanted to do, but of course, she couldn't say that. "Sure. Put him on."

Even over the sound of the wind, she could hear the muffled noise as Mrs. Wright passed him the phone. He would be talking on the wired handset. He hated wireless phones. Always said he couldn't hear through them.

"Maggie?"

"Hi, Dad. How are you doing?"

"Where are you?"

"I'm just sailing into the anchorage at the Saintes. You know, off Guadeloupe."

"What the hell are you doing down there?"

She had to laugh sometimes. Her father had been such a proper man, never swearing before this dementia changed his personality. It seemed to have erased all his protocol filters. "I'm having a grand sail, Dad, on the *Bonefish*. Remember my boat?"

"I've got a boat named *Bonefish*."

"Not anymore, Dad."

"No? I'll ask your mother when she calls."

Her parents had been divorced for more than a decade, and he would be waiting a long time before his ex-wife, now remarried and living in France, was likely to call him.

"Where did you say you are?"

Most of the time now, she told him anything, true or false. It didn't matter. He wouldn't remember the next time she talked to him. She tried to find something that would connect in his muddled memory. "Yesterday, I was in Pointe-à-Pitre."

"What for?"

"If you can believe it, I ran into someone I knew. He's a Yale man like you, Dad."

"Yale? Maybe I knew him."

"I don't think so, Dad. You were there a long time ago."

"You make me sound like an old man."

She reached for the autopilot to adjust her course. "You are an old man, Dad."

"I'm a Yale man. What's his name?"

"Diggory Priest."

"You met a priest?"

She took the phone away from her ear and looked skyward. You had to laugh or you'd cry. "No, Dad, Diggory Priest is the man's name."

"I once knew a priest."

She rolled her eyes. "Did you, Dad?"

"He was a Yale man. He knew Michael."

She shook her head. This disease mixed everything up in her father's head. Dig had been more than five years gone by the time her brother went to the school. "Not the same man, Dad."

"I didn't think much of him. Priests are supposed to be men of God."

It was strange how there were moments like this when his voice sounded so sane, and she could almost forget that he was so ill.

"Dad, the man I know once told me that his mother named him after the hatter who sailed from England on the Mayflower."

"I don't remember that."

She laughed out loud. "No, Dad, you're not quite that old. Is Mrs. Wright taking good care of you?"

"Damn woman won't let me smoke a cigar."

"It's your doctor who says you can't smoke."

"There's something I need to tell you, Maggie."

"No, Dad, don't worry about it."

"I can't keep the secret any longer."

She heard his voice crack and knew where the conversation was headed. Every time she spoke to him now, no matter where she steered the conversation, it always came back to this.

"It was all my fault."

"Dad, don't worry about it."

"They called me. Told me they were going to throw me out if I said anything. I had to go along with it."

"Dad, it's over now. Everyone has forgotten."

"Not me."

"I beg to differ, Dad. You've forgotten most things."

"But, Maggie, I was so angry. After everything I had done for them, to ask for that sacrifice." He stopped, choked on a sob.

"Dad, I know. It was a long time ago." Truth was, she didn't know. She had gone through everything she knew about his diplomatic service career, and she couldn't come up with anything this story could be based on. He never went into specifics. His doctor told her it might even not be a real memory at all. This was not unusual in dementia patients. They often started inventing stories. On one call, her father told her that the State Department had just phoned him and asked him to be the new US ambassador to Taiwan.

He was crying now, sobbing into the phone. Before this illness, she had never seen her father cry. Not even at Michael's funeral. But now most calls ended with him blubbering like this.

"I'm sorry. If I had only known, I would have stopped him from coming. Please, Maggie, please, say it wasn't my fault. Maggie? Maggie?"

She bit her lower lip and squeezed her eyes tight, not knowing if her eyes burned from tears or salt spray. "Dad, it's OK."

Mrs. Wright was on the line then. "I'm putting him to bed. He wouldn't get this worked up if you'd call him once in a while." She rang off without saying good-bye.

CHAPTER TWENTY-THREE

Grand Terre, Guadeloupe

March 26, 2008

As he undressed in his own room this time, Diggory set out the two phones, the disposable local cell and the satellite phone, as well as the Baby Glock. He usually carried the weapon in an inside waistband holster, but he had slipped it into his jacket pocket when he'd disrobed with the German woman. He also removed the small, custom-made leather-and-lead blackjack from his pants pocket and set it on the nightstand with the other articles he always liked to keep close at hand.

He had selected his own hotel, l'Auberge de la Vieille Tour, both for the impressive amenities and the discreet staff who were accustomed to keeping quiet about the hours their guests kept. He stretched out nude on the Egyptian cotton sheets and tried to sleep for several hours, but his mind kept circling around images and memories of Riley. She could be a threat, yes, but once whatever was on that submarine was in his possession, he would be immune to threats. He didn't want to eliminate her immediately, and it pleased his sense of symmetry that he should have this power now to decide her fate. Some religious types might call it karma, but in

Diggory's mind, they owed him this. Do unto others as they have done to you.

After all, how many times over the years had he suffered at their hands? Belittle him? How dare they? The truth was, they saw it in him. That was why they always tried to keep him down. They knew he was extraordinary, and they feared him. His father refused to acknowledge or even meet him, but Priest still had his father's blood in his veins. He was born to lead. The others didn't even know what it was to work hard. Yet from the time he had first been accepted at Yale through his years with the Company right up until now, he had often heard the remarks reminding him that he was not really one of them. Of course, Yorick, who had tried to make him his lapdog, had been the worst.

The first time Diggory had been invited to spend a few days at Deer Island, the private island owned by Skull and Bones on the St. Lawrence River, he had not known what to expect. He had packed his bags as though headed for a country estate. It was during "Dead Week," between having finished his exams and before graduation. He'd brought the new Brooks Brothers slacks and the blue blazer he'd purchased with money his mother had given him for graduation. But he was startled to find the conditions on the island nearer to summer camp than weekending at an estate.

When several of his classmates yelled for him to join them on the lawn for a game of football, he declined, saying he didn't feel well—when in fact he didn't want to damage his new clothes. That night in the dining hall, he was sitting at one of the long rough-hewn tables with a group of young men whose faces glowed bronze from their afternoon in the sun. Their khakis and polo shirts were faded and frayed around the edges from years of wear. Diggory was the only one wearing a jacket and tie, and his clothes felt as new and stiff as he did. While he sat there hoping no one would notice such details, Yorick stopped by their table, slapped him on the back, and hollered, "Our boy here looks like he's on his way to the prom!" The whole dining hall roared with laughter, and Dig finally got some color in his face.

That was more than fifteen years ago now, but the memory still stung. After college, while he had willingly taken advantage of Yorick's recommendations and connections, he had succeeded at the Agency on his own. He owed the man nothing. He no longer had to worry about looking or sounding out of place at any level of society. And very soon, he would ascend to his rightful position as head of the organization.

When he had almost fallen asleep, he was awakened by a call on his local cell from the barbarians alerting him that Riley was on the move, headed for the Îles des Saintes. With sleep no longer an option, Diggory got up and packed his bags. He would travel to the islands and find her, and she would be in his bed by nightfall.

On his last check of the room, he heard his sat phone ring.

"Yes," he said into the phone.

"Thor, we need to meet."

Diggory checked his watch. It was past one. "I was on my way to St. François to catch a ferry for the Saintes."

"Meet me at Pointe des Chateaux at three o'clock," Caliban said and rang off.

* * *

He drove the rental car to the meeting place. It was during the drive and his stop for lunch in Sainte Anne that he contemplated the true meaning of this phone call. Something had gone wrong. Caliban had had no problem meeting with him in the open in Pointe-à-Pitre only the day before. Why this sudden need to drive out to the secluded point at the far eastern end of the island? Had his superiors somehow connected him to Ulrika? Who were they to deny him these little pleasures? They feared he was becoming too strong. Either they wanted to put him back in his place, or Caliban had decided to clean the cleaner.

Diggory arrived early and parked among the half dozen or so vehicles in a dirt lot by the beach. Before leaving his room at l'Auberge de la Vieille Tour, he had unpacked his laptop and googled the location of the meet. He read several online tourist guide descriptions of the place and examined it via satellite photos in Google Earth. Pointe des Chateaux was a rocky spit of land that jutted out at the easternmost tip of Grand Terre where the Atlantic Ocean and the Caribbean Sea met in crashing surf. The wave action had sculpted the limestone rock into dramatic formations resembling stone castles—hence the name—and created several small half-moon beaches of white sand along the Atlantic side. A marked trail led off toward a hill at the end of the point topped by an imposing white cross that had been erected in the nineteenth century.

On this afternoon with brisk trade winds dotting the ocean with whitecaps, he did not see a single person walking out to the cross. The waves breaking on the rocks all around the hill sent towers of spume more than twenty feet into the air. Anyone exploring out there was bound to get wet on the slippery rock. He had forty-five minutes to scope out the terrain, and assuming Caliban didn't also arrive early, he intended to use every second.

He was leaning on the fence that surrounded the parking compound when Caliban drove up in a Mercedes. The older man was fifteen minutes early, but Diggory had expected that.

"Shall we walk?" Diggory asked, indicating the cross on top of the hill. "I imagine the view from up there must be spectacular."

"Yes, let's."

The two men walked in silence for a time. Diggory set a brisk pace. Caliban was the first to speak.

"You've had quite an impressive career, Thor."

"Thank you, sir," he said, bowing his head to indicate his deference to the older man.

"You've become an extraordinary asset to the organization." They walked along, shoulder to shoulder, both of them focused on the path just ahead of their feet. "This morning, though, Thor, I saw something disturbing on the television news. A young woman was killed in Le Gosier last night." He lifted his head and looked into the face of the younger man. "Did you see it?"

"On the television? No. I rarely turn it on." Diggory stretched his mouth in a wide smile.

The silver-haired man paused, turned away, and looked out to sea. "I just wondered. We've noticed, you see."

Diggory walked ahead several steps then turned. "Noticed? What are you talking about?"

"Your little hobby. This time, it surprised me, though. They said she hanged herself by accident, playing sex games. Sound familiar?"

"Was it our people?" Diggory chuckled. "The ones who did Thatcher?"

Caliban resumed walking and caught up to him. "You and I are the only ones on the island, Thor."

"I see. Then maybe she *was* playing sex games."

"Hmm. I suppose. The whole thing made me a bit curious, you see."

"Really?" Diggory stopped walking and looked at the other man, raising one dark eyebrow. "Are you interested in those sorts of games, Caliban?"

The older man looked away, shaking his head from side to side. They had arrived at the place where the dirt path ended. To continue up the hill, they would have to pick their way across an outcropping of jagged limestone rock. The surf thundered against the rocks to their left. Caliban turned back to face him, his mouth smiling, his eyes not. "After you?" he said.

Diggory did not hesitate for even a fraction of a second. He plunged forward, stepping carefully from rock to rock, his arms outstretched like a tightrope walker. The rocks were covered with algae because, Diggory knew, the tide was at dead low.

"There's something else, Thor," Caliban said, and Diggory was surprised that the voice was right behind him. The older man was having no trouble keeping up. "It's about the woman sailor."

That nearly stopped him. "What about her?" Diggory chose the rocks he stepped on with great care, inching the two of them closer to the tide line.

"Her name is Marguerite Riley." A fine mist floated over them from the waves crashing to their left, and white foam swirled around the rocks at their feet. "Does that name mean anything to you, Thor?"

This time he did stop—without warning. He turned and saw Caliban almost lose his balance as he tried to refrain from running into the younger man. Diggory kept on pivoting out and around, and simultaneously he heard the pop of the other man's gun and saw the barrel pointing skyward as Caliban struggled for balance. Diggory's own hand flew out of his pocket. The sap came down hard on the back of the silver-haired skull, and the big man collapsed into a pool of receding foam.

Diggory looked around to see if there were any witnesses, but he saw no one on the isolated peninsula of rock. The beach was more than half a mile away and hidden behind several sculptured rock spires. He bent to the other man and felt for a pulse. Beneath his fingers, the warm skin on the man's neck throbbed with life. The half-opened eyes suggested it would be a long time before he regained consciousness. Diggory went through Caliban's pockets, removing the secure satellite phone. He retrieved the gun from a pool of water. He left the wallet.

Sliding his fingers into the silver hair, Diggory gazed at the face in his hands. It was a handsome face with a strong chin like his own. He could not see the weakness, but it was there or it would not have been so easy for him. He wrapped his hands around the neck, then fought the urge to squeeze. No, that would not look like an accident. Dig grabbed the ears in both his hands, lifted the head, stretching the neck to its limit, and then slammed the head down on a sharp pinnacle of black limestone. He heard the bone crunch and saw the blood seeping down the slime-covered rock. He checked his watch. The tide would turn in the next few minutes, and soon these rocks would be covered with water.

Diggory stood, cocked his head to one side, and looked down at the crumpled form. Already, the man looked smaller, as though some part of him were now gone. Dig sighed and shook his head. "These rocks are slippery, you know," he said aloud. Then he turned, and smiling, leaped from rock to rock back toward his car.

CHAPTER TWENTY-FOUR

Fort Napoleon
Îles des Saintes

March 26, 2008

Riley stepped into the weeds on the side of the road as a bus lumbered up the hill, engulfing her in a cloud of hot diesel fumes. She turned her head and held her breath for a few seconds but kept on walking. A French family with two slender teenage girls stood on the other side of the road, hands on their hips, wheezing and coughing in the cloud of exhaust. Aside from a single man who was several switchbacks behind them, they were the only ones attempting the climb on foot. Riley was pleased to note that she was more than halfway up the hill to Fort Napoleon, and she didn't even feel winded. The daily exercises and morning swims were paying off.

The island of Terre-de-Haut, the largest of the eight small islands that make up the archipelago known as the Saintes, wasn't all that large. Three miles long and less than half a mile wide, with only the one village, Bourges des Saintes, it was small enough that Riley figured if *Bob* was there, she'd run into him eventually. She'd started at the dinghy dock shortly after her noon arrival and roamed the streets of the village, looking in the doors of restaurants and touristy souvenir shops, chatting with other yachties, asking about this guy she had met in Deshaies who had a tattoo on his collarbone and shaggy brown hair. No luck. In the bakery, she'd lingered a little longer admiring the pastries and breathing in the smell of the fresh baguettes, querying the teenage girl clerk, but she was met with a blank stare. On the beach, the local wooden racing sloops with bright, candy-colored hulls and yellow, green, and blue sails were the object of many a tourist's camera, but Riley had not seen a glimpse there of the one tourist she sought: *Bob*.

So her next goal had been to search the fort. She knew it was a crazy long shot. But all afternoon, buses had picked up hordes of tourists hurrying off the ferries from the main island. With their cameras at the ready, they rode up the many switchbacks that led to Fort Napoleon with its commanding view of the channel between Les Saintes and Vieux Fort on Guadeloupe.

Nearer the top, the road widened a bit where the tour buses stopped, turned, and disgorged their cargo. At the front of a tiny clapboard shack, Riley bought an orange Fanta and stopped to watch the mobs. The French family passed her, continuing on up the hill, but the other intrepid hiker, the man who had been far behind her, stopped at the lookout point just beneath her to admire the view.

She'd noticed him only because she felt a camaraderie with the others who had climbed up the long hot hill—even with the two French sisters who had complained the whole way using language so vulgar it shocked Riley—and because she thought, judging from his ratty-looking shorts, red tank top, and green Crocs, that he looked like an American. She could tell from the charcoal color of his skin and the texture of his ponytail that he was of mixed race, but there was something in the way he carried himself that screamed Yank—not French—in spite of the shells in the braids on either side of his face. She'd waited for the fellow because she wanted to congratulate him on the climb, but after ten minutes, she gave up.

The elderly woman in the ticket kiosk nodded her head in the direction of a group of people and told her the tour was starting *tout de suite*. Taking her change, Riley thanked the woman but headed off past the potbellied guard. She knew it was unlikely she was going to find *Bob*, especially by traipsing from tourist attraction to tourist attraction, but she wasn't going to give up yet.

Keeping to the paths, she climbed past the door to the sod-covered ammunition bunker and on to the highest part of the bluff. The point formed one-half of the protected bay off Bourges des Saintes. The cliff plunged down to the open sea. The view of the channel was her reward for the climb. Off to her right, on the other side of the point, was another sheltered bay where a lone commercial fishing boat lay at anchor. The boat was odd for these waters, with her dark-blue hull and tall outriggers. While Riley watched, the tiny figure of a man came on deck and launched a toylike rubber dinghy. He climbed in and began to row toward shore. She thought it odd that such a big boat wouldn't have a better dinghy—something with an outboard on it—for getting to shore.

Looking back out to sea, she identified Guadeloupe's other outlying islands of Marie-Galante, where the villagers grew sugar cane, and Îles de la Petite Terre, which consisted of two uninhabited islands connected by a reef. As she surveyed the broad maritime battlefield, she tried to imagine what it would have been like to stand on this headland, cannons at the ready, watching an enemy fleet of over thirty ships of the line sail into range. How on earth did they aim these cannons?

When she turned to face the cannon behind her, a flash of red slipped behind the bunker below her. That was him, wasn't it? That ponytailed guy who had been behind her on the climb? She turned back to face into the trade winds again, feeling rather exposed up here like Kate whatshername on the bow of the Titanic. What was Mr. Ponytail's story?

Then from behind and off to her left, she heard a footstep on the gravel. Riley spun around, only to see more of the view over the anchorage off the town. There was no one there. She could feel her heart thudding in her chest, and she coughed out a half laugh. That guy was probably exploring like she was, and he just happened to move when she turned around. That was it, right?

No. She didn't think so. Why did she feel so spooked? But she was certain she had heard something. She was puzzling over it when she heard it again, right at her feet. She looked down to see a prehistoric-looking, three-foot-long iguana advancing on her boat shoes.

Laughing, she said, "So you're my stalker, eh?" She took a step toward him, and he skittered off over the edge of the cliff. She would have leaned over the edge to see where he'd gone, but she still felt a little too spooked to venture beyond the safety ropes.

As she walked down the grassy slope toward the two-storied stone structure that housed the maritime museum, she glanced at the side of the bunker. There was a white cigarette butt in the grass. It was the only piece of trash she had seen on the immaculate grounds.

A French-speaking tour guide was just exiting the museum building along with her charges, so Riley took the opportunity to wander the rooms alone. She loved exploring among the glass cases. With Michael, she'd wandered through dozens of museums from Barbados to Paris to Madagascar, always feeling safe from the children who made the streets their turf.

The Fort Napoleon museum contained an odd combination of treasures from a stuffed mongoose to Louis XV furniture. As she walked into the second chamber, she saw Ponytail enter the museum through the opposite end of the building. He hadn't seen her yet, and he was swiveling his head all around. He moved on to the next room, but he wasn't looking at any of the exhibits. Riley walked to the far side of the diorama room, out of his line of sight.

Who was he, and what was he after? She was certain he had not been following her when she first came ashore. She would have noticed. Was he just some creep who was following her to get his rocks off, or did he have some other purpose?

She looked around the room, trying to decide whether she should try to ditch the perv, confront him, or simply ignore him, but her attention was drawn to an elaborate ship model. Here she was—in a neat museum—and she wasn't going to worry about some weirdo who was following her.

She walked over to the display and thought about how much her brother would have loved the intricate model.

"*Hey, bro, look at this!*" she whispered as she admired the three-foot-tall replica of one of French Admiral de Grasse's ships at the Battle of the Saintes. When she and Mikey first started sailing, their father had introduced them to the Hornblower books, then O'Brian, then Bernard Cornwall. Mikey had read them all, while she soon tired of the exploits of the all-male cast. But her brother would have loved this place.

"*Awesome, eh?*" she said in a low voice. From a placard in front of a huge model of the battle with dozens of tiny ships on a painted blue sea, she read about the French defeat. They didn't have any large models of Admiral Rodney's ships there in spite of the fact it had been his victory.

There it was again. That feeling, as if someone were breathing on the back of her neck, watching her. She whirled around and saw a flash of red as the man ducked out of the doorway that led to the costume room. OK, she thought. Enough. Time to have a little talk with Mr. Ponytail.

The exhibition hall was the old fort's former barracks. Essentially a long barnlike structure with walls dividing the space

into different rooms, it had doors in the center of each wall, forming a corridor down the center of the structure. Riley crept forward
on the wood floor so as not to make a sound. As she moved, her
view into the next room panned across half the space, but there was
no sign of Ponytail. She imagined he was hiding farther from the
door, outside her line of vision, but off to her left.

"Hey," she said in her loudest "giving orders" voice. "You want
to talk to me? Here I am. Let's talk."

When she stepped into the room facing her left, she realized
she had guessed wrong when a mannequin crashed against her
back, knocking her to the floor. She struggled in the folds of velvet
fabric as the sound of Ponytail's retreat pounded across the floor.
By the time she got to her feet, he was entering the next room,
with only a hundred feet between him and the museum's entrance,
going as fast as his Crocs would let him.

From MSG School at Quantico to all the years at the different
posts, Riley had trained to take down intruders in a secure building and to protect embassy employees. She didn't make a conscious
decision to go after the man; she simply reacted.

She was on her feet and running flat out within seconds. As the
man entered the last room, a large woman with a sign at the top of
a long stick entered the museum, and behind her flowed a crowd of
Japanese tourists. Half the group had already entered the building
when Ponytail plowed into them, sending them scattering in and
out of the museum. When he made the door, he glanced over his
shoulder. Riley was right behind him. The tourists had slowed him
down enough and cleared an open passage for her. He made it only
about a dozen steps outside the building when she hit him from
behind, and the two of them went sprawling in the dirt.

Riley landed on top of the man's back. His body broke her fall,
but he outweighed her by at least thirty pounds, and she hadn't even
knocked the wind out of him. Ponytail managed to roll out from

under her, scramble to his feet, and take one step when she grabbed one of his shoes. She lifted and twisted it almost 180 degrees, and he fell to the ground again with a cry.

Riley got to her knees still holding the shoe, but he squirmed his foot out of the plastic clog and rolled away again. She threw the shoe, aiming for his head, but it only bounced off his ear. He let out a grunt and grabbed at the side of his head. It slowed him again for a second or two, long enough for Riley to get back on her feet. Then she lunged for him and slid her fingers into his shorts back pocket. She was about to pull him down again when he kicked back with the foot that was still wearing a clog. The fabric ripped free from his shorts when his blind kick connected with her bad shoulder.

Riley cried out at the explosion of pain and fell into the dirt.

Ponytail struggled to his feet, scooped up his other shoe, and took off running through the gate.

The blow had knocked Riley onto her side, where she curled into a fetal position and squeezed her eyes shut to block out the throbbing agony.

* * *

"Mademoiselle?" The man standing over her was the museum guard. His belly hung so far over his belt that the belt disappeared—even when viewing it from the ground. "Mademoiselle?" He reached down and shook her shoulder hard. She hissed between clenched teeth, batted his hand away, and rolled up to a sitting position. Off in the distance, she could already hear the two-toned pitch of the gendarme's siren.

The guard grabbed her by her upper arm and lifted her to her feet. One knee was skinned and bleeding, and her once-crisp white polo shirt was covered with dirt and grass stains. The guard was chastising her for being the aggressor and explaining about charges for disturbing the peace.

"The other man," she asked him in French. "What happened to the other man?"

"*Il a disparu*," he said.

Right, she thought. Disappeared.

A crowd had formed a circle around them. The guard yelled at them to step back as he led her through the gate and toward the bridge over the moat. It was difficult to think through the pain. She looked down at her right arm and realized her hand remained fisted. She uncurled the fingers that still grasped the scrap of fabric from Ponytail's back pocket. Beneath the fabric, she saw a scrap of folded paper. Riley heard a siren stop and the sound of car doors slamming. Two gendarmes were hurrying toward her. Looking back down at the paper in her hand, she unfolded it and saw a photo printed on regular white typing paper. The photo was of a gold coin, and it was the exact same gold coin *Bob* had been wearing around his neck.

CHAPTER TWENTY-FIVE

Bourges des Saintes

March 26, 2008

Spyder Brewster sat on the side of the hill thinking that the bitch was pretty dumb if she thought she could kick his ass. Hell, he'd been in more fights than she'd had pairs of shoes. But all the while he'd sat hiding in the bushes outside the fort, waiting for the cops to cart her off to jail, he'd been thinking hard about what that dude had said in the bar the night before.

Keep an eye on her. Covertly. Report every morning and night to his cell number, and so this morning he had called him, but only after Pinky woke him up to tell him the chick's sailboat was gone. They'd upped anchor and hauled ass out of the town anchorage in time to see a small white sail on the horizon. That was when he called the dude. Told the man she was headed for the islands called the Saintes. The man said to stick to her, and they had. Though when they got here to the islands, they'd just watched for a while, and then Pinky had stayed on the boat on account of his condition, and he don't do too good out in the noontime sun.

That Bertram was a great old boat, but she sucked fuel like a thirsty bitch, and they didn't have the bucks to refuel her. It had been easy enough to steal the boat in St. John's, Antigua. Him and Pinky had just gone in and chartered her for a day. They put half down, told the guy they'd give him the other half after they got back with fish. Said they wanted to give him an incentive. They caught a mahi, and when the captain was leaning over the transom to gaff the fish, Spyder nailed him in the back of the head with the fish billy.

The mate was the captain's seventeen-year-old kid, and he jumped in after they pushed the old man overboard. Saved them the trouble. Seeing as they were about ten miles offshore and the old man's head was bleeding, Spyder figured there weren't any witnesses left to worry about.

Him and Pinky found an anchorage off a place called Great Bird Island. They tore off the tuna tower and slapped some epoxy over the holes where all that tubing had been bolted to the bridge deck. They beached her, changed the color of the boot stripe, and repainted the name: *Fish n' Chicks*. He'd seen another boat with that name and thought it sounded pretty good.

Whilst he was sitting there remembering how cool it felt to have his own sportfish, he almost missed the cop car. They didn't have the siren going like they did on the way up. After they passed, he stood up and stuck his neck out as the little car slowed to make the last switchback. Yup, that was her in the backseat. The little cop car entered the main drag along the beach and speeded up in the straightaway. Spyder stretched, brushed the dirt off his shorts, and felt where the pocket had been ripped off.

"Bitch," he said. "I liked these fuckin' shorts." After they had repainted and renamed the boat, they'd explored all the lockers, and he'd found that he was almost the same size as the kid who'd jumped overboard. He'd been wearing the kid's clothes, even his shoes, ever since.

He stepped onto the road and started down the last hill. He limped because his knee hurt where she'd twisted his leg, and he felt a blister forming on the big toe. He'd been able to grab his shoes before he ran out of the fort, but his bare feet in the kid's Crocs didn't do so good at running.

She'd anchored her sailboat around noon and gone ashore in her dinghy right away, and that was the first time him and his brother had got a look at this chick they'd been sent to follow. He was surprised to find she was a hottie, and he wondered why in hell a woman who looked like that couldn't find a man to sail with her. He wouldn't mind getting a little piece of that, and he hoped it would come to that before this business was over.

Shit. He was sweating like a stuck pig, and people was starting to look at him funny as he passed the fancy restaurants and tourist shops. He stopped to look at his reflection in a shop window. His shirt was covered with dirt. He slowed his pace and started pulling the tank top away from his sweat-slick chest, fanning it like to try to let some air in there. The damn shirt was already soaked through. His feet were sliding around on the soles of the plastic shoes, and every once in a while the raw skin on the top of his toe would make contact with something hard.

OK, bitch, this ain't funny no more. Spyder stopped in the shade of a bright-blue awning with French words on it. He looked both ways on the street, and he didn't see anyone who resembled the woman. Maybe they really were gonna put her in jail. Just for fightin'? He doubted it. She looked like money anyway. People like that never went to jail. Leastwise, he'd never seen any when he was on the inside.

He never done this kind of work before. *Covert* work. Back home in Buxton, he'd done just about every job a man of his many talents could do, from fishing, shrimping, running dope, or working in town at stuff like construction or selling shit to tourists on the streets. But this kind of detective thing was a new one for him. He'd been having fun earlier up at the fort sneaking around watching the bitch, but now he was hot and tired, and his feet hurt.

Well, shit, she got to come back to her boat sometime. Spyder turned and headed back to the dinghy dock.

* * *

Pinky was sitting in front of a laptop computer at the table in the Bertram's main salon, headphones on his head, the generator running, and the AC cranking the temperature down to sixty-five degrees. He looked up when Spyder slid the aft door open.

"So?" Pinky said, sliding the big headphones down and hooking them around his neck.

Spyder stepped into the cabin and crossed the carpet, concentrating so he wouldn't limp. He turned his face away so his brother couldn't see him mimic his whiny-ass voice saying the word "So?" like he was his old lady. "Bitch walked all over the fuckin' fort. Didn't meet with nobody or do nothing special. I got tired of playing tourist with her. What you doing?"

"Checking her out. I got on a local Wi-Fi network and checked the Coast Guard documentation database for her boat name. She's Marguerite Riley, from Washington, DC. Found some stories about her and her family. Her old man's some kind of big cheese with the government, like a ambassador or something, or leastwise, he was. Nothing recent on him."

"I don't give a fuck who she is. She's nothin'." Spyder walked over to the coffee table in front of the couch and stared at the little black and stainless gun sitting there. When they'd first searched the boat, they'd found the little Ruger .22 in the owner's cabin along with a couple of magazines of ammo. He'd hid it in a towel drawer in the forward head so it would be easy to get at without being seen. "What you get that out for?"

"Just lookin' at it."

"You don't know shit about guns."

"Like you do?"

"More'n you, dumbass. Enough to know we don't want nobody seeing we got a gun." He lifted the gun up and pointed it out the back window of the yacht. He sighted down the barrel, imagining he was pointing it at the bitch on her sailboat. He made a soft "Pkew" noise and bounced his hand up in recoil from the imagined shot. The day would come when he would show her. With a curt nod, he bent down and scooped up the ammunition and returned it and the gun to the bottom of the towel drawer in the head. Then, he went into the kid's cabin and grabbed some clean clothes before his brother had a chance to notice the torn shorts and dirty shirt.

"There's something here, Spyder," Pinky hollered so his brother could hear him down in the master cabin. "Something bigger'n just getting paid a few extra bucks to follow this chick. First, they pay us to follow the doc around, a guy we know from back home is after some treasure. But this dude don't want the doc to find the wreck. Then you get this bonehead plan to grab the doc yourself, and you almost fuck it all up. Then they change again, and now it's this woman. I don't know, man, but there is something big going on here. This one might be the jackpot. We do not want to mess this one up."

Spyder stepped back into the salon zipping up the new clean shorts. "What ch'you talking about. We ain't gonna mess up nothing."

Pinky stared at him without blinking, looking at the clean shorts and shirt. Spyder had to turn away. He didn't want to look at that ugly face. His brother knew he could always win in a stare down. The little fucker looked like a tarpon his underbite was so bad, and with all those pink patches on his brown skin and the clumps of frizzy white hair—sometimes Spyder just wanted to smash his fist into his brother's face.

"I'm just saying," Pinky continued, "that sometimes you don't listen to me, and when you go off and try to do things your way, it don't always turn out so good. Like back in Oriental."

"Fuck that shit, you little freak. You're always making out like I'm the stupid one. Like I'm the fuckup. You just wish you was me, that you wasn't some raggedy-ass, patchy-lookin' nigger. You just lookin' up that shit on that woman 'cuz you seen her and you want to fuck her. Shit. You never touched a woman in your life, 'cept maybe Crazy Matilda back home, and she don't count." Spyder crossed to the galley, grabbed a beer, and stole a quick glance at his brother to see if his words were having any effect. As usual, Pinky was ignoring him, which pissed him off even more.

The little freak lived in his own world with that computer and his headphones. Spyder collapsed onto the couch. Fact was, he knew his brother was a whole lot smarter than him, but he'd never admit it out loud. Though they looked nothing alike, Spyder was barely a year older than his half-brother, and growing up with that crackhead they called Mama, they'd learned to depend on each other for survival.

Spyder chugged his beer and then squashed the can in his fist and threw it behind the settee. "I ain't no dummy. I figure, why walk all over town? She'll be back to her boat soon." Spyder leaned forward and examined his blistered toes. He wasn't about to tell his brother that the bitch had jumped him, and he'd had to bolt before she kicked his ass.

CHAPTER TWENTY-SIX

Îles des Saintes

March 26, 2008

After more than an hour in a hot, airless room, the gendarmes finally came in to talk to her. Turned out she was a "person of interest" thanks to the still-missing *Bob*. Seemed they'd decided *Bob* was the fellow she had been rolling in the dirt with. After repeating the same questions over and over, hoping for different answers, they cut her loose with a fifty-euro fine for disturbing the peace. She stomped her way through the quaint streets headed toward the quay, muttering half sentences to her brother.

"French *flics* are even worse than in New Haven, Mikey."

When she'd enlisted, before heading off to boot camp at Parris Island, she'd spent a couple of weeks in New Haven talking to the cops about what happened to Yale student Michael Riley. The way the local and campus police stonewalled her made her certain they'd helped cover up the whole thing due to prestigious old family names (some of which were on campus buildings). One piece of evidence had pointed toward another on-campus organization, but every time she tried to get someone to talk, her inquiries were blocked. Riley hadn't had a high opinion of cops ever since.

Now she was worried about her boat. When she'd left it, thinking that she would be in view of the anchorage most of the day, she hadn't bothered to lock it. She also had left no anchor light on. It was late enough that several shops were closed, but the restaurants she passed were full of talking, laughing people, and their waterfront patios were strung with colored lights and vibrating with music. Along the main street, couples strolled arm in arm reading the menus posted in the front windows of all the restaurants. God, the food smelled good. She hadn't even stopped for the lunch she'd dreamed of while sailing over here.

The sky was still a pale, whitish blue when she arrived at the waterfront, but the boats in the anchorage were mere dark silhouettes against the lighter sky. She searched the fleet for the familiar outline of her *Bonefish*. She almost looked right past it because something wasn't right. She had been searching for an empty boat, but there was a dark shadow moving under the bimini in her cockpit. Someone was on her boat.

Riley ran for her dinghy but decided against using the outboard. Though she couldn't make out the features of the person, she was certain it had to be Ponytail. She was finished messing around with this guy. She wanted to confront him, talk to him, and she wouldn't mind knocking him on the side of the head a few times as payback. As she untied the dinghy painter and stepped into the little boat, the figure opened the double doors, slid open the main hatch, and proceeded down the ladder into the cabin. He was lucky she didn't have any firearms on her, because though she hadn't been to a range in months, she'd once been able to outshoot every marine at every post she'd been assigned to. She shoved the boat away from the dock, fitted the oars into the oarlocks, and began to pull.

As she rowed, the inflatable bounced over the wind chop. She remembered that she had left the forward hatch over her berth open. She'd go in that way. When she pulled alongside her boat, she noticed the intruder hadn't brought a dinghy. Had he bummed a ride? Swam out? She headed her own inflatable to the anchor chain.

Her boat's foot-wide teak platform extended out from the bow, supported beneath by stainless steel tubing called a dolphin striker. Riley tied her dinghy to the anchor chain with a quick bowline, then stepped up onto the rubber boat's seat. *Bonefish* was rocking gently in the swell, and she used the boat's natural motion to help her as she boosted her belly onto the anchor platform by stepping on the striker. She slid under the bow pulpit and pulled herself to a stand with her hand on the roller-furled sail. She stood for a moment waiting to see if the intruder noticed the change in the boat's balance as she came aboard. After several seconds, she figured she was in the clear.

By now, the night had grown dark, and she no longer had to worry about the man seeing her outlined against the sky. She squatted on the foredeck, and her line of sight through the forward hatch showed a cabin that was dimly lit at the aft end. He had a small flashlight. She got down on all fours, then crawled on her belly to the hatch and lowered her head inside for a better look.

She couldn't make out the man, only the dark bulk facing outboard, seated at her chart table. She could see the flashlight's beam dancing around under the lifted lid, searching the contents. She almost yelled out in her fury, but she didn't want him to get away this time. She slid her feet through the narrow hatch and eased her deck shoes onto the berth. Then, ducking inside, she slid to the floor and stood just inside the cabin door.

This was her home, her bed, but for a moment, she felt disoriented. Pressing her body against the drawers under the bunk, she was out of his line of sight, hidden by the bulk of the open door. She scanned the cabin, remembering more than seeing what was there. By her bunk, behind the door. She needed a weapon. She kept a ten-inch aluminum Maglite flashlight in a pocket on the bulkhead for nights when she had to get out on deck in a hurry. She reached in and eased the flashlight out, then gripped it in her right hand, bottom up, measuring the weight of it.

From aft, she heard the sound of the chart tabletop dropping into place. She eased to her left and saw his shadow pass in front of the open cockpit companionway. She ducked back behind the door. Would he see her outline in the dark? No, especially not after losing his night vision from the light he was using. After sliding her butt onto the high bunk, she swung her legs up and crawled onto the mattress.

The floorboards between the settees in the main salon creaked. The thin beam of his light danced around the woodwork in her cabin. He was coming forward. The sound of the wind moaning in the rigging masked any noise she made as she shifted her legs across the mattress until she was kneeling on the bunk behind the open door.

She saw the flashlight appear from around the corner of the door and she knew his body would soon follow. She raised the Maglite over her head and waited. She sensed his bulk more than saw him, and that was when she struck.

CHAPTER TWENTY-SEVEN

The Atlantic south of Bermuda

February 12, 1942

After several seconds' silence, all three men began shouting at once. McKay's voice, the loudest of the lot, drowned out those of the captain and young Mullins.

"Bollocks. S'not true. There's no bomb. He's nothin' but a shit stirrer," he said.

The captain quieted them by turning off the torch and plunging the hold into darkness. When he had their attention, he clicked it back on, illuminating Woolsey in a column of light. "This is true, Lieutenant?"

Woolsey blinked and turned his face aside. He could hear the other men shuffling in the dark, moving in closer to hear him. "Captain, we don't have time for the why and wherefore. Suffice it to say that this afternoon, on orders, I brought aboard and armed an explosive device that is set to go off within twenty-four hours of arming." He tilted his wristwatch toward the torchlight. "That was roughly three hours ago."

"Why you—" McKay started toward him, but the captain reached out and shone the light on his face.

He barked, "Monsieur McKay. *Arrête.* Stop."

Woolsey was surprised that the big signalman followed the Frenchman's orders.

The captain swung the torchlight back round on Woolsey's face. "You say we don't have time, but I say you have sufficient time to explain this to me. Who gave you your orders?"

"I am not at liberty to say, sir."

"*Non. Ça ne suffit pas.* I will not accept that. It cannot be true that the British plan to destroy this magnificent boat."

Woolsey tried to laugh, but it sounded more like a gasp. "Captain, do you have any idea of the gross tonnage of ships we're losing daily in this Atlantic war? You're nothing but a gnat in their eye. It's all about money and goods, man. When the cost of her upkeep exceeded her usefulness to the Allies, *Surcouf* was doomed."

"If this is true, Lieutenant, why not take her out of service?"

"Do you really think de Gaulle would let us? She's become a bloody symbol for the Free French, sir. But a damned expensive one."

The captain turned his back on the British officer, and his torch lit the far side of the hold. Woolsey saw McKay glowering at him between slugs of drink, his cheeks reddening with each swallow. He was seated atop an enormous stack of crates of wine. Mullins sat on the floor not far from him, his head swiveling back and forth between his lieutenant and the angry telegraphist. Woolsey saw his lips move, but he couldn't hear what he was saying. Either he was trying to calm McKay or he was praying.

Captain Lamoreaux turned back to face Woolsey. "You were ordered to place this bomb and then leave this boat and all of my men, as well as your own, to die?"

Woolsey spread his hands, palms upward. "Men are dying every day in this war. Ordered to do so. This isn't personal. There are some documents aboard this boat. The Americans need them. My orders were to set the explosives so the world would think *Surcouf* was the victim of a U-boat, and then get these documents to the Americans." Woolsey hoped the captain would leave it at that. If he started asking him any more questions about who had issued the orders, he would have to lie. And he knew he was a piss-poor liar.

"How convenient for you that you were the one man who was supposed to survive."

Woolsey wiped his palms on his pants leg. There was no heat in the hold, and his hands were cold, yet wet with sweat. "Just following orders, sir."

For such a big man, McKay's moves were both fast and silent. The first sound Woolsey heard came only a couple of seconds before the big man's head and shoulders plowed into his gut.

The two of them went down in the pool of spilled red wine. He thought maybe the other men, Lamoreaux and Mullins, were yelling since their mouths were moving, but he couldn't hear anything over the roaring in his ears.

McKay had him pinned to the floor. Woolsey tried to use his arms for protection, but it was to no avail. The big man concentrated on his body, and the blows to his ribs and abdomen made it impossible to breathe. As the darkness round the perimeter of his vision began to close in, Woolsey registered a different sort of look in McKay's eyes. They changed from dull, unseeing brutish eyes to green pools sparking with light and interest.

McKay froze with his fist drawn back, then he leaned down over Woolsey and reached out his arm. When he raised back up onto his knees, he held a dark, round piece of glass. It was part of the wine bottle's bottom, and attached to it was a long, slender shard, two inches wide at the base and tapering off to a perfect, razor-sharp point.

"Gonna leave us to die, was you?" McKay asked, turning the glass in the torchlight, staring at it and grinning as he watched the faint emerald shadow dance across the deck.

Woolsey opened his mouth, but nothing came out.

"Havin' a little brown trouser moment here, eh, Lieutenant?" McKay pressed the point against Woolsey's neck, and the lieutenant felt the sharp pain as it pierced the surface of the skin. "You yellow-bellied piece of shit, let's see if you can take a little of what you was plannin' for us. Them bombs dismember, ya know."

At that moment, Woolsey found his voice, but to his profound embarrassment, what came out was a high-pitched scream. Or so he thought at first. Then, when a blur of a shadow knocked the big man off him, Woolsey realized his barely audible "Please!" had been drowned out by the screams of Walter Mullins as he had launched himself at the big telegraphist. The two of them disappeared into the shadows beyond the column of light, and with them went the sounds of their scuffling. The captain's voice was now penetrating the roaring in Woolsey's ears, but the man seemed to have forgotten how to speak English. He was hollering "*Arrête!*" and other words the lieutenant could not comprehend.

Woolsey sat up and touched his neck where the point of glass had pierced his skin. His fingers slid, smearing the blood that trickled from the wound. But his whole arm felt wet inside his sleeve, and when his fingers continued to probe the arm, he found another small shard of glass that protruded from the back side of his upper arm. When he touched it, pain shot down the length of his arm.

At once, all the yelling stopped, and all Woolsey heard was the ever-present rumble of the big sub's diesels.

Woolsey looked up as the captain played the light around the compartment. Finally, it found the two Englishmen, still and quiet and prone on the deck. Woolsey was surprised to see Mullins lying flat across the bigger man, pinning him down. For a moment, a small smile played around Woolsey's mouth until he saw the growing pool under McKay's shoulder, soaking his sweater. For several seconds neither man moved, then McKay sat up, pushing the younger man away, rolling him onto his back. McKay leaped to his feet, his breathing hard and noisy in the cavernous compartment. The front of his heavy wool sweater was stained dark, and his face was spotted with blood.

"Jesus," he said, wrapping one of his big arms across the top of his head. "Jesus Christ." He turned away and bent over from the waist, his hands on his knees.

McKay's movements had settled the younger man in an awkward, splayed pose revealing a long gash that traveled from his jawbone across the front of Mullins's throat, down his chest to its finish, where the glass shard remained stuck in the body, its traverse stopped by the bunched fabric of the young man's woolen shirt.

"What the fuck were you thinking, Wally?" McKay flung his arms wide, entreating the body on the floor. "Stupid kid. I wasn't *really* gonna hurt him."

McKay turned and faced the two officers, his head angled to one side as though he could no longer support the weight of it. The tears on his face glinted in the torchlight. "He's just a fuckin' kid."

* * *

A loud clank from the far side of the compartment startled them, and they turned to the entrance. Lamoreaux swung the torch away from the body. They saw the wheel turning on the watertight door. When the door swung open, Ensign Gohin peered into the darkness for a moment, then jerked his head to one side, indicating that someone should enter.

"*Dix minutes,*" he said.

It was Kewpie, the telegraphist, who entered carrying a tray of food, a big smile on his face.

"Ah, Michaut," the captain murmured.

"*Bon soir, mes amis*," the young man said as the door swung closed behind him. From outside, someone switched on the overhead lights, illuminating the entire hold.

CHAPTER TWENTY-EIGHT

Îles des Saintes

March 26, 2008

Cole opened one eye. The searing pain in the back of his head and behind his eyeballs made him squeeze it shut again. Light, bright light. Where was he? He reached up and touched the back of his scalp.

"Ow."

"Wake up, *Bob,* or whatever your name is. I didn't hit you that hard."

When he heard her voice, he remembered. He was on her boat. That woman. Citrus scent. Riley. He had swum out to get the coin, but it wasn't where he'd left it. He'd started to search the salon and then decided to see where she lived, where she slept. Bad move.

He grew aware of the rest of his body beyond the center of pain that throbbed at the back of his head. He was sprawled on the floor, his cheek and chest pressed against something cold and hard. Wood. Opening one eye again, he rolled onto his side, careful not to press the back of his head to the floor. She was sitting on a bunk, her bare feet dangling above him, and a fluorescent light on the overhead behind her made it impossible to see her face. How had she gotten aboard?

Raising an arm to shield his eyes from the glare, he said, "That light up there's killing me."

She twisted her torso around, and he heard a click, followed by another, and the overhead light went out. The cabin was now lit by the softer glow of the bunk reading light. At least it wasn't shining in his face.

"Thanks," he said as he rolled over and curled up into a sitting position. As he bent his bare legs in front of him, he realized that he was again confronting this woman almost naked. He had swum out wearing only his Speedos. "What did you hit me with, Magee?"

She lifted her right hand. In it was a long, black Maglite flashlight, and she slapped it into the palm of her other hand like a beat cop with his baton. "If I'd known it was you, I might have hit you a little harder."

Cole's fingers explored the painful lump on the back of his skull. "Any harder and you might have killed me."

"Stop whining and get up."

She slid off the bunk, her firm thigh brushing his shoulder, and she walked aft through the main salon to the galley, turning on an overhead red-colored light. Sailors used them to move about without impairing their night vision. She knew the bright light hurt his head, and she was being kind to him. That was a good start. And now, watching the way she moved—silky, like a panther stalking its prey—he didn't care how much it hurt. He didn't want to close his eyes anymore.

After filling the teakettle from the sink, she lit the burner, then looked up at him. "Come on, off the floor and onto the seat. There." She pointed. "You've got some explaining to do."

This woman always seemed to be ordering him around. He picked himself up off the floor, his body stiff and sore, and he hobbled his way into the salon. He looked at the neat, tufted-velvet upholstery. "My swimsuit's wet," he said, rubbing his hand across his hip and feeling the wet nylon fabric.

She stepped out of the galley, cocked her hips to one side, and placed a hand at her waist, then threw a dish towel, hitting him on the side of his head. He spread the towel on the edge of the cushion and perched, wishing he had at least worn swim trunks over the Speedos. If she kept moving her body like that, things could get embarrassing real fast.

He needed to get his mind onto something else. Reaching back, he probed the lump on the back of his head. The pain had slowed to a dull throb. He needed to get back on track. Forget the woman, he told himself. Stop thinking about her. He peered around the boat's interior. He hadn't found the scrapbook where he'd hidden the coin, so had she moved it?

She lifted two heavy white mugs off hooks and dropped teabags into them. "So? What do you have to say for yourself?"

He looked up at her and shrugged. What could he say? That he'd broken into her boat to steal back the gold coin that was the key to the location of a sunken treasure? He was pretty sure he knew how *that* would go over.

Before he could come up with some clever retort, she said, "I should report you to the police for breaking and entering."

He felt as if he were back in eighth grade and Mrs. Laughlin was threatening to report him to the principal for cutting school to go fishing. Riley sure as hell didn't look like Mrs. Laughlin though. The thought struck him as funny, and he began to smile.

"You think this is funny?"

He lifted his shoulders in a shrug. Well, yeah, he wanted to say. She had just slid a potholder shaped like a shark over her hand, and the fish now looked as if it were trying to bite a chunk out of her hip. He couldn't help it. He tried to stifle the laugh, but it bubbled up the back of his throat until he sounded as if he were choking on something.

Stepping out from behind the galley counter, her feet planted apart like any good sailor, she glared at him. She was wearing some very short navy cargo shorts, and it took all his strength to keep looking at her face and ignore those legs as she advanced on him, taking another step with each point she made.

"First," she said, "you disappear off my boat, leaving me to try to explain to the French immigration authorities what happened to the American man I claimed I had brought into the country." The shark oven mitt bit her second finger. "Then I find you gave me a fake name. After that, of course, the French authorities accused me of trafficking in illegal aliens and took away my passport. And let's not forget that you stole my only handheld VHF radio." The teakettle started whistling, but she ignored it as she continued advancing on him. "Then you have the nerve to come back and break into my boat and go rummaging through my things. And every damned time you come on my boat, you seem to forget your clothes." She was standing just in front of him by now, the shark oven mitt scrunched up into a fist.

"Please, lady," he said, widening his eyes and holding his hands up in mock surrender. "Don't hit me with that fish."

She looked down at her half-cocked arm, then she seemed to hear the squealing kettle. For just a second, a look of disappointment flashed across her face before she stepped to the galley and turned off the gas. Damn, he thought. She really *was* going to hit me.

As she poured the steaming water over the tea bags, he could hear her breathing, trying to get herself under control. He took the moment to scan the books behind the settee opposite him. He didn't see it there. He wondered if he had just missed it in the chart table because of the dark.

When he glanced back at her, she was stuffing the shark oven mitt into a cabinet. "Borrowed—the radio, that is," he said. "They took your passport?"

She nodded while she continued to work.

He watched her face with fascination. He knew that getting caught aboard her boat should be a major setback for him. It was all about the coin, decoding the journals, the submarine, but he had to admit it—he was glad to have another chance to watch how her lips moved when she talked to herself or how she used one finger to tuck a short strand of hair behind her ear.

The silence stretched out as she collected spoons and a sugar bowl and placed it all on the table. She sat at the end of the dinette table and looked at him through the steam as she blew across the top of her mug.

"I'm sorry I caused you so much trouble," he said.

She took a slow sip of the hot tea before she answered. "You should be."

Man, he thought, she had this tough guy act down pat. He wondered how long she had been using this routine to keep the world at arm's length. He watched her ramrod-straight posture, lips pressed together in a tight line, the graceful way she held her arms when she lifted her cup. He suspected if any man could get past the marine sentry, she could be one hell of a woman.

"Would it help if I told you I had my reasons for doing the things I've done?"

"Probably not."

"Listen, Magee, things aren't always what they seem. Please, just hear me out on this. We think we know what reality is. We think we understand the world and know right and wrong, black and white. Then we learn something that changes everything. You know, people once thought the world was flat, and then ol' Chris Columbus came along."

"So you're going to tell me that's your name now? Chris Columbus?"

"No," he said. "But Columbus did have to break a few rules to do what he did. Like me." He took a deep breath, then tried again. "Is there anything I can do now to make you forgive me?"

"Could start with your name. Your *real* name."

He stood up and with an exaggerated flourish bent over in a deep bow from the waist, his arms bent across his body fore and aft. When he stood up again, his head throbbed anew where she'd hit him, but seeing the faint crinkle of laugh lines around her eyes made it worth it. "Let me introduce myself, Captain Maggie Riley. My name is Cole Thatcher." He held out his hand.

Before she could take his hand, the *Bonefish* heeled over and began to rock and roll so violently, Cole almost landed in her lap. She was too quick, though, and before he regained his balance, she was up the ladder and out into the cockpit.

CHAPTER TWENTY-NINE

Îles des Saintes

March 26, 2008

Spyder watched as the old island fishing boat plowed through the anchorage throwing up a three-foot wake. Starting at the outer anchorage and continuing right up to the sailing dinghies just off the wharf, he heard the sound of hatches slamming open, swearing in all different languages, and rigging creaking and clanking as the waves spread out and spars swung in crazy arcs through the sky. He had to give this Thor dude credit, man. Fucker could make an entrance.

The face behind the glass at the fishing boat's inside steering station was lit up as the old guy at the wheel neared the yellow lights on the wharf. Guy looked like one of the rummies you saw hanging out around the fish market and the main town waterfront back in the capital. Dude's boat looked worse than he did: peeling paint, weed and moss all along the waterline, and the smoking exhaust had stained the entire back half of the hull almost black. And the fish stink was stronger than the stench of diesel. Spyder smiled at the thought of the tight-ass Thor dude having to spend several hours on that old tub.

Standing by ready to take a line, Spyder soon realized that Thor was the only passenger, and the old rummy captain seemed to want him off his boat ASAP. The captain spun the boat around so he wouldn't have to bother with tying up. He put his aft quarter up against the dock, and Thor stood on the bulwark, his small duffel tucked under his arm and the strap of a computer case across his chest. He tossed the duffel at Spyder, then jumped onto the wharf. A black cloud of exhaust rose as the water roiled at the stern. The rummy goosed the throttle, and the fishing boat took off into the night.

Spyder thought about tossing the dude his duffel bag right back. He wasn't this guy's boat nigger. He had a bad feeling about this dude—was beginning to wonder if it had been such a great idea for him and Pinky to get mixed up with these freaks Thor and Caliban. He didn't want nothing to mess up this chance to score.

It had started back home in Buxton out on the Outer Banks. Pinky was working as a busboy at Teach's down at the marina in Hatteras, and one Sunday afternoon when he was filling the bar bins with ice, he heard these two guys talking 'bout a wreck. Pinky's ears pricked up when the drunk one whispered the word *gold*. Pinky went back to the kitchen and called Spyder on the phone inside the manager's office, told him to get his butt over here and sit next to the tall, skinny nigger at the bar and listen to everything he and the drunk dude said. Spyder'd been working as a deckhand on a sportfish right there in the marina, but they didn't have no charter that day, so he was there in five minutes. He slid onto the empty stool next to them, nodded, and asked about the weather. Then, he bought them a round of rum, followed by another.

Soon Spyder learned that the drunk one was named Dr. Thatcher, but he wasn't the kind of doctor that give out pills. The tall, skinny black dude was the deckhand on his boat, but it seemed to Spyder that Doc was treating him pretty decent for a deckhand.

In all Spyder's years of working boats on the Outer Banks, he'd never once had the owner buying him drinks in the bar.

The doc couldn't hold his liquor, and he was slamming 'em back that day over some woman who'd left him, saying he was crazy. The deckhand was an uptight island dude, and he kept trying to get his boss to leave, but the doc was on a roll. He started shooting his mouth off about how he'd show her when he found this submarine that got sunk in the World War with a ton of gold down in the Caribbean, and 'bout how they was fixin' to go on down there and get it. He never said so, but Spyder just knew he had a map or something that was gonna show him to the gold. Finally, the island dude just about dragged him outta there, but Spyder had heard enough. He knew he was gonna stick to this guy like mud on a pig.

When the island dude paid the bill with the doc's credit card, Pinky took a side trip on the way to the cashier and took down his name and numbers. First thing Monday morning, they were on the library computers, and Pinky found out the name of this boat he had and where he docked it over in Oriental. Him and Pinky both quit their jobs in Buxton, moved to Oriental, and started digging for every bit they could learn about the guy and his submarine. Spyder followed the doc round and spied on him. The guy wore a gold coin round his neck, and when Spyder got a picture of it, Pinky looked it up on the Internet and printed out a copy for him. Thinking back on what the dude said, Spyder figured out that the coin *was* the treasure map, and he decided to steal it just to see. But it wasn't long before the doc caught on to the fact he was seeing Spyder around, and the *Shadow Chaser* moved south. Pinky still blamed him for that one.

"Report," Thor said as he moved out of the glare of the wharf lights and into the shadows.

"Guess you missed the last ferry, man."

Thor stretched his arm out and looked at his watch. Spyder thought the dude looked pissed. Must not have liked his stinky boat ride.

When they'd first met the other dude couple of weeks ago, him and Pinky figured they'd found themselves a good gig. They'd been watching Thatcher from a bar in the marina in Guadeloupe when this guy got up from another table, came over, introduced himself with a stupid-ass fake name—Caliban—and said he was looking to hire a couple of local fellows. They were supposed to follow this Thatcher guy who was looking for some wreck that Caliban and his guys didn't want nobody to find. Spyder'd been about to tell the rich asshole that it would be easy, seein's as how they already knew the doc from back home, but when he looked at his brother's face, it was like he had them light-up letters on his forehead with the words *Shut Up* written there. It was a good deal getting paid to do the exact same thing they woulda been doing anyways. Leastwise, it was until last night when this Thor dude showed up.

"I said, report." There was something about Thor's voice that told him not to mess with the guy.

"Last night, I put the oars on the chick's boat just like you said." He decided to leave out the part about invading the powerboat's liquor cabinet the night before, getting sick after drinking a bottle of some kind of sweet French liquor, and sleeping in well past dawn. "This morning we followed her boat over here, then I walked all over the island playing tourist with her."

"Did she see you?"

"Hell, no," Spyder said.

"Where is she now?"

"Out on her boat. But just before dark, Pinky said he saw some dude swim out there. It might have been the doc. He was about the same size, but it was too dark to tell for sure, and by the time he got the glasses out, dude was gone—down below probly. Near's we can tell, he ain't come out yet even though she come back awhile ago. Pinky's watching whilst I come in to get you."

"Put my bag in your boat. Stand by here while I find a meal—then we'll go out to your boat and regroup."

"You don't want me to go check out the guy over there?"

Dude who called himself Thor smiled and shook his head. "Try hard to remember these two things. No questions. No thinking for yourself. Give me an hour."

As Spyder watched Thor's back disappear around the corner toward the village, he was pretty sure the man had just called him stupid. For that, he was gonna make him pay.

CHAPTER THIRTY

Aboard the Bonefish

March 26, 2008

"What the heck was that?" Cole asked, clinging to the companion-way ladder on the rocking boat.

Riley was standing behind the wheel, squinting into the darkness. "It's some jerk," she said, pointing at the offending boat. But she didn't finish, as all around her shouts were flying from the other cruising boats. Riley reached for the binoculars she kept in a teak rack near the helm.

"I guess he doesn't understand the concept of a no-wake zone," he said as he grabbed the stainless arch over the binnacle to steady himself. "No wonder you sailors get so upset. These things really roll."

Riley ignored him and held the glasses to her eyes. It was a grungy-looking local boat, and she was surprised that a local fisher-man would come into the anchorage so hot. What was his hurry? The boat was nearing the town wharf, and a man was standing on the rear deck. She swung the glasses over to check out the dock, and there standing under the light was the ponytail guy.

"Shit," she said.

"What is it?"

She lowered the binoculars and looked at him. What had he said his real name was? Cole. She had no reason to trust him. He'd lied to her, stolen from her, and broken into her boat. But it was like she'd told Hazel last night: in spite of the deceit, there was something so earnest about him. And now even his speech had changed—he no longer sounded like the opening act for Larry the Cable Guy.

After she'd swung the Maglite, then turned on the overhead light and discovered her intruder wasn't the man she'd expected, she'd also had about five long minutes before he came around to take a good look at him. He might spout some weird ideas, but he sure looked great in nothing but a little red Speedo. His shoulders were broad and well-muscled, and his torso tapered to a slim waist and hips. Maybe Hazel was right, maybe she was just swooning over the closeness of so much masculinity.

At Quantico when she'd first attended MSG School, they had been trained in many ways to assess people, from body language to known facial tells that indicate whether a person approaching a sentry is a friendly or not. Such assessments had become second nature to her, and in spite of the lying, her assessment of Cole was that he meant her no harm. He had owned up to everything—hadn't tried to deny it. He'd even apologized, which was rare enough in her experience with men. She thought about the scrap of paper with the photocopy of his coin—the coin he was no longer wearing. He might be a harmless kook, but he was somehow involved with some dirtbag characters, and she needed to find out what the connection was.

She handed him the binoculars. "Check out that man on the dock. The slender guy with a ponytail standing under the light."

When Cole centered the glasses on the man, his reaction matched hers. "Oh, crap."

"You know him," she said, more as a statement than a question. The fishing boat was now backing and filling to bring the stern around into the wharf so that the passengers could disembark. The roar of the diesel filled the anchorage.

"Afraid I do." Cole lowered the glasses. "How do *you* know him?"

"I came over here today hoping to locate you, to get you to come back to Pointe-à-Pitre to deal with Immigration. Went up to Fort Napoleon and had a little run-in with him."

"What happened?"

She thought for several seconds about how she could say this without sounding like a raving lunatic. Then she decided what the heck, she was talking to a lunatic. "He was following me in the museum, and when I went to confront him, he shoved this dummy at me."

"A dummy?"

"Wearing a costume, you know, like a mannequin. Anyway, he ran, I chased him, tackled him, we fought, he got away. Then the cops came and got me."

"What?" His mouth gaped.

"Well, I would have taken him, but I have this injury. He kicked me in the shoulder here." She touched her collar. "It's an old injury from my days in the service, but it still gives me trouble."

"You must be one hell of a fighter, Magee," he said. "That guy in there is no one to mess with. I know him from back in North Carolina, and word is he's killed at least one guy, probably more. I'm sorry I got you involved."

"What do you mean—got me involved?"

"I didn't think he saw me on your boat." He raised the glasses again and scanned the dock.

"What?" Riley could see that another man had joined Ponytail, but she couldn't see much more than a silhouette without the binoculars. "What's happening? Let me see the glasses."

Cole lowered the binoculars and said, "How am I going to get back to my boat without him seeing me?"

She started to reach for the glasses, then stopped. "Your boat?"

"Yeah, I'm anchored in the bay on the other side of the fort."

He handed her the binoculars, but she just held them in her lap as she stared at him. "You have a boat?"

He shrugged. "A trawler—converted shrimper. Sixty feet. Dark-blue hull."

Riley had started to lift the glasses for another look, but she lowered them again and looked at him. "I saw that boat when I was up at the fort. That's *yours?*"

"Yeah. *Shadow Chaser.*"

Riley was having a difficult time changing gears and reevaluating who this Cole guy was. That boat was a serious boat, not some plastic toy. Who was this guy? She lifted the glasses to look again at what was happening on the wharf, hoping to give herself time to digest this new information. Ponytail Man and the new arrival had moved into the shadows, and she could barely make out where they stood, much less any recognizable features. It looked as if Ponytail was now carrying the other, bigger guy's bag.

When she dropped the glasses back into her lap again and looked at Cole, he looked different somehow. "Listen," he said, "that guy in there, his name is Spyder Brewster, and he's bad news. I feel awful that I've somehow got him looking at you. You want to stay away from him. He's a poacher, a pirate, and he's after something I've got. Crap. I need to get back to my boat."

Cole took the binoculars back from her, then trained them on the wharf. "It looks like the new guy is going off into town, and Spyder is standing by on the wharf." He lowered the glasses. "I suppose I could swim to the beach—"

The words came out of her mouth before she was aware of thinking the thought. "I could sail you around to your boat."

He was seated aft of her on the cockpit cushion, and he lowered the binoculars and swung round with a huge grin on his face. "Miz Maggie Magee," he said, "you'd do that for me?"

"Well, I mean," she stammered, "I enjoy night sails. It's no big deal."

"OK," he said, turning away from her. "Then let's do it."

They sprang into motion at the same time and nearly collided, then did that little dance people do when they both step in the same direction while trying to pass. Finally, Cole laughed, took her by the shoulders, and moved her a step to one side, then waved his hand through the air with another exaggerated flourish and said, "After you, Miz Magee."

Riley began coiling the main sheet as she issued orders, telling him what to do before they could depart, but even as she spoke, she felt dizzy, like when she hyperventilated just before a free dive. Her heart was beating like a runaway engine with a faulty governor. She looked up at the star-filled sky and took a slow, deep breath.

What was wrong with her? So he'd touched her. Obviously, it had been nothing more than a joke to him. Then why did she feel so angry? Was it because of what had just happened—or because of what she wished had happened?

CHAPTER THIRTY-ONE

Aboard the Bonefish

March 26, 2008

She decided to sail *Bonefish* out rather than use the boat's engine, so as not to attract any undue attention. The forecast had been for winds outside the bay blowing twelve to fifteen knots out of the due east, but inside the bay they had less than ten. While she readied the interior for sailing, stowing things that might fly when they heeled over, Cole climbed into her dinghy, rowed aft, and tied it to the stern.

As soon as the anchor was off the bottom, she unfurled her headsail. Gradually, the boat gained steerage as it fell off the wind. The only noise was the sound of the water under *Bonefish*'s transom or the occasional music that flowed from another sailboat's open hatches. The waning moon was due to rise soon and would aid them as they picked their way into the next bay. For now, she was thankful for the cover of darkness, wondering if she was succumbing to Cole's conspiracy fears.

Once Riley completed the turn, the boat ran almost dead downwind out of the anchorage, picking up a little speed as she ghosted past the last of the anchored sailboats in the bay. There were not as many boats as she had thought—maybe a dozen sailboats with flags from nearly as many different countries, and one big sportfisherman. They were gliding along at three knots when Cole came aft and slid onto the cockpit seat ahead of her.

"I can see why sailors love this," he said. "No engine noise. Just the sound of the wind and the gurgle of the water in our wake."

"Yeah, it's addictive. I've been hooked ever since my dad taught me."

"Does your old man still sail?"

"No, my father's got dementia. So bad now he can't take care of himself, much less sail."

"Sorry to hear that."

Riley shrugged. "He was always older than my friends' fathers, and his work kept him away so much of the time, so it wasn't like we were close. But sailing was the one thing we had together."

"You were lucky to have that."

Luck. She leaned back to check the set of the jib, and the sigh that escaped from her lips was louder than she'd intended. It was time to change the subject. "I don't think we'll bother to raise the main. We're only going around the headland and into the other bay." She switched on the autopilot and pulled her legs onto the seat, crossing them Indian style. "So, tell me about this guy. Why is he looking for you?"

He spread his arms out atop the coaming behind him. "It's complicated. I'm not sure I know where to begin. My boat, the *Shadow Chaser*, is a former shrimper that I converted for wreck diving and salvage up in North Carolina. We ran into Spyder in Hatteras." He sighed. "See, my mate and I, we're searching for a wreck."

He paused, then crossed over to the opposite seat and scanned the anchorage with her binoculars.

So he was one of those guys chasing treasure. Figured. She wanted to ask him more about this "mate" of his, like whether it was a he or a she, but she didn't want to give him the wrong impression.

"This wreck—would it be the *Surcouf*?" she asked.

He dropped the glasses to his lap and stared at her, naked suspicion in his eyes. "How did you know?"

"That was the name you gave me. Robert Surcouf. When I mentioned it to the Immigration guy, he told me some story about pirates and submarines."

Cole laughed. "I forgot about that—the fake name. Sorry. But this submarine is more than just some story. It's an amazing tale of treachery and treasure."

"When I tumbled with that Spyder guy, I found this picture—"

Before Riley could finish, the headsail fluttered in a wind shift, and she reached for the winch handle to trim the sheet. They had to tack their way east before they could turn into Marigot Bay, and for the next half hour or so, working the boat required most of her attention. The short tacks gave them brief moments of quiet broken by the noise of the slapping sails and ratcheting winches as they brought the forty-footer around through the eye of the wind.

When they cleared the point under the fort, the three-quarter moon was rising ahead of them, looking like a piece of yellow sea glass worn down on one side. Then Cole asked if he could steer, so Riley turned off the autopilot. The boat began leaping over the swells, and his teeth shone white in the moonlight. He stood behind the wheel flexing his bare legs to stay upright in the growing swells, his shaggy hair blowing back around his ears, a big grin on his face. With the dark tattoo of the words *Carpe Diem* across his collarbones, he looked every bit the raffish salvage diver.

Riley looked away. Damn Speedo. She wished she had something to give him to cover himself with, but she had exhausted her supply of man-sized clothes on his last visit. A towel at least—because she was a normal woman after all, and given all these months of sailing solo, how could she not look?

She jumped up and hurried below to search for the biggest beach towel she had aboard. When she climbed back into the cockpit, she tossed it onto the seat next to him. "In case you get cold," she said.

Though he glanced at the towel, he didn't touch it.

"The wind, you know," she said. The temperature was still in the low eighties even at night, but she was starting to shiver a bit from the breeze. "It gets chilly on the water."

"Thanks," he said. Then he lowered himself to the cockpit seat and peered up at the sky beyond the bimini cover. "Great night, eh?" He spoke with a note of something close to reverence in his voice.

"Yeah," she said, and leaning far back to look out from under the bimini, she felt something in her gut loosen up a little. She sighed. Riley thought about all the times she had seen this southern sea and sky and had no one to share it with. She'd almost forgotten what it felt like—that vibration of connecting with someone.

OK, so he was a powerboat kind of guy who could appreciate the subtle beauties of a night sail, but that didn't change the fact that he had lied to her.

"Are you going to tell me the truth about what you were doing swimming off the island yesterday?" she asked.

"Well," he paused and looked back into the bay they had just left, "it's complicated."

She said nothing. She let her silence work on him.

"That guy back there, Spyder Brewster, he has a brother named Pinky."

"Pinky Brewster? You're kidding."

He smiled again. "Yeah, I know. Not exactly the golden age of television. But, I guess they grew up with the TV as their babysitter. That's the only thing I have in common with these two. Pinky's a nickname he got because of his skin disease. Vitiligo. He's got patches of skin with no pigment, and they look kind of pink."

"Kids can be cruel."

"Yeah, well, he's a pretty creepy guy. Voice sounds like Peter Lorre, and he has these pale-blue eyes that look dead. Like nobody's home. Anyway, back to yesterday. I'd been diving, and I'd stripped to rinse off in a stream when these guys showed up. Not friendlies. I took off running and then swimming. I'd known I was being followed. I could feel it. Didn't know it was them until yesterday. They're definite bad guys—poachers—and they intend to get to the *Surcouf* before I do. Right now, I've got something they want."

"What's that?" she asked, but she already knew. She thought about the photo she had ripped out of Ponytail's—or rather Spyder's pocket. She wanted to see if he would tell her the truth. Before he could speak, she heard an explosive exhalation of air and a splash not more than five feet from the boat.

Cole straightened up and pointed. "Dolphins!" he said.

Two of them darted away and then came zooming back in alongside the boat trailing streaks of bluish-white phosphorescence.

"Make a wish," Cole said. "They're a sign of good luck."

"Yeah, right. Luck."

"It's true, I swear. Didn't you ever watch *Flipper*? Dolphins grant wishes. But, whatever you do, you can't tell anyone your wish. It's just between you and the dolphins."

Riley stared at him, his face aglow from the moonlight, the dolphins' ephemeral trails, and the compass light.

"Make a wish," he insisted.

Damn. He was serious. Luck *and* wishes. "Fine," she said. Just this once, she'd humor him. She thought about how good he was at dodging her questions—and at poking fun at her. She squeezed her eyes shut and wished—but she sure as hell didn't need to be told to keep it a secret.

* * *

When they made their turn easing out the big headsail, Cole steered them close by the trawler anchored out near the mouth of the bay. Riley was surprised at the relief she felt when the first mate stepped out of the wheelhouse and he was a tall, young, black *man* with scholarly looking gold spectacles. He raised a slender arm and waved at them as most boaters do. It wasn't until they sailed abeam that the mate recognized his captain, and he began shaking his head.

This time it was Riley who readied the anchor after showing Cole how to operate the furling gear for the headsail. When she'd let out sufficient scope for the anchor and rigged her snubber, she stood on the bow for a few minutes enjoying the night sounds of birds, insects, and the lapping of the waters around her bow. The moonlight looked like a trail of glittery gems across the water. She picked out the Big Dipper, one of the few constellations she could find without a star chart, and she shivered in spite of the tropical night.

Last night she'd been in tears, and now with the moonlit sail and the dolphins and this crazy man who believed in the gospel according to *Flipper*, here she was stargazing and sighing and wishing for the impossible. She shook her head back and forth, not sure if she was losing her mind. One thing she knew for certain, though: she wasn't going to say a word about him to Hazel. Riley knew if she let slip one kind word about any guy to her best friend, Hazel would be making wedding plans.

She turned aft to see if Cole was going to join her, but there was no one in the cockpit. She tiptoed along the cabin and peered down into the hatch over the main salon. The light over the chart table was on, and Cole Thatcher's bare back was bent in a curve, the hinged chart tabletop resting on his head as he dug around inside.

CHAPTER THIRTY-TWO

The Atlantic south of Bermuda

February 12, 1942

Michaut's smile wilted as he began to take in the tableau before him: McKay's tear-streaked face and bloody shirt, and the still body on the deck.

"Capitaine. qu'est-ce qui se passe?"

Lamoreaux sighed, his eyes fixed on Woolsey. *"Un accident,"* he said. Woolsey thought the captain was trying to convince himself.

"Fuck," McKay said again, and he walked as far as he could get from the other men. He slammed his palm flat against the bulkhead, then buried his face in his sleeve.

Henri Michaut stood frozen to the spot. The birthmark glowed red against his pale skin as he stared at Mullins's still form. *"Mon Dieu,"* he said.

"Bloody hell," Woolsey said when he again noticed the blood dripping down his hand from inside his sleeve. He reached over his right shoulder and hissed through his teeth when his fingers found the glass shard embedded in his upper triceps. He pulled it free and threw it into a stack of crates.

The captain took the tray of food from the young signalman, and after crossing the hold to put distance between himself and the body, he set it on one of the cases of wine. He slid a couple more wine crates close to the tray, then said, "Come, let's sit. Henri, join us, please?"

Without a word, Michaut crossed the hold. He lowered his body and perched on the edge of the crate. Woolsey, who had taken off his coat and was tearing his shirt to bandage his arm, thought the young man looked as though he were going to vomit.

"What are the men up to out there, Henri?" the captain asked in English.

The young man turned his head, looking over his shoulder at the corpse.

The captain grasped the signalman's forearms. "Michaut!" he shouted.

Michaut turned back and looked at Lamoreaux. His eyes shone.

The captain spoke in a softer voice. "Ah, you worked with him in the radio room. You knew him well, *non?*"

Michaut nodded and lowered his eyes. A tear slid onto his cheek.

Woolsey took the fabric in his teeth and pulled the bandage on his arm tight. As he eased his coat onto his wounded arm, he said, "What do you expect, man? This is a war, Kewpie. Men die. Now, let's get on with it. We haven't much time, you know."

The captain glanced at McKay, the concern apparent in his wrinkled brow. The big man still had his face buried in his sleeve. Turning back, Lamoreaux said, "Lieutenant, you are not making this any easier. If not for you, we would not be in this trouble."

"I'm the one who's wounded, and now you're saying your men's mutiny was my fault?"

Michaut raised his head and began whispering to the captain in French.

"What's he saying?" Woolsey pointed at the young Frenchman. Lamoreaux waved his hand in the air, shushing Woolsey until Michaut had finished. Then he raised his eyebrows and lowered his jaw with a look of incredulity. The captain turned to Woolsey. "It seems the men who took my ship have made enemies already. Henri thinks there are more who would like to see me regain my command. They fear Gohin cannot get control of the men to run the boat."

"You see?" Woolsey said as he reached for one of the lengths of baguette on the tray. "There is more than one man on your side. We've got to get out of here and get to that bomb."

The captain ignored him. "Michaut, how are things with Gohin's men?" He spoke in English this time.

The young man spoke in slow, accented English. "Not good. Many are drunk. Many fight. They destroy the radio equipment. Is very dangerous. Gohin ask me to spy on you."

"*Quel surprise*. Gohin's a fool. What about weapons?"

"Gohin open the gun cabinet with your keys. Only he has pistol."

Woolsey fingered the knot on the side of his head. "Had the gun when he escorted me here. Made me intimately aware of it."

The captain ignored him. "*C'est bien*. He does not trust any of the others with sidearms."

Michaut continued. "The doctor say something to him, and Gohin beat him unconscious. The men are now afraid."

Lamoreaux rubbed his hand across his chin. "They should be. Without the radio, we have only signal lamps for communication."

"You can't just sit there," Woolsey said. "You know how desperate the situation is. We haven't much time—and no idea at all how reliable that timer is."

Michaut's eyes darted back and forth between the two men. "Captain? What—"

"No time, Henri. They will come for you soon. Tell Gohin you found me drunk and depressed that I'd lost my ship. Then, listen, can you come back alone? *C'est tres importante.* No one can see you. With so much wine, the men will be sleeping soon."

"Yes, sir."

The wheel controlling the waterproof door creaked as it began to turn. Henri Michaut jumped to his feet.

"Return within the hour," the captain said when the signalman passed him on his way to the door. "Alone."

The door closed, and the lights went out again.

After the sound of scraping on the deck, the captain's torch clicked on. Woolsey and the captain resumed talking in low voices. McKay wandered over, leaned down, and tried to push a wine crate toward the other two. He couldn't budge it. He stood up, saying, "What the bloody hell?"

The captain jumped up and offered McKay his seat. "Here. Sit down. Join us."

"We're trying to work out a plan here," Woolsey said.

"I heard ya."

"The captain and I—" Woolsey began.

"I said I heard ya. I'll take care o' yer bomb." McKay stuffed some bread and cheese into his mouth and began to chew. "Stupid fucking war," he said, spewing bread crumbs.

"We could use—" Woolsey said.

"We din't learn nothing from the first one," McKay said, ignoring Woolsey. "Mullins brought me a message yesterday. Jerries dropped a bomb on the house. All dead. My mum, sister, her boy, Fred. He was six. His dad died at Dunkirk."

Woolsey sighed. "Sean, I'm sorry."

McKay grimaced, his eyes fixed on the still form on the other side of the hold. "Mullins told me when this war is over, I could go live with him and his mum."

"Sean—"

"Shut up. It's McKay to you."

"Look, man, we could use your help here and now," Woolsey said.

"Naw," the big man said, then tore off another piece of bread with his teeth. "Don' trust you." He swallowed and ran his tongue over his teeth before continuing. "You get control, mate, and yer likely to leave the rest of the crew to go up in smoke. I'm goin' fer the bomb. Fer Wally."

McKay picked up a mug of cold coffee and drained it. Then he walked around the hold until he found a tarp covering a stack of crates. He pulled it free, then, crossing to the body, he knelt down and pulled the shard of glass out of Mullins's chest. He wiped the glass on the young man's trousers, then draped the dark oilskin over the body and sat on the floor to wait.

Woolsey turned back to face Lamoreaux.

The captain was still watching McKay. "Do you think he will do as he says?"

Woolsey didn't trust McKay, but he tried to push his doubts aside. "Of course he will."

CHAPTER THIRTY-THREE

Aboard the Fish n' Chicks

March 26, 2008

Diggory settled onto the front seat of the Boston Whaler as Spyder started the outboard engine. His thoughts were still roiling, as they had throughout his meal. What was Cole Thatcher doing on Riley's boat? Assuming it was Thatcher—but he had to assume worst-case scenario here. If she had just picked up the guy swimming at sea as the immigration officer had stated, why would Thatcher return to break into her boat here in the Saintes? What did she have that he wanted?

As the dinghy approached the sportfishing boat, lights came on illuminating the aft deck. There, leaning over the transom, was one of the ugliest men Diggory had ever seen. That he was fat and out of shape was obvious in spite of his loose-fitting clothes. He had a protruding lower jaw and a broad nose, but his Afro-style hair was pure white. The hand that held the door to the swim platform had brown skin down to the knuckles, then pinkish-white fingers out to the nails. It looked as though he were wearing brown gloves with the fingers cut off. The skin of his face and neck above the collar of his shirt was mottled and splotched with patches of brown and pink.

When the Whaler nudged the bigger boat, the repulsive man called out. "Where you been, man? She left half an hour ago." His nasal voice seemed not to fit the fleshy body.

Spyder spun his head around and squinted into the dark. "Shit!" Turning back to Diggory, he said, "This here's my brother, Pinky." Spyder struggled to hold on to the bigger boat as the dinghy bounced in the wind chop. "Open the fuckin' door and take the man inside, Pinky."

Diggory stepped through an opening in the stern of the boat, his bag under one arm. He didn't like boats—hadn't spent much time on them, and it was one of the few areas where he had to admit to a lack of expertise. When he'd been a boy, his father had kept a sailing yacht in Newport, and the local papers often ran photos when he won in the yacht club's races. He'd only seen his father in the flesh once. He'd been thirteen years old when he rode his bicycle to the club and approached his father in the parking lot. Before Diggory could get a word out, his father motioned to a security guard and had him physically thrown off the property. The guard threw his bike too, and bent the front wheel. He'd had to walk it the whole eight miles home. Diggory used to dream of the day when he would be a part of that yachting world and beat his father on the racecourse, but once he had the money, his time for learning to sail had passed. Besides, by then his skill for exacting revenge had grown far more sophisticated.

Diggory followed the man named Pinky up several steps and into what looked like a living room with a couch and a kitchen just beyond. Dirty clothes and towels lay scattered about the floor, and the stuffy interior stank of sweat and cigarettes. In the kitchen sink, stacked dishes teetered several inches higher than the counter level. Pinky sat down in front of a computer on the dining table and slid large earphones onto his head. Diggory stood there surveying the mess as Spyder came in the door.

"You want sumptin' to drink?"

"You're living like pigs," Diggory said. "Doesn't this boat have air-conditioning?"

"Hey, you want to pay for the fuel, I'll be happy to fire up the generator and turn the AC back on. We ain't been running the AC at night."

Pinky pulled off his headphones. "Didn't you guys hear me? She left. And a guy was with her. The doc, I think."

"First, get the AC running and clean this place up." Diggory went down the steps into the accommodation area. One of the brothers had already settled into the master stateroom. He took the man's things and tossed them into the hall. He set his own bag on a bench at the foot of the bed and retrieved a small black case from his shoulder bag. Had Thatcher been the man on Riley's boat? If only he had told the barbarian to plant a listening device in the cockpit of her boat. He would like to know what those two had to talk about.

When he returned to the living room, the generator was running and the vents were blowing cool air into the cabin. Both brothers now held cans of beer. Diggory set the black case on the table, then pulled the headphones off Pinky's head. "Go down to my cabin and put clean sheets on my bed."

The man glared at him. "What you talking about?"

Diggory grabbed Pinky's throat in his right hand and lifted him out of the chair until the barbarian's face was mere inches away from his own. Dig saw that his irises were such a light blue they looked almost white—just before the man squeezed his eyes shut. Shame, that, Diggory thought. The pudgy limbs flayed about ineffectually and odd clicking noises came from between his clenched teeth.

Spyder looked up from the TV remote control he'd been studying, then jumped to his feet. "What the fuck? That's my brother! Put him down, you son of a bitch!"

Diggory dropped the splotchy man to the floor. He lay crumpled on the carpet gasping. "Remind him who gives the orders here."

Spyder helped his brother to his feet. The two disappeared down the stairs, and Diggory heard them moving about and talking, but the low rumble of the generator prevented him from hearing what they said.

Yorick had taught him the importance of establishing dominance during his first dinner at the Tomb. Diggory had arrived early and was wandering the rooms alone. The building held him with an almost erotic fascination, as it was filled with hundreds of artifacts, some of which dated back to the founders in 1832. There were bones, including real skulls—both human and animal—paintings, images on crockery and silver, and quirky, odd mementos dating back to the Civil War that all depicted and glorified death. Most of his fellow Bonesmen got a laugh out of all the paraphernalia. It wasn't unusual to find them tossing footballs or playing Hacky Sack around the many valuable objects. They had no doubt grown up in grand old homes decorated with original oil paintings and ancient objets d'art. They found the death motif amusing. They didn't walk through the rooms as he did, feeling the low, warm tingling of power growing in his groin.

That night he had been standing in front of the fireplace in the library admiring an enormous painting of a nude woman hanging above the mantle. In the painting, a small red man with pointed ears and an oversize erect penis was dragging her toward a gaping, glowing hole in the earth. The woman's white belly and thighs were scratched and bleeding, but she continued to claw at the dirt. Her mouth was open and round, and Diggory imagined he could hear her screaming.

"Like that one, do you?"

Diggory jumped. The voice was at his shoulder, but he hadn't heard anyone come into the room. An older man stood behind him, his chin lifted, hands clasped behind his back, staring up at the painting that stretched all the way to the fifteen-foot ceiling. When the man turned to face him, Diggory saw the wandering eye and knew this was the man who had played the part of Uncle Toby at his initiation. Without warning, "Uncle Toby" crashed his forearm into Diggory's neck, pinning him to the stone fireplace mantle. He felt the older man's hot breath on his cheek. He concentrated on staring at the one good eye.

"So, you think you're one of us now, Priest?" The man pressed harder, trying to make him squirm. He seemed intent on crushing Diggory's larynx, but Dig tried not to struggle. He could go a bit longer without air. "I know your old man, and he doesn't want you here either. How are we going to turn a half-Irish bastard like you into a Bonesman?"

The edges of the room began to disappear into the creeping blackness.

"I decide when and if you breathe. Understand?" Yorick said. He released the pressure on Diggory's throat and stepped away, as if from something distasteful.

* * *

Dig settled into a chair at the yacht's dining table. He opened the black case, and the small flat screen glowed blue. He was adjusting the settings when the brothers returned to the salon.

"You don't need a little DVD player, man. This boat's got a whole entertainment center." Spyder slid open a teak panel to reveal a flat-screen TV and an array of black boxes. "We even got satellite TV, but my brother said not to use it 'cuz they could probably track us with it."

Pinky gave Diggory a wide berth when he came upstairs. He headed straight for his laptop, but when he saw the small black case and screen, he edged closer to take a look. Diggory saw that the whites of the freak's eyes were bloodshot.

"That ain't no DVD, Spyder," Pinky said. "It's a computer." He blew out air and waved his mottled hand dismissively. "We got one of them on this boat already."

"Not like this one."

Pinky took another step closer to look over Diggory's shoulder as he removed the voice encryption module and plugged a cord into the data port on his sat phone.

"So, we gonna up anchor and follow that bitch's boat or not?" Spyder asked.

Diggory placed his finger on an icon on the touch screen, and the zoom changed. He was now looking at the northeastern end of the island Terre-de-Haut. The wedge-shaped icon of a boat was located off the entrance to the next bay to their east, and it crawled across the screen, turning into the anchorage.

"Not tonight," he said. "We won't have any trouble finding them in the morning."

CHAPTER THIRTY-FOUR

Aboard the Bonefish

March 26, 2008

"What the hell do you think you're doing?"

Cole sat up so fast, the chart table lid slid off his head and slammed down on his hands. "Ow!" He lifted the tabletop, extracted his hands, then grinned sheepishly up at her. "This looks bad, eh?"

Riley pulled the dive knife out of the scabbard on the bulkhead. She took the companionway steps one at a time, keeping the knife between her body and his. When she reached the bottom of the ladder, she eased her way forward to the settee. She motioned with the knife. "Get up and go sit down over there." Her voice was flat, a soldier's voice. Giving orders. But she felt as if she were going to be sick. He had conned her so easily.

The corners of his mouth dropped, and the look that replaced the smile was difficult to decipher. Sad? Scared? She wasn't sure. *Who was he?*

He sat down on the settee, and she switched on the overhead florescent light.

"Yesterday—" he began.

But before he could go any further, she said, "Quiet."

She held the knife on him, remaining absolutely still as she thought it through. Under the settee, she had a package of large wire ties. She would bind his hands, his feet. Then sail back to Pointe-à-Pitre, back to that snooty immigration officer. Once she had her passport, she'd be off to Dominica to her job appointment and get back to the life she'd had before she plucked Cole Thatcher out of the sea.

"Riley, let me explain."

The knife in her hand twitched. But he didn't look at the weapon. He kept staring into her eyes.

"When you picked me up out there in the water..." he continued.

Dammit, she'd been conned enough by this Speedo-clad character. She wanted to tell him to shut up, but her lips wouldn't move.

"The coin I was wearing. You saw it?"

She didn't move.

"It's an 1899 fifty-franc French Angel. Very rare. This one was given to me by my father. The Brewsters want it." He paused but held her gaze.

She'd had many a stare down as she stood sentry in front of her embassy posts. But this time, when she attempted to force her mind into that cool void, images of his bare chest and smooth shoulders popped into her head. Damn. She turned away, relieved to preserve some sense of dignity.

She shifted the knife from hand to hand, wiping her palms on her shorts. "What does that have to do with you digging through my chart table?"

"I hid it in there. The coin."

"What?"

"Before I hitched a ride back to my boat yesterday. I couldn't take a chance they were watching. Can't let them get their hands on it. So I hid it inside some sort of scrapbook that was in your chart table. The book was there yesterday, and now it's gone."

Behind him, tucked in among the books on sailing, emergency medicine, 12-volt electronics, and sail repair, she saw the scrapbook.

"Turn around," she said. "It's behind you. Next to the red book, *The 12-Volt Doctor's Practical Handbook*. I moved it last night."

He twisted at the waist. "Damn. It's hard to recognize spine out." He pulled it out and handed it to her. "Look in the back," he said. "Inside the last plastic sleeve. I hid it with a bunch of newspaper clippings in Spanish."

She took the scrapbook from him but hesitated before opening it. The newspaper clippings were stories from *La Republica* and *Diario del Sol* she had saved but never looked at once she'd returned stateside. That was nightmare country. She patted the last page and felt the bulk of the coin and chain. It slid out when she tilted the book on end and fell out with a solid clank onto the teak table.

He didn't move to take it. "Pick it up," he said. "Look at it."

Riley set the knife down on the settee beside her. She picked up the coin. The heft of it was surprising. There were those words again: *Liberté, Égalité, Fraternité*.

He said, "It's almost half an ounce of ninety percent fine gold—minted in Paris in 1899. There are plenty of the twenty-franc ones around, but they didn't make many of these fifty-franc pieces. Hardly any made it into circulation."

Riley turned the coin over and examined the design. It showed an angel depicted in profile, a male nude, well-muscled in the style of Greek statuary, with feathered wings sprouting from the back and a cloth thrown over one shoulder. The angel was writing on a stone tablet. The first word was *Constitution*. Beneath that there was something else, numbers maybe, but the print was too small to read. On the right of the angel was a rooster, and on the left, a cup.

"It's beautiful," she said.

"There are tons of legends about these French Angel coins. They're supposed to provide protection, good luck, health, you name it."

"Back to luck again."

He hunched his shoulders and spread his hands palms up. "It all started with the coin's designer, Augustine Dupres. He was a medalist to King Louis XVI. After making several medallions in honor of the newly minted French Constitution, Dupres fell out of favor and was sentenced to death. According to the story, on the day of his execution, he knelt in his cell to pray, clutching the coin in his hand, and when the executioner saw a flash of sunlight reflected off the gold, he broke into tears and allowed Dupres to escape." Cole chuckled.

"Quite a story," she said.

"Oh, it gets better. See, it's more likely that Dupres used the gold to bribe the guard, but from that day on, this design was known as the Lucky Angel. It wasn't used again until 1871, when France started minting the twenty-franc coins. Those coins became good luck talismans for sailing ship captains, and fighter pilots have carried them from World War I to Vietnam and even now in Iraq."

"So where are you going with all this history?"

"Give me a chance to finish. These fifty-franc coins were only minted intermittently between 1878 and 1899. Few were ever released into circulation. They were kept in the vaults of the French National Treasury—that is, until the Nazis invaded, stole the gold, and sold it to the Swiss to finance the German war machine." He paused, and when she looked up at him, he said, "Or so the story goes."

"And you know another version?"

He grinned. "Indeed I do."

She didn't know whether this was going to be another of his paranoid conspiracy tales, but the historical connection was intriguing. "OK, you've hooked me. What happened?"

"Well, my father was British, you see, and a bit of an amateur historian. He wrote about this in his journals. His version states that in June 1940, as the Nazi Panzer tanks rolled toward Paris, a French submarine was in dry dock in Brest. A small group of Free French patriots, one of whom owned a small winery outside Paris, did not want to see their country's gold fall into Nazi hands. They had been planning for this day, and they had made several hundred special champagne bottles. They loaded several trucks with what looked like a simple wine shipment. They took off on a dash for Brest." He paused and grinned.

She couldn't help it. She had to ask. "Did they make it?"

He nodded. "Although there are no reports or cargo lading documents, my father claimed to have found proof that in the dark of night, with no help from the crew, they loaded all the wine crates into the sub's cargo hold. On June 18, 1940, she sailed for England. Those resistance fighters who stayed behind were killed as the Nazis rolled across France. But, on June 20, *Surcouf* arrived in Plymouth, England, and tied up at the Devonport Naval Dockyards, and no one but her captain knew she had more than a thousand pounds of gold from the French National Treasury hidden in her hold."

CHAPTER THIRTY-FIVE

Aboard the Shadow Chaser

March 26, 2008

Cole climbed up the rope ladder that he had left rigged off his trawler's starboard bulwark earlier that afternoon. After helping Riley swing her bare legs over the rough metal, he hollered out. "Lucy, I'm home!" in his best Ricky Ricardo imitation.

Theo's lanky frame appeared in the doorway of the pilothouse, and he gave a brief shake of his head as he took in the fact that his captain, who was wearing only his Speedos, had brought along a guest. "Late for dinner, Captain, as usual."

"Food is exactly what we need. We're starved." He grabbed Riley's hand and led her forward. "Theo, meet Captain Maggie Riley, who prefers to be called Riley, of the good ship *Bonefish*, yonder. She sailed me home this evening when our friends the Brewsters showed up again."

Mention of the Brewsters did not deter Theo's interest in their guest. "Welcome aboard," he said. After shaking Riley's hand, Theo pushed his glasses up his nose to get a better look at her. He stood a full head taller than Riley, and Cole watched him lean back and give her body a quick up-and-down assessment. Even in the weak light from the pilot house, she was bound to notice, and Cole hoped she understood what it was like for a couple of guys to spend all these weeks on a working boat with no women around. And certainly none who looked like she did.

"Glad to be here," she said.

Theo bent down and in a stage whisper said into her ear, "Be careful." He pointed to Cole. "You do him one little favor and in his world, you're his ally for life."

Cole saw Riley smile. Theo, with his clipped, British-Caribbean accent, had that effect on people.

"Thanks for the warning," she whispered back.

"I made the mistake some months back," Theo said, "and he shanghaied me proper. Been shackled to this bloody ship ever since."

Cole waved Theo aside. "Blasphemy!" He leaned in and whispered. "Don't mind him. He thinks I don't pay him enough. Fact is, I can't afford what he's worth, but we can't let him know that." Then raising his voice, he said, "Come along, I smell young master Theo's cooking, and it is not to be missed."

* * *

Either the meal of grilled mahi-mahi, rice and peas, and fried plantains was one of Theo's best efforts, or it was the company. Cole tended to think it was the latter. After pouring Riley a glass of chilled chardonnay, he had slipped into his cabin and changed into his best pair of cargo shorts and the one clean T-shirt he had left. Then by turns, he and Theo regaled Riley throughout the meal with stories of their adventures and misadventures in rebuilding the *Shadow Chaser* and designing her for maritime salvage work. They told tales of the Outer Banks and the Brewster brothers. They were acting a little like Peter and the Lost Boys fighting for Wendy's attention. But it was terrific to have a woman on board. She smelled good, and she laughed at his jokes. Right there, he thought, it was a massive improvement over Theo.

But more than that, she was smart, and Cole couldn't wait to get her take on their code problem. She might see something they had missed. Another pair of eyes looking at things was just what they needed.

Theo began to clear the dishes off the table.

Riley lifted her plate. "Let me help you."

"Not on this boat, lady," Theo said as he took the plate from her hand. "You are our guest."

Cole slid out of the dinette. "I'll be right back. There's something I want to show you."

He entered his cabin and sat on the bunk. With the door ajar, he could still hear the clank of Theo stacking the dishes and the voices coming from the galley.

"Well, Miss Riley," he heard Theo say, "it looks like you've had quite an effect on our Dr. Thatcher. Most of the time, he is so suspicious of people he won't even talk to them."

"Doctor?"

"Well, don't ask him to write you a prescription, but he does have a PhD."

Cole listened. The silence on the other side of the bulkhead stretched out for several beats. He wished he could see her face. He grabbed the box that held the journals and returned to the galley.

When he set the box on the table, she stared at it. Then she lifted her eyes and squinted as though trying to focus on his face. "Theo tells me you have a doctorate?"

"Yeah."

"In what?"

"Maritime archeology."

"From where?"

"Texas A&M."

"I…" she started to say, stumbled, and tried again. "I didn't figure you for an academic."

He shrugged. "I loved the learning part, but I can't say as I've figured out the making a living part. Tried teaching at East Carolina University, but it seems the rest of the department thought I was a nutcase. I hated meetings. Never went to their faculty parties or the get-togethers at the local pub. Weekends, I was always out diving or fishing. Did three years, long enough to know I'd never make tenure from that lot. Then Theo came along, and I quit for good. I've never regretted it."

Theo turned from the sink, wiping his hands on a dish towel, and announced in a loud voice, "I feel like a walk." When Riley wasn't looking, he flashed an exaggerated wink in Cole's direction and grabbed his backpack. "Riley, would you mind if I take your dinghy ashore? That way I can fetch our rubber ducky at the dock when I make the return trip. Dr. Thatcher here has a way of losing dinghies."

"Sure, Theo. Take it."

Cole asked his first mate to retrieve the shoes and clothes he had left hidden under a sea grape tree on the beach, as well. Once Theo had disappeared out of the galley, Cole shifted his position on the vinyl settee seat. He knew he should say something, but he wanted it to be the right something, and he was drawing a blank.

"So, is North Carolina home?" Riley asked, finally breaking the silence.

"No. I was raised by my mom in Fort Lauderdale. Like I said, my dad was British, but he and my mom broke it off when I was a baby. He moved back to England."

"Did you know him?"

"I only met him once." He was conscious of his hands resting on the metal box in front of him. "He sent cards and letters from abroad, but when I was about twelve, he came to the States."

"That's tough on a kid—growing up without a dad."

"So they say." Cole shrugged. "I didn't think I was deprived. Adults lived on the periphery of my world. My mom worked at the hospital all the time, so I didn't see her much either. I just wanted to go surfing and fishing and diving. Can't say I missed him until I actually met him."

"Really? Why?"

"Well, when he showed up, I thought he was great! You know, the accent and all. He took me out to a fancy restaurant on the ocean and told stories about his travels through Europe, behind the Iron Curtain, tales of close calls with military police, secret codes, and smuggled packages. He never admitted it, but I figured him for a real-life James Bond."

"Was he?"

"Not quite Bond, but I did learn later, after he died, that he *had* worked for MI-6 in the eighties. He was a courier and cryptanalyst. Must have been something he didn't like about the business, though, because he spent the last twenty years of his life writing books and articles that ripped the international intelligence community—and he especially ragged on the Brits and their Official Secrets Act."

"You seem to know him pretty well."

Cole opened the box and pulled the journals. "You know, I never saw him again. But after that one night, we stayed in touch through the mail. No e-mail. He was old fashioned, you know. Bit of a Luddite. He sent me stuff—packages with books about codes and ciphers. After that, he included secret messages in all his letters. Taught me to decipher his letters and how to encrypt my own to send back. All that stuff about secrets and spycraft was pretty cool to a twelve-year-old. When I got older, in high school and later in college, his letters became these rants about what was wrong with the world, and well, I stopped writing back."

"Why?"

"I thought he was crazy. My father had this worldview that I found very disturbing at first—about how this small minority of superpowerful, wealthy people have been attempting to control Western civilization for hundreds of years."

"So that's where you get it from."

"It? What do you mean 'get *it* from'?" Cole stopped and took a deep breath. He could feel his pulse pounding in his neck. He had to stop the knee-jerk defensive reaction this time. "Riley, I realized I was wrong. He wasn't crazy. He wrote about them in his books, too, and they killed him for it."

She looked away then. He was losing her. It sounded nuts when he said it out loud. "Listen, I know how that sounds, and I know that crazy people always insist they're the sane ones. But these people, they've counted on that. They've gone by different names. Everything from the Illuminati to the Masons, but names don't matter; they're still all *secret societies*. These guys are from old money. They've infiltrated the CIA, NSA, NRO, DIA—the entire alphabet soup of intelligence agencies, including the secret ones people like you and me have never heard of. They own Homeland Security. Hell, they created it. These aren't just some guys with a fancy handshake who meet at the lodge to drink beer. We don't know what *really* happened at Pearl Harbor, the Gulf of Tonkin, the Kennedy assassination, or even on 9/11—these guys have been controlling the flow of intelligence for decades and all for one end: to make sure our country gets into another very profitable war, and another after that. My father showed me *they have not gone away*." He took a deep breath; it had all poured out of him in such a rush, he hadn't even paused to inhale.

She didn't say anything. Seemed to be a habit of hers. She wouldn't speak until she had thought about what she wanted to say. Any other time, he'd find that quality refreshing. But not today. The silence dragged out. Then she pushed back her chair, stood, and headed for the door.

CHAPTER THIRTY-SIX

Bourges des Saintes

March 26, 2008

"Who the fuck does he think he is?" Spyder said when he jumped from the *Fish n' Chicks*'s aft swim platform onto the town wharf. "It's our boat, and after we do all the work of upping the anchor and docking alongside, he sends *us* to town to fetch *his* shit."

He watched as his brother reached for the stone pier. The mottled hand missed the steel cleat he'd been aiming for, and Spyder had to grab at the waistband of his brother's pants to keep him from falling into the water. "Jesus H. Christ, Pinky. You'd think you never been on a boat." He dragged his brother up onto the concrete surface of the commercial wharf.

"He wants some privacy," Pinky said. He stood and brushed bits of gravel off his white pants.

"I don't give a flying fuck. It's *our* boat. Leastwise it is now." They headed up the wharf to where it intersected the village's main street. Spyder wanted to get this errand done quick. He didn't trust that Thor dude on his boat all alone.

"He's got a sat phone," Pinky said when they arrived at the intersection. "I saw it. And he won't eat that crap you bought. He wants some decent food and wine, and he gotta make a phone call."

After Thor had settled in the master stateroom, he came out into the galley and started opening lockers. A quick check of their supply of cocktail sausages and cheese puffs, and the neat freak asshole had demanded they take the big boat in and tie up to the main dock. That way they would be able to run the AC without running the generator.

Spyder reached into his shorts pocket for the money and shopping list Thor had given him. "It's the middle of the fuckin' night! I can't even read what he wrote on here."

"It's OK. The French stay up late. That's some kinda grocery store just up there." Pinky pointed toward the center of the town.

Spyder counted the bills. "Two hundred. Looks like there's enough for a tip for us, bro."

"You go. I wanna walk. I'll be back in about an hour." Pinky turned and plodded off down the sidewalk that led away from the lights and sounds of town.

Spyder stood in the middle of the deserted street and watched the eerie white outline of his brother's silhouette as he slid off into the darkness. The bushy Afro, long-sleeved shirt, and cotton pants, all white, made him look like a fat freakin' ghost. His brother's weird behavior still creeped him out. He knew there were two main reasons Pinky loved the night: for one, his skin just couldn't take the daytime sun, and second, when it was dark, people couldn't see him, didn't laugh at him, or point and call him a freak.

Inside the place Pinky called a grocery, a runt Frenchman with Coke-bottle-bottom glasses stood behind a counter scooping ice cream out of a bin for a kid who wasn't even tall enough to see through the glass. The two of them were jabbering in French. In the middle of the single room, there were four standing shelves with a mishmash of wine, school supplies, and packaged goods. A small cooler held bottles of beer and wine. At the end of the refrigerated section were several wooden boxes filled with fruits and vegetables. Half the wall behind the counter was covered with different kinds of cigarettes, rolling tobacco, and papers, and on top of the freezer were boxes of cigars.

Spyder wasn't sure they'd have the kind of fancy food this Thor dude was looking for, but as long as it was French, the asshole would probably like it.

When the kid left, the old man said something in French, and Spyder handed him the list. The old guy pulled out a cardboard box and began collecting bottles and cans from the shelves, so Spyder stuffed a cigar in his pocket when the owner wasn't looking, pulled a can of Heineken out of the fridge, and went to the door. He figured he might as well kick back and let the old man do the heavy lifting. In the restaurant across the street, a bunch of customers sat hunched over the bar. The music had quit, but the serious drinkers were still out.

From the corner of his eye, he noticed movement back down by the wharf. When he swung his head that way to look, there was no one there. What was it that attracted his attention? He hollered into the shop that he would be right back and headed down to the corner to take a look at the boat.

The *Fish n' Chicks* was docked about fifty feet up the pier, and though there weren't many lights in the area, he saw the outline of a man on deck. Keeping to the shadows, he edged closer to the boat. The figure stepped around the cabin headed for the afterdeck, and Spyder recognized him. It was just Thor, and now he was climbing up to the fly bridge. What the fuck was he doing? Guy didn't know squat about boats. He watched as the man settled into the helmsman's seat. Had Thor been talking to somebody? Was that what he'd seen? He closed his eyes and tried to pull up a clearer image of what had attracted him. Yeah, it had been somebody hauling ass off the wharf. It wasn't a woman, he was sure of that. A man, then, walking fast. Too fast.

Spyder returned to the main street, then entered the alley that led up the side of the hill between the dark cottages. This was definitely the direction the shadow man had gone. Spyder stepped softly, listening for footsteps, ducking overhanging branches heavy with sickly sweet flowers. The windows he passed were all dark and dull like the eyes of old blind men. After about fifty yards, he came to another cross street that ran parallel to the little shopping and restaurant district below. The houses on the back street were larger and fancier, with second-story wrought-iron balconies and whitewashed brick walls surrounding front courtyards. A narrow concrete sidewalk ran alongside the cobblestone street beneath the high branches of the poinciana trees. He turned right and started to circle the block when he felt a hand fall on his shoulder.

He spun around fast, spilling beer down the front of his shirt from the can he had forgotten was still in his hand. "Shit, Pinky! I almost crapped my pants. What are you creeping around here for?"

"Just walkin'."

"You seen anybody come by here?"

"Just a dog. That's all."

Maybe it was just a dog. But he didn't trust Thor, that was for sure, and if they were going to make out on this deal, he'd have to watch him.

"I found where the woman's sailboat went to."

"You seen it?"

Pinky nodded. "Just where that dude's GPS thing said it would be."

"Yeah?"

"Unh-huh." He pointed down the street that led out of town. "Off that way. There's another boat there, too. Can't make it out, though. Too far out. I just seen the white anchor light."

Spyder chugged down the last of the beer and burped loudly. He was trying to think. He knew that knowing stuff was always worth something. Now Pinky'd seen the chick's boat, and they had that. But what they didn't know was who had been running away from their boat. Had the dude got rid of him and his brother just so he could meet with somebody?

"Spyder, you don't look so good."

"Shut up, bro. I'm trying to think."

Pinky chuckled and scratched at a scab on his cheek.

"I said shut up, man." Spyder hated it when his brother laughed at him. "Fuck this. Come on. Let's go get the asshole's food and get back to the boat. I don't like leaving him alone with our shit. Who knows what he's doing. He might be going through our drawers and shit. We got our own secrets, right bro?"

CHAPTER THIRTY-SEVEN

Aboard the Shadow Chaser

March 26, 2008

Riley leaned over the stern bulwark and peered across the water toward her boat lying at anchor farther inside the bay. Above her loomed the cables and dark shadows of the former shrimper's outriggers. Though she knew sailboats, she was unaccustomed to work boats, and she felt like a foreigner aboard this one.

Where was Theo? With her dinghy gone, she had no way, aside from swimming, to get back to her distant anchor light. But at that moment, she wanted more than anything else to get off this conspiracy nut's boat. Her father made more sense than this guy.

"Mikey, what was I thinking?" she whispered to the wind.

Closing her eyes, she reached out to her brother. She needed that connection to him. A sudden thought popped into her mind, and she opened her eyes. "You agree with him?"

Though she hadn't heard anything, she felt his presence behind her. He exhaled a long breath.

"Mikey?" She started to turn.

"I don't blame you for wanting to bolt," Cole said.

"Oh," she said. "It's you."

"Who did you think it would be?"

She turned back to the rail and stared out at her boat's distant anchor light. "Nobody."

He rested his forearms on the bulwark next to hers, and he didn't say anything for several long minutes. His voice was soft when he began to speak. "I talk to myself all the time too, Magee."

She wasn't about to correct him—to tell him that she wasn't talking to herself.

"I know how all this must sound to you."

She thought for a moment before speaking. She had to phrase this right. "Cole, I grew up in embassies. My father was a career diplomat. After that, I spent nine years as a marine, six as an MSG stationed in Cairo, Honduras, Lima. I grant you, in all that time, I've seen some pretty bad stuff from our government. But they're not even organized enough to get the right units assigned to the proper stations, much less to pull off any big conspiracies. I don't see how you can believe that."

"I was a skeptic too, at the beginning. After I outgrew the whole hero worship thing, I decided my old man didn't have both oars in the water. But then it happened. I came to believe."

She shook her head, but he continued.

"A little over five years ago, my father sent me an autographed copy of his latest book. It was about a submarine. The book was called, *Surcouf: The Disappearance of the Greatest Submarine in the World*. I never wrote him a thank-you note. The package arrived when I was still teaching at ECU, trying to fit into that world. It was some tiny publisher—more like a vanity press. But it got reviewed, and people in my field knew about him. I was ashamed of him. Early on in my career, I discovered that a mere mention of my relation to James Thatcher made people look at me as if I were a crackpot."

When she turned to look at him, his profile was silhouetted in the moonlight. His chin was up, his eyes on the stars, his soft words swallowed up by the dense marine air. She leaned forward, trying to hear him better. For some reason she didn't understand, his stories seemed both to repulse and attract her.

"It was after he sent the book that his letters dried up. I'd stopped writing back. We had no communication at all the last three years of his life. The last message I got from him was a birthday present when I turned thirty." Cole lifted the coin on its chain to his chin and looked down at it. "This. I didn't bother to save the card. He'd written a message in it saying something to the effect that this coin was a key."

He ran his thumb over the face of the coin as she'd seen him do that first day.

"What did he mean? A key to what?"

"I didn't know back then," he said.

"And now?"

He nodded. "It's why they killed him."

She brushed her hair off her forehead and rested her palm against her brow. Oh, Mikey, she thought. I know what that is like to have suspicions but not be able to prove anything. The sense of déjà vu was making her feel nauseous. "What makes you so sure he was murdered?"

Cole took a deep breath. "Will you come back inside? There's something else I want to show you."

* * *

"Nobody contacted me at first when he died," he said after they had both slid back onto the benches of the dining booth. "It was several months after his death when this package arrived in the mail from Bodwin, England." He opened the box, lifted the journals out, then retrieved the yellowed clipping from the bottom of the box. "Inside were these old leather-bound books," he said, tapping the journals. "There was also a note from my father's solicitors saying the old man had specified in his will that he wanted his son in America to receive these. Tucked inside one of the volumes, I found this article from the *London Times* about his death."

He unfolded the newspaper clipping and placed it front of her. She began to read.

"Bodwin, Cornwall. Late Thursday morning, James Thatcher was found hanging from a skylight in his loft at his house in Cornwall. When the body was discovered by a housekeeper, Thatcher was dressed in a green hazmat suit for use in nuclear, biological, or chemical warfare, green overalls, a black plastic mackintosh, and thick rubber gloves. His face was covered by a gas mask, and he was wearing a sou'wester. His body was suspended from two ropes, attached to shackles that had been fastened to a piece of wood, and he was surrounded by pornographic photos of women in bondage. According to consultant pathologist Dr. Jonathon Yates, Thatcher died from asphyxia in what is now called autoerotic asphyxiation."

She opened her mouth to say something, and then she closed it again. She didn't know what to say. What did he want from her? Why was he sharing all this? Where the hell was Theo with her dinghy?

"Riley, I may not have spent much time with my father, but I knew him well enough." He shook his head and pointed his finger at the clipping. "I can't buy that story. It's not the lurid sex part of it. It's too over the top. I mean, it's not even practical if you think about it. Thick rubber gloves? And you know, there couldn't have been a more effective or symbolic way to silence and discredit him. He wouldn't write any more books or letters throwing scorn on the British Official Secrets Act. No more investigations into Britain's World War II code breakers or the real reasons for the invasion of the Falklands or the secrets kept by the royal family. And the body of his life's work, like the body dangling from those ropes, had been made a mockery."

"Cole, I'm sorry, but—"

"I didn't communicate directly with my father the last three years of his life, but when I met Theo and decided to start my own exploration company to do underwater archeological work, we got a large anonymous donation that allowed us to buy *Shadow Chaser* and fit her out. That was our seed money. After he died, I discovered something. That anonymous donor was my father. He sent the money—not because he wanted to help me out. He wanted *me* to help *him*."

"What do you mean?"

"He wanted me to find *Surcouf*."

CHAPTER THIRTY-EIGHT

Aboard the Shadow Chaser

March 26, 2008

Riley sat looking down at the hands folded on her lap and tried to digest everything he had told her over the last couple of hours. Far-fetched was the word that kept coming to mind. Cole Thatcher might be attractive, well-educated, funny, and a good boatman, but—and this was no small item—*the man was nuts.* He didn't have so much as his big toe grounded in reality. She reached across the table, picked up the heavy gold coin, and turned it over in her hands.

"I know the answer to *Surcouf's* location is on that coin," Cole said, staring at the coin. "And that's why the Brewsters are following me. I was stupid enough to tell them as much." He glanced up, met her eyes. "Alcohol was involved." He attempted a smile, his lips pressed together in thin lines.

"You must have been a pretty convincing drunk for them to follow you this far."

"And an idiot."

He stood up then and began pacing in the confined galley like a figure skater doing figure eights. He stopped and stabbed his finger at the chart. "It's got to be there. Everything points to it. There's something in the old man's journal—a cipher or code—and that coin is the key!" Then he added, "I *know* it."

She was about to respond, to shift the subject matter to something that made her a little less uncomfortable, when he spun on his heel, braced his hands on the doorframe, and leaned out into the night.

"She's out there. *Surcouf.* Close by. It's like I can smell her."

The deck breeze ruffled his shaggy hair and rippled his T-shirt where it hung from his arms. She was fascinated by the pent-up, almost manic energy in him.

"Why here? Why Guadeloupe?" As soon as the words were out of her mouth, she regretted them. Why was she encouraging him? Maybe she was nuts, too. But she had to admit she was curious about this code thing. She'd always enjoyed a good puzzle, and like her brother, she was pretty good at them.

He swung around to face her again. "In the last eighteen months of his life, my father flew down here twice, landed at Pointe-à-Pitre, stayed several weeks. It's all in the journals here." He picked up one of the volumes and began to thumb through the pages. "It was right after his second stay that Theo and I got the anonymous donation. He found something here. Maybe it was the actual wreck. I don't know. There were only two more journal entries after that. But those two entries don't read like the rest of the pages. The words don't make sense; the sentences don't connect, and sometimes the words aren't even words. It's got to be a code. Take a look."

He placed the open book in front of her. The handwriting on the page was uneven, almost chaotic. It leaned left in places and to the right in others. In some places, the letters were neat, and in others, the script was barely legible. Riley knew nothing of handwriting analysis, but it didn't take an expert to see that this was the writing of a disturbed individual. On the final page, she read:

Dear Son,

Wit's end is where I am. Spent a bit of time there. Expect to be there 'til the end of days. Got to stop. Them. American president is part and parcel. What goes up must come down. Not a nickel to my name. It's all yours now. Got to stop. Them. The Creoles sing a song in the islands. It's called Fais pas do do. Like this.

Fais pas do do, Cole mon p'tit coco
Fais pas do do, tu l'auras du lolo
Yayd d'dir
Y'did yd
Jamais fais do do.

Cole leaned back in the seat opposite her, and his shoulders slumped. "But I've tried everything. I've searched the text for a hint that he used a book code, tried various field ciphers. For a while, I thought the coin's date was a key to the cipher. Then I figured that a letter/number substitution was giving me the longitude and latitude of an area off the west coast of the island. That's why I was diving out there yesterday. None of it's worked."

"This is a weird version of a well-known French lullaby. *Don't go to sleep, Cole my little coconut, Don't go to sleep, you will have a treat,* then those weird letters as a chorus, and finally, *Never go to sleep.*"

"I know. I had a friend translate that much. Give me some credit. I get that he's telling me to never be caught sleeping. But the code? I don't have a clue. Yet I know it's the key to this thing."

He lifted the lockbox aside, and there were still a few objects in the bottom. Riley leaned in to look. "What's that?"

"It's just some other stuff the old man sent me over the years. Kid's stuff."

"Anything might be relevant."

"No, it's this coin," he said, pointing at the heavy gold piece. "I'm sure of it."

She picked up the coin again. "Have you got a magnifying glass?" Riley asked. "There's a mark here, a scratch or something that I can't read."

"Sure." He disappeared into the wheelhouse, and when he returned, he handed her a small leather case. Inside was a round brass magnifier. There was a ring around the lens with three slender legs that kept it about an inch off the table.

"Nice," she said. She turned the ring round the lens and saw that it adjusted the height to focus the lens. "I've never seen one of these."

"It's an old chart magnifier I found at a nautical flea market. My eyes aren't so good when it comes to the fine print on charts— or anything else, for that matter."

Riley slid the coin under the lens. The nude angel's arm crossed the tablet, and he held a pen of some sort in his hand. She saw the big letters above that hand that spelled out the word "Constitution." But there was something else. Beneath the angel's hand where a drape of fabric crossed the tablet, there appeared to be something scratched into the gold. She moved the coin back and forth hoping to make it clearer in the reflected light.

"What's that written on the tablet?" she asked.

"Like I told you, Dupres designed this coin to honor the new French Constitution."

"No, under the word. Beneath the angel's hand. In tiny script."

He leaned forward, his arms resting on the table, his head touching hers as he peered at the coin. "What are you talking about? There's nothing under it."

"Yes, there is." She adjusted the outer ring on the chart magnifier, trying to bring the image into focus. "I think it's a number."

"What? Let me see." He took the magnifier from her hand, slid the coin across to his side of the table, and squinted into the eyepiece, one eye closed. "I don't see anything."

She put a hand on her hip and leaned back. "OK. You think I'm making it up? Aren't you the one who told me you can't make out the fine print on charts?"

He sat up straight and without a word pushed the coin and the magnifier back across the dinette table.

She lined up the coin and the eyepiece. "Have you got any better light?" she asked.

He got up and brought over a flashlight, a sheet of paper, and a pen. She repositioned the magnifier and coin on top of the paper while Cole angled the beam under the lens. "There," she said. "That's it."

"What is it? What does it say?"

"It's three digits." She stopped before saying any more. Her pulse began to throb in her neck, and she tried to slow her breathing.

"Yeah? I'm listening. What three digits?"

There had been an inquest after her brother's death. She'd read the court documents that described how the frat boys had tied off the end of the old musty sleeping bag so he couldn't escape, the signs of his struggle as his asthma made his throat constrict, the condition of the body. She'd once teased her brother about that pocket pencil protector with his collection of pens and pencils. He'd used one of them to write on his hand.

"Are you OK?"

She was sitting up, staring into space. His voice brought her back. She blinked. "Sorry." She ran her hand over her eyes, then picked up the pen and started to write. Three numbers.

Three-two-two. She was looking at what she had written, but she was seeing the police photo of the pale hand, hearing the husky voice of the New Haven detective asking her parents if the number meant anything to them.

"Riley? You look like you're going to throw up. What's wrong?"

She realized she'd started rocking and rubbing her hands on her thighs as though trying to warm herself up. Forcing herself to stop, she laced her fingers together, rested her hands on the table. "It's about my older brother," she said. She took a deep breath. "He died his freshman year at college. A fraternity hazing. It was his asthma. He suffocated trapped inside a sleeping bag. Didn't have his inhaler. Before he died, he managed to write three numbers on his hand."

In the distance, she heard the whine of her outboard approaching. Finally. Theo returning with her dinghy. She'd been afraid he would stay away all night. But maybe Theo understood more than she was giving him credit for. Maybe he knew that after hearing all these tales about gold coins, shipwrecks, murder, conspiracies, and secret societies, she would be counting the minutes until he returned.

"There's Theo," she said. "I need to go. Now." And, she thought, I need to figure out how or if any of this connects to Michael.

Cole reached across the table and placed his hand on top of hers. "I'm sorry about your brother."

She glanced at his sea-green eyes, but she had to look away. He was much easier to take when he was joking around.

"I need to get back to my boat."

He squeezed her hand. "No, please. Riley. Don't go. This is the first break we've had in weeks. We're close, I know it."

She slid her fingers out of his grip and moved her folded hands to her lap. She stared at the coin, unable to look at Cole. She, too, wanted answers. But hers were different questions.

Through the open galley door came the sputtering sound of the outboard shutting down, then the thudding of scrambling feet.

"Riley, I need your fresh set of eyes. I still can't see those numbers. Theo never picked up on it. Stay and help me figure out what they mean."

"Cole!" Theo called.

She glanced across the table and saw worry lines appear between his eyebrows.

He lifted his chin toward the open door and called out, "We're in the galley!"

Theo appeared in the doorway, his glasses askew and his breath rasping in his throat. His elbows were both raised over his head as he attempted to take off his backpack.

"They're here," he said. "I saw them both in town. And another fellow on the powerboat." As he spoke, Theo untangled his arms from the straps, swung the backpack onto the table, and unzipped the front compartment.

"Slow down, Theo. You talking about the Brewsters? We know—we both saw Spyder."

The younger man nodded and pulled a small digital camera from the backpack's pocket. He pushed a button on the camera, and the LCD screen lit up. "Check this out. I couldn't use the flash—obviously—but I thought you'd like to get a look at this guy." Theo handed the small camera to Cole. "The brothers went to town to buy provisions. I saw them leave, so I went down to check out the boat. Then this other chap comes out. Push that silver button on the back of the camera to scroll through. I got three different shots of him before I took off."

Cole moved the camera farther away from his body, then tilted the little screen, squinting to see the dark images. "He doesn't look like he'd be friend or family of the Brewsters, that's for sure."

"Not a boatman either, judging from the leather-soled loafers," Theo said. "Pricey ones, I bet. When the brothers left the boat, they were complaining about him bossing them around."

Cole looked across the table at her. "Check this guy out. Looks like he stepped right out of an ad in *GQ*." Cole set the camera down in the middle of the table and spun it around so that Riley could see the image on the screen.

She glanced at it more out of politeness than interest. She had been listening for a break in the conversation so she could make her excuses. She hadn't at all expected to recognize the man in the photos.

She didn't say anything.

"Riley? What is it?"

She said nothing. She couldn't breathe.

"Cole," Theo said. "She doesn't look too good."

Cole slid off the table bench and stood. He put his hand on her shoulder. "Riley?"

She looked up and blinked at him. "Yeah," she said, her voice sounding stronger than she felt.

"You know him, don't you? You recognize this guy."

When she had first agreed to meet him in Pointe-à-Pitre it was because she needed answers, but all she kept finding was more questions.

She reached for the pen, underlined the number she had written on the paper. "Let me tell you about this number three-two-two."

CHAPTER THIRTY-NINE

The Atlantic south of Bermuda

February 13, 1942

By the time Michaut returned to the hold, they had armed themselves, Woolsey with his pocketknife, Lamoreaux and McKay with broken bottle glass. They waited in the darkness with only the occasional cough or shuffling feet to indicate the state of their nerves. Their plan was to go straight to the bridge, take out Gohin first, and then hope the others would return to their senses once the man who had bullied them into this mad mutiny was out of the picture.

"When I leave the radio room," Michaut said, speaking in his broken English so they all could understand, "Gohin go up to deck to take some air and smoke." He pointed up with his index finger.

"What about the others?" Lamoreaux asked.

"Most men is sleeping from wine, *Capitaine*. Gerard is the helm and Fournier *navigateur*. No diving, so no one do planes or vents."

"Reckless way to run a boat." Lamoreaux's eyes locked on Woolsey. "*Bon, Lieutenant, allons-y*. Let's take back my boat."

The four of them stayed together as they headed forward through the compartment containing the auxiliary pumps, hoses, and motors that brought fresh air into the sub when she ran at the surface. Their path would take them to the ladder just aft of the control room. Michaut went ahead to distract the men on watch there, and McKay followed him. Just before the big man peeled off into the radio room, a sailor stepped out of that compartment and into the companionway. His wide eyes registered surprise at seeing the captain there in the company of the two Brits. Before the seaman could open his mouth, McKay stepped behind him, wrapped one of his ham-sized arms around the man's neck, then lifted, bending his head back and pressing the sharp glass against the taut skin.

"*Non!*" the captain rasped in harsh whisper. He glanced forward toward the control room. He could hear Michaut chatting with the other men on watch just a few feet away. He lowered his voice. "*C'est pas necessaire, n'est-ce pas, Bertrand?*"

The sailor attempted to shake his head in spite of the glass at his throat and the meaty hand clamped on his forehead.

The captain held his finger to his lips while staring at the sailor's face. "Release him," he whispered to McKay. When the big man obeyed, the captain stepped up and spoke in low, rapid French as the sailor gasped for air and clutched his throat.

The captain's words seemed to calm him, but when the old man finished, the sailor turned aft and took off at a dead run. Woolsey said, "That was a mistake, Captain. You should have let McKay kill him."

McKay stepped up to Woolsey and backed him into the bulkhead. "Sod off," he whispered. "I wasn't gonna kill him. No more needless killing on this boat." The spray of spittle caused Woolsey's right eye to blink. McKay spun away and disappeared into the radio room.

Lamoreaux grabbed the side of the steel ladder, and Woolsey watched as he climbed through the first of three hatches that would take them to the conning tower. Looking straight up, he saw only darkness above the captain, but he knew the conning tower hatch was open. He smelled the sea air. Woolsey was glad to let the French captain take the lead. No sense being the first to poke his head out there, since Michaut had told them that Gohin was now armed. Their weapons would work up close, but they would have no effect at all against bullets.

Woolsey began to climb once Lamoreaux disappeared. When he got closer to the hatch, he could make out the stars. Then, the captain's head appeared. Putting his finger to his lips, the captain pointed aft. Woolsey eased himself onto the conning tower deck and remained in a crouch. Even behind the bridge, the cold wind lifted his hair and whistled around his ears. Looking aft, he saw the silhouette and the red glow of the cigarette on the gunnery deck just below them. Gohin had his back turned as he leaned over the rail and dragged deeply on his smoke.

The weather was on the mild side for February in the North Atlantic, but the sub's forward speed of ten knots, coupled with the ten knots of breeze over the bow, resulted in a stiff and loud wind. Woolsey shuddered when he looked down at the black water rushing past the hull. One slip and he'd be in that water, drowning. He stifled a groan. Woolsey feared that any sound would carry straight back to Gohin. There was no moon, but the stars seemed all the brighter in her absence.

There were only two ways off the conning tower: back down the hatch or down the aft ladder to the gun deck. They would be totally exposed in the event that Gohin turned, but he hoped the noise made by the sub slicing through the water would offer them a chance—as long as they moved before the big man finished his cigarette.

Woolsey kept his eyes on Gohin as the captain eased himself down the ladder backward. When it was Woolsey's turn, it took all his willpower to turn his back on Gohin, but it was the only way to get down the ladder. He stepped gingerly, testing his footing on each rung before shifting his weight. Though there were only five steps in all, Woolsey felt his chest loosen a bit when his foot touched the flat steel deck.

Then he felt the sharp jab of a gun barrel thrust against his ribs.

From the corner of his eye, Woolsey saw Lamoreaux backed against the guardrail, his hands raised over his head. Gohin barked something in French. The press of the pistol on his side eased, then something slammed into the side of his head, causing him to stumble and fall to the deck at Lamoreaux's feet. Damn, he thought, not again. Gohin kept yelling, but as Woolsey's head cleared, he realized the Frenchman wasn't directing his words at him. Gohin had turned his back to them. He was pointing the gun upward at the conning tower.

Woolsey pushed himself to a sitting position, and from there he could see what had distracted Gohin's attention. Sean McKay stood atop the conning tower ladder, the wooden crate held tight against his chest.

Lamoreaux shouted over Gohin's tirade. "He's telling you to come down here, or he will shoot."

"Bugger him," McKay said.

"Sean," Woolsey yelled, "for God's sake, do as he says, man. He shoots that box and we're all dead."

McKay just grinned and raised the box over his head like a prizefighter hoisting the championship cup.

Gohin never stopped yelling, but his voice was drowned out by the explosion from the gun.

CHAPTER FORTY

Aboard the Shadow Chaser

March 27, 2008

"You two have lost me here," Theo said. "What number? What are you talking about?"

"She's discovered something." Cole grinned, then he picked up the coin and held it out to his first mate. "Did you ever notice something written on the tablet under the word *Constitution*?"

Theo assumed a mock shocked expression. "Me? You're going to let me touch it?" he said, taking the coin. He paused and turned to Riley. "He's been a bit territorial about the thing. Never takes it off."

The two of them continued talking, but Riley had ceased hearing them. Her mind felt like a cotton candy machine spinning wispy fragments. Ponytail man was following her. Cole said Ponytail's name was Brewster and he was after the coin. The coin that was a key. A key to the location of some old submarine. A submarine full of gold. And now, Diggory Priest lands in the middle of it all. Why? What's the CIA's stake in this? Did his handlers even know about it? She was certain Dig didn't always play by the book, and it took a great deal of money to support him in the lifestyle to which he had grown so very accustomed. Had Diggory turned pirate? Traitor? And where did Michael fit in?

"I see something." Theo's words brought her out of her reverie. He held the coin up close to the right lens of his glasses, squeezing his left eye shut. "Can't really make it out, though. It looks like a scratch or a flaw on the coin. Are you telling me that's a number?"

"So you can understand why I never saw it before," Cole said. "Here, try this." He handed Theo the magnifier, then grabbed the flashlight and shone it on the coin.

"Good Lord. You're right. Even with the magnifier, it's difficult to make them out. How did your pop make such tiny numbers?"

"I have no idea," Cole said.

Riley interrupted them. "Micro etching with electron beams or lasers—we've been doing it for quite a while, but it's not technology that just anybody can put their hands on. Your father put some effort into keeping that number hidden. Does it mean anything special to you?"

Cole shook his head.

"I'm a little surprised," she said.

"What do you mean?"

"Well, you've just been going on for the last hour or so about secret societies, so I figured you would have heard of Skull and Bones."

"Of course I've heard of them."

"You've never seen their insignia, then?"

"Well, sure. It's a skull and crossbones. Like the pirate flag."

"True. But that's not all. Under the skull and bones, in small print, is the numerological symbol of their society—that number," she said, pointing to the coin. "Three-two-two."

"Oh great," Theo said, throwing his hands into the air. "Now she's into secret societies and numerology. You two were made for each other."

Riley stepped back, her hands up, palms open. "Wait a minute. I didn't say I was into this stuff. I consider myself a rational person."

Cole rolled his eyes. Then he took a deep breath and said, "But you seem to know quite a lot about this society."

Riley shrugged. "I told you about what happened to my brother."

"You said he died in a fraternity hazing and he had written this number on his hand."

"Was the fraternity Skull and Bones?" Theo asked.

"No, Bones isn't a fraternity. They're a senior society. Future Bonesmen are tapped in the spring of their junior year at Yale. Their on-campus membership only lasts through their senior year. Of course, they stay members the rest of their lives."

"I'm still not getting the connection here," Cole said.

"OK. Once I realized the significance of those numbers on my brother's hand, I read everything I could get about them. The number three-two-two comes from the year Skull and Bones was founded, 1832. It was started by a Yale student, William Russell, who went to Germany for a year and joined this dark, Goth-like secret society over there. When he came home, he started the second chapter in the US, named it Skull and Bones, and made their symbol three-two-two. The first two digits, three-two, are for the year they were founded, while the last number two signifies that it was the *second* chapter."

Cole nodded. "OK. I get it."

Then his eyes met hers, and she felt that jolt again.

"Did you ever figure out what your brother was trying to tell you?" he asked.

She dropped her eyes and shook her head. "No."

"I'm sorry."

"Yeah." She paused as she took the coin from Theo, then stared down at it in her hand. "But maybe we'll have better luck with this coin," she said.

"We?" Cole said.

When she glanced at his face, his smile was so big his dimples looked like craters.

She cleared her throat. "Wipe that grin off your face," she said. "We have work to do."

* * *

Riley glanced at her dive watch, then flopped back against the dinette seat. The table in front of them was covered with a chart of the island of Guadeloupe and several pieces of scribbled-on paper. Pencil scratchings covered the chart, and the table was dusted with the pink fibers of a much-used eraser.

"We can't give up," Cole said.

Riley massaged her shoulder and rotated her head in a circle to stretch the muscles in her neck. "We've been at this for almost two hours, and we've got nothing."

"I wouldn't say that. We've figured out lots of ways that you *can't* use three-two-two on this island."

She laughed, and in spite of the look of exhaustion on his face, he started to laugh, too. Soon, he clutched at his side, and she felt her eyes fill with tears as she continued to giggle and gasp for air.

Theo stood up from the stool he'd been perched on. "You two need coffee. I'll put the kettle on." He crossed to the opposite side of the galley and lit the stove.

Riley wiped her eyes. "It's ridiculous to drink coffee at two in the morning."

"Not really," Theo said. "Not with the Brewsters creeping around this island. Captain, we need to be gone by sunrise. Remember?"

Cole nodded, his laughter subsiding at last.

"Where will you go?" Riley asked.

"Well, let's see." Cole reached into the lockbox at the edge of the table and pulled out a small coin. "You want to call it?"

"How am I supposed to know where you want to go?"

"Just call it, Magee."

She sighed and shook her head. "OK," she said. "Heads."

Cole flipped the coin high into the air and caught it in his right hand. He slapped it onto the table.

"Heads it is," he announced when he lifted his hand.

Riley stared at the coin, her mouth open. He had taken the coin out of his lockbox. "You said your father sent that coin to you?"

"Yeah," he said. "They aren't all that rare, but I hang on to it anyway. It's a 1915 Indian Head nickel. Cool, huh?" He leaned over the table and pulled the box toward him. "There's another one in here he sent me when I was a kid." He dug around in the box. "This one's a Kennedy half dollar." He held it up. "This was the first coin he ever sent me."

"And so this one was the second." She stared at the image of the Indian with a braid flowing down his shoulder and the feathers in his hair. She whispered, *"Not a nickel to my name."*

"OK, but," he said, "I don't see what that gives us."

She looked at Theo, who was leaning against the counter waiting for the kettle to whistle. "Forget the coffee, Theo," she said. "Can you find us a chart of Dominica?"

Theo stepped over and looked down at the coin on the table, then he nodded and chuckled to himself. As he walked into the wheelhouse, he said over his shoulder, "You know, Cole, I like her."

Cole looked at Riley. "I don't get it. What is it?"

She picked up the nickel. "This," she said, waving it at him and bouncing on her seat. "This is what three-two-two takes you to." She grabbed the pencil and one of the pieces of scratch paper on the table. Turning the paper over, she began to write. "Look," she said, and she wrote out the figures 3+2=5. "Three plus two equals five. Five cents is a nickel. That takes care of the first two digits." Then she wrote the number 2 followed by a small *nd*. "And the last digit two signifies second. Like Skull and Bones was the second chapter? This is the second coin your father sent you. This one," she said, holding the French Angel coin on the flat palm of her left hand, "is the key that takes us to this one." She opened her fist to display the Indian Head nickel. "Remember your father's last journal entry? He wrote he didn't have a nickel to his name. That's because he had sent it to you."

"So what? What does that old nickel tell us?"

Theo appeared then with a large chart, and after sweeping the rest of their debris to the far end of the table, he spread the new chart out on top of the marked-up one. It was a chart of the large, nearly oval-shaped island of Dominica.

"Captain," Theo said, "it's an *Indian* Head nickel."

"Yeah, so what?"

"Dominica, mon, it's my home. And the number-one most photographed spot on the island, the place where Johnny Depp came and played Captain Jack Sparrow in *Pirates of the Caribbean II*, the place on every tourist's itinerary, is none other than…" He stabbed his finger on the chart. "The Indian River."

CHAPTER FORTY-ONE

From Bonefish to Shadow Chaser

March 27, 2008

Cole paced the foredeck of Riley's sailboat while she packed her rain gear, set a second anchor, and locked up all the hatches and ports. She wasn't telling him everything. She knew more about this connection to Skull and Bones, and she recognized something in that photo on Theo's camera. He watched her rigging a second anchor light in her cockpit. She was so damned methodical, and he feared that pushing her to talk to him might wind up pushing her away. He'd just have to wait until she was ready.

Riley had only agreed to accompany them to Dominica after Cole had assured her that the twenty-mile crossing would be no more than a three-hour trip in the big trawler and they would be back by nightfall. He stopped pacing and watched her as she started toward him. Even in the dim starlight, he admired the confident, fluid way she moved. Again, he thought of a dancer. He'd promised her that he would see to it that she and her boat were safe—because he needed her. He blinked his eyes and looked away. He needed her to help him find the *Surcouf*.

"You ready?" he asked when she joined him.

She gave a curt nod. "We've still got a couple of hours before dawn."

"I hope to be long gone by then."

When they arrived back alongside *Shadow Chaser*, the aft crane was ready, and Theo had fashioned a lifting harness for Riley's inflatable. They'd decided to take her dinghy with the outboard engine instead of attempting to paddle ashore in Cole's rubber ducky. Riley helped him get the boat on deck while Theo lounged in the wheelhouse doorway and raised the anchor with his tablet computer. Fifteen minutes later, they had cleared the headland and were beginning to feel the slow rise and fall of the open ocean swell.

Cole secured the pilothouse house door behind him and hung his yellow oilskin jacket on a bulkhead peg. Theo sat in the helmsman's chair, his bare feet propped up on the dash, his tablet on his lap. Cole rested his arm on the back of Theo's seat and stood still, checking the glowing red instruments and admiring the dark sea visible though the wheelhouse windows. The big six-cylinder Cummins purred along as she always did under Theo's care.

"Can you take the con for a while?" Cole asked.

"Sure, Cap'n. Why don't you try to get some sleep?"

He glanced back through the bulkhead door into the galley. Riley sat on the dinette bench, her head bowed over the chart, her hair hanging forward shielding half her face. She'd ducked back into the galley as soon as everything on deck was secure. Now, she was poring over the chart, trying to narrow the search area. Cole watched her slide the tip of her forefinger in a quick half circle, tucking the hair behind her ear. He saw a flash of white where her teeth pressed into her lower lip.

Without turning to face his first mate, he said, "I don't think I could fall asleep right now."

On the periphery of his vision, he saw Theo twist around and glance aft.

"Yeah," Theo said. "Sure has improved the scenery around here." He made a couple of loud sniffing noises. "And the smell."

Cole lifted his arm in a panic and pulled the fabric of his T-shirt to his nose.

Theo dropped his head forward and his shoulders bounced with his quiet laughter. He looked up at Cole and shook his head. "Oh, mon," he said. "You got it bad."

With his open hand, Cole thwacked his first mate on the back of the head, but he could still hear the muffled laughter when he left the wheelhouse for the galley.

"How's it going?" he asked when she looked up at him.

"OK," she said. Then, after dropping her gaze back to the chart, she added, "Do you always beat your crew?"

He sighed. She didn't miss much.

"I've been thinking," he said.

"That's a good start."

He thought he could see a hint of a smile on her face when he sat down on the bench across from her. Leaning over the metal box, he withdrew one of the leather journals. "It might help if you read some more of this. You'll get an idea of how the old man thought." He fanned the pages with his thumb. Less than half of the book contained his father's neat writing. "This is the last one. He started it in the fall of 2002. The world was still reeling from September 11. This was before the Iraq invasion, but the no-bid contracts to rebuild were already a done deal." He shook his head. "The old man was really on a roll." Cole sat next to her. He spread the book out on the table and flipped open the pages. "Start here," he said.

Dear Son,

Your country is now asking itself how such a thing could have happened without the intelligence services having foreseen it. The finger-pointing has started. Many are using the phrase "Faulty Intelligence" to lay blame at that fraternity's door. You may wonder why the brethren don't object? Because in peacetime, much attention had been focused on the vast secret budgets of the intelligence infrastructure. But this event now offers them the opportunity for a counterargument. They can give the excuse that their warnings could have come sooner had not their budgets been slashed and their needs for new technology and manpower been ignored. Also, the warnings they did give were ignored by politicians who chose not to listen. Or so they claim.

In fact, what intelligence was handed over to the decision makers of both your country and mine was filtered through THEIR hands. Their numbers are small and they dwell in the shadows, but their influence is vast. Our leaders can only make decisions based on what they know— and the members of this inner circle decide what flows through that pipeline. One would think that the Americans would begin to wonder why it is that every time some significant military event takes place, the American intelligence community is wrong-footed. Pearl Harbor, the Gulf of Tonkin, 9/11. Faulty intelligence, indeed. But the fault is not a cock-up nor a lapse of any kind. It is intentional and secretive. It is THEIR work. Secrecy is power. It puts this power in the hands not of democracy, but of this moneyed aristocracy that profits from their advance knowledge of when and where your country will go to war.

I know you will find this difficult to believe. How could THEY have known and allowed thousands to die just to persuade your country to go to war? Take this from an old hand who has seen it all. My experience shows that with intelligence matters, the more bizarre the claim, the more likely it is to be true.

Cole placed his finger on the last sentence on the page. "Every time I read that last line, I think about the way my father died. I think about Alexander Litvinenko, the Russian spy who died of polonium poisoning in London, or the story of the Bulgarian killed by the umbrella that shot poison pellets. I know it sounds mad to say that this old British gentleman was assassinated by the members of some secret cabal simply because he had discovered the whereabouts of a sixty-year-old submarine, but there it is: *the more bizarre the claim, the more likely it is to be true.*"

"Cole, listen," she said. "I'm willing to spend this day with you guys looking for whatever this is that your father wants you to find. I'll be honest; the connection to Skull and Bones has piqued my interest. But I don't think the *them* you're talking about is Bones. I just can't swallow this whole conspiracy theory that you and your father have inhaled without chewing. I'm a slow eater, Cole. Anyway, why don't you go get some rest and leave me to read this." She flipped to the first page of the journal and started to read. After a few seconds, when he had not moved, she turned to him. "Go on. If I find something, I'll call you."

Cole closed the door to his cabin, lay down on his bunk fully clothed, and laced his fingers behind his head. He stared up at the overhead. Sleep, he thought. Yeah, right.

CHAPTER FORTY-TWO

Portsmouth, Dominica

March 27, 2008

Riley awoke to the loud rattle of the anchor chain feeding out through the steel hawse pipe. She'd fallen asleep facedown on the table, and when she sat up, she had to peel the damp paper chart off her cheek. James Thatcher's journal lay open atop the chart, her right wrist still resting in the center of the pages. She checked her watch—it was after eight o'clock. Stretching her arms high over her head, she opened her mouth in a big, ear-popping yawn. Sunlight streamed in through the exterior door that led out to the side deck, and she heard unintelligible voices outside. It must be the guys up on the foredeck, she thought.

She slid off the bench, stepped through the forward door, and admired the view through the eight windows that graced the rounded front of the *Shadow Chaser*'s classic pilothouse. She saw the two of them standing out in the brilliant glare on the fore-deck—Cole in khaki shorts, white T-shirt, hiking boots, and a faded blue baseball cap, and Theo in long plaid shorts bunched at his waist with a length of rope and sporting dark mirrored sunglasses. They were an odd pair, she thought. Theo was tall enough to be a professional basketball player, but the bit of leg showing between his shorts and his flip-flops looked bird thin. Cole's legs, on the other hand, were thicker, his calves knotted with muscle.

She chuckled to herself and wondered what her friend Hazel would say if she could see her here gawking at those shoulders and the waistband where Cole's T-shirt was tucked into his shorts. She would undoubtedly ask why Riley had sent him packing last night, and then add that if she was going to turn *that* down, she really should go buy a cat.

"It's not that simple," she said aloud, and she wasn't at all sure if she was speaking to Hazel, her brother, or herself. She remembered the light in Cole's eyes a few hours ago as he spoke about his father's journals and this crazy theory that somebody, somewhere had known what al-Qaeda was up to and had suppressed the information. And somehow, that was tied to some World War II wreck? One minute, this whole thing seemed possible, even logical—and the next minute, she felt as if she had fallen down the rabbit hole.

Beyond the two men rose a jungle-covered headland with the ruins of another stone fort. Beneath that, the bay swept round to the buildings of the town nestled at the base of the green hills.

So they'd arrived in Prince Rupert Bay, and that was the town of Portsmouth on shore. Her memories of this place harkened back to a much simpler time in her life. Back when her father was posted in Barbados, her dad had taken them on a business trip. They'd flown in a seaplane to Antigua so he could visit the consular offices there. He'd done his business in the morning in St. John's, and by afternoon, they were aboard a borrowed sloop headed down island.

That had been a glorious week. In those days, she and her brother still reveled at the chance to spend time alone with their father. Once they managed to separate him from his briefcase, they had gone for morning swims in the crystalline water and laughed while cooking fresh-caught kingfish and fried plantains. They'd climbed to spectacular waterfalls and stood still in the cool mountain air waiting with binoculars for a glimpse of the native wild parrots. Here off Portsmouth, their little sailboat had been accosted by dozens of boat boys offering to row them up the Indian River. Michael had selected the littlest boy, Galen—she remembered the odd name—and it had taken him more than an hour to row them up the dark jungle tunnel that was the river.

Where twenty years ago theirs had been the only sailboat in the anchorage, the big trawler was now anchored among dozens of yachts, and the only boat boys were older men in wooden fishing boats that sported big Yamaha or Honda outboards on their transoms. Even Dominica changed.

Out of habit, Riley looked around the wheelhouse for the GPS to check their position. Above the helm, a big computer screen displayed a color chart of the anchorage. In bold black letters along the bottom of the screen, she read their position in latitude and longitude: **15°34'45.07N: 61°27'39.12W**.

She was still staring at the numbers a couple of minutes later when Cole walked in.

"Good morning, Miss Maggie Magee," he said.

"Hey," she said without taking her eyes off the instruments.

"How are you feeling this morning?"

She heard his question, but her mind was elsewhere. She wondered if it was possible. Though reading those pages in Thatcher's journal had given her a sense of one facet of the man, she still wasn't sure about these puzzles. He had been meticulous about building his arguments about the cabal. He had cited names, dates, places. Were these numbers just a coincidence, or was this going to tell them where to look on the Indian River?

"It's amazing the way you do that," Cole said.

When she turned to look at him, his face was no more than six inches from hers. She took a step back, her heart hammering, and she felt her face flush with heat. The tufts of brown hair that poked out from under his baseball cap were damp, and she could smell the fresh scent of his shampoo. "What? What are you talking about?"

"The way you focus like that. You shut out everybody and everything."

"But…" she pointed at the GPS screen, then cleared her throat. "Look at our latitude."

"OK. I see it. That's supposed to mean something?"

"You didn't spend all night looking for patterns or repetitions in numbers or text like I did. The first number is fifteen. Make you think of any of the coins?"

"You're kidding, right? It is a 1915 nickel, but he sent that to me years ago."

"But I'm sure he remembered. The man who wrote the journal pages I read last night didn't forget any details. What about the next number—the minutes?"

"'Thirty-four? I don't see what that has to do…" he stopped, and Riley saw the creases around his eyes deepen. He relaxed the squint and smiled. "OK. It's three-two-two again, isn't it? This time we add the digits differently. Keep the three, then two plus two equals four."

"Good. You're starting to get the hang of this."

"I was a little rusty. It's been a few years since the old man sent me puzzles like this. But I think you're definitely on to something here."

"Remember in the old days of sailing ships, how sailors were not able to calculate their longitude? They used to just sail a latitude heading straight east or west until they hit land. Maybe this time, we sail the latitude until we hit the river."

"We need the big-scale chart of the bay," Cole said. At the rear of the wheelhouse was a small chart table. He pulled out a wide drawer beneath the table and began thumbing through a thick stack of charts. When he found what he wanted, he pulled it out, grabbed some navigation tools, and headed into the galley.

Rather than showing the whole island, this chart showed only the big crescent-shaped bay and several miles of coastline on either side. Cole placed his fingers at the side of the chart about two inches apart, like the legs of a little man. "This," he said, "is one minute of latitude, which is equivalent to one nautical mile." He dragged his fingers from west to east across the chart, and the spread included the whole of the Indian River and half the town of Portsmouth. "It's not precise enough."

"Right. We got the first number from the nickel, and that gives us the degrees. The French Angel gives us the second number, which is the minutes. But latitude is measured in degrees—each of which is divided into sixty minutes, and then the minutes are divided into sixty seconds. If we can figure out what number to use for the seconds, we'll have it down to within one-sixtieth of a mile."

"Do you think we use the third coin?" Cole asked.

Riley lifted the big silver half dollar out of the box. "The year is 1964," she said. "That doesn't work for minutes. Sixty-four is too high a number."

"Should we add six plus four?"

"That might work," she said. Riley picked up the stainless steel dividers and spread the two legs of the instrument like the legs of a geometric compass. She then positioned the instrument on the latitude markings at the edge of the chart. She measured and found the mark for **15°34'10.00N.** Cole set the parallel ruler on the mark, and they saw that it ran south of the river and did not intersect.

"That won't work either," Cole said.

"What else is in that box?"

Cole dragged the box closer to him. "My father used to send me letters with some kind of surprise inside. It was sort of like getting the prizes in the cereal boxes. It wasn't valuable stuff. Just cool. Like this." He lifted out a St. Christopher's medal. "Maybe this is telling us to go to the island, St. Kitts? The real name of that island is St. Christopher."

"It's possible."

"The problem with that theory, though, is that the old man never went to St. Kitts. And he sent me that medal when I was twelve—before he even started his research about the *Surcouf*. See the phrase on the medal—*Saint Christopher Protect Us*? That was the key to a simple alphabet cipher. I wrote the letters of the alphabet above those letters and then deciphered the text to read his letter. He started with simple ones like that, and as the years went by, they grew more challenging."

"What about the coins? How did he use them?"

"Well, the first one was the Kennedy fifty-cent piece. For that one, I had to use a bifid cipher. You know, that's where you create a five-by-five matrix of numbers. In that case I used the date, 1964, and for the fifth number, I had to play around with the fact that it was a fifty-cent piece. I eventually tried 19645, and that worked. You write those five numbers down and across, and it produces twenty-five squares. Then you fill in the alphabet, and each letter winds up with a pair of coordinates."

"OK. And what about the Indian Head nickel?"

"That one? Let's see. That one was more complex, and he used it twice. The first time, it was a Gronsfeld cipher using the word *Indian* and a key series of numbers."

"Wait a minute," Riley said. "You say he used the Indian coin twice?"

Cole opened his mouth to answer her, but he froze and then reached for the dividers.

Riley beat him to it. She scooped up the instrument and placed one point on the latitude line that crossed the chart, then she squeezed the legs until the other leg was right on the mark for **15°34'15.00N**. She slid the instrument across the chart and placed one leg on the black latitude line that ran beneath the Indian River. With that leg anchored, she swung the other in an arc as though drawing a circle. When her arc touched the line on the chart that indicated the river, she stabbed the end of the dividers into the chart. "There," she said. "I don't know what it is we're looking for, but I'm willing to bet we'll find it right there."

At that moment, she heard Theo's feet padding down the side deck. He poked his head in the door. "Dinghy's in the water, Captain. All's ashore that's goin' ashore. My cousin Zeke's waiting with his van. A quick trip through customs and immigration, and we're off. "

"Oh shit," Riley said. She'd known this moment was coming, and she'd been dreading it.

"Did I say something wrong?" Theo asked.

Riley wiggled her hand back and forth in the air. "It's just that I've got a teensy, little problem with my passport."

"Like what?" Theo asked.

Cole sighed. "Like she doesn't have one."

CHAPTER FORTY-THREE

Aboard the Fish n' Chicks

March 27, 2008

Diggory awoke to the sound of a man's voice shouting in French. In response to the Frenchman, he heard the whiny shrieking of the brother he had come to think of as the Freak.

He rose and pulled on the khaki pants that he had folded with care and hung up in the cabin's tiny closet. He grabbed his wallet and slipped it into his back pocket. Shirtless and in bare feet, he climbed the steps, crossed through the main salon, and opened the sliding door to the aft deck. Some four feet above the Freak on the stone quay stood a heavyset man wearing a white uniform with brass buttons and epaulets. His face flushed red as he shouted that because they were docked there, he had to put his ferryboat on the end of the quay. There would be other ferryboats arriving soon, he screamed while shaking his fist at the blotchy-skinned barbarian, and they needed to move their boat now.

Diggory stepped out into the bright morning light and slid the door closed behind him. He introduced himself in his flawless French, then apologized to the ferry captain for creating such a problem. He assured him that as soon as they had taken on fuel, they would be moving the boat. From his wallet, he removed a crisp new hundred-euro note and handed it to the man.

"I understand that it is only fair that you should be compensated for your inconvenience," he said in French.

The captain snatched the note from Diggory's hand and slid it into his pocket while mumbling about how he guessed he could wait a few more minutes before moving his boat.

Diggory turned to the Freak. "Where is your brother?"

"He took off at first light to go scout out the chick's boat. Make sure she's still there. He reckoned you'd want to know if the doc spent the night there."

Dig sent the man off to find the dockmaster so they could start fueling. Soon, a young, efficient Frenchman came down the pier dragging the fuel hose. He jumped aboard and began the process himself when it became apparent the Freak had no clue what to do. The half-breed was worse than useless, Diggory thought. He was an abomination, a crime against nature. When would the human race wise up and realize that not every child should be saved? This piece of excrement was a waste of resources. Diggory removed his wallet again and took out another bill. Handing it to the Freak, he sent him to a village café for coffee and croissants. Perhaps he could be made to have some use.

If the one called Spyder did not return in the next few minutes, Dig realized he would be forced to try to drive the boat out into the bay and anchor it himself. He climbed up the ladder to the bridge and sat in the helmsman's seat as he had the night before. Before him was an array of buttons and switches, levers and screens. He understood none of it.

The French boy manning the hoses called up to Dig, asking if he should fuel the port tank also. Dig looked around again for Spyder. Though there were a few locals riding bicycles down the village main street, there was no sign of either brother.

"Yes," he called down. "Top it off." If it turned out the tank was empty and the boy said something about his ignorance, Dig would just take it out of his tip.

He leaned back in the comfortable helmsman's seat, rubbed his fingers across his day's growth of beard, and contemplated the sailboats anchored out in the bay. What the devil was Riley doing mucking about on a sailboat in the Caribbean? For a moment, a picture of her nude body lying on his bed flashed through his mind. He thought about what she had said when they met in Pointe-à-Pitre. He'd often wondered what she remembered about Lima. She'd answered that question last night. What had she said? *Those flames haven't stopped burning.* He knew her well enough to realize she would stop at nothing to get at the truth. She had become a dangerous liability. Now that he had taken care of Caliban, he had to move, he thought. With the girl right here within his grasp, the next step was his for the taking.

"*Monsieur,*" the boy called from the lower deck. "The port tank, it is full. I will go make your receipt."

Dig stood and walked to the ladder. Just before he turned around to descend, he saw the two brothers up at the head of the pier. They appeared to be arguing. The Freak was cringing as Spyder flailed his arms, pointed at the powerboat, and shouted words that Dig could not understand at this distance. Then Spyder turned to look in the direction he was pointing, and he saw Diggory staring at him.

When the brothers returned, Spyder's manner was so obsequious, it turned Dig's stomach. Spyder said he had taken a long, hot hike over the hill, but he was pleased to report that her boat remained anchored in the other bay. "No sign of the doc, though," he reported. Then he asked if there was anything else he could do.

Dig ignored him and, after settling the bill, gave orders to get off the dock and anchor out in the bay. Meanwhile, he went below to shower and enjoy his morning coffee away from the sight of that human rubbish. When he emerged from his stateroom forty-five minutes later, he had a plan.

Dig could feel the Freak's eyes on him as he crossed the salon. The man didn't even bother to remove the bulky headphones that made him appear like a giant insect from one of those old Japanese horror films Dig's mother used to watch when he was a child.

It was Spyder, though, who spoke first.

"Too bad that machine of yours don't work."

"And what machine would that be?"

"You know, that satellite tracker thing over there." He flung his arm in the direction of Dig's GPS tracking unit.

"When we got up this morning," the Freak said. He had pulled one of the earphones off his ear, and it now dangled around his neck. "The fix was all wrong. That's why Spyder went to check on her boat. Just to make sure."

In spite of the air-conditioning and his recent shower, Dig felt a flush of heat. He strode across the cabin and tilted up the screen of the small black unit. With one finger, he tapped the key to wake the machine, and he realized at once that his plans would have to change.

"How long has this machine been *malfunctioning*?"

"I dunno," Spyder said. "It was like that when I first got up this morning."

"And it didn't occur to you to tell me about this?"

"I thought it'd be better to go check on her boat right away. I done that."

"You're a moron." He turned to the Freak. "You both are."

Spyder swung around from the galley counter where he had been slathering jam on a croissant. "Mister," he said, his voice tight. He clutched the wood-handled knife in his right fist, his knuckles white from the strain. "That ain't right. There's no need to call us stupid."

"When you went to check on her boat this morning, did you happen to notice if her dinghy was there?"

"No, I ain't seen it. I wasn't particularly lookin' for it neither."

"And if her dinghy's not there, the oars aren't there either."

"Shit," the Freak said. "Last night when I walked over there, I seen another anchor light way out in the bay. What's this about oars?"

"Your brother helped me place the GPS transmitter inside her oars. That's why I had you return them to her boat. Which means there is nothing wrong with this GPS tracker, you moron. The other boat was likely Dr. Thatcher's boat. Because of your stupidity, they are now," he said, pointing to the screen, "somewhere down off the island of Dominica. If you two don't get this boat moving in the next five minutes, I'll be forced to shoot one of you, and I'd be hard pressed to choose which one."

Spyder glanced at his brother, and Dig saw the question pass between them. The Freak moved his head in a sideways twitch, but the tendons in the bigger man's forearms relaxed. Spyder set down the knife, picked up the croissant, and stuffed the entire thing into his mouth. He walked past Dig without acknowledging him and stepped out onto the deck.

Interesting, Dig thought. He now knew which of the brothers was really in charge.

CHAPTER FORTY-FOUR

Portsmouth, Dominica

March 27, 2008

Theo pointed to the rungs of a rusty ladder clinging to the side of a crumbling stone pier, and he shouted to be heard over the noise of the outboard engine. "The dinghy will be safe over there."

"Yeah," Cole said. "But will we?"

"Long as your tetanus shot is up to date," Theo said as he lowered a small stern anchor to keep the inflatable dinghy from rubbing against the sharp, rusty steel.

The Portsmouth customs and immigration offices were located in a waterfront warehouse just beyond the stone pier. The facility serviced the small cargo freighters that transported Dominica's banana crop and the few remaining sailing cargo boats that traded between the islands. Open on one side and littered with the old lumber from abandoned cargo pallets, the place reeked with the sickly sweet smell of rotted fruit. Riley tried hard not to wrinkle her nose in disgust as they stepped into the shade.

Sitting on a couple of wooden cable spools that looked like the kind found in her mother's sewing box—but on steroids—two bulky men in green, military-issue uniforms stared at the game of dominoes on the table between them. One man wore a sidearm at his waist, while the other had some sort of semiautomatic rifle resting in the shadows across his knees.

"Do you know these guys?" Cole asked Theo under his breath.

The men had not yet noticed the three newcomers. Theo lifted his arm to stop his companions. "Afraid not. Wait here a bit."

When he was within about thirty feet of the two officials, Theo spoke in his proper, clipped baritone. "Good morning, gentlemen."

The two men jumped to their feet. Riley hadn't been aware just how tall the man wearing the pistol was until he stood up. She guessed his height at somewhere close to six foot eight, and with the bulk on his frame, he would have felt at home in any NFL locker room. The "smaller" of the two, at a mere six feet tall, now held his rifle at an angle aimed at Theo's feet.

"I am Theophilus Spencer," he said. Then, with a little half turn, he pointed at Cole and Riley and said, "And this is Captain Thatcher and his girlfriend. We came in on that trawler out there from Guadeloupe."

Riley turned to Cole and raised her eyebrows at the term "girlfriend."

Cole lifted his shoulders and cocked his head to one side as if to say, "Whatever works."

The giant walked up to Theo and motioned for him to remove his backpack. Theo extracted his passport and handed it over to the man who examined it for several minutes as they conversed in the local patois.

"Which do you think is worse," Riley whispered, "the jails in Guadeloupe or in Dominica?"

"Definitely Dominica," Cole said.

"Thanks a lot," she said.

The big man extracted a cell phone from his pocket and dialed a number. He stepped away and turned his back to Theo as he spoke into the phone. When he finished his conversation, he pointed to a crude bench nailed together out of old palette wood. "Wait over there," he said. Then he and the other official returned to their game. Soon the warehouse was echoing with the sound of dominoes slapping against the table.

The three of them settled on the bench.

"Theo—" she started, but he cut her off.

He shook his head. "Trust me."

She'd never been good at sitting and doing nothing. Riley saw the mosquitoes hovering around her ankles, and she hoped the repellent Theo had offered her was working. It was beastly hot with no breeze whatsoever, and she was beginning to wonder what had made her decide to join this motley expedition.

She slapped at a mosquito on her calf. "I thought we were supposed to be looking for a submarine."

"We are," Cole said.

"Well, if we're right about this, and your dad did put something up the Indian River, obviously it's not going to be a submarine."

"No," Cole said. "It's not." He reached up and pulled the gold piece out of his T-shirt. "The old man was here in these islands, Guadeloupe and Dominica, about three years ago. He found something. Maybe it wasn't the sub. Maybe it's something that will lead us to the sub."

"So I'm risking life in a Dominican jail for a treasure map?"

Theo started laughing. "You think—" he began, but he didn't have a chance to finish because at that moment the door at the back of the warehouse flew open, and a short, thickset man wearing a loud tropical-print shirt, cotton pants frayed at the cuffs, and flip-flops burst in and bellowed "Theo!" loud enough that Riley reckoned all the boats in the anchorage heard him. The domino players glanced up, then went back to their game.

Theo stood up smiling, shaking his head, and walked over to meet the other man saying, "Uncle Reggie, thank you for coming so quickly."

When they met in the middle of the warehouse, the two men embraced. Theo towered over the portly man. After they exchanged a few quiet words, they strolled over to Cole and Riley.

"I'd like to introduce you to my uncle, the Honorable Reginald Blackmore, Minister of Public Utilities, Energy, Ports, and Public Service in the Government of Dominica. Uncle Reggie, this is Captain Cole Thatcher and our friend, Maggie Riley."

Riley caught the look Cole gave Theo.

Theo shrugged. "Like we say in the islands. No problem, mon."

* * *

Less than ten minutes later, the three of them had "cleared immigration" and packed themselves into a miniature van, which took off careening through the streets of Portsmouth. Theo's cousin, Ezekiel Blackmore, his dreadlocks streaming in the breeze, sang along with the reggae music that blasted from the van's tinny speakers. "Gonna mek yuh feel more steam dan rice wa jus cook."

One minute they'd be flying down the narrow paved road, then Zeke would brake, swerve, and stick his head out the window to converse with pedestrians. Half the time, he nearly clipped them on the roadside swale, but they always just smiled and waved. Riley tried hard not to think about Cole's thigh pressing against hers and not to lean too hard against him as the van swerved. But she was disoriented by the right-hand drive and the fact they were passing other vehicles on the wrong side of the road. She found herself twitching with body English in the backseat as Zeke, swerving around people, chickens, and goats, kept up a nonstop, one-sided conversation.

"Your mama, she gonna kill you, Teo, you don't go see her after you been gone almost two years. I know you say you in big hurry take your American friends up the Indian River, but, mon...yoo-hoo, hello, Mrs. Robinson. How's de leg? Auntie gonna skin you, Teo. Hey, Mr. Joseph. Look who here in my van. Yeah, mon. It's Teo. De prodigal son."

At last, they pulled over into a dirt lot before crossing a bridge. Several dusty taxis were already parked there. The drivers squatted in the shade of a big banyan tree on the riverbank above a rickety-looking wood dock.

Zeke shut off the van, and they climbed out. "My boat dat one over dere," Zeke said, pointing to a fifteen-foot dory with a yellow hull and bright red-and-blue interior seats. "She call de *Providence.*"

"She turned out nice, Zeke," Theo said. Then to Riley, he added, "He had just started building her when I left the island."

The boat had four athwartships seats and enough room to carry a group of six to eight tourists. Once they were aboard, Zeke untied the dock lines and pushed off. He perched his backside on the high transom and took his place at the oars facing forward, looking over the heads of his passengers in the fashion of all the Indian River boatmen.

At the beginning of their journey, the river was nearly a hundred feet wide, and they could still see the peaks of the Diablotin Mountains. Theo explained that they were headed for the dock upriver where the boat boys took all the tourists, but they'd have to leave the boat there and go on by foot, as there were rapids just beyond.

At Theo's instructions, Zeke was rowing hard. Soon the river narrowed, and they entered the shadows as the rain forest canopy closed over them. The sunlight filtered through the trees only in rare, narrow shafts that appeared like the beams from tiny spot-lights. But this wasn't any man-made Disney jungle boat ride, Riley thought. Flowering vines and prehistoric ferns made the scene even more fantastic than anything Hollywood could dream up. From both sides, they heard the calls and cries of far more birds than they were able to see. And the only real wildlife in evidence was the moving mass of land crabs that crawled in the crevices between the giant buttressed roots of the trees at the river's edge.

"These trees are amazing," Cole said, looking at the swirling designs formed by the sharp-edged roots. "What kind are they?"

"We call them bloodwood trees." Theo had removed his backpack. From inside, he withdrew a handheld GPS and the folded chart. He handed the chart to Riley, then pointed at the trees. "If you cut them, the sap flows red. The Caribe Indians used to have a camp here on the river before they moved to the other side of the island. They still say it's bad luck to make the trees bleed. That's why these trees are so old. No one dares to cut them."

"There are still living Caribe Indians here?" Cole asked. "I thought they were all dead."

Zeke laughed. "Dat's Dominica, mon. De land of de living dead."

* * *

No other boats were tied to the dock when they arrived at the river terminus, but in the clearing, perched on a stool in the shade of a palm frond lean-to, Riley saw an older man weaving a green palm frond hat similar to the one resting on his head. His back was bent, and his clothes hung loose on his thin frame. When he looked up, all Riley could see under the brim of his hat was a yellow-toothed smile.

"Is that who I think it is?" Theo asked.

Zeke's dreads danced when he nodded. "Yeah, mon. Talk about living dead."

"I can't believe Galen's still alive," Theo said as he stepped out of the boat.

CHAPTER FORTY-FIVE

Indian River, Dominica

March 27, 2008

Cole heard Riley suck in a deep breath. "I was here twenty years ago," she said. "There was a boat boy named Galen who rowed us up the river." She pointed to the lean-to. "Is that his dad?"

Theo and Zeke exchanged looks. "That's him," Theo said. "Same fellow. About ten years ago, he left the island for the States. Found work in a boatyard in Miami. Once he got his residency, a US Marine recruiter talked to him, and the next thing he was in Iraq. Something happened over there. He came home like that," he said, tilting his head in the direction of the clearing, "with a belly full of shrapnel and looking more like he'd aged thirty years than ten."

Cole regarded Riley's face. She squinted her eyes and stared at the distant man.

Zeke said, "I keep Galen company. Be here when you get back."

Cole watched Zeke as he crossed the sunlit clearing. All around them, the jungle now looked dark and impenetrable. "Do you know where we're headed, Theo?"

He held up the GPS. "Follow me."

At first, their track was a narrow trail that wound through the trees at the top of the riverbank. Along this stretch, the river narrowed to a fast-moving stream and was often obstructed by large granite boulders. Boats would never make it up this far.

Cole was pleased to see that Riley, in spite of her much shorter legs, had no trouble keeping up with them along the stream bank. She was taking two strides for every one of Theo's, but she wasn't even breathing hard. It was tough going, and he was glad he'd decided to wear the hiking boots. To make it even worse, the air around them was so heavy with heat and humidity, his shirt was already soaked with perspiration. He knew how much worse he was going to smell in an hour or so.

They heard the rapids before they saw them. It started as a soft chuckling sound as the water dodged around the stones in the shallows. As they hiked closer, the jungle sounds of birdsong and underbrush skitterings were drowned out by the roar of the rushing water. Then the trail came to an abrupt end on a dirt patch high above the rapids. Below them, white water gushed over boulders in the middle of the stream while dark pools and eddies swirled nearer to shore.

Cole had to shout to Theo. "Where to now?"

Theo consulted the map. "The location is a little southeast of us," he said, pointing off to the right of the river. "I used to play up here when I was a kid. It's easier to follow the river than to go overland. The brush is too thick." He reached down, removed his flip-flops, and wiggled his big brown toes in the dirt. "Be careful on the rocks. Algae makes 'em slippery."

* * *

About twenty minutes had passed when they came to the edge of a deep, blue pool into which rushed a magnificent waterfall that dropped from a cliff fifty feet above them. From where they stood atop a boulder, Cole saw rainbows in the mist at the base of the falls.

"What now?" he shouted so they could hear him over the noise of the water.

Theo pointed into the jungle. "There used to be a trail—over there. Come on."

"I've got a better idea," Cole said. He knew his clothes couldn't get any wetter, and he could use any hygiene help he could grab. "*Geronimo!*" he yelled as he leaped and cannonballed into the pool. The water was icy cold and remarkably deep. He stroked his way to the far side of the pool and pulled himself out of the water at the base of the trail. He grinned at Riley and Theo, who had just arrived by hiking the perimeter of the pool. "Shortcut," he said.

* * *

The trail was a series of switchbacks up the side of a jungle-covered cliff. In places, someone had buried round tubes of bamboo in the slick mud to be used as steps. The person who had placed the steps had legs as long Theo's, and while his Dominican friend climbed on ahead, Cole's pace slowed as he followed behind Riley. Given the view from that angle, though, he wasn't about to complain.

"That name you hollered." She paused then to gulp in air. "It has special significance for Skull and Bones, you know."

"What name?"

"*Geronimo.*" Although they could still hear the rush of the falls off to their left, the noise was muffled, and they didn't have to shout anymore. "The real one, the Indian, he plays a part in the whole mythology about Skull and Bones. I did a lot of research about Bones when I found out what Michael had written on his hand. Most folks claim there is more fiction than fact in the Geronimo myth, but according to the story, Prescott Bush, father to one president and grandfather to another, had a bunch of his fellow Bonesmen visit him when he was stationed at Fort Sill in Oklahoma. Their weird idea of a prank was to dig up Geronimo's grave, steal his skull, and take it back to New Haven as some sort of trophy."

"Fun bunch of guys."

"Yeah." Riley stopped on the trail, bent at the waist, and rested her hands on her knees. Then she straightened up and took a deep breath. "They're supposed to have quite a collection of them in the Tomb. Skulls, I mean."

"The Tomb?"

"That's the name of their headquarters on campus. Silly, isn't it? That's why I can't really see this bunch of boisterous, grave-robbing frat boys as the engineers of some New World Order."

Cole knew it would take time to make her understand. There was nothing funny about these guys. "According to my old man, there was another, not-so-silly side to Prescott Bush. He was a director of a bank that was seized during the war because it was owned by Nazis."

"Really? I'd never heard that."

"Good old capitalism. Make money where you can. Morals be damned. In the journals, my father never points fingers. He kept everything either very vague or enciphered. Otherwise, I never would have gotten my hands on the journals. And he wasn't sure. See, according to him, these guys aren't spies for the other side. They're not enemy sympathizers. They believe in the strength of the US. In fact, they build the weapons and equipment that make us strong. But the last thing they want to see is the world at peace because then there is nowhere near the consumption of goods and services like there is during a war."

When they reached the top of the trail, Theo was waiting for them at the edge of the stream. The water flowed deep and fast just before plunging off the cliff. He held up the GPS and shouted. "Hey, it's less than a quarter of a mile ahead now. Come on."

CHAPTER FORTY-SIX

Indian River, Dominica

March 27, 2008

When Cole first saw the tree, he knew it had to be the one. He was starting to think like the old man—and he knew he would have picked that tree. Above the falls, they had found more rapids, and while there were stretches where they were able to hike up on the dirt banks, too often the shrubbery and low-hanging trees forced them onto the slippery, algae-covered rocks at the edge of the stream. Theo had been calling out their lat and long, and then Cole saw the biggest tree trunk he had seen yet.

The old man would have chosen an attention grabber like that. It was his style. The massive roots covered an area at least twelve feet in diameter. He didn't know what kind of tree it was, but the proportions were so fantastic, he half expected to find a small door between the roots with Bilbo Baggins's name on it.

He felt Riley looking at him as he stared at the enormous tree. "Wow. That's an impressive tree," she said.

Theo picked his way through the underbrush and stood next to the giant trunk. "According to the GPS, we are now on the latitude fifteen degrees, thirty-four minutes, and fifteen seconds." He began to hike around the trunk, and he was out of sight when he yelled, "It would be nice if we could find a big red X on the ground right about now. This looks like a rather large area."

"Cole," Riley said, "now that we're here, it seems a bit stupid to ask, but..." She made a little half turn and pointed. "Why here? If your father was hiding instructions on how to find a submarine, why hide it halfway up a mountain in the middle of a jungle?"

"I don't know what to tell you that won't make you think I'm even crazier. But my father saw the world differently than anyone I have ever known. Three years ago when he was here in the islands, he was already paranoid. But then again," he tried to smile at her, "is it paranoia if someone really is out to kill you? He believed that his research had attracted the attention of these people. James Thatcher lived in a place he called the *'tween*. It was a world of shadows. I guess he knew *I'd* figure it out and find my way here, but he was pretty sure *they* wouldn't."

"You make me wonder what the hell I'm doing here when you talk like that."

"Hey, Cole. Over here. Look!" Theo was perched on one of the huge razorback roots, and he had been unloading gear out of his backpack. Now his nose was an inch from the bark, and he was tilting his glasses up to see something.

Cole and Riley pushed their way through the underbrush to join him. The writing was crude. His father must have done it with a small knife. Carved in the bark of the tree was the word *Liberté*.

He held up the coin to show her in case Riley didn't remember. Then he picked up the folding shovel from Theo's pack and struck the ground between the roots. His arms felt the impact when the shovel clanged against hard wood. There were more roots under the surface that he couldn't see. He tried again in another spot. It seemed the whole area—even ten feet away from the trunk—was a part of the massive root system. He was still searching for diggable dirt when Riley called out.

"There's another one over here."

Cole handed Theo the shovel and then made his way through the underbrush to the smaller tree where Riley stood. She pointed. There, carved in the same crude letters, was the word *Égalité.*

"Good find," he said. "That's two, but there are three words on the coin."

Riley swung her head around and surveyed the surrounding trees. "And with three, you could get a precise triangulated position."

"You stay here," Cole said. "I'll go look. Theo," he called. "Stay by that tree."

It only took him a couple of minutes to find the word *Fraternité* carved into the bark of a large gumbo limbo.

"OK, now let's all walk the shortest distance to the center."

Theo still had the shovel, and there was very little underbrush at the point where they met. "Looks like the ground has been cleared here," he said as he thrust the spade into the ground. "Ground's soft, too." He tapped the overturned spade, and a handful of dirt fell to the ground alongside the small hole.

Cole grabbed the shovel. The dirt was soon flying. The muscles in his back were feeling the strain of bending into the deepening hole. He knew his father would have been more than thirty years older than Cole when the old man was here. That is, if he was here. Cole had hit more dry holes than he wanted to think about since coming to these islands.

He had dug down over two feet, and he was beginning to doubt that they had found the correct location, when he heard a clink as his shovel struck metal. He saw something shiny through the dirt.

He dropped to his knees, and then, almost standing on his head, he shoved his hands into the black soil at the bottom of the hole. Riley handed him a pocketknife, and he used the blade to clear away the dirt from the edges of what looked like a rusty, round Danish cookie tin with a shiny bright slash where the shovel had scraped through the dirt and corrosion.

Theo and Riley crowded him, blocking his light, and he blinked as the sweat dripped into his eyes. He thumped the box with the heel of his hand, trying to loosen it from the earth. When it broke free, he lifted the box out of the hole and sat back on his heels. For a moment, he felt light-headed after hanging upside down in the hole. The shafts of sunlight that filtered through the trees danced with Tinkerbell-sized balls of sparkling light.

"So, come on. Open it," Riley said. "What are you waiting for?"

He closed his eyes for a second trying to clear his vision, hoping the dizziness would pass. "Wait a minute," he said, trying not to smile. "Didn't we skip lunch? Maybe we should take a break. Theo, what have you got to eat in that pack of yours?"

"Are you nuts?" Riley asked.

Cole opened his eyes in time to see the look Theo gave her.

Theo said, "Riley, do you have to ask that question?"

Cole smiled at the two of them, wanting to savor the moment but unable to keep his fingers from working to loosen the tight-fitting lid. He slid the blade of the knife under the lid and wiggled it to break loose the bond of rust.

"OK, OK, boys and girls. Let's not squabble." Cole yanked the top off the tin. Inside was what looked like a wad of old newspapers. But it was too heavy for paper. He dropped the tin and began to unwrap the layers of newsprint. Inside, he found another package wrapped in an olive-green oilcloth. He turned it over and unfolded the flaps of the cloth.

"I was really hoping," Riley said, "that it would turn out you were just crazy."

CHAPTER FORTY-SEVEN

The Atlantic south of Bermuda

February 13, 1942

Woolsey saw Sean McKay stagger back a step when the bullet struck him in the shoulder. McKay managed to stay on his feet, and he hung tight to the crate. The growing bloodstain on his sweater appeared black in the starlight.

While Lamoreaux babbled away to the ensign, Woolsey remained on the deck where he had fallen, nursing the bloody mouth Gohin had dealt him. Woolsey hoped the captain was persuading Gohin not to take another shot. If that bomb went off out here, just over their heads, it would kill them all for certain. Woolsey watched as McKay tucked the crate under his wounded arm. He then climbed down the ladder to the gun deck. No one tried to stop him. Gohin was still covering him with the pistol, but his eyes bulged with apprehension now. Lamoreaux must have succeeded at explaining the situation.

"Mister McKay," the captain said. "Put the box down. Ensign Gohin here will shoot you again if you don't comply."

The big man twitched as though to repel a mosquito buzzing about his ear. McKay paused at the bottom of the ladder, his dark hair fluttering in the wind, his eyes focused on something in the distance back in the boat's white wake. The two Frenchmen were quiet for a change, waiting to see what McKay was going to do next.

Gohin broke the silence first by shouting what sounded like orders. The man couldn't seem to comprehend that his French was no good at all with the Englishmen.

McKay shook his head, as though waking himself from a reverie. He walked straight across the deck, a trail of black-looking blood following him, his eyes focused on the distance as though the other men were not even there. He ducked around the 37-mm cannons, staggered to get his balance back, then headed for the rear of the gun deck. The ladder down to the main deck was off to the port side, but McKay didn't head for the opening to descend.

Injured as he was, Woolsey wondered if Sean McKay would be able to throw the bomb far enough away from the sub to prevent damage in the event it should go off.

When McKay stopped at the far starboard aft corner, Gohin began shouting and raised the pistol to aim at the English sailor.

"*Arrête*," he yelled. "*Arrête*."

"McKay, you fool," Woolsey said, more to himself than with any hope that the signalman would hear him.

McKay turned round and faced the opening opposite him. He spread his legs wide for balance and wiped the sweat off his face with his sleeve. His mouth was a thin, straight line, his cheeks creased from the effort of holding on. He swayed, unsteady on his feet.

Gohin shouted more French gibberish, but McKay appeared not to hear him. The French ensign was working himself into a lather over the Englishman who would not recognize him as commander of the submarine.

McKay stood stock-still for several seconds, and Woolsey watched, waiting for the shot.

Then, McKay threw back his head, opened his mouth, and let loose a wounded roar as he launched himself into a dead run. He crossed the twenty feet of deck that separated him from the opening in the railing in seconds. Gohin fired, but the shot went wide as McKay hurled himself into the air in a powerful rugby player's leap that carried him over the side deck and into the sea.

Woolsey scrambled to his feet just in time to be blown back onto the deck again as the bomb exploded in the water off the boat's port side. The submarine rocked as though it had been hit with a depth charge. Seawater and bits of what was left of Sean McKay rained down on the deck around them.

CHAPTER FORTY-EIGHT

Indian River, Dominica

March 27, 2008

"Did you hear that?" Riley asked.

Cole stopped shoveling the dirt back into the hole where he was burying the newspaper and the tin. He cocked his head to one side. "I don't hear anything."

"Forget that." Theo waved his hands at Cole's efforts with the shovel. "It's *too* quiet, mon."

Theo was right, but Riley felt certain that, before the silence descended, she had heard some noise that didn't belong out here. Perhaps it had been a land crab or some small animal that had come to drink at the stream and been startled by the three humans there. Or maybe it was her nerves.

She shrugged, then extended her hand palm up, nodding at the bundle in Theo's hands. When he handed it to her, she turned back the flaps of oilcloth and examined the device more carefully this time, wondering what new games Cole's father would put them through now.

She had no doubt that this was something buried by James Thatcher. It was some sort of fancy desktop paperweight. More numbers. The small object was the size and shape of a hockey puck, and the outer casing looked like green marble. Felt cushioned the bottom, while the top facing was covered by two layers of brass plate; the uppermost plate was more like a ring with holes punched in it that revealed the dates and the days of the week that were engraved on the lower plate. She rotated the upper plate, and it revealed dozens and dozens of numbers. At the center were written the words "40-Year Calendar, 1998–2037." Cole stood, folded the shovel, and stuck it into Theo's pack. He turned to her, brushing his hands on the sides of his shorts. "What do you make of it?"

Theo answered first, his voice still low. "Looks like a cipher disk to me, or that's how your old man meant for us to use it. Plenty of time to examine it when we get out of here." His head swiveled around, his round eyes staring into the woods around them. "I don't like this. Come on. Let's get moving."

Riley lifted her head and listened again. She agreed with Theo. Something wasn't right.

Cole put out his hand to take the device from her, and this time all three of them froze at the loud *crack* of a branch breaking and the anguished word, *"Fuck!"*

Cole shoved the device deep into Theo's rucksack and slung the pack onto his own back as Riley scanned the jungle around them searching for an escape route. She waved her finger back and forth in the air to signal the others to move out, then she started into the bush, leading them, stepping to avoid hard wood and turning her body sideways to ease past the bigger branches of the trees, palmettos, and ferns. The Indian River followed the narrow, rocky ravine until it reached the coastal plateau and the broad forested swamps. Up here, the rain forest canopy was high, but the brush on the ground was still thick, prickly, and almost impenetrable. She didn't want to veer too far from the streambed for fear they would get lost.

They were only about fifty feet away from the stream, and she could hear the noise as she and her companions passed through the woods even with them. She guessed there were two of them. She could hear heavy breathing and grunting as they jumped from boulder to boulder following the streambed up the ravine. And there was the occasional guttural curse, but otherwise, not a word. They weren't tourists who had decided to hike upstream for fun. Nothing about them said fun. These guys were hunting.

Through the trees, she glimpsed a flash of white, perhaps a T-shirt. The men were close. Too close.

She wondered if they should continue in stealth mode like this or say the heck with it and haul ass back down to Zeke's boat at the river landing, hoping they could outrun them. But Zeke had rowed them up the river, and he didn't have an outboard on the back of the *Providence*. Who knew what kind of boat the hunters might have.

The decision was made for her two minutes later when Theo stumbled and crashed into a thicket of bamboo.

"Over there!" a man shouted behind them.

Cole yanked Theo to his feet.

"Follow me," Riley said, and she took off running, oblivious now to the noise, as they angled back toward the riverbed and down toward the falls. She kept her ears tuned to the regular breathing of her companions. She'd lost men once, and she wasn't about to let that happen again.

Ahead, she could hear the roar of the water over the rasp of her ragged breaths. The air grew more humid as they neared the churning stream. They'd have to go back down the trail they had climbed on the way up. The walls of the ravine narrowed to sheer rock, leading them to the switchbacks alongside the waterfall. It had taken the three of them an hour to climb up the cliff, but she didn't see any other way.

Riley broke through the underbrush and leaped onto a rock that protruded above the fast-moving water. She leaped to another, and a third, and paused to check on the men behind her.

Cole jumped first, and with his arms spread out like a tightrope walker, he wobbled, then found his balance. He stepped to the next rock.

Theo stood on the bank of the river and stared at the rapids.

"Go on," she said. "You grew up here. You should be used to this."

He looked up at her and smiled ruefully. "Yeah, but I always hated doing this," he said, and he jumped across to the first rock. He teetered for a moment. "Because when I hurry," he said, one long leg extending outward as he tried to counterbalance his tilting body, "this is what always happens." He crashed sideways into the rushing water.

"Theo!" she called, reaching out to him. "Grab hold!"

His fingers came within inches, but not close enough. "Shit!"

Then behind her, she heard another splash, and she turned in time to see Cole's head surface as two men, one she recognized as Spyder Brewster, busted through the brush and stepped onto the stones fifty feet upstream. Riley stretched her hand out to Cole, and when her fingers closed around his, she braced herself to pull him to safety. She did not expect the quick tug that produced a burst of pain in her shoulder and pulled her off balance, plunging her into the freezing cold water.

When she surfaced, she couldn't see Theo's head anymore. Cole was pulling ahead of her.

"When you go over the falls," Cole called back to her, "be ready to break your fall with your feet in case it isn't deep enough."

Then he was gone, lost in the white water at the head of the falls.

And seconds later, the white foaming water sucked her down before she'd taken a proper breath, and she was free falling. She wanted to follow Cole's advice, but she was disoriented and could not tell if she was falling feet first or not. Then she hit the water and plunged down and down until her feet touched the soft, silty bottom. She pulled for the light above her, but she wasn't making any progress. The downward current at the base of the falls forced her down, and the light remained out of reach. The pressure in her chest was building as her body craved oxygen. Realizing she had to get out from under the falls, she let the water force her deeper, and then she swam parallel to the bottom. After traveling no more than twenty feet, the pressure changed, the surface brightened, and she swam up and finally broke into the air, filling her aching lungs with a loud, rasping gulp of air.

Theo was already on the bank at the edge of the pool, and Cole was hauling the dripping rucksack out behind him. She stroked over to join them.

"That's always been the fastest way down," Theo said.

She glared at Cole. "Thanks for the warning."

He looked up at the top of the falls. "Think they'll try it?"

"I suggest we don't wait around to find out."

* * *

Zeke and Galen were sitting cross-legged on the dock next to the boats when the three of them ran, still dripping, into the clearing. Zeke shook his dreads and called out, "Theo, how come you not tell these people nobody care if they skinny dip?"

Cole's boots thudded down the dock. He stopped in front of the two men and bent forward, hands on knees, gasping for breath, and struggled to say, "Did you see two guys come through here a while ago?"

"Yeah, mon. Red Man brought dem up in de *Sally B*." He indicated another of the boats tied to the dock. "Dey axe about you."

Riley cut in, "Zeke, we've to go. Now." She leaped into the boat. Cole followed her.

Zeke looked at Theo, who nodded. "We go, den," he said, and he stepped into the *Providence*.

Riley glanced up and saw Galen's face under the brim of his palm hat. His left cheek and neck were marred with lumps and craters. Patches of skin stretched smooth and red in a way she had come to know well during her stay in the burn unit at Bethesda.

Theo untied the dock lines and pushed them off.

"Galen," she said as their boat drifted away from the dock. He didn't seem to hear her. She looked back the way they had come, and she could hear the others crashing through the bush beyond the clearing. She turned back to Galen. "Marine!" she shouted in her best drill sergeant voice. "We need a distraction. Something to hold them up here long enough for us to get back to our boat. Can you handle it?"

Galen jumped to his feet. He straightened his back and snapped her a salute. "Yes, ma'am. *Semper Fi.*"

* * *

They passed two boatloads of German tourists who glared as Zeke splashed them with his oars, but the boat boys pulling the tourists upriver merely nodded at Zeke. Cole opened the bag and showed her that he had not lost the paperweight. He handed the yellow GPS to Theo. The younger man groaned when he held the electronic device up and water dribbled out of the plastic case.

There were only two taxis parked under the banyan tree at the Indian River Boat Tours dock—Zeke's and one other. The second one had the engine running, and Riley could see the driver sitting in the air-conditioned interior. The man glanced up at Zeke's arrival but went right back reading his newspaper. Riley was first out of the boat. The sun was brutal. She stepped into the shade to wait for

Zeke to finish securing his boat, then pulled her cell phone out of her pocket. She didn't have to open it to know what condition it was in. She was peeling wet bills out of her pockets to pay Zeke when she felt a hand on her right elbow, and a familiar voice spoke her name.

"Riley."

She knew who it was even before she turned around. She tried to yank her arm out of his grip. "Let go of me." It was crazy, but she was certain her arm burned where he touched her.

His hand opened, releasing her, and she backed away rubbing her hot skin. He stood there in his creased khaki Dockers, white Polo shirt, and yellow-and-navy Henri Lloyd jacket, looking as if he had stepped right out of the pages of *Yachting Magazine*. Diggory the chameleon. He was no yachtsman. His eyes traveled up and down the soggy length of her, and a slight smile flashed across his features.

She slid between Cole and Theo, who had come over to join her. She squelched the desire to reach up and attempt to tame her unruly hair. She thought her pulse must be throbbing cartoon-style in her neck.

"You're coming with me," Dig said, all traces of the smile gone.

She wanted to smash her fist into that smug cleft chin of his, but she wanted even more to run.

"How did you find me?"

"That's irrelevant. We have to go."

"I'm not going anywhere with you, Diggory."

"Yes, you are." He sighed and turned to face downriver toward the sea. His eyes narrowed. He wasn't looking at her when he said, "It's about your father, Riley. They sent me to get you."

"What? Who sent you?"

He turned and looked at her with a face that asked her why she was even asking. "You know—State."

"What are you talking about?" Her mind whirled with thoughts of her passport, her father's dementia, the possibility of another terrorist attack somewhere in the world outside these small islands.

"He's had a stroke, Riley."

His words hit her like a physical blow, and she took a short step back. "What? When?"

His blue eyes seemed to sear into her, burning even more than her skin. "He's asking for you. The doctors say it doesn't look good."

"But—" She wanted to say something intelligent that would make him be quiet, but she couldn't find the words. She bit the insides of her cheeks when she felt her throat tighten. She'd be damned if she'd let any of them see her cry. Her father? But they said he'd live another ten years.

"Riley." Cole put his arm around her shoulders as though he expected her to swoon. He steered her away from Dig. "If what he says is true, then I'm very sorry about your father. But you don't know what's true for the moment." He glanced back over his shoulder, then turned back to face her. "Who is this guy?"

"It's a long story, Cole."

"It's the guy from the photo, isn't it? The one on the boat with the Brewsters."

She nodded. She was looking for the pattern in all these connections: Dig, the Brewsters, her father, Michael, and now Cole Thatcher.

"How can you believe what this guy says?"

She couldn't. She knew that. Dig was the most talented liar she'd ever known. But she couldn't entirely *not* believe him either. She'd been looking for an opportunity to get answers out of this man. So maybe this was it.

Diggory called out to her. "Phone him, Riley. Call your father's townhouse."

She went for her pocket but remembered that everything, including her phone, was soaked. Her mind felt waterlogged, too.

She walked back over to Diggory. "My phone's dead. Can I use your cell?"

He cocked his head to one side and stared at her for a few seconds. "You know very well I can't let you use *that* phone. You can call from the airport."

"Dig, I don't think I *can* get on a plane right now. I don't even have my passport. I have to be in Pointe-à-Pitre on Monday for a hearing, and I have—"

While she was talking, Diggory reached inside his jacket and produced a small blue folder with gold lettering that read US Passport. He handed it to her. "I took care of it. Here."

She opened the cover and saw the old photo taken before she left for her first posting at Cairo. She thumbed through the dozens of visas stamped in the back. It was hers. She looked up at him. "I don't understand."

"I have us booked on this afternoon's American flight to San Juan. We'll get into DC before midnight. Let's go."

She clutched her passport to her chest. "Diggory." She wondered again if she knew who was playing for what team. She held up her passport. "How did you get this?"

"Riley, we don't know how much more time your father has. We can talk about this on the way."

She turned away from Dig and saw Cole's green eyes fixed on her. She walked up and stood in front of him. "It's my father," she said, her voice soft.

Cole glanced over her shoulder, then took a deep breath and turned back to her. "Even if it's true, Riley, you don't have to go with him. I can get you to the airport."

She saw the pain in his eyes.

Dig's deep voice intruded. "The flight is overbooked already." He coughed as though to clear his throat. "I had them bump two passengers to get us on. We miss this flight and the next one's not until tomorrow, and *that* might be too late."

She mouthed the words, "I'm sorry." She wanted to tell him she knew what she was doing. That she knew better than to trust Diggory Priest, but she hoped to find more answers down this path. Then she spoke aloud without turning to look at Dig. "What about them?" She pointed at Cole and Theo.

"They're free to go," Dig said. "They've nothing to do with this."

She placed a hand on Cole's shoulder. "Take care of my boat, OK? I have no idea when I'll be back."

He reached up, covered her hand with his. "Don't go with him, Magee. Please."

She gave his shoulder a squeeze and withdrew her hand. "The combination for the hatch padlock is 1996, the year she was built. I've got business cards on my chart table with my contact information. I'll get a new phone in DC."

"How do you know he isn't lying to you?"

She glanced at the waiting taxi and then turned to meet his gaze. "I don't. But I'm not a fool. I can take care of myself. I'll call my father's housekeeper before I get on the plane." She leaned in and brushed her cheek against his for an air kiss. "I'll be fine," she whispered.

Diggory took her arm and led her to the minivan. He slid open the side door, and Riley climbed inside without looking back.

CHAPTER FORTY-NINE

Indian River, Dominica

March 27, 2008

The taxi van had long since disappeared from view, but Cole stood in the middle of the parking lot staring at the patch of road where he had last seen it.

"Sorry, mon," Theo said.

"I can't believe she left."

"If you want, Zeke could drive us to the airport, and you could try—"

"No," he said, shuffling his feet in the dirt. "It's not like he kidnapped her. She made her decision. Come on. Let's get out of here."

He was still carrying the soggy backpack, and he slung it off his shoulders and extended it to his friend. "Here," he said as they walked toward Zeke's van.

"I'll take that." It wasn't Theo who answered him.

Cole spun around. Walking up the dirt embankment from a boat that was now tied to the wooden dock were Pinky and Spyder Brewster. Spyder's T-shirt was caked with mud, and his yellow teeth flashed in a wide grin when he waved at them with the gun in his hand.

"What's up, Doc?" he said.

"You look like hell, Spyder," Cole said. "What happened to you?"

The grin faded when he looked down at his shirt. "Some old fart jumped us upriver there."

"Looks like he got in some pretty good licks." As the two men got closer, Cole saw that one of Spyder's eyes was swollen. Pinky, in his long white clothes, looked unscathed. "And it looks like your brother didn't exactly jump in with his support. No surprise there."

"Shut up about my brother. He don't need to get dirty. He's smart enough to bring a gun." Spyder tried to brush some of the dried mud off the front of his shirt. "That dude knew karate or some shit. Fought pretty good for a old guy."

Theo said, "You didn't shoot him, did you?"

"Nah. Pinky might've winged him. Didn't kill him, though. Dude disappeared into the jungle. He run off our boat and driver, but we stole another one from a bunch of foreigners." He smiled wide, and Cole could see the dark gap where one of the man's upper eyeteeth was missing.

Spyder pointed the gun at Zeke. "You. Get in your van and get out of here."

Zeke turned to Cole.

"Do as he says," Cole said.

Zeke climbed behind the wheel and drove out of the dirt lot, leaving a dust cloud in his wake. They were alone now—no cars, no buildings, no witnesses.

"So what do you want, Spyder? Riley already left with your buddy there."

"I don't give a rat's ass about them—neither one of them. It's between you and me, Doc. Always has been. You found something upriver there, didn't you? Gimme that bag of yours."

"What if I say no? What are you gonna do? Shoot me?"

It was Pinky who answered. "No. But my brother'd have no problem taking out one of your buddy's knees."

Spyder laughed. "I like that, bro." He swung the gun around and pointed it at Theo's lower extremities.

Without a word, Cole held out the bag.

Spyder stepped forward and wrenched it from his hand. He tossed the backpack to Pinky, who unzipped it and began to rummage inside.

Pinky threw the folded shovel to the ground. "That's what made it so heavy. Ain't no gold in here."

Cole laughed. "That's what you thought?"

Spyder shrugged. "Hoped, maybe." Spyder stepped closer to his brother. Pinky was now examining the 40-Year Calendar. Spyder glanced back at Cole. "What's that thing?"

"Don't answer him," Theo said.

Cole shrugged. "You need your knees, my friend." He took one step closer to Pinky. "That's what we found up the river there. When we get out to the boat and get some charts, we'll use it to figure out where the submarine is."

"How's it work?" Pinky asked.

"We've still got to figure that out, but we're pretty sure this is the key we've been looking for. It's a cipher disk that'll give us the exact coordinates of the sub. Then, we just dive down and get the gold."

"Then let's go," Spyder said. He waved the gun, directing them toward a path that led past an island sloop, her keel resting on some rotting timbers in the weeds, several wooden props holding her upright. Vines crawled up her hull, and termites had taken up residence.

They walked single file along the narrow trail, Cole in the lead, followed by Theo and then Spyder, who held the gun aimed at Theo's back. Cole searched the ground under the old boat hoping to spot a tool or something he could use as a weapon, but all he saw was tangled underbrush. He felt inside his pockets. He had nothing but a waterlogged cell phone. Beyond the sloop was another small wood dock, and tied to it, he saw his own Boston Whaler dinghy.

"You guys been enjoying my boat?" he asked.

"It's all right," Spyder said. "Too small, though. Should'a got the one with the steering wheel."

"You can pick the model you want when you're buying."

Spyder coughed out a laugh that sounded more like the grinding gears of a manual transmission. "Me and Pinky don't never *buy* boats."

Waving the gun in the air, he directed Theo to get into the Whaler first and start the outboard.

Cole sidled up next to Pinky, who was still examining the marble paperweight. The man turned the brass plates and cocked his head to one side.

"Figured it out yet?" Cole asked.

Pinky shook his head.

Cole glanced up and saw Theo pulling on the starter cord for the outboard. The engine wasn't starting. Theo hadn't pulled the choke out far enough. He was buying time.

"See where it says you're supposed to turn the top plate until you get the year over the month? So you've got to find the year 2008, and then line it up with the month, which is February. Here—look, I'll show you." Cole took the paperweight from the man's mottled hands.

Theo continued to pull at the starter cord, and the engine coughed but would not start.

"It's hard to read the numbers. I can't tell if that's 2008 or 2003. The brass is corroding." Cole pulled up his shirttail and attempted to polish the brass plate. Then he looked up and shouted, "Theo, give her more choke, man."

Pinky turned to look at Theo in the Whaler, then he turned back to Cole.

"Hey, man, give me the fucking disk back."

Cole raised his arm over his head and said, "You're not using this cipher disk to find my wreck, man. I've worked too long for this. If I don't get it, nobody does." Cole lobbed the object far into the bush just as the outboard roared to life.

Spyder ran into the underbrush, the gun dangling in his hand, forgotten. Cole looked at Pinky's open mouth and eyes and said, "Sorry about this, man." It only took one punch to the man's chin, and he went down like a sack of cement.

Cole slipped the dinghy's bowline off a piling as he leaped into the Whaler. He heard a gunshot just as Theo gunned the engine, and the dinghy leaped onto a plane headed downriver. Theo zigged back and forth as bullets zinged past. Then they rounded a slight bend, and the gunshots stopped. Beyond them, the mouth of the Indian River emptied into Prince Rupert Bay. Theo cranked up the throttle, heading straight out into the blue water, then turned the Whaler in a wide arc to head for *Shadow Chaser*. Neither man tried to speak over the screaming outboard engine.

Theo didn't throttle down until they were a hundred feet off the stern of the trawler. The Whaler slid up to the big boat's stern on a wave of white foam. Cole grabbed the ladder and motioned for Theo to climb aboard first. "You go on, get her ready for immediate departure."

"We just leave? Let the Brewsters have the cipher disk?"

Cole nodded. "We're leaving as soon as I come back with Riley's dinghy." He reached into his pocket and extended his closed fist to Theo. "Here, put this somewhere safe."

Theo reached out and Cole dropped the marble and brass calendar into his palm. "We don't have much time. I want to be gone before Spyder finds my drowned cell phone out there in the bush."

CHAPTER FIFTY

In the air

March 27, 2008

Diggory was unable to stop staring at her small hands, at the pink, close-cut, but clean fingernails that drummed on the tray table in front of her seat. Ever since takeoff when the flight attendant had come through the first-class compartment taking drink orders, she had remained silent, her head turned aside, staring out the window at the cloud tops and the distant blue sea. Sometimes, she tugged at her still-damp T-shirt or reached up and tried to smooth down the wild spikes of her hair. Most of the time, though, she stared out the window, her body and face turned away from him. But those tapping fingers told him all he needed to know.

He'd gotten to her. Not that he'd ever had any doubt. He knew the power he had with women. She was refusing to talk to him. For now. It was all part of the game, and it was so much more interesting when the stakes were high.

At the airport, she had insisted on finding a pay phone and placing a call to her father's home number, but she got no answer. After that, she tried calling the hospital, but she had been making her way through the voice mail when the attendant announced the final boarding call for their flight over the airport PA system. He'd known she would follow him on board.

He watched out the window as the plane flew over a corner of the island of Guadeloupe. Soon, very soon, it would be his time. He would get his hands on the documents on that submarine, and then he would be the one calling the shots. No more errand boy, cleanup man. He winced as he remembered how Caliban had refused to tell him what it was they were after. The man had paid for that lack of respect—as they all would. A little more time, that was all he needed. Time enough to pay one last surprise visit to Yorick, and to allow Thatcher to find the wreck while he was gone. Then he'd go back to the islands, collect what was his, and return to DC—not as a janitor, though. Once he'd *paid his respects* to Yorick, he thought, smiling in anticipation, and taken control of the situation in the Caribbean, they could kiss his shoes.

Diggory remembered the first time Yorick had visited him after graduation. The Company had recruited him in the final weeks of his senior year, and he'd moved straight to DC with his few possessions in a cheap suitcase. He hadn't known what to expect when he heard the three knocks on his door. He'd moved into the rented room in a house on Seventeenth Street SE across from the Congressional Cemetery. The row house was owned by an obese Ukrainian woman, and the hallways, wallpapered with horrid floral patterns, always smelled like cooked cabbage. But it was the only room he could afford that wasn't being rented out by blacks, and while he was poor, he wasn't that desperate.

Opening the door, he first saw the sleeve of the Italian Merino wool navy suit, followed by the striped tie and then Yorick's puckered countenance as he surveyed the tiny room. He slid his one good eye up and down Diggory's worn slacks and polo shirt.

"A Bonesman living in squalor," he said. "You're a fucking disgrace, Priest."

"It's only temporary, sir."

Yorick pulled out a fat gold money clip and began peeling off the hundred-dollar bills and letting them fall onto the threadbare carpet.

"That's not necessary," Priest said. "I start on salary next week."

"Pick it up," Yorick said.

The older man focused his eyes on Diggory, who glanced back and forth, trying to remember which was the good eye. Then the lazy eye jerked away. The good eye seared into him. Dig dropped to his knees and began collecting the bills.

"It's going to be a while, Priest, before I can pay you any respect—as long as I have to pay to pull you out of the gutter."

By the time Dig had collected the last bill, Yorick had started down the stairs. He did not look back.

* * *

Diggory sipped his wine, then turned back from the plane window and sighed. "It's going to be a long flight, you know," he said to her. "Do you want to talk? Just to pass the time?"

She didn't reply. In fact, she'd ignored him so long, he was beginning to think about sleep. The nice pinot noir they served in first class was making him drowsy.

Then the tapping of her nails stopped, and she placed both her hands palms down on the tray table. She faced the seat back in front of him, still not looking at him. "I'll talk if you'll give me some answers," she said.

"All right. What do you want to know?"

"I've been thinking about it since we were in the cab. It doesn't make sense. Why would they send you to find me? Why not have Eleanor Wright contact me?"

"She tried. You weren't answering your phone. I gather you were outside their signal area. Offshore, perhaps? Anyway, she called the State Department for help locating you. The French authorities had informed our embassy in Barbados when they relieved you of your passport, and since Barbados is my home base these days, they called me. They knew I was in Guadeloupe on Company business."

"And how did you find me?"

He smiled. "That, my dear, comes under the heading of trade secrets."

She turned to face him for the first time since boarding the plane. He noticed two vertical creases between her eyebrows when she spoke.

"You trusted me in Lima," she said.

"Ah, well," he said. "That was different."

"How so?"

"Things were different then."

"Between us, you mean?"

"Well, yes." Sex made all the difference, he thought.

"We knew what we were doing was wrong."

He ran his finger over the skin on her forearm. "But it was right in so many ways."

She shivered and drew her arm back. "I wasn't supposed to know your real job. You were just another trust-fund Yank playboy enjoying the lower cost of living south of the border. And yet you asked me to do things for you." She jerked her head in his direction and flashed him a quick look. "And I'm not talking about *those* things. I mean work things."

He chuckled at her discomfort. She never could talk about sex. She'd done all sorts of things to please him. "You were a great help to me." If you only knew, he thought.

"I'd convinced myself I was only doing you little favors—but," she said, lifting her eyes to his, "it was more, wasn't it? That last day." She turned away and spoke to the back of the seat in front of her. "I want to ask, but I'm afraid of what your answer will be."

He pasted a wounded expression on his face and leaned forward to try to get into her field of vision. "Riley, I don't know what you're talking about. I cared for you. Really. I was in—" He stopped. "You're not going to hit me again if I say that word?"

"I might. Don't say it. You know you don't mean it."

"What makes you so sure?"

She made a noise as though something had caught in her throat. "The flight's not *that* long," she said.

Neither of them spoke again for a long time. He ordered another glass of wine. He would answer her questions. Soon. But not here. She was petite, but strong and skilled, and he couldn't afford to have her go ballistic on the plane. She flipped through the pages of the in-flight magazine not even looking at the print on the pages. He could feel her mind crawling all over him.

Still, she startled him when she spoke. "So when we get there, are you going to disappear again?"

That's it, he thought. He'd won. She wanted to be with him. She *wanted him.*

"We won't get in until midnight. I have a car and driver meeting us. The weather forecast is for snow. I'll drive you home so you can get some rest and change."

She tugged at her shorts with one hand and felt her tousled hair with the other. "I'm not even dry yet. I'll freeze dressed like this."

"My driver will have blankets in the car."

She bit her lower lip and tucked a strand of hair behind her ear. The worry lines appeared again between her brows. "If I go with you, Diggory, there won't be any surprises, right?"

"Absolutely not."

CHAPTER FIFTY-ONE

The Atlantic Ocean

February 13, 1942

"Bloody hell," Woolsey said as he wiped the cold seawater off his face.

Gohin was the first among them to stagger to his feet. Woolsey saw that the muscular French ensign looked dazed, and he was no longer carrying the pistol. As the man standing closest to the rail when the bomb went off, Gohin had been blown back halfway across the deck, and his face was covered with blood. He may have been hit with a bit of shrapnel or bone, or his nose was just bleeding from the concussion. Either way, he looked a fright.

Michaut was the first man out of the conning tower, but he was followed by a handful of others. Though Woolsey could not understand what they were saying, he was glad to hear Captain Lamoreaux answer them with a steady voice. But when Woolsey looked into the captain's eyes, he saw they were focused not on Gohin, but on the gun that lay on the deck between the two men— the gun that was closer to Woolsey than to either of the Frenchmen.

The three men on the lower deck moved at once. Woolsey was at a disadvantage because he was sitting on his backside, but he tried to crawl on all fours across the slippery deck. The big French ensign landed on top of him as Woolsey's fingers closed around the gun, but after receiving a couple fierce jabs to the kidney and a crushing blow to his wrist, Woolsey gave in. He wasn't much of a fighter. Gohin pulled the gun from Woolsey's limp fingers, and the big Frenchman got to his feet. He delivered one final kick to Woolsey's ribs as he muttered the word "*Salaud.*"

Woolsey lay curled in a ball struggling to breathe. At Gohin's order, Michaut and one of the deck officers pulled him to his feet while a couple of sailors grabbed the captain's arms. They half dragged the two of them across the deck to the ladder, then with Gohin pointing the gun and shouting orders, the men herded Woolsey and Lamoreaux down the various ladders and along the passage to the door to the hold.

Inside, Mullins's body lay where they had left it. Woolsey felt Michaut's grip tighten on his arm as they entered. When the sailors released the captain, Gohin pointed the gun at his midsection and said something in French. The captain answered him.

"Michaut, what are they saying?" Woolsey whispered.

"*Capitaine* tell Gohin that he know a secret about this place. That he want to talk to Gohin alone."

"What's Gohin saying?"

"He say Captain want to play trick. He must talk in front of all the men."

Lamoreaux began to speak, and Woolsey heard several men gasp. Then the captain walked over to Woolsey and held out his hand. "Give me your knife," he said in English.

Woolsey drew the folded rigging knife out of his pocket. He handed it to Lamoreaux. Walking to one of the wine crates, the captain crouched down and proceeded to pry open the rough wood. He removed what looked like a large, antique, hand-made champagne bottle and held it up for Gohin to see the label. There was something odd about the way he handled the bottle—he held it with two hands as though it were very valuable. Lamoreaux kept talking, explaining something in French, but when Woolsey looked to Michaut for a translation, he saw the young man's mouth hanging open and slack, his eyes wide in anticipation. Woolsey was trying to figure out what the old man was up to when the captain lifted the bottle with a sharp jerk upward, then frapped it down hard on the steel deck. The dark green glass shattered, and dozens of shiny gold coins clattered to the deck.

For several seconds, it was as though they were in a film and the reel had stopped. Then, in a single instant, the film started up again, and they were all thrust into motion. Officers and sailors alike, they ran to the crates and began pulling them apart with their bare hands. Gohin stuffed the pistol into his back waistband and fell to his knees with the others. Bottles crashed and broke as the men scrambled across the floor shouting and laughing and stuffing their pockets with the bright, shiny coins. Broken glass soon covered the deck, but the oblivious sailors ignored the red stains at the knees of their white duck trousers as they rushed to open more crates.

Though the men holding his arms had forgotten about him and released him, Woolsey stood there watching the pandemonium, trying to make sense of it. Did they know about this back in New Haven? Or was it possible their intelligence was not so accurate after all? With the bomb gone, Woolsey had failed in his mission to destroy the sub. Might he rise in their estimation if he could deliver them a fortune in gold?

The sound of the gunshot was deafening in the relatively small chamber. Woolsey swiveled around, unsure, at first, who had fired. Then he saw Captain Lamoreaux standing over Mullins's body, the gun in his hand pointed at the dead man's torso.

Gohin slapped at his empty waistband, then scowled at the captain. Woolsey figured that the captain had shot into the body to avoid killing anyone else with a ricochet. It worked, and he now had their attention. He turned the gun on them and spoke in French. One by one, they began to empty their pockets and place the coins on the bloody, glass-strewn deck.

Lamoreaux pointed the gun and barked an order. The men started toward the door. When the last of them had exited, the captain turned to Woolsey and said, "The men will get their way. We go to Martinique."

"And what about your orders?"

The captain spit on the deck. "After the Allies tried to sink *Surcouf,* you think they deserve my loyalty?"

"And what about me?"

"When we arrive in Martinique?" He shrugged. Then he rested one hand on the edge of the door. "You will hang," he said, giving the door a strong push.

The door slammed closed and the lights shut off, plunging the hold back into darkness.

CHAPTER FIFTY-TWO

Îles des Saintes

March 27, 2008

Cole sat on the bench seat of the galley dinette with his left leg stretched out straight, his foot braced against the doorway so he wouldn't slide off the seat as *Shadow Chaser* rolled in the southeasterly swell. He bit his lower lip and turned the brass plate on the green marble calendar for the hundredth time. On the table before him lay various charts of the area, the lockbox, and his father's well-thumbed journals.

He had told the Brewster brothers that the object was a cipher disk that would give him the exact coordinates of the location of the submarine. Talk about wishful thinking. He had no idea how the thing might work. As far as he could tell, the purpose of the calendar was to learn the day of the week for any given date. First, you had to know the date—month, day, and year—and then the calendar would tell you what day of the week that date fell on. As for how that could be translated into a cipher disk, he was stumped.

He thought about setting it to his own birthday, November 19, 1971, and then realized that the calendar only started in 1998, so that wouldn't work. Most of the possible dates were in the future.

Assuming his father wanted him to set it to a certain date, what date did he have in mind?

Cole turned his attention back to the books and picked up the last of the journals. He opened it to the last page and read the words there for the umpteenth time.

Dear Son,

Wit's end is where I am. Spent a bit of time there. Expect to be there 'til the end of days. Got to stop. Them. American president is part and parcel. What goes up must come down. Not a nickel to my name. It's all yours now. Got to stop. Them. The Creoles sing a song in the islands. It's called Fais pas do do. Like this.

Fais pas do do, Cole mon p'tit coco
Fais pas do do, tu l'auras du lolo
Yayd d'dir
Y'did yd
Jamais fais do do.

His old man was trying to tell him something secret here, but doing it in such a way that it wouldn't be clear to others who might look through the journals. Cole had tried everything to decode those words during these past months, and when he was trying to use the French Angel coin as key, nothing had worked. Not until Riley came along, that is.

Cole shook his head to try to clear it. He hadn't been able to concentrate on the problem at hand all night. His mind kept returning to her. What was happening to her? Had she arrived in Washington? He thought about the way she tucked her hair behind her ear, how she smelled like the orange blossoms he remembered from his childhood, and the way the light danced in her eyes when they dug up the calendar.

The calendar. *Concentrate*, he told himself. This blasted calendar paperweight that his father thought he would understand, and yet, though he'd been at it most of the night, he still had no idea how to use it. What was the connection to the journals or *Surcouf*? The calendar had the names of the months written in the center, the years on the background plate, and the day names and numbers on the two plates. How did that relate to his father's cryptic note and this odd French Creole song? Or did it relate at all? In the end, the message of the French Angel had nothing to do with this journal, other than maybe the reference to the word nickel.

He started to read the page through one more time, and he paused at the end of the second sentence. His father had used the word "time." Wit's end. Where on a calendar is wit's end? How much time had he spent there? He had written *expect to be there 'til the end of days*. Cole sighed and rubbed his tired eyes with both hands. The old man could never make anything easy for him. Wit's end. Cole felt as if he were already there. He wished he could understand what his father was trying to tell him.

"Cole," Theo called from the bridge. "We're approaching the bay. Do you want to take her in?"

He closed the journal, slid off the bench seat, and made his way to the wheelhouse. Through the forward window, he saw Riley's boat at anchor deep inside the moonlit bay. Cole checked his watch: eight thirty.

"We made good time," he said.

"Helps to have the current and the wind on our tail."

Cole stared at the sleek white sailboat. "Glad to see her boat looks fine."

Theo glanced at Cole over the tops of his glasses. "It's not her boat you're worried about."

"I told Riley I'd look after it. We'll drop the hook close by. I'll take her in. You go ready the anchor."

Thirty minutes later, the *Shadow Chaser* was anchored with the little sailboat tied to her port side, fat fenders preventing the two hulls from bumping together. Cole stood, his forearms resting atop the bulwark, and stared down at the deck of the *Bonefish*. Theo appeared at his side, and the mate handed him one of the frosty beer bottles he was carrying.

"How's it going with the calendar thingy?" Theo asked.

"I don't have a clue what to do with it. It's got to refer to some future date."

"Hmm," Theo said, and then he took another long pull from the beer. "Do you think that Spyder is still searching in the weeds back on Dominica?"

"I doubt it."

"Think he'll come after us?"

"Maybe."

"You worried?"

"Not about him."

"Ahhh," Theo said, dragging the sound up and then down the scale.

The two men stood there for a long time watching the moonlight trail travel across the bay. Finally, Cole broke the silence.

"Theo, what do you think of when you hear the phrase *end of days*?"

"Why?"

"I hate when you do that. You answer a question with another question. Just answer it. *End of days*. What does that mean to you?"

"Cole, my mama took me to church every Sunday of my childhood, and I heard many preachers refer to the *end time* or *end of days*. They meant the return of Christ, you know, the second coming."

Cole squeezed his eyes closed. "My mom never once took me to church, so excuse me if I ask some stupid questions." He peered at Theo. "But, like, is there a specific date associated with that?"

Theo laughed. "There's more than one preacher who's claimed to know, but no, I don't think any of them really do."

Cole nodded. He rubbed his hand across the stubble on his chin. "I remember there was an old Schwarzenegger movie called *End of Days*, but I can't see Pops as an Arnold fan."

"What's this all about?"

"We have to figure out what date to set the calendar to so we can try to understand what my crazy old man is trying to tell us. I thought the answer might be in the journals—you know, on that last page with the nursery rhyme we were trying to decode. He wrote, "Expect to be there until the end of days." I don't think it was a mistake—that he forgot to write end of *my* days. He meant *end of days*—as if it was some special date. But what date is that?"

"Well, I know of one possibility."

Cole straightened up and turned to face Theo. "What?"

Theo didn't look at him; he continued to stare across the water at the sailboat, a small smile on his face.

Cole said, "You want to share it with me, or are you just going to stand there grinning?"

"I thought I'd relax here for a bit and enjoy the moment. I know something that the brilliant Dr. Thatcher doesn't." Theo tipped his bottle to his lips. Before he could take a drink, his teeth clinked against the glass when Cole slapped the back of his head. Beer sloshed down onto the deck. "Hey," Theo said. "You're wasting perfectly good beer."

"You don't speak up, and I'll be throwing you over the side next."

"Oh captain, my captain. I was getting to it."

"Sometime before those two morons get here?"

"All right, all right. According to the Mayas, the end of days is going to be December 21, 2012."

"The Mayas?"

"Yes, you know, indigenous people in South and Central America?"

"I know who the Mayas are, numb nuts, but what's this about them and the end of days?"

"I'm surprised that a know-it-all archeologist and conspiracy buff like you doesn't know about the Mayan calendar."

"Hey, I'm a *discerning* conspiracy buff. Not my specialty anyway—I stayed away from all that pre-Columbian stuff. But I remember now. The Mayas invented a super accurate astronomical calendar, and according to the New Age wackos, the world is going to end when that calendar ends. I need to get to a library—a big, decent library, not one of these dinky island places."

"Yeah, it's all over the 'net. There are people who are so into this they believe your government is building underground shelters in preparation for a great celestial event on that date."

"You've got to be kidding me. People believe that hooey?"

Theo sniffed. "Well, if it isn't the crackpot calling the kettle black," he said—and then he ducked.

CHAPTER FIFTY-THREE

Washington, DC

March 28, 2008

Riley followed Dig through the empty corridors of Reagan National as though she were in a dream. She supposed she must look like some refugee with her bare legs and the thin airline blanket draped over her shoulders, but she was too exhausted to care. She doubted whether the late-night floor polishers and bathroom cleaning ladies were paying any attention to the crazy woman whose only baggage was the passport in the back pocket of her shorts.

The car waiting outside in a cloud of steaming exhaust was identical to the thousands of black Lincoln Town Cars one saw all over the city. When she stepped into the frigid winter night, Riley gasped and stopped short. Dig took her by the elbow and steered her to the car door, placing his hand on her head like a cop settling a prisoner. She sank into the soft leather, thankful the car had seat warmers. Dig covered her with another blanket, tucking the edges around her legs, and she leaned her head back to watch the city lights and the barren, leafless landscape as they drove toward the river.

She wanted to think, but her brain felt fuzzy. She and Cole had slept little the night before as they'd sat in the galley on his boat and pored over that chart of Dominica. Now, here it was after midnight by the digital clock on the car's dash, and still she had not even dozed. Her brain wasn't working right anymore. Thus far, Dig had brought her to Washington. Nothing more. No secret agenda in evidence. If it turned out that he was telling the truth about her father, she would need to make plans for her father's care, for the townhouse, for her boat back in the islands. If it turned out that he had something different in mind for her, she needed rest to be able to take Dig on both mentally and physically.

Her mind kept flashing images of the sparks in Cole Thatcher's eyes as he held up that damned calendar device. The man was obsessed, but she was beginning to understand it. She felt it, too. She wanted to be there with him—to solve the puzzle, that's all. No other reason. Had he solved it without her? Or had he gone back to the Saintes to look after her boat as he'd promised?

Don't be a fool, she thought. Did she really believe he could leave Dominica if he had discovered where the *Surcouf* was located?

For the second time since they'd landed, Dig's satellite phone buzzed. The first time, she'd been struggling to keep up with his long strides and hadn't heard a word of the conversation. This time when he answered, he said, "Yes. Mm-hm. All right." She was not able to hear any of the caller's side of the conversation. Dig pushed a button to end the call, and as he leaned forward to slide the phone back inside his coat pocket, he said, "Your father is home now."

"What? They've already discharged him?"

"Seems so."

"But I thought he was at death's door."

"Riley, you never know how it is with these things. Given his age, they may have sent him home if there was nothing more they could do for him."

"I want to talk to his doctors."

"In good time. Tomorrow." He stretched his arm out to bare the watch on his wrist. "Or rather, later today. You get cleaned up, get some rest. I'll come back in a few hours to take you to the hospital."

The car turned into the familiar street, and Riley felt her stomach churn. "I can walk in the morning. It's not that far."

"As you wish. I'd be happy to drive you if you want, but I don't mean to intrude on your life."

If she hadn't been so tired, she would have laughed at that.

There were no inside lights visible when they pulled up in front of her father's brick two-story townhouse, but the dim porch light was lit in the alcove at the top of the steps. As usual, the street was lined with parked cars—they hadn't built garages in the late 1890s when these row houses were built. Riley patted her shorts and realized she didn't have her key with her.

As though he could read her thoughts, Dig said, "Mrs. Wright will let you in. Just tap on the door. She's awake." He reached across her and opened the door. "Hurry," he said. "Or you'll freeze."

Riley climbed out of the car, and her sneakers crunched on the thin layer of snow that covered the pavement. The frigid night air stung her bare skin like a thousand icy needles. She trotted across the sidewalk, opened the black iron gate, and rushed up the steps. As she was lifting her hand to knock on the door, she heard the sound of the lock turning, and the door swung open. Riley tilted her head back to look up at Eleanor Wright, who filled the doorway in her flower-print robe, a white scarf tied round her head. Behind her, the house loomed dark and silent. All Wright needed was a kerosene lamp in her hand, and she'd look like a king-size version of the original residents of the house from the turn of the last century.

"Thanks for waiting up for me, Mrs. Wright," Riley said as she stepped into the dark foyer and closed the door behind her.

She stomped her feet on the front door mat and tried to remember where the light switch was.

The older woman looked her up and down in the dim light that shone through the windows from the street, frowning at the way Riley was dressed. She grunted, then turned away and passed into the kitchen where she turned on a light. "There's hot tea left in the pot there," she said, "and you can warm the soup on the stove if you're hungry."

In the harsh kitchen fluorescent lights, the ancient appliances and the deeply etched butcher-block countertops were familiar in their shabbiness. Between her father's postings, they had sometimes returned to Washington for a few months, and her father would allow the children into his personal domain. Her parents divorced after she joined the Corps, and since her mother had moved back to France, whenever Riley returned stateside, her father's spare bedroom was hers. After her discharge, she had moved in for good.

The housekeeper lifted the heavy lid off a mammoth pot on the stove and swirled the contents with a ladle. Wright always seemed to cook enough to feed an army. She stood nearly half a foot taller than Riley and probably weighed twice what Riley did. She wore no makeup, and her cheeks hung down in overlapping jowls on either side of her thin, pursed lips.

The woman had seemed like a godsend when she arrived. Riley had been advertising for a day nurse, and the old battle-ax had arrived at the door one day, saying she had a recommendation from one of her father's old school friends. When Wright moved in, Riley was able to move out.

"Thank you, Mrs. Wright, but I'm not hungry. I just want to know about my father. What can you tell me about his condition?" Riley hugged the blanket tighter around her shoulders in spite of the oppressive heat in the house.

The older woman sighed and pressed the knuckles of her right fist into her hip. "You never call him, and now you want to chat at nearly one in the morning? I don't think so." She started to turn toward the door.

Riley reached out and grabbed the woman's arm through her robe. "I know you don't think I'm much of a daughter, but he is my father. How is he? I can't believe they've just sent him home from the hospital to die."

Wright stared down at Riley's hand on her arm, then looked up and locked gazes with her.

"Turns out he didn't have a stroke after all."

"What?"

"Doctor said it was a problem with his sodium or some damn thing. He drinks too much water. Other than that, there's been no change in your father's condition."

"But he," Riley pointed toward the front door, "told me you'd been trying to reach me to tell me about the stroke."

Wright turned and stared at the door for a moment, then shook her head. Turning back to face Riley, she said, "I was wrong, that's all. Your father is still the same ornery son of a bitch who can't remember who I am most days or how to find his own goddamn way to the bathroom. Don't know what they been telling you, but if that's the only reason you came home, you can call that limo and head back down to the islands." Eleanor Wright turned and lumbered out of the kitchen, leaving Riley stunned, the blanket still draped over her shoulders.

CHAPTER FIFTY-FOUR

McLean, Virginia

March 28, 2008

Diggory leaned forward and gave the driver an address on Old Dominion in McLean, Virginia. It wasn't far outside DC, but he would have enough time to sort through the information he had received and make plans. Back in the airport, he had been surprised when his sat phone rang shortly after landing. He realized then he would need to delay his plans.

He could tell from the echo on the line they had him on speakerphone, but he didn't know where they were calling from, nor who all was in the room. They asked about Caliban—said their man in Guadeloupe had gone missing. Beelzebub, the old politico, wanted to know if Dig knew anything about it. Dig, glancing past his shoulder at the blanket-clad girl shuffling behind him, kept to one-word answers.

"When did you see him last?"

"Friday."

"And everything was normal then?"

"Yes."

"And the target. Has he found anything yet?"

"No."

"You've been watching him?"

"Yes."

"We're going to have to consult the others. Our methods may have to change. We didn't think the target had the potential to do damage, but if he is responsible for Caliban's disappearance, you might have to take him out. Understood?"

"Yes."

Dig knew what that meant. They had already called a meeting, and he knew where. Once, Dig had driven Yorick to this meeting place. That was ten years ago, but he doubted the location had changed. It was a small British pub not far from Langley, owned by a Bonesman. Because some, like Beelzebub, often had Secret Service escorts, they met well before daylight, when only the night-shift workers and insomniacs might take note of the collection of limousines parked in the lot of a small pub.

There were twelve of them, and they called themselves the Patriarchs. In fact, in Bonesman terms, they all became patriarchs upon graduation, including Diggory. This group, however, did not include every Bonesman. They were a highly selective inner circle of the most prominent and powerful men in the country, and at the pub where they met, there was a circular table with twelve chairs. Dig was going to get a seat at that table. In ordinary circumstances, they would never include a son of a waitress among their ranks. Every man at the table could trace a bloodline to one of the most wealthy and powerful families in the country: Whitney, Harriman, Vanderbilt, Bush, Kellogg, Goodyear. But Dig would not give them any choice.

He signaled the driver to pull over when they were a quarter mile short of the pub. He gave the man specific instructions and dismissed him, then climbed out of the car and shivered. The freezing night air penetrated the light jacket and khakis he had put on that morning aboard the barbarians' boat. After dropping off Riley, there had been no time to swing by his apartment to change—not if he expected to get there before them. And if he wanted to hear what they were planning, that was what he had to do.

The last time he'd traveled this way was in summer, and the trees had been in full leaf. The country houses set back from the road had not been visible. Now the ground shone white in the moonlight, and the houses looked cheapened by their nudity. He took long strides along the shoulder of the two-lane road, his breath puffing white, his shoulders hunched up against the cold. When he reached the small intersection and came upon the now-empty strip mall, he recognized the old brick building. The night of his last visit came back to him.

He'd been sent to pick up the old man at the Capital Yacht Club down on the Potomac in the wee hours of the morning. Yorick and a pair of congressmen had been out sailing all afternoon on a racing sloop that belonged to the president of a company that manufactured body armor. They had been enjoying the owner's hospitality at the dock half the night.

Dig remembered the smell of alcohol on Yorick's breath, the rosy glow of the man's cheeks, the cell phone call that led him to say that they weren't going home after all. Dig would never forget a word of it, including the conversation Yorick started from the backseat, where he always sat.

"I knew your father, you know."

Dig glanced up at the rearview mirror and saw the white-haired patrician watching him with his one good eye. "Yes, sir," he said. "You've mentioned that before."

"I met him in school at Choate. We weren't the same year, mind you. He was older, but I knew him by reputation. Everyone did. Good-looking fellow. He claimed to have set the record for the senior with the most notches on his bedpost. Produced the most bastards, too. He liked to go slumming. I suppose you've got quite a number of brothers and sisters swilling beer in Connecticut's trailer parks."

Diggory had said nothing, but he'd opened his right hand and one by one closed the fingers and squeezed.

* * *

The restaurant was on the ground floor of an older brick building that stood alone at the corner of a large asphalt parking lot. Dig remembered how they had driven around behind the building to a delivery access door. He cut through the parking lot alongside a hardware store, a chiropractor's office, and a Chinese takeout, then kept to the shadows as he approached the back of the brick building. He checked the few parked cars, watched the roofline, and checked his watch: 2:10. The last time they hadn't met until four; however, that didn't mean there was no security at this hour.

After watching the building for twenty minutes, he decided it was safe to take the next step. He followed the power and communications lines that hung low where they crossed the street. An outside staircase offered him access to the second floor offices as well as the junction box. Twenty minutes after he had cut the phone lines, he left the hiding place in the trees where he had been waiting across the street. Cutting the wires had not triggered any silent alarms; no security had arrived.

The upstairs office windows opened onto the bleached wood gallery that surrounded the second floor. He extracted a pair of thin plastic gloves from his wallet, then, without making a sound, he began to move from window to window, checking them to see if any were unlatched. Wasn't it always the way, he thought, when the last window on the gallery slid upward an eighth of an inch— enough to slide a credit card under it and turn the old-fashioned latch. He pulled the window up and the warm air spilled out from inside.

The last door he had passed outside bore the name of an accounting firm, so he was surprised when he found himself inside what appeared to be a linen room. Shelves lined the walls covered with folded white napkins, tablecloths, chefs' aprons, and kitchen towels. An antiquated time clock was affixed to one wall, along with a large metal rack filled with cards and a cork bulletin board. The cigarette-burned table with several chairs round it took up most of the center of the room.

Dig had been hoping merely to get into one of the building's offices, but here he was in the restaurant's staff break room. After closing and latching the window behind him, he crossed the room and peered out the door. The hallway was lit by a red glow that flowed up the stairs from the restaurant below. To his left, two doors led to what looked like bathrooms, though it was too dark to see if the doors were marked. On his right and across the hall, the third door opposite the top of the stairs sported a plaque he could read in the dim red light: Office.

Dig stood listening. He heard the muffled whoosh as the fan started up in the building's heating system, but nothing more. He stepped into the hall. The wood floor creaked as he crossed to the office, and he winced. He was, he figured, directly over the kitchen. Better not be anyone down there preparing food for the upcoming day. He tried the office door. The doorknob barely budged, and he cursed under his breath. He hadn't brought any tools.

Then, through the door, he heard the noise of a car pulling up outside the back of the restaurant. The office must have windows overlooking the rear of the building, he thought. He glanced down the staircase into the pub. From there, he could see most of the interior of the restaurant—the gleaming mahogany bar with leather-capped stools and the round table with twelve chairs.

He had to get inside the office. It would make a perfect vantage point for watching and listening. He jiggled the knob again. Then the heating system fan shut down, and the restaurant interior grew so quiet, Dig could hear his own breathing.

From outside, he heard men's voices and the thunks of car doors slamming.

Dig dashed across the hall back into the staff break room. He glanced at the window, and for a brief moment, he considered leaving the way he had come. The Patriarchs would not be pleased if they found him there.

No. Luck was on his side. He was sure of it. He started round the room, searching the shelves, patting down the linens, feeling under the table, examining the time clock. There had to be something there he could use. He moved to the bulletin board and grabbed one of the pushpins. No, too short; it would never work. He let the pin fall to the floor when he heard the sound of a door opening below him, and he felt the air pressure in the building change. They were coming inside.

Then he saw it. One of the time cards had a folded sheet of paper affixed to it with a paper clip. He yanked the card out of its slot. The torn card and note fluttered to the ground as he stepped into the hall.

The floorboard creaked, and the voices downstairs ceased. Dig froze. They would send someone upstairs to check it out. Soon. He straightened the paperclip and felt the chill air roll up his sleeve as he straightened his arm to reach for the doorknob. He slipped the shaft of the paper clip into the lock on the old round doorknob. The cold air reached the sweat-soaked fabric beneath his underarm, and he shivered. He'd handled locks like this a hundred times during his years with the Company. He stilled his breathing, closed his eyes, and jiggled the pick. With a soft click, he felt the lock give. He turned the knob, then lifted his foot and froze. They would be able to break in as easily as he had if he confirmed his presence to them. One creak meant it was an old building. Two and you knew you were not alone. Standing there balanced on one foot like a bloody flamingo, he realized he had no idea if the floor would creak again if he stepped into the office.

With a loud whoosh, the heating system started up again, and Dig slipped into the office without a sound, closing and locking the door behind him.

CHAPTER FIFTY-FIVE

Foggy Bottom

March 28, 2008

Riley sat on the flowered couch in their old family apartment in Paris. A tattered Scrabble board rested on the cushion between her and Mikey. The odd thing was that she was having one of those dreams where she knew she was dreaming, and she kept looking around the apartment thinking, *I want to be sure to remember all this when I wake up.*

It was Mikey's turn at the game. He arranged his tiles to spell the word *beware*. She started laughing because she thought it was so melodramatic of him—something right out of a horror movie. If they were in a movie, she thought, the music would be slow with lots of bass about now. Bum, bum, bum, bum…then Mikey looked up from the board and instead of smiling, his eyes grew wide and his mouth opened in a silent scream. His gaze traveled past her, over her shoulder, at something or someone who stood tall behind her. She started to turn—

Riley lurched up into a sitting position as though someone were pulling at the center front of her nightgown. She gulped air and brushed the sweat-slicked hair off her forehead. Moonlight streamed through the lace curtains at the window.

She pressed her fingers to her temples as the dream came back to her. She did not ever remember seeing such a look of terror on her brother's face.

"Oh God, Mikey? What was that all about?" When she spoke, her throat felt raspy and sore from sleeping in the dry, overheated house.

The bedside clock read 4:03. It had been nearly two in the morning by the time she settled into bed. That meant she'd slept only two hours, but now she felt wide awake. She swept aside the covers and swung her feet to the floor. Getting up and moving was the key to throwing off these night terrors.

She looked at the hardwood floor beneath her bare feet and thought of Mrs. Wright sleeping downstairs. The woman was nowhere near as adept a liar as Diggory. Riley didn't believe her father had ever left the house. Assuming this was all some ruse by Diggory Priest to get her to Washington, the question was why?

She remembered the argument on the quay in Pointe-à-Pitre and her exact words about how she wanted the truth. Then she'd said, *There's more you and your kind aren't telling me. And if you won't tell me*—Was this all a reaction to that half threat?

She eased the door to her father's room open and found it much darker inside than in the hall. The room's stuffy air had that sickroom smell of disinfectant and urine. She crossed to the window and drew back the heavy black drapes, allowing the moonlight to fall across the floor at the foot of his bed. The covers clung to the outline of his body, and he looked smaller, thinner than she remembered.

On the nightstand, she saw a photograph in a frame, and when she carried it to the window, she was surprised to see that it was a shot of the four of them taken in Paris when she was about sixteen years old. She remembered that day. Her mother had hired a professional photographer to get a family portrait. Her father traveled a great deal in those days, and her mother had started trying to make them all the über family whenever he was home. That day, her mom was furious that Riley refused to wear the designated photo shoot dress and instead wore a polo shirt and jeans. Printed on the front of her brother's T-shirt were the words, "Gravity, what a downer." Both Riley and Mikey wore goofy grins in the photo. They were that age when anything that irritated their parents was vastly amusing.

Now, with the benefit of years, she saw the sadness in her mother's eyes. Riley knew that their marriage had gone wrong even before Mikey's death. Within three years after this photo was taken, Michael was gone and her father had returned to Washington without his wife.

She heard the bed creak behind her as he rolled over.

"Maggie? Is that you?"

She turned toward the bed. Because she had been examining the photograph in the bright moonlight, she'd lost her night vision. She had difficulty making him out in the shadows. "Yeah. Hi, Dad. Sorry to wake you." So this was going to be one of his good times. At least he knew who she was.

"I'm glad you're here. I've been wanting to talk to you about something."

"Dad, it's late. Go back to sleep. I was just checking on you."

"There's something I have to tell you."

Here we go, she thought. "Dad, we'll talk in the morning."

"It's about Michael. I was ashamed."

"Dad, you're not making sense."

"He was such an odd child."

Riley felt her throat tightening. Her defenses were down, but she was determined not to let him see her cry. "Dad, I know. Let's stop talking about this now. It's the middle of the night. Time for you to go back to sleep."

"I wanted to make a man of him." She heard the covers rustling and saw the vague outline of him trying to sit up in bed. "Thought Yale would do that."

She heard a click and the bedside lamp lit the room. She saw his disheveled white hair, a bony wrist protruding from the sleeve of his maroon satin pajamas, but it was his face that appeared most changed. Where he once had plump pink pouches under his eyes, his skin now sagged in black craters. His cheekbones carved sharp angles above more sunken shadows. He motioned for her to sit in the chair.

"They made me do it."

He always came back to this story about something he had done, but like the offer of a position at the Taiwan Embassy, it seemed to have been created in the twisted depths of his dementia.

"It's all history now, Dad. Let the past lie."

"Please, Elizabeth. Say you forgive me."

That was it. Her mother was remarried and living in Paris. Now, he forgot even that, and he didn't know his own daughter. Riley went to the bedside and eased her father back down onto the pillow. His shoulders felt so thin, she wondered if he was eating anything at all. The bubble welled up her throat again. She swallowed. "Dad, we'll talk about this tomorrow."

She smoothed his hair down and trailed her fingers across the paper-like skin of his cheek. His eyes were open wide, and as usual, whenever he got upset like this, his lazy eye rolled around the eye socket, looking everywhere but at her.

"Shhh," she said. "Go to sleep." She clicked off the light and backed out of the room, closing the door behind her.

CHAPTER FIFTY-SIX

McLean, Virginia

March 28, 2008

There were two of them. Diggory stood behind the desk and listened to the footfalls outside the door. The one at the end of the hall by the restrooms hollered, "Clear!" Dig heard the other man jiggle the office doorknob.

"Door's locked," he told his partner. "Do we know where the keys are?"

"Pick it or kick it."

"They're not going to like it if we break the place up."

"So pick it. It's a friggin' office door, Johnson."

Dig looked around the office. There was no closet, nothing to hide behind. Just a tall file cabinet in the corner behind the desk.

He wished he had a weapon. Too late now.

Then he saw the recessed panel in the ceiling above the desk. An attic access panel.

One of the men outside shouted to the others a floor below. "We're coming. Just a minute." Then, lowering his voice, he said, "Hurry up. They want us downstairs."

Dig slipped off his shoes, took them with him as he climbed onto the desk, and stood on the papers scattered across the desktop. With the low ceiling, he had to bend his head to one side. The panel was stuck with paint.

"I've got ears, you know. This pick's stuck in my wallet. It's like it's embedded in the leather."

"News flash. Time to go on a diet."

"I wish we had another man, tonight. I don't like coming out here like this."

Dig hoped that between the heating system and the men's voices, any noise would be covered as he gave the panel a sharp push. One small flake of paint fluttered onto the desk when the plywood panel broke free. No time to clean it up. He placed the panel aside, shoved his shoes inside, then pulled himself up through the opening. There was barely room for him to sit up on the rafters. He pulled his legs up just as he heard the men's voices below.

"You go on down. I got this."

Dig lowered the panel back into place.

The lock clicked, and he felt the atmosphere in the room below change when the door opened. Warm air blew up through the cracks around the attic panel. Footsteps circled the room and stopped beneath him. He thought of the paint chip and wondered if he had left footprints on the papers with his sweaty socks. Then, just as quickly, he heard footsteps again, and the door slammed.

"All clear up here," he heard the man yell.

Dig exhaled, and the floor in the hallway creaked as the agent walked toward the stairs. That man should be fired, he thought. Certainly not up to his standards. He would have noticed the tiny fleck of paint. But he knew there weren't many operatives of his caliber, no matter what branch of service.

He set the panel aside and dropped down onto the desk— didn't bother closing it up. He might need it again.

From down below, he heard their voices and the scraping sounds as the men pulled out chairs. They were greeting one another and chatting, and the odor of cigar smoke wafted up the stairs. While they were still making lots of noise, Dig climbed down off the desk. Leaving his shoes off, he took slow and cautious steps across to the door.

Dig gripped the doorknob, rotated it one-half inch, then another, and another. He felt the latch give way, but it made no noise. Squatting down, he eased the door open and put his right eye to the crack.

His vantage point provided him with an excellent view down the staircase. Someone had covered the round table with a black cloth, and at the center, a candle burned in a crystal skull. Of the twelve chairs, all but one were occupied. He identified Beelzebub to the right of the empty chair, and there was Magog and Hellbender. Several of the others he recognized as well, although he did not know their Bonesman names. A cloud of smoke hung near the ceiling, and each man had a cut-crystal highball glass on the table filled with ice and amber-colored liquid.

"Let's get started," Beelzebub shouted over the din of voices. "Agents, you may leave us now." Dig heard the back door open and then close. The room quieted.

Beelzebub produced a short staff and pounded the heel of it on the table. "Hear ye, hear ye, by the power conferred upon me in the absence of our leader, Yorick, I do hereby call to order this convocation of the Patriarchs of the Order of Skull and Crossed Bones. If there be any man present who objects to my assumption of command, let him speak now." Dig noted that Beelzebub waited three seconds before continuing.

A man Dig did not recognize said, "I think the first order of business should be filling that chair." He pointed to the empty seat.

"You know we can't do that," Beelzebub said.

Magog asked, "Well, what's the story with Yorick's health now? Is there any chance of improvement?"

Beelzebub shook his head. "It's not good. He's in a wheelchair now. Some days when I visit, he doesn't even know who I am. But his doctors say he could live another ten years."

A man Dig recognized from a network television news desk said, "Lord, if that happens to me, I hope someone will take me out and shoot me." He drained his glass.

"Surely we can't leave the head chair empty for another ten years," Magog said. "Can't we change the charter?"

Side conversations broke out around the table.

Beelzebub raised the staff to quiet them. "I know Yorick's health is a problem, but remember, the man sacrificed a great deal for this organization." At that the others stopped speaking. "And our forebearers knew what they were doing when they decided that those who sit around this table will do so for life." He looked around at the other men. "The only way to quit our august body, gentlemen, is through death. You know that. And that will come to Yorick in due time. At that time, we will choose his successor. Until then, we continue as we are, holding his place as chair should he recover sufficiently to resume. Agreed?"

The group responded with a low rumble of inarticulate voices. Most of the men round the table looked at their drinks or their watches, or the ceiling.

They want him dead, Dig thought, and I'll be happy to oblige them.

"So on to the real reason I called this meeting. I received word within the last couple of hours that Caliban's body washed up on a beach in the northeastern corner of Guadeloupe." The murmuring rose in volume. "It's not clear what he was doing there, outside Pointe-à-Pitre, nor have they established a cause or time of death.

However, Caliban's associate Thor could not rule out that that this might be Thatcher's work."

Magog chimed in. "This has gone on far too long, been far too costly. I say we eliminate Thatcher and forget about the submarine."

"I wish it were that easy," Beelzebub said. "Thatcher has been in contact with too many others. We can't kill them all, can we?"

"I don't see why not," Hellbender said.

Diggory watched the faces around the table. Hellbender was a political cartoonist with a distinct pro-life view, but no one else seemed to see the humor in his comment.

"Be serious," their leader said. "What if we miss one? To make it worse, there are all these damn rumors of gold. I swear the Brits started those rumors after the war to goad the public into searching for the boat. They want to know what happened to their men."

"Maybe that's all Thatcher knows. Those rumors."

"Doubtful. We know the father knew more. But have any of you contemplated the consequences if this sub were to be found? What if proof of Operation Magic were to go public?" The man's voice had been rising, and he took a long swallow of his drink. He looked from one end of the table to the other.

"It's not as if we could fall much further in the polls," Hellbender said.

"This isn't just about the legacy. The future is at stake, too. We want our man in there," the news anchor said.

"After two miracles, we'll pull out a third."

A few men at the tabled chuckled.

Beelzebub stood up. "Think of all the Americans who died that day. My God, men, think about it. Think about the fucking reporters who couldn't wait to start digging for other similar cases related to Korea, Vietnam, the Gulf. And let's not even discuss more recent events. Do any of you want to be publicly connected to an organization responsible for that?"

The room went silent.

Finally, Magog spoke. "So, Bee, what do you suggest?"

"Thatcher knows something. That much is clear. Nobody else has searched that part of the Caribbean. Everyone else believed the story—that the sub went down off Panama. The problem with a salvage operation has always been the fact that we'd have to eliminate all involved with the operation. And the location was too close to the island of Guadeloupe. I say we give Thor the green light. Let Thatcher locate the sub first, and then have Thor destroy it and him. If there's anyone else around who Thatcher talked to, no one will believe them once the evidence is gone."

"And what about Thor?"

Diggory gripped the edge of door and leaned forward.

"You all know that only the men who sit at this table can know about what we do here. Yorick once had to sacrifice a child because of it. We never even told Caliban the truth about Magic, and he was our most trusted agent. No, we can't trust a man like Thor with that kind of information."

"But he's a Bonesman," Magog said.

Beelzebub closed his eyes and sighed. "Yes, but not a Patriarch. He has served us well. It's my job to act in Yorick's place, and I know what he would say. A Bonesman, yes, but…" His voice rose on the last word and hung there.

Several of the others laughed and nodded. Hellbender said, "Sounds like Yorick."

"I don't like killing one of our own," Magog said.

The TV anchorman said, "Thor might be Bones, but he's not one of us."

Beelzebub said, "Shall we vote, then?"

Dig eased the door shut and rose to a standing position. He'd seen every hand go up. His skin felt hot, and he pressed his forehead against the cool wood of the door. He raised his right hand

and began flexing the fingers, forming a white-knuckled fist and then releasing the grip and spreading his fingers wide, over and over again. He filled his lungs and then exhaled.

That empty chair? Thor intended to be Yorick's successor before the day was out.

CHAPTER FIFTY-SEVEN

Foggy Bottom

March 28, 2008

Riley stepped out of the shower, grabbed a towel, then stopped and stared at herself in the full-length mirror on the back of the bathroom door. On her boat, the only mirror was a small framed 9" x 12" rectangle that hung on the bulkhead inside the head. It had been many months since she had seen herself naked. From the front, she reckoned she didn't look half bad, in spite of the farmer tan. Her small, firm breasts and flat belly gave her a shape that was more streamlined than voluptuous, but she was proud of her lean body. She worked at it. It served her purposes on the boat, and since sex had not been one of her purposes since that day in Lima—and considering her scars, she supposed it never would be again—sexy was not something she needed to be. She turned sideways to check out her profile and winced.

Twisting, she leaned in over the vanity to take a closer look in the well-lit mirror over the sink. The scar tissue that stretched from the top of her shoulder to a point halfway down her back looked like an angry alien creature that had attached itself to her. The skin was mottled: red, brown, and bumpy. The scars weren't getting any better although her surgeons had claimed they would. She should put any thoughts of Cole Thatcher's sweet dimpled smile right out of her mind. Flipping the towel over her head and sliding it down the skin on her back, she thought if things ever were to go that far, the man would take one look at this body and flee.

Ten minutes later, when she opened the bathroom door onto the upstairs hall, she was dressed in some old winter clothes she had stored there when she'd moved aboard her boat. The jeans were loose, and she had smiled when she'd pulled on the Margaritaville long-sleeved T-shirt. She'd had to squeeze her feet into her sneakers after so many months of not wearing shoes. She collected her dirty clothes and transferred her passport to the back pocket of her jeans. Until she got some kind of a bag, she would just have to carry it in her pocket.

Across the hall, her father's bedroom door was ajar, but his bed was empty, the covers already drawn smooth. She had slept in until after ten, which was very unusual for her. The smell of fresh coffee wafting up the stairs tempted her, but after a brief debate with herself, she walked straight down the hall to the upstairs living room, where her father sat with his wheelchair drawn up to the window.

The townhouse was an odd design with the kitchen, dining room, and small bedroom downstairs. Upstairs, the bedrooms were at the back of the house while the living room stretched all across the front. She entered the room and felt a frisson of déjà vu. His back was to her, his chair angled so he could look down on the gray street through the big bay window. The weather had not improved overnight. Snowflakes drifted past the glass. Her father was dressed in a plaid sports shirt, dark slacks, and a cable-knit cardigan sweater. As his dementia had progressed, so had his incontinence. She winced at the smell as she rested her hand on his shoulder.

"Good morning, Dad."

"Elizabeth?"

"No, Dad. It's me, Maggie. How're you feeling this morning?"

"I'm fine." Her father twisted around in his chair to look at her. "It's Michael I'm worried about."

Riley turned away from him.

After Lima, when she had come back for good, she had tried moving in with him. But she learned soon enough that she made a lousy nursemaid. When she came home from work, after cooking her father's supper, she would go up to her room. He went into the sitting room and watched CNN nonstop. She didn't want to spend her evenings with him—not after what he'd done to her brother. She simply could not let go of that. If he hadn't forced Michael to go to Yale instead of MIT, her brother would still be alive.

When she turned back to him, he was watching the falling snow again. She studied the back of her father's head, wondering when his hair had gone pure white. She felt an ache in her chest. It had taken the threat of his death to dissolve some of that anger. He was still her dad, and she would lose him one day. She hadn't realized before yesterday how much that would hurt.

When he spoke again, he startled her. "I'm frightened for Michael."

"Dad. Shhh. Mikey's long gone, you know."

"He shouldn't have come to Washington." Her father's hands waved in the air as though shooing away flies. "If only he hadn't come, Elizabeth. It's all my fault."

She pulled the wheelchair a few inches back from the window so she could sit on the window seat. She put her hands on his knees. "Shhh, Dad."

"Numbers. Michael and numbers."

"Yeah, Dad. Mikey was the brilliant one."

"Just a glance, but he figured it out. Shouldn't have done that."

She felt helpless when he went off like this. He sometimes rambled for hours making no sense whatsoever, getting more and more agitated. Downstairs, she heard the door open and then voices. She wished Mrs. Wright would get rid of whoever it was and come up here to help her.

"Ugly little runt. Not like other people. But a good boy, I told them. He would listen." His voice had been steadily rising in pitch.

She pushed away the lock of hair that had fallen onto his forehead and tried to get him to look at her. Both his good eye and his lazy eye seemed to be rolling around in their sockets. She patted his cheek. "Dad, please. Don't get yourself worked up."

"They said he was dangerous. Knew too much. They wouldn't listen." His hands picked at the fuzz on the bottom hem of his cardigan.

"Shhh. I'll call Mrs. Wright."

"No, I said. Please. He's my boy."

This last came out as a wail and his eyes were glossy with tears.

Riley heard footsteps on the stairs. "Dad, listen. Mrs. Wright's coming. It's going to be OK."

He grabbed both her arms and squeezed so tight it hurt. "I *told* you, Elizabeth. There was nothing I could do. They wouldn't listen. I tried to stop them. They said *he had to die*."

"What? Dad, what are you talking about?"

Riley jumped when she heard a voice from across the room. "You know better than to speak of these things, Yorick."

Her father's eyes grew wide, and he moaned, then let go of her arms. She stood up and saw Diggory standing just inside the doorway.

CHAPTER FIFTY-EIGHT

The Atlantic Ocean

February 17, 1942

By the fifth day, Woolsey decided he might go mad before they ever got to Martinique.

When they first locked him in the hold with only a corpse for company, they left him in darkness for what seemed like a fortnight. But once they opened the door on him blinking and shivering, he learned it had only been about twelve hours. That first time, the captain came down to the hold and oversaw things himself, the pistol displayed on his waist. Lamoreaux only allowed two men into the compartment, and though he ignored Woolsey, he watched his crew's every move as they walked among the crates that contained the gold. The men removed Mullins's body, swept up the broken glass, and allowed Woolsey to go to the WC under guard.

After that, it was only Michaut who was allowed into the hold. They left the lights on for him during the day, shut them off at night. Michaut came in with his food rations and escorted him to use the toilet twice a day. The young man wasn't as friendly as he had been before the bomb. Woolsey ate in silence while Michaut waited for his dishes. If the two of them happened to pass another sailor in the confines of the sub's passages, likely as not, the Frenchman would curse under his breath or spit on the ground at Woolsey's feet.

After they turned the lights on and cleaned away the glass, Woolsey had played with the gold coins to amuse himself. The captain had collected the coins from the broken bottles and placed them in a cloth sack inside one of the crates. Woolsey took it out from time to time and poured the coins into his hands, letting them clang on the deck. Though his was a wealthy family, and he had never lacked for anything, still there was something glorious about feeling the heft and mass of that much gold. He passed the hours trying to calculate just how many coins were there in all the cases.

But after four days of not talking to another human being, he decided he just might be going crazy. When Michaut entered the hold, dropped his tin plate and mug onto a crate, then began to unload cutlery from his various pockets, Woolsey leaned against the bulkhead, his arms crossed. He watched the heart-shaped birthmark on the young man's face grow brighter under the scrutiny. Woolsey said, "So, have you got orders against talking to me?"

Michaut shook his head, but he refused to look at Woolsey. He sat down on another crate, his back turned.

Woolsey sat down on the crate next to his food and rubbed the stubble growth on his chin. "Any chance you could get me a razor, Kewpie?"

Michaut sighed and shook his head. Without turning around, he said, "Lieutenant, why do you want to blow up this boat? You hate the French people?"

Woolsey picked up a fork and wolfed down a couple of bites from his plate of stewed beef and potatoes, soaking up some of the rich wine gravy with a slab of French bread. He wiped his mouth on his sleeve.

"Michaut," he said at last. "This is war. It's not personal."

"But if you kill me, I think that is very personal."

"Yeah, well, I was following orders. Like you're following orders now."

Woolsey drained the mug of water while his young companion stood up and wandered over to one of the cases. Michaut pulled out the cloth sack and looked inside.

"You do realize, Henri, that by turning me over to the authorities in Martinique, you're killing me? They'll hang me for trying to blow up *Surcouf.*"

"Yes, but there is nothing I can do." He reached inside the bag and pulled out a handful of coins.

"Just as there was nothing I could do when I received my orders."

After another period of quiet, the young man said, "I hate this stupid war." He let the coins fall back into the bag, and the soft clinking noise sounded almost like music.

Woolsey smiled. "Not everyone feels that way. Some men are making a great deal of money off this war."

Woolsey watched the young man reach back into the bag, take several coins out, and place them in his pocket.

"That's what doomed *Surcouf,* you know. Not that gold. No one knew about that except your captain. But all the money the Allies have put into this old boat. No return on that."

Michaut replaced the bag in the crate.

Woolsey continued. "It's always about the money, isn't it? And politics. Power."

Michaut shrugged.

"Kewpie, what would you say if I told you that I'm not only a lieutenant in the Royal Navy?"

"I don't understand, sir."

"Neither do I sometimes. But I also work for some Americans. Got involved when I went to university in the States. A place called Yale. Ever heard of it?"

Michaut shook his head.

"Doesn't matter," Woolsey said. "They don't want you to know who they are. Very hush-hush, you know. They invited me to join their lot in the spring of '40. Anyway, lots of money to be made in a war like this, and these Yanks, boy, they know how to do it."

"I do not understand."

"Listen, man, somebody has got to build all these ships and planes, make the bombs and the bullets. They sell them to the government and make a fortune, and they know there will always be a need for more as long as we are at war."

"But many men are dying."

Woolsey shrugged. "Not their problem. But one thing they're not interested in is seeing America pour millions of dollars into an old French submarine. The problem is, General de Gaulle would never stand for seeing this boat retired. So she must be martyred."

Michaut turned to face Woolsey. "No. Is not necessary. That is why we go to Martinique."

"I'm not so sure we'll make it, my friend. When the Americans don't hear from me, they will send out planes looking for the *Surcouf*. There is something aboard this boat they do not want to see fall into the enemy's hands. In fact, I'm certain they are searching for us right now."

It was less than an hour after Michaut had left with his dirty dishes when the door to the hold opened again, and Gohin entered with Michaut. It was exactly what Woolsey had predicted would happen.

Gohin shouted, "*Allez. Vite.*"

"Come with us," Michaut said. "Le Capitaine want to talk to you."

The captain's cabin on board the *Surcouf* was quite large for a submarine. It contained a small writing desk and another sitting chair opposite. The bulkheads were paneled in rich, varnished wood. The captain turned from where he had been working at his desk when Woolsey entered. He lifted a white ceramic coffee mug, took a drink, then indicated the extra chair by gesturing with the mug.

"Sit down, Lieutenant."

Woolsey eased himself into the chair. He saw the plate on the desk and realized they had interrupted his meal.

"What's this Michaut tells me about something else on board this vessel that I know nothing about?"

"Do you remember the mail bag we got from that Canadian frigate a couple of days before we arrived in Bermuda?"

"Yes."

"There was a diplomatic pouch from London with highly classified documents in there. My instructions were to set the device aboard the *Surcouf* and then to deliver those documents to America. It's been several days now, and they have not heard from me. They will have figured out that something went wrong—that I'm still aboard this boat. I don't know what's in that pouch, sir, but I'm certain the Yanks are scouring the Atlantic right now looking for us. When they see you're headed for an enemy port, they won't hesitate."

"And where is this pouch now?"

"In the safe in the radio room."

"Michaut, take the lieutenant, get the pouch, and both of you come straight back here."

Ten minutes later, Woolsey placed the heavy canvas bag on the captain's desk. The pouch was of the sort often used for top-secret documents. The canvas was rubber-coated on the outside to make it waterproof and lead-lined to assure that the fabric could not be cut. Also, if the ship were to sink, the pouch would not float to the surface later. The top of the pouch was folded over several times and was secured with a steel bar and a combination lock.

The captain sat down and rubbed his own day's growth of stubble as he stared at the pouch. "You do not know what this contains?"

"No, sir. But I do know that it was sent by a special envoy to the American president. They only told me the code words for these documents. They called it Operation Magic. I know that neither one of us would be permitted to read it. But if you are headed to Martinique to surrender this boat to the Vichy government there, you will be passing top-secret classified material into German hands. The Yanks know this, and you can be certain they have every ship and plane they can afford out looking for us." Woolsey knew that only a few select Americans knew about the pouch, but they wielded enough power to make this threat very real.

"I have been worried about being spotted, so I have taken an unconventional route. At present, we are passing between the islands of Guadeloupe and La Désirade. It is one of the last places they would look for a submarine."

"I hope you're right."

"So, you are certain you do not know the combination to this pouch?"

Woolsey looked at the numbers on the combination lock, and he wondered. The special envoy did have a sense of humor. Woolsey asked himself if he really wanted to know what was inside. And did he want the Frenchman to know? Lamoreaux was the enemy now, but he could also torture Woolsey. He knew himself well enough to know that he would not hold out for long. He was no hero. And Woolsey suspected they would never make it to Martinique.

"I suggest you try the numbers three-two-two."

CHAPTER FIFTY-NINE

Foggy Bottom

March 28, 2008

Riley was still trying to comprehend what her father had just said. She felt as though she were being carried along by the swift-moving current as she had in that river on Dominica, with the scenery flashing past before she could take it all in. What had her father just said?

Diggory stepped through the doorway, and Mrs. Wright followed behind him, a smug smile on her face.

"Dig?" Riley said. "What are you talking about? Who's Yorick?" There were so many other questions she wanted to ask him, such as why he had lied to her about her father's stroke, why he wanted her there in DC. But she couldn't stop thinking about her father's words. *I would have stopped it if I could—he had to die.* Was he talking about Michael? No, it couldn't be true. It was the illness talking, making him say crazy things.

Looking at Dig, she pointed at her father. "Did you hear what he just said?"

Dig crossed the room and stood behind her father's wheelchair. He pulled the chair back from the window a little, then walked around in front so her father could see him. "I believe he mentioned something about approving the murder of his own son."

"That's crazy. No way that's true."

"I'm afraid it is, my dear. There is a lot you don't know about this man."

Her father had loosened a piece of yarn from his sweater, and he pulled at it, refusing to look at Diggory.

"Dad?"

He would not look up at either of them.

"Isn't that right, Yorick?"

"Diggory, leave him alone. And stop calling him that."

"But that's his name—his Bones name."

The current was pulling her under again. She could not breathe. "What?" No. She would have known if her father had been in Skull and Bones. He would have told her.

"I've known your father much longer than I've known you, Riley. He was a sort of mentor to me in Skull and Bones. Helped get me on at the Agency."

Dig appeared to be addressing her, yet his eyes were on her father as though he really intended the words for him. Riley tried to process what he was saying.

"Yes, Yorick used to be a very powerful man, before he became this pathetic, simpering, mindless shell sitting here in his own urine. And to think he's a Patriarch."

"What are you talking about? Dig, I don't know what you're playing at with this stroke story and luring me up here."

"Don't flatter yourself, Riley. You're only a pawn in this game. This is between me and Yorick."

"Then why did you go to such lengths to get me here?" Riley placed her hands on her hips, trying to appear more in control than she felt. "It's time for answers, and no cock-and-bull story about Skull and Bones or my brother."

His eyes remained on her father. "You've been asking me for the truth, darling, so here it is. Fourteen years ago, when I was getting started with the Agency, I got a call from one of the Patriarchs. They had a little problem. The son of one of their own was some sort of math genius."

She stumbled back a step, as though his words had delivered a physical blow. "Stop that. You're lying," she said. She wanted to cover his mouth, but she could not move any closer to him.

"The young man had found some documents while skulking about in his father's study. Not only did he manage to decode them, but he was also able to extrapolate what they meant in the bigger picture."

She thrashed her head from side to side saying, "No, no, no."

Dig continued speaking to her, but staring at her father. "The son told his father that he intended to go public with it. Something had to be done, and the men your father associates with never get their own hands dirty. They always call in someone else to clean up their messes. Someone like me."

Her father lowered his face into his hands, and his shoulders shook. "No," she said, unable to take her eyes off her father. "You're a goddamn liar," she said, but she was thinking *I slept with him—I slept with my brother's murderer.* And she felt the acid rising in her throat.

Diggory turned away from the old man and walked to the center of the room. "It has to be unanimous, you know." He spoke to the back of her father's head. "Doesn't it, Yorick? When the Patriarchs vote to have someone killed, I mean. What's one life when there are dollars to be made, empires to build? And in your father's case, they rewarded him for his vote." He lowered his voice and said, "You earned first chair with that vote." And then he shouted, "Didn't you, Yorick?"

Riley slid around behind her father's chair and stood between the old man and Diggory. "Shut up and get out of here." Her voice came out in a whisper.

"Couldn't do the dirty work yourself, though, could you, Yorick? You always had me to call on. Well, all that's finished now. I'm not your janitor anymore. Today, I'm taking your chair."

Riley turned to the housekeeper. "Mrs. Wright, call the police. Tell them we have an intruder."

"Silly girl," Dig said.

The woman glanced at Dig, and a look passed between them. Mrs. Wright came up to her and clamped a large hand around Riley's arm.

He laughed. "She works for us. Always has, you know. Someone had to keep an eye on this demented old fool—make sure he wasn't babbling about former projects or trying to confess his part in his son's murder."

Dig walked past her, clutched a handful of her father's white hair, and jerked his head back. "That was a stupid move, Yorick."

Riley lunged forward, but the housekeeper grabbed her other arm and held her.

Diggory leaned in close and spoke in a hushed tone. "Deathbed confessions won't do your soul any good, old man. If there is a hell, your reservation is confirmed. And you know what? You're about to find out—"

Riley struggled to free her arms.

The old man's good eye stared at Dig. He hissed one word. "Bastard."

Dig's open hand smacked across her father's face so hard the old man's head bounced off the handle of the wheelchair.

"No! Stop!" Riley broke free and launched herself at him, but Dig was too fast.

CHAPTER SIXTY

The Library of Congress

March 28, 2008
Earlier that morning

Cole Thatcher climbed out of the cab at the corner of Independence Avenue and First Street, pulled the collar of his yellow rain jacket tight around his neck, and hoisted his small duffel bag onto his shoulder. Even with his old fisherman's knit wool sweater, he was freezing in this weather. And though he had relented and put socks on, his boat shoes weren't working to keep the cold out either.

He stepped gingerly onto the icy sidewalk that led over to the foot of the steps and then looked up at the massive edifice: the Library of Congress. He'd told Theo he needed a bigger library, and this was the biggest library in the country. That it happened to be located in the same city where Riley was had not influenced his decision to drive *Shadow Chaser* from the Saintes to Pointe-à-Pitre all night in order to catch a predawn flight to San Juan then on to DC. Not a bit.

He trotted up the steps, eager to get inside out of the cold. Cole knew the library building well. His work on the Ocracoke

Shipwreck Survey at East Carolina had brought him here on many occasions to search old maps, ships' logs, personal accounts, etc., as they'd worked to identify the thousands of ships that had foundered off Cape Hatteras.

Today was different, though. He nodded to the librarians behind the counter in the Main Reading Room, then headed for the stairs to the second floor and the Hispanic and Early American collections. Today, he was here to learn what he could about this End of Days business.

* * *

An hour later, Cole leaned back in his chair and sighed. This was getting him nowhere. There was far too much information on this Mayan calendar. Most of what he'd been reading here had little to do with the sky-is-falling-mania he had read about on the Internet. He'd learned that the Mayan calendar was also sometimes called the Aztec calendar, and it was all based on the Aztec Sun Stone that was discovered in Mexico City in 1790. In fact, though, the Mayan calendar was really three calendars: the 260-day religious calendar, the solar calendar, which divides the years into 365 days, and the long-count calendar. That's the one, Cole discovered, that is supposed to end on 12/21/12. That calendar started counting off the days on Day One and continued to an end date. The Mayans noted all the important days in their history by that long count calendar. By correlating some long count dates inscribed in stone monuments of known Mayan historical events, archeologists were able to fix the start date for the long count as August 11, 3114 BC.

He didn't see how the Mayan long-count calendar could relate to the forty-year calendar they had found on Dominica. He had entered the 12/21/12 date into the device and learned it would fall on a Friday. But how did that help him? There had to be something more here. He rubbed his hand across his forehead. His temples were throbbing, and he hadn't eaten anything since the nighttime run on *Shadow Chaser* up to Pointe-à-Pitre. They no longer served anything resembling food on airplanes.

He wanted to talk to Riley about this Mayan calendar stuff. But more than that, he *needed* to know that she was OK. He reached into the pocket of his rain jacket and fingered the business card he had picked up on her boat. It only had an e-mail address and a cell phone number. He checked his watch and saw that it was almost noon. He wasn't sure she wanted to see him, so he was reluctant to call. She might be at the hospital. Probably was. But he could find out where she was staying. He knew that her father had worked for the US Foreign Service, and it was a good bet his name was Riley, too. How difficult could it be to locate his address? After all, here he was in the largest repository of information in the world—and there were plenty of computers available.

Twenty minutes later, Cole was riding in another cab, and he asked the driver to let him out a block past the address he had found for Richard Riley. The street was lined with two-story attached houses that looked as if they were at least a hundred years old. He wanted to get a good look at their place first. He wasn't sure yet what he intended to do. He wouldn't be able to stay out here in this cold very long. Should he walk up and knock on the door? What if she answered? What would he say?

He paid the driver and climbed out onto the sidewalk. Theirs was the brick front with the bay window upstairs and the black iron gate that separated the little front yard from the street. He supposed it was a lovely neighborhood in the summer, but now the trees that lined the street stretched their bare black branches toward the sky like spindly thorns. It had started snowing during the drive, so Cole dropped his duffel and pulled the hood of his rain jacket up over his head. He cinched the string tight under his chin.

He was still standing there staring down the street a block away from the house he presumed belonged to Riley's father when he saw a black Lincoln Town Car pull up from the opposite direction. The door to the backseat opened, and a man climbed out and hurried up to the house. Though he was now wearing a heavy overcoat, Cole recognized him as the same man Cole had last seen on Dominica ushering Riley into that taxi van.

Cole began to walk down closer to the two-story house. He wondered if they would be heading out to the hospital soon and he might catch a glimpse of her. As he drew closer to the house, he saw the ground floor windows were all covered with heavy curtains. He tried to look nonchalant so the neighbors wouldn't think he was some kind of peeping tom. Perhaps if he crossed to the opposite side of the street, he would be able to see through the upstairs window. When he stepped up onto the far curb, he turned, and he could make out the form of a person, a man he thought, sitting in a wheelchair facing the window. He could barely make out another figure standing behind him. The man sitting in a wheelchair appeared to be crying.

Then Cole recognized the hair and the profile of the woman standing behind him. Riley.

Her body was turned away from the window as though she were talking to someone else in the room. He saw another woman step up behind her and take her arm, then another man moved between the window and the old man.

Cole was trying to decide what he should do, knock on the door or wait and observe—when he saw a flash of movement and heard her voice shout loudly enough to penetrate to the cold outside air. Just two words.

"No! Stop!"

CHAPTER SIXTY-ONE

Washington, DC

March 28, 2008

Dig caught Riley's arm and twisted her around, and with his forearm pressing against her larynx, he held her tight against his body. His other hand was smashed against her cheek, turning her head so she could see his face. The bastard was smiling.

From downstairs, Riley heard the sound of the front door opening. A voice called out, "Hello?"

Dig jerked his head toward the stairs, and Mrs. Wright left the room.

With her one free hand, Riley pulled at the arm across her throat, trying to open up a small airway. The harder she struggled, the tighter his grip. When the black started closing in, she stopped fighting him. He loosened the pressure on her neck. She sucked in air.

"You see, Yorick? Your daughter is here in my arms." He jerked her around so her father could see her.

The left side of her father's face still showed red where Dig's hand had struck. His good eye glared at Dig.

"Don't we make a lovely couple? We did once. Down in Lima. She didn't tell you? Once I realized who she was, it was easy. She wasn't a bad lay, but knowing I was fucking the great Yorick's daughter made it all the sweeter."

"Kill you," her father's words came out in a breathy hiss.

Dig laughed. "Your time is done, old man. With you gone and proof of Operation Magic in my hands, no one will oppose me. I'll have taken everything that was once yours. Imagine—first your son, then your daughter, and finally, your *bastard protégé* sitting in your chair."

While Dig was talking, Riley had forced her body to go limp. Then, when Dig was concentrating on her father, she slammed the heel of her sneaker down on his foot. He groaned, and the pain caused him to loosen his arm enough for her to continue her downward motion into a squat. She slipped right out from under his arm. Pivoting around and shooting upward, she brought her knee up into his groin with every bit of anger and strength she had in her.

Again she heard him moan as his body bent. She stepped back, trying to get out of his reach, but his arm shot out. He grabbed a handful of fabric at the front of her shirt. He straightened up with effort and pulled her to him. Though she hit back and landed several good punches to his body, he didn't flinch.

Then both his hands were around her throat, and she could not breathe. He pulled her face so close to his, she could see the watery tears shining in his blue eyes. Dig's attempt to smile through his own pain turned his face into a horrible grimace of clenched teeth and drawn cheeks. She didn't want to look into those eyes, but he held her so close, there was nowhere else to look.

In the distance, she heard another voice she thought was her father's, but the roaring in her ears made it too difficult to hear.

Dig's nostrils flared, and she felt the hot breath on her face. He was taunting her. He had air, she had none. His fingers tightened on her throat, and she felt his fingernails dig into her skin. She punched at his body with both her hands, tried to reach up, to get past his forearms and elbows to scratch at those eyes that were burning into her.

"Yorick," Dig shouted. "I've been waiting for this day. You didn't get to watch me kill your son." His spittle sprayed her face. "But this time, you'll get to watch it all."

Riley did not want to die. Not like this. Not staring at this man, her heart filled with hate. Her chest felt as if it were going to explode, while at the same time she grew weaker. With no idea whether it would work or not, she unbuckled the big dive watch on her left wrist and laced the strap through the fingers of her right hand, the big glass and metal dial on the outside of her knuckles. Then, with every bit of strength she had left in her, she swung her fist at Dig's head. Just as she struck, she saw her father standing, launching himself onto Dig's back.

The pain in her fingers was excruciating, but Dig's eyes went unfocused for a second, and blood smeared down from his temple. In the next moment, his face reddened with rage. He roared and flung her away. In the second before she hit the wall, she sucked in air before the impact knocked it out of her again.

The side of her head struck the wall first. The blow didn't knock her unconscious, but she couldn't move for several seconds. She was aware of lying there in a heap on the floor, helpless, but there seemed to be some disconnect between her brain and her limbs.

She opened her eyes and saw Dig's back. He was leaning over her father's wheelchair. Her father's legs were twisted.

Riley heaved herself to her knees and crawled over to the couch. From that angle, she could see the hands around her father's throat, just as they had been around hers. She saw her father's red face, the fear in his eyes.

"Dad," she croaked as she used the couch to pull herself to a standing position. She picked up the ceramic lamp, raised it above her, and brought it crashing down on Dig's head.

He released her father and turned to face her. Another gash in his forehead dripped a jagged line of blood.

"You bitch," he said before he went for her.

She didn't have enough strength left to put up much of a fight. He knocked her to the floor again with one backhanded blow to the face. When she got up, she licked her lip, tasted her own blood. The room was tilting, her vision blurred. Where was he? She blinked her eyes, trying to clear them.

Then she saw him. He was standing behind her father's wheelchair now, his big palms gripping the sides of the old man's head like a pair of earmuffs. Her father's lazy eye shone white, while his good eye danced in the socket as he tried to see what Dig was doing.

She pushed against the floor and struggled to her knees.

Then her father's good eye focused on her, and he said, "I'm so sorry."

Dig roared, "Yorick!" and twisted the head around to the right with a sickening crunch.

Riley screamed, "Dad!"

Dig released his grip and jumped back, his hands high in the air like those of a runner who had just won the race of his life. He danced back and forth from one foot to the other, his bloody face alight with laughter.

Her father's head fell on his chest at an unnatural angle, the lock of white hair falling forward again. More than anything she wanted to run to her father, to fix him, to straighten his neck and brush back that lock of hair.

When Dig lowered his arms and looked at her, she knew he intended her to be next.

So she leaped to her feet and ran.

Riley made it into the hall before Dig reached the door. He was so much bigger and faster, though; she could never outrun him. She would have to outmaneuver him.

When she reached the top of the stairs, he grabbed the tips of her fingers on her arm's backswing. She whipped around and smashed her free hand down onto his, breaking his grip. Dig howled with rage. He lunged after her, but she dodged his grip, pivoted around, and started down the stairs, taking them three at a time.

But Dig must have been taking four steps with each of his strides because when they reached the bottom, she felt the backward tug as his fingers closed around her shirttail. She dug her shoes in even harder, thinking that if only she could make it to the door and scream, someone might hear her on the street and come help her.

That was when something flashed past her right side at the farthest edge of her field of vision. She heard a metallic clang and a crack at the same time. The pressure pulling at the back of her shirt released, nearly causing her to fall face-first onto the floor. She slowed, glanced over her shoulder, then came to a complete stop inside the front door.

There, at the bottom of the stairs, was Cole Thatcher standing over Dig's crumpled body, holding the lid to Mrs. Wright's soup pot in his right hand.

CHAPTER SIXTY-TWO

Washington, DC

March 28, 2008

All Cole could think of as he looked at her standing in the entry like a frightened fawn ready to bolt, was *what has that son of a bitch done to her?* Riley's lower lip was swollen and split, her chin streaked with blood. Her neck shone with the imprint of fingers and thin red slits where fingernails had pierced the skin. A big knot of a goose egg swelled on her right temple. She stood there, unmoving, staring at him. He heard the sound of traffic outside, the ticking of a clock somewhere in the house. In the seconds that passed as he tried to think of what to say to her, her blank eyes filled, and tears dripped down her already-wet cheeks.

"Cole?" she said. She sounded confused.

He walked to her and put his arms around her, inhaling the scent of her. He touched her hair and attempted to lay her head on his shoulder, but her body remained rigid. He slid his hand from her hair to the silky soft skin of her neck, and he felt the flutter of her runaway pulse. His own heart and body were reacting to the closeness of her, and he felt the fierce heat of anger together with an overwhelming need to protect her.

Cole would have been willing to stand there for hours sheltering her in the safety of his arms, but from the kitchen he heard a dull thudding, like someone pounding on a door. A muffled voice called out for help. Riley's body jerked away from him, ready to run.

He held her at arm's length and moved his head back and forth as her eyes darted around the room. He tried to get her to focus on him. "It's OK," he said, keeping his voice soft. "She can't get out. That's the woman who came downstairs when I let myself in earlier. She tried to stop me, and we had a little disagreement," he said.

He didn't tell her there had been a moment when he thought the old Amazon was going to get the better of him. She was a fighter, and she had both a height and reach advantage on him. But his high-school wrestling career had come back to him, and he'd managed to force a biceps slicer onto her arm and got her elbow into a compression lock. The old gal did as she was told after that. "She's in the pantry, which for some reason, has a bolt and hasp and a padlock on it. If you tell me to let her out, I'll go do it, but I wouldn't recommend it."

"We have to go," Riley said.

He noticed she would not look at the unconscious figure on the floor. "What about your father?" he asked.

She jerked out of his arms and turned away to face the front door. "We have to go," she repeated.

Cole decided not to ask again.

He rummaged in a coat closet in the entry and found a man's heavy coat and a hand-knit scarf. At his bidding, she threaded her arms through the sleeves. She was barely tolerating his ministrations, he thought as he wrapped the scarf round her neck, covering the purpling bruises. She was desperate to get out of that house.

Grabbing his duffel, he led her to the front door. Before turning the doorknob, he glanced back once at the still form on the floor. He thought of the marks on her throat, and his grip on the duffel strap tightened until he felt his fist trembling. The man was still breathing. Cole saw the heavy metal pan lid, and for the first time in his life, he considered taking another man's life.

As though she could read his thoughts, Riley said, "We have to go. Now."

Cole glanced around for something he could use to tie him up, but Riley tugged at his arm. The man might regain consciousness at any minute. He wanted her to be gone, their trail cold.

He hustled her down the sidewalk toward the major thoroughfare at the end of the block. At the intersection, he hailed a cab. When they'd both slid into the backseat and closed the door, the driver turned around and asked, "Where to?"

Cole was starting to consider the possibilities when Riley surprised him by speaking in a clear voice, "Thirty-four ten Prospect Street, Georgetown."

The cab driver nodded and pulled away from the curb.

Cole turned to Riley and raised his eyebrows.

"It's my sister's place," she said, and angling her body toward the window, she rested her cheek against the glass and closed her eyes.

Cole opened his mouth, then closed it. Sister?

* * *

When the cab pulled to the curb after what seemed like an interminable, silent ride through the city's traffic, Cole peered out the window at their destination.

"Dang!" he said, staring up at the immense, five-story, brick Georgian mansion. The front of the home was festooned with white windows in different shapes, from round ports to the large multipaned sash windows on the lower floors. Next to the front door, he saw a bronze plaque with the date 1787.

Riley sat up straight, tucked her hair behind her ear, and said, "Let's go."

She opened her door and climbed out, so Cole paid the driver and followed. Riley was already at the front door ringing the bell.

"Do you want to tell me what's going on? I didn't know you had a sister."

Before she could answer him, a young, slender African American woman with close-cropped hair opened the door. She wore a black turtleneck sweater with black pants and black-framed glasses with narrow, rectangular lenses. When she smiled, her teeth were so white they seemed almost to light up the gray day. Her smile faded when she got a closer look at Riley's face.

"Miss Riley," she said. "My gosh, are you all right? Please, come in out of the cold. Oh my god, she'll be so happy to see you!"

"Thanks, Kayla," Riley said. "So she is here? I need to talk to her."

"Of course. I'll clear her calendar for the rest of the day. Just let me take your coats."

From upstairs, a voice called out, "Kayla?"

The young woman rolled her eyes. "Hang on," she said to Riley. "I'll go tell her you're here." She hurried down the hall and disappeared.

"What is this place?" Cole asked as he hung his oilskin jacket in the entryway closet.

"I told you. My sister lives here."

Riley had no sooner finished speaking than Cole heard shrieks from somewhere inside the house. When he turned to look, a tall, light-skinned African American woman wearing a bright-pink blouse and flowered pants came running down the hall, her sandals clacking on the polished wood floors.

"That's Hazel," Riley said.

"Mmm. I can see the family resemblance."

The woman scooped Riley up in her arms and shrieked, "Girlfriend!" Cole could not help but notice the woman's voluptuous, hourglass figure and the low-cut blouse that revealed her ample cleavage. With black hair that fell in soft waves around her shoulders, he thought she looked like a human defibrillator—she could jumpstart the heart of a dead man. After she'd spun Riley around once, she set her back on the floor, held her at arm's length, and looked down at her.

"What happened to you?" Hazel's voice had changed to a very businesslike tone. "Kayla, back bedroom bath. Get the kit." She glared at Cole. "Did you have anything to do with this?"

Riley patted Hazel's shoulder. "No, no. He's a friend. I don't think I'd be here if it weren't for him."

Hazel nodded, then put her arm around Riley's shoulders and began ushering her down the hall. Kayla took up position on the other side. Glancing back over the top of Riley's head, Hazel said, "Come on. You, too."

Cole followed the women down the hall, through a larger entry, and past a huge grand staircase with gilt banisters. They continued down another hallway to a small bedroom that overlooked an empty swimming pool. Hazel directed Riley to sit on the bed, while Kayla slipped into the bathroom. She returned seconds later with a large plastic case.

Cole sat on the edge of a plumped armchair by the window and leaned forward, his hands clasped between his knees. He felt awkward and helpless as he watched Hazel rip open packets and swab at Riley's facial wounds.

After examining the lower lip, the lump on her temple, and the bruises on her neck, Hazel said, "Looks like you were lucky, sister. The last woman I saw with marks like these on her neck was dead. Do you want to talk about it?"

Riley sighed. She wet her lips with her tongue. "Not really."

"If you want me to keep on helping out here, you need to tell me what happened. I've got Kayla's safety and mine to consider, too."

Riley's shoulders sagged even lower. "You remember Diggory Priest? He's the guy—"

"I know who he is. The asshole from Lima."

Riley nodded. "He claimed my father had had a stroke, but it was all a lie."

Cole cursed under his breath.

"Dig wanted to lure me back up here from the islands," Riley continued, her voice even, almost a monotone. "This morning, Dad was saying a lot of crazy stuff." She paused and closed her eyes, licked her lips. "Then Dig showed up. He said he'd known my dad for years, that they were both in Skull and Bones at Yale. He said..." She covered her mouth with her hand.

At the words Skull and Bones, Cole sat up straighter.

She lowered her hand to her lap and looked at Hazel. "*My dad a Bonesman?* I would have known. And he said..."

It can't be that bad, Riley, he thought. Say it. He wanted to take her in his arms and tell her he would never let anything hurt her again. If she'd let him. But he was the outsider here, and for the moment, as far as the women were concerned, he might just as well be invisible.

She took a deep breath and continued in a monotone. "Dig said awful things. He talked about taking over Skull and Bones and something about Operation Magic. The way he looked at my dad— it was awful. And he kept saying crazy things. About Michael. He claimed he did it, and Dad knew all about it." She grasped Hazel's arm and bit her lower lip. "That's not possible, is it?"

Cole wasn't sure what she was talking about, but he couldn't bear watching her suffer like that. He stood, took a step toward the bed, and called out her name.

Hazel waved him back. He clenched his fists, stepped back, and perched on the edge of the chair again.

Riley shuddered and her eyes focused on something in the distance as though she were reliving the afternoon's horror. "Dig told my dad he seduced me in Lima. Fucked *me* to get back at *him*. Said he was going to kill me and make my dad watch." Her hands went to her throat and touched the bruises. "But I fought back. And he..." One tear rolled down her cheek. She closed her eyes. "Dig killed my father." The last three words came out without emotion.

Cole jumped to his feet. "I knew I should have killed that son of a bitch."

Hazel's eyes flashed him a warning. She turned back to Riley. "Shhh, baby," she said, pulling Riley's head to her chest and rocking her back and forth.

Cole strode to the window and looked out at the empty pool. He put his hand over his mouth and pulled it down across his chin, feeling the rough stubble of his day-old beard. The trees on the grounds beyond the pool were black and barren against the gray sky. He turned back around to look at her. He had never felt so helpless in his life. He swore he would make this guy pay.

Riley's eyes were wide open, staring but unseeing.

"Shhh," Hazel repeated. "There was nothing you could do." He read her lips when she mouthed to Kayla, "She's in shock." Cole could see Riley's body trembling, see the built-up tension in the taut tendons of her neck.

He was wondering how much longer he could just stand there, watching these women, doing nothing. He saw Kayla hand Hazel a couple of pills and a glass of water. "Now, honey," Hazel said, placing the pills in Riley's palm, "go on and take these. It'll help you sleep."

Riley shook her head and turned away from Hazel.

"You need to get some rest. Kayla will stay with you."

Cole saw Riley's shoulders lift and then fall. "All right," she said, and then she tossed the pills into her mouth.

The two women stretched Riley out on the bed, removed her shoes, and covered her with a blanket. At first, she lay there, eyes wide open, staring at the ceiling, but within less than a minute, her breathing slowed and her eyes closed.

CHAPTER SIXTY-THREE

Washington, DC

March 28, 2008

Dig groaned when he brought his right hand up and touched the knot on the right side of his skull. What? He opened his eyes, but all he saw was a white ceiling. He rolled his head to the side and tried to focus his blurry vision on the stairs and a doorway beyond.

Pain stabbed at the back of his eyes when he tried to sit up. He screwed up his face and pressed the heels of his hands against his eyelids, then he looked up and shook his head, trying to clear it. He remembered where he was: the Riley house. He spread the fingers of his right hand, then squeezed them into a fist. Yorick. He flexed his hand again. Dig remembered the satisfying crack the old man's neck made when it broke—and the intense pleasure that had flowed through him from his head to his groin. He stared at his fist. He had felt the power pass into him. Then he'd seen Riley, and he had never wanted a woman as much.

But she ran—and he chased and nearly caught her. Then it was a blank.

He should have finished her in Lima. That was how he had planned it. Then, he was going to squeeze the life from her as Yorick watched. And again, she had thwarted his plans.

There was another noise in the house. Pounding. Cries. He was not alone.

When he stood, the dizziness made him wobble, and he reached for the banister to steady himself. The nausea was so strong he thought he was going to vomit.

"Help! Somebody get me out of here!" He could understand the words when he stood in the kitchen doorway. He recognized the voice. It wasn't Riley.

She was gone. Again. He would find her and finish this now.

He walked to the front door, opened it a crack, and looked out into the front yard. The bright light seared his eyeballs. It had stopped snowing. He looked both ways. No sign of her. He had no idea how long he had been unconscious.

Back inside the house, the shouting was louder.

"Hold on," he said.

Inside the kitchen, he found a door with a hasp with an unlocked padlock hanging loose. He lifted the lock, and the door swung into him hard. He stepped aside, and Mrs. Wright tumbled out. She caught herself and lifted a hand to push back the gray hairs that had fallen loose on either side of her head.

"What happened to you?" he said.

"Where is he?"

"Who?"

"That fella. You were upstairs, and I went down to see who was at the door. Fella came barging in asking to see Riley. I tried to stop him—"

"Describe him."

"Shorter than you. Brown hair, stocky build. Wearing a yellow-and-blue rain slicker. Like to broke my arm before he locked me in there." She pointed to the pantry. "Had to put a lock on that door to keep old Mr. Riley from eating all the cookies. I found him drinking maple syrup from the bottle once. Crazy as a loon, that one." She pulled at the tails of her shirt and straightened her sleeves. "Never expected I'd be the one shoved in there."

"Shut up," he said. The woman was getting on his nerves.

It had to be Thatcher. In Washington. He was more resourceful than Dig had expected. So, they were together now, Riley and Thatcher. The son was turning out to be even more of an irritant than the father had been. He would see to both of them.

"You've got no reason to talk to me that way," the housekeeper said. "Not after all I've done for you. That fella's gone, then? Is the daughter up there with her father? I'm surprised the old man's not hollering down here for his lunch."

This woman talked too much. Then, in another one of those serendipitous moments, his mind flitted to the elder Thatcher, then back to Yorick. Dig smiled.

"Follow me upstairs," he said.

* * *

Just over an hour later, Dig pulled off his gloves and surveyed the scene in Yorick's bedroom, imagining the ideas that would be running through the minds of the rescue workers who would be called to the scene—by the smell if nothing else. He flexed the fingers of his right hand and nodded, pleased with his work. This was getting to be a theme for this whole affair. A signature. But he was so much more adept at staging than those yokels in Cornwall. Yorick was thin enough, he'd almost fit in Riley's underwear. It didn't matter, though, that the panties and bra had ripped when he'd dragged them on the old man's corpse. It was all part of the scenario. And Dig had been surprised—and not a little disgusted—to find that the Wright woman had drawers full of black, lacy things and various electric apparatus. He hoped it would make the press. He could see the headlines now. Murder-suicide death pact between former ambassador and housekeeper.

At the bottom of the stairs, he looked around, thought back over his entry. No, he hadn't touched anything else. Before going outside, he pulled his gloves back on and checked the coat closet for a hat. He found a black cap with a short bill that he pulled down over his eyebrows, and he turned up the collar on his jacket.

He exited the house at a fast, steady pace and turned right, following the street to the end of the block, where he turned right again. There, idling at the curb where he'd told him to wait, was the black Lincoln with his driver reading a newspaper behind the wheel. Dig opened the back door, slid inside, and leaned his aching head back against the warm leather.

"Georgetown," he said.

CHAPTER SIXTY-FOUR

Georgetown

March 28, 2008

Hazel turned to him. "Follow me," she whispered.

Cole allowed her to lead him away from Riley's room, down hallways and through several rooms. He wondered how big the house was; already, he wasn't sure he could find his way back to Riley. When they got to a library with windows that overlooked the street, Hazel closed the door and crossed to the bar.

"I don't know about you, but after that, I could use a drink." She pulled out a bottle of Maker's Mark and poured several fingers into two crystal glasses. She handed him one, then pointed toward a couple of chairs in the corner.

"What was that you gave her?"

"Just a mild sleeping pill. She never takes meds, so it doesn't take much to knock her out." Hazel shook her head. "That woman is the toughest person I know, male or female." She took a long drink. "It must have been pretty damn bad to shake her up like that. I've got a feeling I should be thanking you for saving her life." She raised her glass as though toasting him.

Cole shrugged. He looked around the room wondering how he'd come to this place. He should have done more, he thought.

"Did you see her throat? The man who had his hands around her like that intended to kill her. He probably still does."

"Hang on," Cole said. "Things have been happening too fast. Let's back up a bit. I'm Cole Thatcher." He stuck out his hand.

"Oh!" she said, flashing him a lascivious smile. "So you must be Riley's buck naked redneck. How d'ya do?" Her eyes danced and sparked, giving his entire body the once-over. Then she took his hand in her strong dry grip. "Hazel Kittredge."

"It seems you know a few more intimate details about me than I do about you."

She laughed and drained her glass in one long pull. "Well, you're wondering who I am and how two so very different people like Maggie Riley and Hazel Kittredge came to be such good friends. And trust me, you are not the first to ask."

"She said you are her sister."

He saw her purse her lips in an attempt at a smile before she looked away. When she spoke, Cole heard the choked emotion in her voice.

"Riley and I met," she said, "when we were nine years old and both our daddies were posted to the US Embassy in Barbados. We looked so much alike back then, people often took us for sisters. I tried to stay out of the sun, but that girl was outside so much, she was darker than me. Some little girls played house or princess, but we played sisters."

Cole watched her throw back the remainder of her whiskey. She swallowed and stared into space as though she were looking back at those two little girls.

"My family was transferred to Cairo for a few years, but I met up with Riley again when we were all posted to Paris. Time and distance hadn't changed a thing. We were still sisters even though we were teenagers, and we didn't look a damn thing alike anymore. She'd stayed small and lean," Hazel said with a laugh, "and I just kept busting out all over." She waved a hand in the air to indicate her body.

"That's not a bad thing," he said. "It looks very good on you."

She dabbed at her eye. "Ooh, Riley was right. You are a Southern gentleman."

"I grew up in Florida. I don't know if that counts as the South."

She smiled. "Honey, if you're black, Florida is the South for sure."

He nodded. "So you've stayed friends since childhood, even though she lives on a boat and you live—" He waved his hand at their surroundings.

"That's right. Granddaddy was an inventor and made a ton of money. All my daddy ever wanted to do was work in the foreign service. So, when Granddaddy died, it fell to yours truly here to figure out what to do with it all. I got myself a little business degree from the London School of Economics while Riley was off playing soldier, and I established the Kittredge Foundation. Philanthropy suits me." She smiled. "And since our primary focus is on black women and girls, getting them through college and out of abusive relationships, this place has served as a shelter for more than a few battered women."

"I thought you and Kayla looked like you'd done this kind of thing before."

She smiled, but there was less sparkle in it. "More times than you want to know." She jumped up and went to the bar, returned with the bottle, and refilled his glass. "So tell me about what happened before you got here."

"I'm not sure where to start."

"Start with what you know about this man. The one who hurt her."

Cole told her about meeting Riley in the islands, going together to Dominica, and then Dig's arrival. He skipped over all the parts about what they were doing there. He explained about flying up to DC, going to her father's house, seeing Dig enter, and dealing with the housekeeper before hearing them coming down the stairs.

"I wasn't even thinking. I just grabbed the closest thing at hand and hit him with it."

"Thank God you were there. From what I know about him, he is CIA. Riley dated him for more than a year, so she may have told him about me—but he also has the resources to find out who her friends and associates are. And that means we aren't safe here. Do you have any idea what this is about?"

Cole wondered what he should say. If he tried to explain it all, he'd wind up sounding like some kind of nutcase. He'd seen the looks on people's faces too many times before.

"Yes and no. I know about his kind, and I know that there is something so important to them, they've killed before to keep the secret buried. I think it's this thing that he was talking about, this Operation Magic, though that's the first time I've heard that name. I can tell you this—I intend to get my hands on it first and to expose it and them."

"Ah, tilting at windmills, that's right. I remember her telling me that. I like that about you, Thatcher. I do a lot of that myself."

"The thing is, I need to get back down to the islands as soon as I can." He wanted more than anything in the world to take Riley back with him. He needed her brain to help him solve the rest of this, and—who was he kidding? He wanted her more than he'd ever wanted any woman before.

And it was because of that, because of what he felt for her, that he had to leave her behind now.

"She's going to be worried about her boat," he said. "But I can take care of it. This guy, this Diggory Priest, what he wants most is this Magic thing, and he knows I'm the only one with a hope of finding it. Once he realizes I'm back down in the islands, he'll follow me. And I trust you'll take care of her, help her deal with the arrangements for her dad, get her whatever help she needs?"

Hazel nodded. "That's what I do best. She's gonna need a lot of rest, but I don't think any of us should stay here tonight. I have a friend. We'll be safe at his place. And I'll call my pilot and tell him to ready a plane for you. We don't have our own jet, but the foundation buys several hundred hours of fly time every year. The pilot needs twelve hours' notice. In the morning, after you're gone, I'll keep our girl here on the move so that bastard can't find her."

After a light knock, Kayla's head appeared around the door.

"Miss Kittredge, I've just seen a black Town Car pass the house for the second time," she said.

CHAPTER SIXTY-FIVE

At sea off Guadeloupe

February 17, 1942

Captain Lamoreaux turned the rings on the barrel combination lock until the four digits lined up as 0322. He pulled on the lock, and it fell open with a soft *snick*. He rose and stepped back from his desk, leaving the pouch lying there. He glanced first at Michaut, who still stood by the door, then back at Woolsey.

"Lieutenant, you go ahead and remove the documents."

Woolsey looked at the pouch. *Lamoreaux's worried that there's some sort of booby trap*, he thought. Actually, it was quite possible. Woolsey knew that this diplomatic pouch was not, in fact, intended to arrive in Washington, but rather it was his job to deliver it to the Tomb in New Haven. *They* played by different rules.

Woolsey removed the metal bar and unfolded the heavy fabric. He eased open the mouth of the pouch, his heart pounding. Inside, he saw a thick tagboard folder marked "Operation Magic—Highly Confidential." He pulled it out of the pouch, untied the string wrapped round it, and removed a thick sheaf of papers. To his great relief, there seemed to be no traps within. The real trap was in going against his orders and reading these papers.

The Patriarchs would kill him for that if the French didn't beat them to it.

Woolsey recognized the sheaves of paper. Though the forms differed for different branches of service, he had been working with communications, codes, and ciphers since he was commissioned. The top sheets were copied messages from GC&CS, the Government Code and Cypher School at Station X. He had spent a little time there at the estate in Bletchley during his training. There were other decrypts from FECB, the Far East Command Bureau in Singapore, and the most recent came from the Americans at OP-20-G, and that meant the American Naval Codebreakers. The British documents were all carbon copies and dated from July and August 1941. The American sheets, however, were original raw decrypts in the hand of the men who had taken the messages— definitely not copies. Across the top of the page was written *Top Secret Ultra*. Below that the date and below that, the code designator: JN-25. Woolsey had no idea what that meant—he had never heard of that code designator, but that was not surprising, as he had never worked in intelligence.

He examined the first of the American decrypts. It was dated 19 November, and it read: "This dispatch is Top Secret. To be decoded only by an officer. Text: *At 0000 on 21 November, carry out second phase of preparations for opening hostilities.*" Another, dated 21 November, was also marked Top Secret and gave instructions that it should be decoded only by an officer. This one gave specific orders for the "Combined Fleet" to move out of Tankan Bay on the morning of 26 November and advance to a refueling position on 4 December. Woolsey could tell from looking at the latitude and longitude that the position was somewhere in the Pacific. My God, he thought. The message discussed various possible targets, including Pearl Harbor. The officer's initials on the American decrypts were always the same.

"Lieutenant," the captain said. "What is it?"

Woolsey glanced up at the Frenchman. He tried to compose his face so as not to give away anything. "Sir, I don't know yet," he said. "Give me a moment."

These had to be decrypts of a Jap code, he thought. *My God.* He wondered how they'd worked it. The Patriarchs had wanted into this war. They must have had their man inside at Bletchley Park and somehow he had figured out a way to secret these out. Woolsey guessed that not even the American president had seen them.

Woolsey pulled the last message from the bottom of the stack. It was dated 6 December. *Oh shit*, he thought as he read. They knew. *They bloody knew long enough in advance, but they let them all die.*

"Lieutenant, I can see from your face these papers are important. Explain to me what they mean," Captain Lamoreaux said.

Woolsey lifted his head and stared at the captain. He had been so amazed at what he was reading, he had forgotten where he was. In an instant, he realized the explosive nature of what he held in his hands.

"Sir, I'm not sure what this is," he began, "but I can tell you they will undoubtedly try to sink us before they'd let this get into Hitler's hands."

"What is—" the captain started to say, but he was interrupted by a sailor who burst into the cabin babbling in French.

When Woolsey turned to look at the man in the doorway, he saw Michaut's eyes focused on the documents.

Woolsey shuffled the papers, moving that last sheet back to the bottom of the pile.

Lamoreaux responded curtly to the sailor, then rose and stepped around his desk, grabbing his coat, which hung from a hook on the wall.

He'd understood one word from their exchange: *Avions.* Planes. Woolsey stuffed the papers back into the envelope and shoved them all into the diplomatic pouch.

Captain Lamoreaux turned from the sailor as he shrugged into his coat. "They have not seen us yet, but there is little time. With the radio gone, I order them to prepare the signal lamp in the conning tower. Come."

Woolsey folded the top of the pouch back to seal it and added the bar and lock. "This is highly classified, sir. You must secure it."

The captain tipped up his mug and drank off the last of his coffee. "Michaut," he said. He leaned down and pulled out the bottom drawer of his desk. Inside was a strongbox. "Take care of it. In there."

The captain stepped out from behind his desk. He placed his hand on Woolsey's shoulder and steered him out of the cabin to the companionway that led to the conning tower. *"Allons-y,* Lieutenant. If these planes are American or British, it will be up to you to save us."

CHAPTER SIXTY-SIX

Georgetown

March 28, 2008

Riley just wanted to sleep. She wanted oblivion. No thinking. Just a deep, dark, dreamless sleep. But instead, Mikey was there trying to shake her awake.

"I tried to warn you," he said. "I couldn't tell you straight out because you'd never have believed it coming from me."

She groaned and rolled over.

He shook her shoulder hard. "He was always a dangerous man. We never knew he could be a danger to us."

"Leave me alone. Let me sleep." She pushed him away.

"I tried to stop them." He touched her hair.

"No," she said, trying to pull the blanket up over her head.

"You've got to wake up." The hand caressed her shoulder.

"Go away," she said, and she pushed at the hand.

"No way. Not without you, Magee."

"What?" She opened one eye. The person with one hand on her shoulder was Cole Thatcher. She squeezed the eye closed again and shook her head, trying to throw off the nether sleep world and come fully awake. When she opened both eyes this time, she saw that, without a doubt, those were Cole's arched eyebrows.

"Hey, sleepy."

She groaned as it all played back to her. Her father. *I would have stopped it if I could, but they said he had to die.* Yorick, his Bones name. Dig's hands on her father's head. That sound. That unforgettable crunching sound as her father's head turned too far. Oh God, Dad.

"Time to wake up."

Cole. He had been there for her. But how? What was he doing here?

"We've got to go," he said. "*Now.* Kayla saw a black Lincoln with tinted windows cruise down the street twice."

Riley sat up, all vestiges of sleep ebbing with the surge of adrenaline. "Shit. Where are my shoes?"

"Right here," he said, handing her the sneakers.

As she laced them up, she asked, "How long have I been asleep?"

"A couple of hours. It's a little after six."

"Where's Hazel?"

"Packing. She's coming with us. She's going to arrange for me to fly back down to the islands, and she's taking you somewhere safe. We're supposed to meet her in the hall by that big staircase."

Riley swung her legs off the bed, but when she stood, the room seemed to tilt. So they had already decided her future for her? She grabbed the bed's footboard and steadied herself. Now was not the time to get into that. "OK," she said. She had learned long ago that a soldier had to pick her battles. If Dig was coming, she had to get them all away from him. "Let's go."

Hazel had changed into black jeans, and she wore a knee-length black suede coat with a fur-lined hood. She was waiting in the hallway with a small leather backpack swung over one shoulder when Riley and Cole arrived pulling on the jackets they'd retrieved from the entry. Cole was still carrying the small, gym-bag-sized duffel she'd noticed when he appeared at her house.

"You OK?" Hazel asked.

"Yeah. I'm solid. We need to go."

"I know. The kitchen. Follow me." Hazel turned and took off at a fast pace through the front living room. When she rounded the corner into another hallway, all the lights in the house went out.

Riley reached her hand out in front of her, probing the blackness, trying to find the wall. So he's here already, she thought, and she knew that she couldn't lose anyone else to this madness of his. Her fingers touched the wallpapered surface. She found the doorframe. Poking her head partway out into the hall, she peered into the darkness. Hazel, dressed in black as she was, had disappeared.

"Hazel?" Riley whispered.

"Down here." Hazel's stage whisper came from far down the hall.

Riley blinked and squinted trying to make her out. A hand touched her sleeve and she jumped, whirled around, and slammed him against the wall, her forearm at his throat. Then she smelled the half-briny, half-musty smell of Cole's foul weather jacket. She felt his breath on her face, and the flip-flops in her belly weren't just from fear. She exhaled and put her finger to his lips to warn him to keep silent before she backed away. Damn, she was jittery.

They had to catch up with Hazel. Riley knew the house better than Cole. She took his hand in hers and pointed with her index finger on his palm in the direction of the kitchen out back. She could barely make out the outline of his body. It seemed to be taking forever for her eyes to adjust to the darkness.

Cole rested a hand on her good shoulder, and she felt the room tilt again, and she knew it wasn't the drugs this time.

They started down the hall, their backs to the wall. Her eyes were growing more accustomed to the dark. Riley hoped Hazel was ahead of them, but she still saw no sign of her. Damn black clothes.

She was about to risk a call out to Hazel when the hand on her shoulder tensed. A cold draft. Riley felt it, too. Somewhere in the house a door or a window had opened and let in the subfreezing air from outside. Riley was certain it wasn't Hazel leaving without them. Besides, it had seemed to come from behind them. He was inside now.

At the end of the hall, she could see a dim red glow from what she thought was the digital clock on the microwave oven.

That it was Dig who'd just entered the house, she had no doubt. The man she had seen dancing over her father's body wasn't rational anymore—if he had ever been. She also knew that the government had trained him to be an effective killing machine. Now he was coming for her, and he wouldn't care about collateral damage. She picked up the pace.

Before they could reach the kitchen, they had to pass the open doors on either side of the hall that led to the dining room on one side, a drawing room on the other. Riley paused, her back to the wall. The drawing room had windows facing the street, and from them a pool of pale light shone across the floor at the intersection. They would have to walk through it. Or run.

She turned to Cole and signaled that they should run on the count of three. She grasped his hand. Holding up the fingers of her other hand, she counted down.

Go! Riley heard the shot and the soft *phhfft* as it penetrated cloth. Cole! *Was he hit?* She ran hard. She did not dare slow the pace. She gripped his hand tighter, and she felt some small relief when he squeezed hers back. If he faltered, she would pull him, carry him if necessary.

They made it through the kitchen door, then turned right and rounded the big butcher-block center island. Riley strained to hear the sound of footfalls behind them. Nothing. Her breathing rasped in her throat, and she could not hear a thing beyond the slap of their own shoes. Cole was keeping up with her. She was headed for the servants' door out back, through the mudroom.

The scarf round her neck tightened so abruptly, her throat closed and her feet nearly flew out from under her. Her neck, already sore and bruised, burned as the scarf dug into her skin. She could not breathe. Cole continued past her, then almost dislocated her shoulder when he pulled up short. She nearly blacked out from the pain, but even so, she wanted to scream at him *No, go on, let go of me. Get out of here!*

In less than a second, Riley regained her balance and whirled around, her hands coming up ready to strike. She would not let Dig get his hands on her again.

"In here," a voice whispered. She paused, her arm cocked back, ready to punch. In the darkness, Riley could make out Hazel standing in a recessed doorway holding the other end of her long scarf.

Behind Hazel, a flight of stairs led downward. Jesus, she thought. She stopped herself from imagining what would have happened if she'd struck Hazel.

Her friend motioned again for them to go down the stairs. Riley hesitated. She didn't like the idea of being caught in a cellar. Then another shot whizzed past them, and she heard it hit the wall next to her head. Night-vision goggles, she thought. Of course. She sprinted down the stairs with Cole right behind her. Hazel slammed the heavy wood door, and Riley heard the bolt slam home. At the foot of the stairs, Hazel turned on a small penlight.

Riley squeezed Cole's hand. "Are you OK?" she asked.

He held up his duffel and searched it with his fingers. "I heard it hit," he said.

Hazel shone the light on a small hole.

"Thank God," Riley said, throwing her arms around him. "I thought you'd been shot."

"Hey," he said, his lips right next to her ear. "You keep this up, and I might go back out there and let him have another try."

Riley released him and stepped back. She brushed her hands off on her jeans. "Don't get your hopes up, Thatcher," she said. "Just glad none of us is injured."

"Don't even joke about going back out there. Not smart," Hazel said to Cole. "I've seen enough of these obsessive nutcases. You, he'll do quick." She pointed at Riley with her thumb. "He wants to take his time with her."

"Enough chitchat, people," Riley said, loosening the scarf round her neck. "He's got us all cornered down here."

From the top of the stairs came a resounding crash. Then another.

"And now he's planning to beat a hole in the door," Riley said. "Dammit, is there anything down here we can use for a weapon?"

"No need. Over here." Hazel led them down a corridor between racks filled with wine bottles. The cellar was large, the air damp and cool, though not freezing. "This whole house used to be heated by coal. The old coal chute is back here."

The pounding continued from the top of the stairs, though it sounded more muffled when they reached the back wall.

In the corner, Hazel shone the thin light on double doors that angled down from overhead. A big rusty barrel bolt held them closed on the inside.

"Boost me up," Riley said.

Cole threaded his fingers together and bounced his eyebrows up and down. "Glad to be of service."

She put her sneaker in his hands. "You'd better not be enjoying any of this, Thatcher."

He grunted as he heaved her up. "Not a bit, ma'am. I promise."

She hit the bolt's raised handle with the heel of her hand. It didn't budge. She hit it again, hard enough to make Cole stagger. "Shit!" she said. "That hurt."

"Let me try," Cole said.

From the far side of the cellar, they heard a muffled gunshot. He was shooting at the door now to splinter the wood.

"I'll get it," Riley said. She hit it again with the heel of her hand, biting her lower lip against the pain.

Hazel appeared out of the dark with a magnum of champagne. "Try this," she said.

Riley grabbed the heavy bottle and tapped the bottom of it against the raised iron knob. After several tries, the bolt slid clear with a shriek.

"Move me closer to the wall," she told Cole. She pushed up, and the wooden door rose and then fell open. When she scrambled out into the freezing night, sirens howled, not too far distant. She spun around and grabbed Hazel's hand, then heard the sound of splintering wood. The pounding stopped.

"Hurry," Riley said as she boosted Hazel up. Cole followed her out and grabbed Riley's hand. Hazel led them at a run across the stone terrace to some smaller brick buildings around the perimeter of the property. When they reached the shadows between two of the brick buildings, Hazel stopped and turned around to look back at her house. The sirens had reached the street in front of the house and then shut off.

"Cops are here," she said.

Riley stood next to her looking back at the house. "You're pretty cool under fire, my friend," she said.

"Not the first time for me either. I'm glad I sent Kayla home early. The bastard cut the power and the alarm system. I called nine-one-one from my cell while I waited for you to get to the kitchen." She tapped Riley's arm with the back of her hand. "You took your time."

"We didn't know the house like you. In the dark, you were invisible in that black getup. I couldn't follow you." Riley realized she and Cole were still holding hands, and she made a show of needing to blow on her hands to keep them warm. "Come on, we need to keep moving." She didn't like standing there talking when Dig might be about to come out of that cellar at any minute.

"I think he's more worried about the cops than us, right now. But come on," Hazel said. She turned and led them down a walkway with old oak trees on one side and a brick wall on the other.

"Where are we going?" Riley asked.

"These are the old slave quarters that I've made into rental apartments. Ironic, eh? I have a car in the garage of a vacant one. This way."

At the end of the walkway between the apartments and the adjoining property, they had to pass through a gate to the street. Hazel opened the wood gate a crack, then pulled it closed again.

"A black car. I know, there are thousands of the damn things here in DC, but let's wait a minute." After they heard the car pass, Hazel hurried them around the side of the brick building and pushed an electronic fob on her key chain that opened the garage door.

Riley knew Hazel collected antique cars like she collected rich boyfriends, but she wasn't prepared for the bright red little two-seater convertible.

"We're going to fit three of us in that?" she said.

"It's all we've got, honey."

"Hazel," Riley said, "it's not what I would call inconspicuous."

"Exactly. Nobody would suspect that the three of us would be driving around in a 1949 MGTC. You either sit on this fella's lap all the way to Leesburg or..." She raised the lid on the back of the car and threw her bag inside. "We can lock you up in here. Your choice."

Cole tossed his duffel inside. He looked up and down the car. "Wire-spoke wheels, tufted red leather seats." He nodded. "We'll fit," he said. He tipped his head toward the car. "Let's get moving."

Riley looked at Cole, then swiveled around to face her friend. She raised one eyebrow.

"A two-seater with right-hand drive?"

Hazel nodded. "Let's go," she said. As she passed Riley going round to the driver's seat, under her breath she added, "The shocks on these old cars suck, so it might get a little bouncy." She winked. "Enjoy the trip."

CHAPTER SIXTY-SEVEN

Georgetown

March 28, 2008

The door must be made of two inches of solid oak, he thought. Dig had tried everything from knives to bullets to a big meat cleaver he had found in a wood block on the kitchen counter. The hole he had made was not yet big enough to reach his hand through, though, when he first heard the sirens. He tried enlarging the hole with a few more shots, but the sirens stopped in front of the house. It was time to leave.

He backtracked the way he had come, passing down the hall, through the day room to the grand staircase. As he climbed the stairs, he heard the voices of the police officers assembled on the front porch, their radios crackling. He had disabled the alarm system, but Riley and the others must have called from a cell phone. He heard the front door open and the jangling of the gear the officers wore as they entered the house.

Earlier in the afternoon, it had taken him more than an hour to find the manhole covers where he could access the power transformer and phone lines. He had his driver cruise the street past the front of the house several times. Twice he caught a glimpse of the

Kittredge woman with Thatcher. Even at such a distance, he could see her animal sexuality. It was common in her kind.

He found his way back to the master bedroom window, and he climbed back out through the broken shards of glass onto the branch of the big old elm tree just as the police were starting up the stairs. The DC Police were a hopeless lot of barbarians. They'd lost all standards through affirmative action. Dig wasn't worried about them, he thought, as he dropped to the ground. He hurried across the neighbor's yard, removing his cell from his pocket, and then slipped out the gate onto a side street. His car met him at the corner and picked him up.

"Circle the block a few times," he told the driver.

In front of the Kittredge house, half a dozen police cars with flashing lights lined the street. The few passing cars slowed, the drivers gawking. A Pepco truck had already arrived and was at work on the power lines. As they drove past the front of the house, he slid down in the backseat and watched out the window. He looked for them in the crowds in front of the house, or through the windows. Once, he saw a small woman about Riley's size, and he told his driver to slow, but it wasn't her. He imagined them down in that cellar, cornered, waiting for the police to arrive and save them. If only he'd had a few more minutes.

Priorities, he told himself. Operation Magic. He had no idea what it was, but he knew it would be his ticket, his reservation for a seat at the table. That was what he must concentrate on now. He'd shot at Thatcher's duffel to motivate him. Let the man think he was out to kill him. In fact, Dig wanted Thatcher back down in the islands as soon as possible to find that submarine.

He had seen the way Thatcher looked at Riley down on Dominica. It turned his stomach, but the fact was that he could put that to good use. Thatcher would do whatever Diggory wanted— hand over whatever he'd found—as long as Diggory had Riley to motivate the man. Then later, when he had Operation Magic in his possession and Thatcher had been dealt with, Dig could take his sweet time with Riley.

Dig told his driver to return to his apartment, then settled back into the seat and removed his gloves. He would fly to Guadeloupe and charter a boat. He spread wide the fingers of his right hand, stretching the aching muscles. Then he would check on the barbarians, he thought, clenching his fingers into a tight fist. He would find Thatcher and his submarine. After closing his eyes, he pictured Riley's naked body, her pale skin and long neck, and he squeezed until his knuckles turned white.

CHAPTER SIXTY-EIGHT

Leesburg, Virginia

March 28, 2008

By the time they passed through the electric gate onto the unplowed road, Riley was beyond worrying what part of her body landed on what part of Cole's. Even though Hazel tried to speed whenever possible, attempting to leave the Washington area during the evening rush hour was a horror, and it had taken them more than two hours to travel about forty-five miles. But thinking about the man's body beneath her had at least prevented her from reliving the events that had taken place earlier in the day.

During those first miles, she braced herself with one arm on the seat back and the other on the dash, her head bent to one side. But she was so tired from whatever medication Hazel had given her earlier that eventually she leaned back against Cole's chest and rested her head on his shoulder. She was beyond caring what he or anyone else thought, and she had to admit, though the old MG was a drafty wind tunnel, the heat they were generating between them was more than enough to keep her warm. She said, "Wake me when we get there." It was the drugs, she told herself.

Of course, try as she might, she wasn't able to go to sleep. Drowsy or not. She couldn't shut off her mind. What was wrong with her? After what she had been through this day, men should be the last thing on her mind. But, there was something comforting about being cradled in his arms. He made her feel safe, and sometimes she opened her eyes in thin slits and watched the curve of his jawline as it hardened when Hazel bumped over the reflectors in the road. Her weight must be crushing his legs, she thought.

The front left tire dropped into a pothole with a jarring lurch, and Riley's butt dropped hard onto Cole's lap. With no more feeling in her legs, she wasn't even trying to make the bumps easier on him. She was pretty sure this had stopped being fun for him quite awhile ago.

He slid his hands under her and cupped her buttocks. "Sorry, Magee," he said. "I'm just going to adjust your position a little."

She lifted her head to look at him, her eyes open wide. She saw his white teeth shining in the glow from the headlights. "Hey," she said. Maybe she was wrong about the amount of fun he was having.

"Well, I reckoned we were almost there, and if I was gonna cop a feel, it was now or never."

Hazel laughed. "Riley, Sweetcheeks here's a hoot. Stick with him, and I won't have to worry about you getting a cat."

Cole said, "A cat? You mean like a boat cat?"

"Ignore her," Riley said.

"Well," Hazel said, "your fella is right about us almost being there. The house is right up here."

"He's not *my fella*." As she spoke the car went over a little rise, and Riley saw the white columns of an enormous old antebellum mansion. "Jesus, Hazel, are you dating Rhett Butler?"

"No, darling, he's an adorable Greek by the name of Niko Boulis, and we're not an item anymore, just good platonic friends."

"He must be gay," Cole said.

"You know those Greeks, darling. They always play for both teams—or at least they're more honest about it than the rest of us." Hazel chuckled. "His father's in shipping, and they have the nicest couple of yachts." She pulled the car up in front of white steps and swung around to face them. "The *Savannah Jane* happens to be in Antigua at the moment, only a few miles from Guadeloupe."

"*Savannah Jane* doesn't sound Greek to me," Riley said.

"Well, he's got this sort of obsession with the Old South. Like this place. Looks historic, right? Nope. It's a reproduction—right down to the last detail."

The front door swung open, and a tall, dark-haired man in a white linen suit came running down the steps. He opened Hazel's door and offered her his hand to help her out of the low car. "Hazel, honey! How wonderful to see you!"

Riley could hear the smacks of the air kisses coming from that side of the car. She felt Cole's hand moving along the outside of her hip, then the door swung open. He shifted his knees, and she slid right off his lap onto the hard-packed snow.

"Wake up," he said. "We're here." After he climbed out, he reached out a hand to help her to her feet.

She rolled onto her knees and made a wobbly ascent to her feet on her own. The pins and needles in her legs were killing her, but she wasn't about to let it show.

In the porch light, she admired the shine on the big, black curls that clung to Niko's head. Platonic, my ass, she thought.

He led them inside the house, and it looked to her like all the furniture pieces were museum-quality antiques. It was as though the plantation owner had just left and handed over the keys.

Their host led them upstairs and showed Riley and Cole to their rooms. "The bathroom is down the hall," Niko said, "as it would have been in the nineteenth century." Riley's room had a four-poster bed with what looked like handmade lace fringing the canopy. Niko explained she should help herself to any clothes in the wardrobe and that his cook had prepared some food for them. They could eat downstairs once they had freshened up from the trip.

Hazel, who was holding Niko's hand, whispered, "I know we're safe here, but are you going to be OK?"

"I'm good. I just need sleep. You go have fun. But spare me the details."

Hazel smiled at her. "See you in the morning." She fluttered her fingers at Riley.

Riley leaned against the closed door. So much for Hazel and Niko's "just friends" status. She flopped down backward onto the bed and stared up at the canopy. As usual, her friend would be having hot sex with some deliciously sensuous man, and here she was back in her Semper Fi Immaculate Heart Convent for Wayward Marines.

Riley closed her eyes, and the image of Diggory Priest standing over her father flashed in her mind.

Her eyes snapped open.

Through the wall, she heard them usher Cole into the room next to hers. With everything that had happened over the last few hours, she hadn't asked him what he was doing in DC. How had he come to be in her father's house today? What made him leave his beloved submarine hunt and come up here?

Time to change the subject again, she told herself. She didn't want to think about him so close on the other side of that wall. But thinking about him kept her from reliving the events of that afternoon.

She got up and explored the room. On a dressing table, she found a pitcher of cold water, soap, and towels. Just what she needed. She pulled her shirt off over her head and splashed her face and hands, then scrubbed her skin with the soap and washcloth. The cold water felt good on her hot skin.

As she dried herself, she looked at her reflection in the mirror above the dressing table. Her eyes darted between staring at her scars and looking into her own eyes.

"Stop dreaming, sailor," she said aloud. "Men aren't interested in women who look like you." She bent her shoulder forward to examine the red skin there again. "He might be attracted to you when you're dressed, but once you take your clothes off?" She held her index finger up straight, then slowly let it droop down. She looked at the grim smile reflected in the mirror. "Better to laugh than to cry, right?" She had cried enough today, she thought as she pulled her T-shirt back over her head.

From the armoire, she selected a white, long-sleeved men's shirt and draped it over a chair to put on before going to bed. She needed a good night's sleep, she told herself.

When she found her way to the kitchen a few minutes later, Riley discovered Cole already standing next to an enormous stone fireplace. He was staring at the spread on a long rough-hewn wooden table. The surface was covered with bottles and dishes including Greek salad, quiche, various cheeses and meats, a bowl of large prawns nestled in crushed ice, warm French bread, and a selection of wines.

Cole looked up when she came in. "Can you believe this spread? Or this house? Not to mention Hazel's house. I feel like I've been dropped into the reality TV show *Who Wants to Visit the Millionaires?*"

Riley looked at the food and felt her stomach churn. "I'm not really hungry."

"How about a glass of wine, then?"

She nodded. As she wandered around the room exploring, Cole opened a bottle of pinot noir and poured them both glasses. He motioned her over to a pair of chairs set up before the big stone fireplace.

When they'd settled themselves, she said, "I still don't understand why you're here."

He puffed out his cheeks and blew out air in a long sigh. "Well," he said, "it's kinda hard to explain."

"Try me."

"OK." He reached into his pocket and drew out the green marble and brass calendar device. "After you left, Theo and I took *Shadow Chaser* back to the Saintes that same afternoon. En route, I kept going over the journals and thinking. Why this device? What is he trying to tell us? The only passage I could find that seems to refer to any sort of date is on that page with the weird nursery rhyme song where the old man refers to the End of Days. Then Theo brought up the Mayan calendar, and I decided to come to DC to do some research."

Riley sighed. "It's difficult to care about those games anymore."

"It matters more than ever now."

She shook her head. "Not to me. Not after today." She set her glass down on the hearth and rubbed her eyes. "I'm not at all sure what matters anymore."

"Riley, I don't believe that."

She felt the tears returning, and she steeled herself against them by taking another big gulp of the wine.

"What about truth?" he said. "Does that matter? Or honor, duty, reason, freedom?"

She sighed. "Cole, I don't want to talk about it."

He stood up and crossed to the table and leaned on it with both his arms stretched out straight. Without turning, he said, "That's the problem these days. Nobody wants to talk about the things that are most important."

"Sometimes it just hurts too much."

He spun around and walked back toward her. "I know you're hurting, Riley. And for good reason. I wish there was something more I could do about it. But it makes me crazy that guys like Priest and the men he represents get away with their crap because people don't question things that are too good to be true—whether it's a subprime loan or the idea that we can keep services without paying taxes. We have our big cars and cheap fuels, all the shiny trinkets they've convinced us we can't live without, and our 'reality' has become what appears on the screens we stare at twenty-four seven." As he spoke, he paced the room, his arms carving his points in the air.

"Jesus, Cole. Enough already." She rubbed her forehead. The man was passionate, all right, but politics weren't what she wanted to think about at the moment.

"I mean, really," he continued as though he hadn't heard her. "You mean to tell me we can find Saddam hiding in a hole, but after all these years our government still can't find bin Laden? Why should we? That might end the war, end all their profits! And the saddest part of all is that we can't claim to be victims. We helped them to it," he said as he pantomimed the motions of throwing something at her. He stopped and slapped his hand down on the table, making the dishes jump. "Well, I'm gonna head back down there and make sure that sonofabitch gets caught—by finding whatever this Operation Magic is."

"That's quite a speech," she said, keeping her voice calm and even. "I'm going too, you know."

"You? No, it's better if you stay here with Hazel. It's safer."

She set down her glass, made an effort to smile, but her lips just stretched thin. "You've got it all figured out, haven't you, Thatcher?"

"Well, yeah. I know who the bad guys are and what I intend to do about them."

She stood. "So it's all black-and-white to you, eh? The big, tough guy goes back down to the islands to search for his submarine while the little women stay home safe. How sweet." She turned her back on him and walked away. At the kitchen door, she paused and turned to face him again. "You don't get it. Your father did. I read in his journal where he talked about living in the world of the *'tween* where things aren't black-and-white, right and wrong—where it's hard to figure out who's good and who's bad. For the last twenty-four hours, I've been deep in that *'tween* world, Cole. I found out for certain, today, that *they* killed my brother—*and* that my father was one of *them*. I'm going, Cole Thatcher, and there's not a damn thing you can do to stop me." She headed for the stairs before he could say another word.

CHAPTER SIXTY-NINE

Leesburg, Virginia

March 29, 2008

Cole leaned back on a pile of embroidered pillows on the big four-poster canopied bed still wearing his jeans, T-shirt, and socks. It was after midnight. There were no lights on in the room, nor was there a fire in the big brick fireplace. The room was cold, and Cole wondered if the Greek guy took his authenticity kick to such an extreme that he had no heat in the rooms. No sense in getting undressed if he wasn't going to be able to sleep. His knees were bent, and one foot rested on the opposite knee. In his right hand, he held the marble-and-brass calendar paperweight. He tossed it into the air and snatched it on the downswing with his opposite hand. Then he repeated the motion.

Through a tall window opposite the door, the light from a slender moon lit the spindly dressing table covered in lace doilies. On it was a collection of antique perfume bottles and an engraved silver comb and brush. The wallpaper was covered with hundreds of little bouquets of flowers, and the dominant color in the room was a cross between purple and pink. On the wall opposite the bed was a portrait of a guy in a military-looking coat with a curl of brown hair falling across his forehead. The guy wore white pants that were so tight they might as well have been a dancer's tights.

God, he thought, it was like trying to sleep in a fifteen-year-old girl's bedroom. He couldn't wait to get on that plane in the morning and get back to his own cabin on his boat. He looked at the paperweight in his hand and turned the brass faceplate. He would do this on his own—no problem. He didn't need anything else complicating his life. As if trying to find the *Surcouf* wasn't enough complication already.

Shit, he thought, what the hell was he supposed to do? What did she expect from him, anyway? Some wack job just killed her father right before her eyes, and now the wacko was out to kill her. Of course, her emotions were overloaded right now, but Cole wanted her to understand that he just wanted to see her safe. He wanted to go after the sonofabitch for her. She could at least give him a little credit for that.

He threw the paperweight into the air again and snatched at it with his right hand. He sat up suddenly, drawing his arm back, poised to throw it at the wall that separated his room from Riley's. Why, he should go in there right now and...

Cole lowered his arm and fell back into the pile of pillows. No, that would be way too dangerous a thing to do: going into her room when all he could think about was how much he wanted to undress her and hold her naked body close, skin to skin? No, what was he thinking? He rested his forearm across his brow, hot in spite of the chill in the room. How the hell was he ever going to sleep? He closed his eyes and thought back to the long car ride, holding her on his lap, drunk on her citrus scent. He'd wanted to bury his face in her hair, then, starting with her ears and that long curve of throat, he would kiss and nibble all the way down to...

"Stop it," he said aloud. His jeans were starting to bind uncomfortably, and this stranger's house was no place to be dealing with that.

"Stop what?" a soft voice said.

He hadn't heard the door open, but there she was, stepping into his room, the moonlight reflecting off the streaks of gold in her tousled hair.

"I need to talk to you," she said, her voice not so soft now. More demanding. "You've got some nerve, you know. I'd like to know where you get off telling me where and when I am allowed to go back down to the islands to my own boat." She stood at the foot of the bed, her hands on her hips the way she had stood on her boat that night with that fish oven mitt on her hand. Only this time, she was wearing a man's dress shirt, the top three buttons open, her suntanned skin glowing in the V formed by the open neckline.

He rolled off the bed in one quick move, landing on his stockinged feet. She was barefoot, and the skin of her thighs showed beneath the dangling white shirttails. The outline of her hard nipples poked out beneath the thin cloth.

"You're not the only one in the whole friggin' world," she continued, "who gives a damn about things like justice and liberty and honor. How dare you? If you think you've got the corner on that, I know a few marines I'd like to introduce you to. You think you know how to keep *me* safe? You do realize that I am a highly trained United States marine, and I *am* going back down to the islands in the morning, and there isn't a goddamned thing you can do to stop me."

"OK," Cole said as he rounded the bed, "but I guess there's only one way to stop you from swearing like a sailor." He scooped her up and engulfed her mouth in a long, firm kiss. Her words turned into a slow moan. The little struggle she gave at first melted away as he tried to find his way back to the bed before his own legs buckled under him.

He could tell from the smooth feel of her body beneath the cotton cloth that she wore nothing under the shirt. His desire for her threatened to overwhelm his willpower. He wanted to see her, all of her, to rip off her shirt and take her, to plunge himself into her. Already his breath rasped in his throat when he broke off the deep kiss to look into her gray eyes. But there, to his surprise, he saw fear.

He had to slow down. Resting one knee on the top of the bed, he set her down amid the mountain of pillows. He stretched out next to her, his elbow resting on a pillow, his cheek against the palm of his hand so he could take her all in. After brushing a loose strand of hair across her cheek and behind her ear, he let his finger curl around her ear the way hers so often did. With a feathery touch, he explored the tiny shell-like opening. He saw the shiver run through her body as his finger traced down her neck toward the half-visible swell of her breast, saw her nipples standing hard beneath the thin fabric.

"Riley," he said, his voice already hoarse. "I've wanted you since that first time I saw you on your boat. But I need to know this is what you want, too."

She rolled onto her side and propped up her head to mirror his. The ghost of a smile played across her mouth. "Does this answer your question?" With her free hand, she reached for the top button of his jeans and slipped her fingers inside, releasing the button that opened with a snap from the pressure within.

He bent his head back and groaned, then reached into the depths of that darkness to reassert control over his body. He wrapped his fingers around her wrist and pulled her hand away.

"Not so fast, Magee," he said, rolling her onto her back and pinning her hand to the pillows next to her head. He looked down into her sea-gray eyes. "Give me a chance to do this right."

Closing his mouth over hers, he explored the moist, soft flesh within, letting their tongues dance round one another, nipping at her lips, then brushing his mouth over her chin. He traced the curve of her jaw with his tongue. Her breath beat a hot rhythm on his face, and he heard it catch in her throat with little sighs of pleasure. He moved down the front of her neck, kissing, tasting, exploring, and when he nuzzled aside her shirt and circled her nipple with his tongue, she dropped deeper into the pillows, arching her neck with a soft gasp.

Cole raised himself up on one arm and began to unbutton the last two buttons on her shirt. "I want to see you—all of you," he said.

"No." She grabbed a fistful of white cloth over her shoulder and held it tight against her neck. "I'll keep the shirt on." She squeezed her eyes shut.

He waited nearly a minute, but it seemed like an hour before he spoke again. "I said *all of you*, Riley." He bent his head down and kissed the white knuckles of her fist. One by one, he unfolded the fingers.

She turned her face away from him as he undid the last button and brushed the shirt aside to reveal her naked torso. In the light of the moon, he saw the pearl-colored skin of her high, firm breasts and the shell-like pink where red angry flesh crept up and over her right shoulder. He knew burn scars when he saw them, and so much about her suddenly made sense to him.

"God, you're beautiful," he said, and he heard the soft wail that escaped from her lips. He began at her neck again, kissing the soft white skin. As he approached the edge of the scar, he felt her body stiffen. But when he did not slow, when he continued on across the pink ridges, he heard her gasp, and he surprised himself with the electric, erotic jolt he felt from it. "So beautiful," he whispered and he kissed her shoulder again. He felt the shudder course through her. His own fingers trembled as they traced the contour of the injured skin. The thrill he felt at pleasuring her in this way surprised him.

He trailed his tongue down and took her nipple between his teeth. She groaned and he released the firm bud. "And you taste like the sea," he whispered. His fingers danced across her ribs, across the taut, smooth skin of her belly and down to the soft shadows of her inner thighs. He traced feathery circles across her burning skin, and waves of pleasure washed through him each time her breath ended with a little cry of delight. She shuddered and writhed as he explored every crevice and peak, and he reveled in bringing her right to the quivering edge, then retreating and exploring some as yet untouched part of her body.

Then her fingers wrapped around his wrist, and she pulled his hand away and rolled him over, pinning his hand to the pillow next to his head. He saw the desire, the hunger in those gray eyes that were locked on his. When she released his wrist, she slid her hand up under his T-shirt, circling his own nipples, sending shock waves to his groin. Then her fingers skimmed across his belly until her hand cupped the bulging front of his jeans. He leaned his head back, mouth open, and the noise that broke from deep in his throat sounded more like a growl. The pressure inside him, the enormity of his wanting was overpowering. Cole couldn't wait any longer to press his bare skin to hers.

Fumbling at the zipper to his jeans, he at last got the pants loose enough to slide down his legs. He kicked the jeans off the bed, then tore the T-shirt over his head. He took her in his arms, pressing his chest to her breasts, and he rolled atop her. Her body was hot and wet and welcoming, and as she wrapped her legs round his waist, he dove into her and lost himself.

CHAPTER SEVENTY

Fort Napoleon

March 29, 2008

Spyder inched his foot forward to the edge of the cliff, his new cheap flip-flops providing little cushion over the rough volcanic rock. Though he hated spending any of their money on shoes in the little French grocery, leastwise this time he wasn't wearing those fucking Crocs. He still had the blisters from that day. How many days ago was it when he had beat down that bitch? That was how he decided he would think of it—him beating her—and that was how he told the story to his brother. With each retelling over the last couple of days, he'd got it better, made himself sound like he had really busted her ass. He was even starting to believe it himself.

They were going fucking ape-shit nuts sitting around waiting for something to happen. Two, three times a day he'd been hiking through the village and around the hill to check on their boats in that Marigot Bay, but nothing ever changed. He'd told Pinky all they needed to do was watch Thor's little GPS gadget, but Pinky said Thor had told them to report on both boats, and if the skinny nigger on the trawler left, or the doc came back without the girl, the GPS wouldn't show no change. So, late this afternoon, seeing as Pinky had never been up to the fort, he'd talked his brother into coming along with him to the top of this big-ass hill so's they could check on the boats from up here. He needed to do something. All this waiting was driving him nuts.

When his foot neared the edge of the cliff, he paused and leaned forward, testing the ground. He had stepped over the chain barrier, and he wondered now if they kept people back because the cliff was crumbling.

The bay below was a brilliant aquamarine, the water so clear he could see the crazy quilt pattern of the grass growing on the seafloor. His mind flashed a picture of the cliff caving in and his body tumbling down the rock face, leaving bloody bits of tissue and bone as he smashed against the black rock.

A hand grabbed his arm, and he jumped back from the edge, nearly tripping on the low chain barrier. "Jesus, Pinky, what the fuck are you doing? You wanna get me killed?" He jerked his arm out of his brother's grasp.

"Just wanted to know did you see something? They still there?"

"Gimme a minute." Spyder pulled his tank top down over the several inches of boxer shorts that protruded above the belt line of his low-riding jeans. He inched back out to the edge and peered over.

The white sailboat was anchored so close to the base of the cliff he had to lean his body way out into space to see if it was still there. He spotted the mast and a bit of the white deck in the late afternoon shadows. The dark-blue trawler was still out in the sunlight closer to the mouth of the bay.

"There she is. See, bro," he said. "I told you they was both still there. Come here and look."

"I ain't goin' out there. I'll take your word for it."

Spyder hopped back over the loop of chain that hung between the short fence posts. "You better, bro. You know I wouldn't lie to you." He draped an arm over his brother's shoulder and thought about how he lied to his brother all the time, but what Pinky didn't know wouldn't hurt him.

Spyder stepped back and looked at his brother. He was wearing a bright-orange baseball cap he had found somewhere on the boat. The words "Bacardi Cup" were stitched across the front. Probably belonged to the old man they stole the boat from. He sure as hell didn't need it anymore. Like the black binoculars that dangled from his brother's neck. Pinky's white frizzy hair stuck out on either side like a pair of fuzzy mouse ears, and he wore dirty white tennis shoes, white pants, and a long-sleeved white shirt. The freak wanted to bring along a fucking umbrella to keep the sun off him, but Jesus, Spyder thought, that would have guaranteed everyone who saw them would remember them. He was working on what that Thor dude had talked about. That covert crap. Maybe they'd like to hire him at the CIA or something and give him some cool weapons and shit.

"Let's go," Spyder said, tipping his head toward the fort entrance.

Pinky pointed back over Spyder's shoulder. "Look there."

Spyder turned around. A big white megayacht had rounded the point and was easing her way into the bay.

"Fuckin' rich people," he said. "These islands are crawling with them."

His brother raised the binoculars. The big white yacht began to turn a wide, slow circle inside the bay. A small figure in a white crew member's uniform appeared out on the foredeck.

"They think 'cause they got money, their shit don't stink," Spyder continued. "Someday, when we get this gold, bro, boat like that won't be nothing to us."

When the bow of the boat pointed seaward, the yacht's engines reversed, and they began backing down.

Without lowering the binoculars, Pinky said, "The boat's named *Savannah Jane*. I like that. Sounds classy. Better'n *Fish n' Chicks*."

By the entrance gate, a security guard pulled on a bell cord, and the sound rang out. The fort closed at 5:00 p.m.

"Hell, Pinky. That ain't nothing compared to the high-class boat we gonna get." Spyder grabbed his brother's arm, forcing him to lower the glasses. "You wait and see. Come on. We gotta go. They're closing."

He steered Pinky back down the grassy hill toward the fort's exit gate. The two of them had slipped through the gate with a large tour group so they didn't have to pay the entrance fee, and he saw now that most of the groups were crowding out the narrow exit. He hoped they could slide along with the crowd right onto their bus so they wouldn't have to hike all the way back down to the town. "Shit, I'm getting tired of all this waiting around," he said as they edged into the crowd. "I wonder what the fuck is going on with the doc? He gonna come back and go after this submarine or not? We need to do something about our cash situation."

"What cash situation?" Pinky asked.

"The *we-ain't-got-none* situation," Spyder said, motioning like one of the rappers he liked to watch.

"Don't go getting ideas, Spyder. That guy told us to wait here for him. Two days ain't so long."

"It's too long to go with no cold beer and no pussy." Spyder nudged his brother toward the crowd of tourists mobbed around the door to one of the buses. They were mostly older, chubby French tourists, but he spied a voluptuous, pouty teenage girl trailing behind her parents. She wore a tight, low-cut tank top, and she was busting out of it. He worked his way through the crowd until he was right next to the girl, and then he turned sideways in front of her.

"Hey, man," he said to the big man on the other side of him—as though blaming him for pushing him—and he fell against her tits.

"*Pardon*," she said, stepping back and glaring at him.

Spyder pretended to stumble again and fell against her for a second go, this time raising his hands to cushion his fall. He gave her tits a good squeeze.

"Sorry," he said.

She was yelling some gibberish at him in French, and her father started their way, so Spyder grabbed Pinky's arm and yelled, "Come on!" They took off running down the steep road.

His damn brother sure as hell wasn't any kind of athlete. He looked like an injured pelican as he waddled down the hill, his arms flapping like wings. Lucky for them, the parents were too busy drying the little cunt's tears to take off after them. Probably decided against it since the day was too hot and they were too fat.

So they didn't get a ride down the hill, but it had been worth it. Once they rounded the first hairpin switchback, he and his brother slowed to a walk, and Spyder began to whistle "The Eddystone Light," a tune he'd picked up one summer working on a shrimper.

From high up on the side of the hill, they had a great view looking down on the harbor. Spyder watched the ferry thread its way through the anchored boats. He hoped Thor was on it. Even if the dude was a total douche bag, it would cure this boredom to have something happen.

"That was a dumb move," Pinky said between wheezing breaths.

Spyder rounded on his brother and grabbed a handful of fabric at the front of his shirt. "Fuck you, Pinky. You just wish you'd got a good feel like I did." He cackled and released his brother. Then he rounded on him again and put his finger in his brother's face. "And don't you never call me dumb again."

"You ain't got no discipline, Spyder. That's your problem. And we're gonna need discipline if we 'spect to take this Thor dude. He knows his shit. 'Stead of sitting around drinking up the last of the liquor on the boat and coming up here to feel up some French chick, you and me need to be figuring our way out of this. It ain't gonna be easy to kill a dude like Thor."

CHAPTER SEVENTY-ONE

Aboard the Savannah Jane

March 29, 2008

Riley sat sideways on the bench seat on the bow of the yacht *Savannah Jane*, leaning back on her elbows, her feet propped up on the cushion. The flight on Hazel's private jet had taken four hours, with another hour spent dealing with the officials on both ends. Niko's captain had arranged for a launch to ferry them out to the yacht. Riley had seen these big, white, multistoried yachts that looked more like wedding cakes than boats, but she had never been aboard one. If Dig was keeping watch on the airport at Pointe-à-Pitre, as she assumed he was, he would never know they were already back down in the islands.

It felt good to get out into the warm Caribbean night once more—to enjoy the star-splashed sky away from the big city lights. From the moment the crew had anchored here in Marigot Bay, she'd been feeling cooped up inside the yacht. Theo told them when they'd contacted him earlier via the long distance single side-band radio that Spyder Brewster was keeping watch on the bay, so neither she nor Cole had dared venture on deck in daylight. They'd decided to wait until well after dark before making the dinghy transfer across to their own boats. Thankfully, *Bonefish* looked safe and secure when they'd entered the bay.

She had left Cole asleep on one of the settees in the cabin below after Hazel and Niko had retreated with their drinks to the afterdeck. She smiled again at the memory of those early morning hours spent in that big colonial four-poster. She had only slept, at most, a couple of hours, curled up in a spooning position in Cole's arms, his cheek resting against her back. She knew she should be inside the cabin catching up on her sleep too, but she was too buzzed. She felt as though electricity were humming through her veins and firing off hundreds of random synapses in her brain.

Much as she wanted to revel in the memory of her early morning lovemaking, Riley could not forget the sound she'd heard when Dig wrenched her father's head to one side. Yesterday, in order to survive and get through the day, she had tried to stuff her sorrow into a compartment and shut it out. It was time to face it. Diggory Priest had murdered her brother and her father. And he intended to kill her next. Not only did she need to stop him, she intended to stop the entire organization that had set this moment in motion. To do that, they would need to get to *Surcouf* first.

She and Cole had spent most of the day with their heads bent together poring over the journals he had brought with him in the duffel he carried. She listened as he explained his thoughts about the calendar paperweight and what this clue from his father might mean. Cole was certain they were looking for a date that when entered into the calendar would produce the name of the day of the week. He showed her how the date when the world was supposed to end according to the Mayan calendar, when entered into the 40-Year Calendar, would fall on a Friday. But what did that tell them?

Riley was more inclined to think the paperweight would relate to one of the coins or an earlier puzzle that the elder Thatcher had sent his son. She'd asked Cole to compile a list of all the types of coins, ciphers, and puzzles his father had sent him. But it turned out all the dates on the coins were outside the forty-year range of the calendar.

From out in the darkness, Riley heard the noise of an outboard cranking over, and when she glanced off the big yacht's starboard quarter, she saw the single white light of a dinghy pulling away from *Shadow Chaser*. That would be Theo coming over for dinner, she thought. Hazel had invited him to join them when they'd spoken on the radio earlier.

Riley got up and headed aft to welcome Theo aboard, but Cole was already there ahead of her, leaning on the aft rail watching the dinghy approach the broad swim step. She admired his dark silhouette backlit by the glow of the underwater lights that turned the water around the stern a brilliant blue.

"Hey there, Sleeping Beauty," she said.

Cole turned around. "Hey, Magee." He opened his arms, and she stepped up and kissed him, placing her hands on his waist and then sliding them up his back as she moved into his embrace. She was only three or four inches shorter than he was, and their bodies fit together so well; she rolled her hips against him in a playful little hula. He broke off the kiss and whispered, his breath hot on her ear, "That's what I like about you, Magee. You get straight to the point."

"We have this Marine Corps motto," she said as she wrapped one leg around his backside. "When in doubt, empty the magazine."

Below them, they heard the outboard engine cut off. That was followed by a thud, then the sound of feet scrambling on the teak swim step and muttered curses. Riley slid out of his embrace and leaned over the rail. Behind her, she heard Cole groan. Below her, Theo lay sprawled on the swim step, the dinghy painter wrapped around one of his legs.

Cole appeared at the rail next to her. He cleared his throat. "Nice landing," he said.

"You can see right into the engine room down here. Damn distracting." Theo untangled the mess, tied off the line, and climbed up the curving staircase to the afterdeck.

"Still don't understand," Cole said, "how you can build almost anything with those hands, but you have trouble putting one foot in front of the other."

Theo wasn't listening to him. He was surveying the large afterdeck with minibar and the glass doors that led into the luxurious interior. "Not bad," he said. "Not bad, at all. These friends of Captain Riley know how to travel."

"She's a Horizon Elegance Ninety-Four. Just launched a year ago," Cole said.

"She's got twin cats with over fifteen hundred horsepower each," Riley said. "We'll introduce you to the captain, and he can show you around the bridge and engine room later."

"Sweet!"

"Glad you approve, my man." Cole slapped him on the back.

The door to the main salon slid open, and Hazel poked her head out. "You must be Theo. Welcome aboard." She stepped out onto the deck and shook his hand. "Your timing is impeccable. Dinner is about to be served." She waved them inside.

When Hazel was out of earshot, Theo whistled a low appreciative note.

"Slow down, island boy," Cole said. "She's got a boyfriend."

"A fellow can look, though, eh? Wow!"

Riley sighed. "She always has that effect on men."

Cole turned to Riley, smiled, and extended his arm. "After you," he said.

As she entered the salon, Riley heard Theo's hushed voice say, "It's about time the two of you figured it out."

"Figured out what?"

"That you two needed to stop knocking heads and start knock-ing boots."

"What are you talking about?" Cole said.

Theo laughed and shook his head. "Mon, it's written all over your face."

CHAPTER SEVENTY-TWO

Aboard the Savannah Jane

March 29, 2008

The meal reminded Riley of the many embassy dinners she had attended with her family when she was a child, only here they were five at a table that could have seated twelve. The stewardess in her crisp white uniform delivered food that looked almost too pretty to eat: fresh conch salad garnished with orchids, spicy callaloo soup, Vietnamese swordfish curry, jasmine rice, chocolate lime rum cake. It had been years since she had seen a spread like that, and judging from the looks on the faces of the guys sitting on either side of her, it may have been the first time for Cole and Theo.

The dining table was separated from the plush couches and chairs of the main salon by a low, burled wood counter atop which sat a gorgeous floral arrangement. Opposite the dining table, a carved wood bar sported a gold-plated beer tap, and throughout the yacht, the teak and holly floors were partially covered with thick Persian rugs. Riley had spent part of the passage across from Antigua roaming the yacht and talking to the crew. Now, she found it awkward to sit and let them wait on her. When the coffee was delivered, she asked Hazel to invite the chef and crew out for their thanks.

"You're kidding," Theo said when the chef turned out to be a pretty, petite redhead named Victoria who looked barely twenty years old. "You did all that?" She blushed crimson at their applause and hurried back to the galley.

Niko offered them after-dinner drinks, but Riley and Cole declined, instead asking for another espresso. "If we're going to sail out of here soon," Riley said, "we'll need clear heads."

Hazel said, "We watched you two all day poring over that book and scribbling on paper. Have you figured out where you're going yet?"

Riley glanced at Cole and then back to Hazel. "Not exactly. But I was thinking about it when I was out looking at the stars this evening, and there is something in the journals I want to check."

Cole stood up. "I'll get it." He returned a few minutes later with the last volume of his father's journals, several sheets of paper, pencils, and the marble paperweight. He pushed their coffee cups aside and spread them out on the tablecloth.

"May I see that?" Niko asked, reaching across the table to indicate the paperweight.

"Sure." Cole handed it to him.

Riley reached for the journal as the two men played with the device. She turned to the page with the odd song and read it over one more time.

"Ah, I see," Niko said. "Hazel, darling, did you see this? Isn't it clever?"

Hazel grinned across the table at Riley. "Where did you say you found this little treasure?"

"We dug it up on Dominica. Cole's father left him these journals and buried that for Cole to find." She pointed to the calendar. "But now, we don't know what he wanted us to do with it."

"What did you find out at the library?" Theo asked.

"Nothing that will help us," Cole said. "Riley and I went over and over that on the plane this morning. Most scientists don't think there's anything significant about the date when the calendar ends."

"Oh yeah," Hazel said. "The world is supposed to end sometime in 2012?"

Riley turned the journal around and slid the book across the tablecloth so Hazel could see Thatcher's last entry.

Theo reached across the table and pointed to the text. "You see this line where he writes, 'Wit's end is where I am. Spent a bit of time there. Expect to be there 'til the end of days.' Cole thought because he mentioned *end of days*, that might mean we should set the calendar for that date."

Cole took the device from Niko and turned the top plate carefully, lining up the months and years. "So, you see that when we set the month for December under the year 2012, we see that the twenty-first day will fall on a Friday. But we can't figure out what Friday might mean—if anything. This afternoon, Riley and I asked your captain for charts and maps of Guadeloupe and Dominica, and there isn't any place name on either island that uses the word Friday."

"Or the French word *vendredi*," Riley added.

Hazel pointed to the page in the journal. "What is this song here?" She read the words aloud.

"Fais pas do do, Cole mon p'tit coco, Fais pas do do, tu l'auras du lolo, Yayd d'dir, Y'did yd, Jamais fais do do. Riley, what language is that middle part?"

"I thought at first that it was some kind of Creole phrase. But I had another idea this afternoon. Let me check." She ran her fingers under the letters of the two odd lines and counted under her breath. "Hmm. Both lines have an even number of letters."

Cole stepped from behind her chair and stood at the head of the table. He pulled the book closer. "So what are you getting at?"

"Well, coordinates on a chart are always in pairs. Like latitude and longitude."

"Oh no," Theo said. "Not again."

"Riley," Cole said, "Theo and I have been trying to get longitude and latitude coordinates out of those two lines for months now. We've tried everything."

"But what if they were coordinates on a different sort of graph? Remember when I was asking you this afternoon about the different puzzles your father sent when you were a boy? You mentioned one called a Polybius square or checkerboard."

"What in the world is that?" Hazel said.

Cole rubbed his hand across the whiskers on his cheek in a gesture she was getting to know that meant his brain was jumping ahead. "It's a bifid cipher that uses a pair of letters or numbers in the cipher text to represent one single letter of plain text," he said. "For a Polybius square, you create a five-by-five grid and fill in the letters of the alphabet."

"You lost me at bifid cipher," Hazel said.

"Here, I'll show you. Riley, grab a pencil."

She picked up a pencil and pulled a blank sheet of paper to her.

"Now draw a big square," he said, "and make five columns, then five rows across."

Riley began sketching the grid.

"That gives us twenty-five boxes, but there are twenty-six letters in our alphabet, so start filling in the squares with the alphabet. You can put the last two, Y and Z, on the same square."

Riley filled the squares with letters as he talked.

"Are you all with me so far?"

They nodded.

Cole picked up the pencil when she had finished and began using it as a pointer. "Then you select two five-letter words and write them along the outside horizontal and vertical edges. So let's say your cipher text is AF; you find the A row in the word on the left side and the F column from the word on top. Then follow down to the square those two coordinates lead you to. The key to the cipher is knowing what those two words are."

Hazel leaned back in her chair. "How on earth are you going to figure out which words to use?"

Theo said, "Too bad Friday is a six-letter word."

The five of them sat there in silence staring at Riley's sketch.

"Wait," Riley said. "Theo's got something. Look at those two lines in the song we have determined are not in French. The only letters used in those two lines are RIDAY. Cole, give me that pencil."

He handed it to her, and Riley added another row and column to her box, making it six by six. Then she wrote the word FRIDAY down the left side of the page. She used the same F in the top corner and wrote RIDAY across the top. When she was finished, she presented the paper to Cole.

F	R	I	D	A	Y
R	A	B	C	D	E
I	F	G	H	I	J
D	K	L	M	N	O
A	P	Q	R	S	T
Y	U	V	W	X	YZ

"Riley, you're brilliant!" Cole said. He leaned down and kissed her on the mouth.

She felt her brain short circuit and flicker for a moment like the lights did during a power surge.

Cole rested his elbows on the table again, pencil in hand. "Theo, read me the letter pairs from the song chorus."

"OK. *Ya.*"

Cole found the intersection of the Y row and the A column. On another sheet of paper, he wrote the letter X.

"Then *yd.*"

Cole repeated the process and wrote the letter W.

When Theo finished reading him the letters, Cole looked at what he had written: XWMFWHW.

"Does that mean anything to anybody here?" he asked.

They all shook their heads, but nobody said a word. Riley felt sure they were close, but they'd missed something.

Finally Cole broke the silence. "Well, it was a good idea, Riley. But you know, it's getting late."

Riley tried to think like James Thatcher, the man who lived in the *'tween.*

Cole pushed the paper aside and stood. "If we want to shake the Brewsters, we've got to leave tonight early enough to get a good head start."

Hazel looked up at him. "But where will you go?"

"Wait a minute," Riley said. She had not stopped staring at the Polybius square she had drawn.

"Riley, it's already nearly ten," Cole said.

She pointed to the grid. "What if we use the coordinates backward?"

"What do you mean?"

"You know, instead of latitude and then longitude, what if we use them the other way around? Your father was trying to prevent people like Diggory Priest from finding this. He wouldn't have made it easy."

Cole shrugged. "It's worth a try." He dropped back into his chair.

"Read me the letters again," she said.

Cole slid the journal across the table and turned it around so he could read it. "OK. *Ya.*"

Riley ran her right index finger across the top of the grid to the Y column. With her other hand, she traced a finger across the A row. She wrote the letter *T.*

"Then, you've got *yd.*"

Using her fingers, she traced down the Y column and across the D row. She wrote the letter *O.*

When she had finished, she looked at the word: TOMBOLO.

"At least it *looks* like a word this time, but I have no idea what it means," she said.

"Me neither," Cole said. He placed his hand on the back of her neck and massaged the tight muscles there. "But again, it was a good idea."

At that moment, Theo started laughing.

"Theo," Cole said. "What is it?"

"You seriously don't know?" Theo said.

"Don't know what?"

Theo closed his eyes and made a *Mmmm* sound as though he had just eaten something delicious. "As I've said, it gives me great pleasure when I know more than you, Dr. Thatcher."

"You know what a tombolo is?"

Theo nodded, his grin so wide his face looked as if it were all mouth.

"Well, spit it out."

"Your dad, Cole, he was quite the funny fellow. Yeah, mon, I know what a tombolo is. You will too if you look it up. In Dominica, we must study our island's geology in third form, and we learn that our island has the only tombolo in the Caribbean. It is a landform where a small island is attached to the mainland with a thin spit of land. People usually call it a *tied* island, but the proper name is tombolo."

"OK, so where is it?"

"At the south end of the island. It's called Scott's Head. There's a village—I have two cousins who live there. You know our islands are on a geological formation called the Caribbean Plate. It is a small and very active plate—that's why we have so many earthquakes and volcanoes in the region. The bay formed by the tombolo is called Soufrière Bay. It's one side of an old volcanic crater, and it's very, very deep."

"Deep enough to hide a submarine?"

"Yeah, mon."

CHAPTER SEVENTY-THREE

The Caribbean Sea off Guadeloupe

February 17, 1942

"Avions au large de la tribord avant!" one of the sailors on the bridge shouted. Another man handed a pair of binoculars to the captain when he emerged through the hatch.

Woolsey climbed out behind the captain, blinking in the bright, slanting sunlight. He stopped for a moment to revel in the warm wind on his face and breathed deep, grateful lungfuls of the flower-scented air. He had been on the French boat long enough to understand *tribord avant* meant starboard bow—and *avions* were planes—but for a moment, he wanted to let the tropical air thaw his bones. Four days in the hold had taken something out of him. Whether it was by the noose in Martinique or from these damned advancing planes, odds were he was not going to survive this war. Any small pleasure might very well be his last.

He swiveled his head around to squint into the sky, trying to get his bearings. He was startled to see the low green hills of an island close off their starboard beam, and the water the sub steamed through was no longer the dark, shadowy blue of the deep Atlantic.

Woolsey estimated they were no more than six miles from shore, dangerously close for a sub the size of *Surcouf.*

The captain was shouting incomprehensible orders, and his second-in-command repeated his words into the voice tube. Woolsey wished he could understand what they were saying.

"Lieutenant!" the captain barked.

Woolsey stepped to the front of the conning tower. "Whose are they, Captain?" he asked.

Lamoreaux did not lower the glasses when he spoke. "*Les Americains,*" he said. "They are searching to the southwest by the entrance to Pointe-à-Pitre. They have not seen us yet, but it will not be long."

Woolsey scanned the sky, but he still saw nothing. The planes were not yet visible to the naked eye. Americans. That was a bloody bit of irony for you. He'd loved America the four years he'd lived in New Haven and attended Yale. And they'd loved him. Enough to ask him to join Bones, anyway. Now there were American planes out there searching for him, ready to send him and the lot of Frenchmen to the deep seafloor.

"Do you think it's a regular patrol, or are they looking for us?" he asked the captain.

"Difficult to say."

Woolsey didn't think it was so difficult. The Royal Navy had not heard from the sub since she'd left Bermuda. The Allies didn't trust the Free French to begin with, and once *Surcouf* went silent, they'd assumed she was no longer a friendly, that she was making a run for the Vichy-controlled islands of Guadeloupe or Martinique. Woolsey examined the shore. He had thought all the islands in the Caribbean were high and mountainous, but this was a lush green strip on the horizon. Clouds gathered above the land like a dramatic dome of white and gray cumulus, and a couple of villages of red-roofed houses squatted along the coast.

"Place doesn't look like much," he said.

Lamoreaux lowered the glasses and wiped his brow with the sleeve of his wool coat. "This is the low side of Guadeloupe. The volcano is under those clouds." He turned and pointed aft. "We came through the cut there." Woolsey followed his finger to the small gray smudge on the horizon. "Between La Désirade and Pointe des Chateaux."

Both men turned back to resume their search of the sky off their bow. Surely, the planes would spot them soon, Woolsey thought. He noticed the gunners had not taken their stations in the big turret. That could only mean one thing. The captain did not intend to fight.

"What's our depth?" Woolsey asked.

"Twenty-five meters. That is what makes this the last place to look for us. Or so I thought."

The *Surcouf* drew nine meters. Woolsey had no idea if the water was deep enough to hide from a plane, but he assumed the captain's rapid-fire orders were readying the boat to dive. If only they could stay hidden the two hours or so until dark. God, he hated this waiting, but with each minute that passed, their chances for survival grew.

They had been running at the surface these last five days for a reason, though. Woolsey had heard there were problems with the sub's electric motors. The mechanics had been working on them since Bermuda, but they were Frenchmen.

One of the sailors shoved a signal lamp into Woolsey's hands, mumbled something about captain's orders, then disappeared back down the hatch.

"A few miles ahead," the captain said, "beyond those small cays called Îles de la Petite Terre, the bottom drops to more than three hundred meters. The question is, will we make it?" The captain turned and spoke orders to his second, who again shouted them into the voice tube.

Woolsey examined the small archipelago off their bow. He could make out palm trees and white sand beaches, but no signs of any human inhabitants. The little islets were perfect tropical deserted islands.

The conning tower shook with the vibration of the diesel engines. The captain was pushing the sub at maximum revolutions in her run for deep water.

Whether or not they would make it in time wasn't the only question, Woolsey thought. "What about the electric motors, sir?" he asked Lamoreaux.

"*Mon Dieu.* Our mechanics were working on farm tractors one year ago." The captain shook his head. "We'll be good for a few hours. On one motor. No more."

Woolsey turned his attention to the device in his hands. They were counting on him to signal the damn planes, if—or when— they came this way. But he hadn't used one of these things since his all-too-brief training more than a year ago. And the one he'd trained on wasn't made by the bloody French.

Henri Michaut appeared at his side. He reached for the lamp. "You want I show you how?"

"Are you good with this thing?" Woolsey asked the French signalman.

He blew air out through his rounded lips. "But of course. It is my job."

"Then you do the signals. I'll dictate."

"*D'accord.*"

Woolsey stepped to the far side of the bridge with young Michaut, and they rehearsed the English spelling of the words so that Michaut could send the signals as fast as possible.

He heard one of the sailors call out the depth: thirty meters. They were getting close.

"*Les avions! Ils arrivent!*" The lookout shouted the warning.

The captain barked, "*Préparez à plonger.*"

Ready to dive. Woolsey kept his eyes on the sky. He wanted to ask for the binoculars, but the captain had them glued to his eyes. The sun slid behind a bank of clouds on the horizon, and while the shadows would work in their favor once they dove, for now, the *Surcouf* still stood out as a huge target on that pale-colored sea.

There. He spotted them. Three small dots in the sky. Flying a V formation. Only they weren't so small anymore.

"Lieutenant, they will make one pass for observations. That is your chance. Tell them we are damaged but are not stopping here. We are Free French, not Vichy."

Right, Woolsey thought. And that's why you're headed to Martinique to surrender to the Vichy authorities there.

Only the helmsman and two lookouts remained with them on the bridge. The others had already clambered below to ready the boat to dive. He began spelling it out for Michaut. The lantern *clacked-clacked-clacked* as Michaut sent out the signal code, and Woolsey felt his heart hammering just as loud.

Who had issued the orders for these planes? Had their orders come from Washington? In that case, they might believe this story Lamoreaux was fabricating. But if their orders were from New Haven, they were more concerned with that pouch below—and not letting it fall into the wrong hands—than with the sub's destination.

Woolsey heard the planes' engines now. The sound started off thin and tinny, like toy planes, but as the V-formation neared, the engine noise dropped in pitch to a throaty roar. He recognized the American planes because of their twin engines. They were P-38s, and they were coming in low. This was no practice run.

"*Plongez!*" the captain yelled into the voice tube. He ordered his men to clear the bridge as he dashed below.

The claxon sounded, drowning out the men's voices as they scrambled after the captain, pushing for the hatch. Their lack of training turned the cramped conning tower deck into a free-for-all. The helmsman nearly knocked Woolsey to the deck when he shoved him out of the way.

As he struggled to regain his balance, Woolsey saw the bright-red tracers seconds before he heard the *pop-pop-pop* of the gunfire. The lantern continued clacking behind him as he struggled to reach the hatch. He saw the water rising up the sides of the sub.

With his feet on the second rung, he turned and looked behind him. "Henri!" Woolsey called. The young man did not stop signaling as the water erupted in a peppering of mini geysers far off the bow of the sub. "Michaut!"

The young signalman stopped and turned at last. His eyes grew huge as the sea rushed up toward him. The lower decks were covered, and the water was nearing the top of the conning tower. If the hatch was not secured, the sub would flood and they would all drown.

Henri threw down the signal lamp and began to run, but those last few seconds of hesitation had made all the difference in the world. Woolsey saw that it was too far, too late. He would never make it. Waiting any longer would doom them all. Woolsey stepped down a rung and pulled the hatch closed behind him. He spun the wheel to engage the airlock.

The diesel engines stopped, and the electric motors kicked in with a soft whine. From two decks down, he heard the captain give the order to take her down to twelve meters. Clinging to the ladder, his cheek resting against the cold steel of the top rung, Woolsey listened to his heart pounding in the sudden silence. *Clang-clang-clang.* It was his heart, he insisted, until the banging suddenly ceased.

CHAPTER SEVENTY-FOUR

Scott's Head Bay, Dominica

March 30, 2008

Stepping into the knee-deep water off the village, Riley thought about the dream she'd had that morning when she'd first arrived in Scott's Head Bay. Cole and Theo had arrived hours earlier, but she told them she needed a few hours in her bunk after the all-night sail. That's when Mikey had come to her in her dream and told her what to do and that she needed to hurry.

Riley knew why, too. She'd seen the fury on Dig's face when they were at her father's townhouse. He was coming for her, and she had no doubt he would find their trail. If they were going to succeed at finding whatever it was James Thatcher wanted them to find, they had very little time. Cole lifted the outboard engine so that the propeller wouldn't hit the stones, and she hauled the dinghy up the rocky beach.

"I think we're wasting time," Cole said. "We have a few precious hours of lead time, and we shouldn't squander it."

She realized she and Cole had been thinking parallel thoughts. "I know we haven't got much time. But it makes sense to ask if anyone in the village was around back then. See if they remember something that will tell us where to look." It was more than that, but she didn't know how to tell him about the dream. About Mikey, who had told her to go ashore and talk to *him*. Only she had no idea who *he* was.

"And if we don't find anyone who remembers, we'll have wasted an hour."

"Cole, they won't know which way we went. And there's no reason to believe they'll come straight to Dominica. But you're right—I think our lead is measured in hours, not days."

"They found us quick enough last time."

"I know," Riley said. "Either it was luck, or I don't want to think about the second possibility."

"What's that?"

"That Dig has somehow placed a tracking device on your boat."

"Why my boat?"

"We only took *Shadow Chaser* to Dominica last time."

"Shit," Cole said. He grabbed the small anchor out of Riley's dinghy and buried it in the black sand and pebbles above the tide line. "I'd much rather be out there helping Theo rig up the ROV. And checking my boat for a goddamned bug." Cole stood up, brushed the sand off his hands, and stared out into the bay. "That's a mighty big search area out there though."

"My point exactly. We don't have time to search it all."

Shadow Chaser had arrived in Soufrière Bay before 3:00 a.m., and the guys had been starting their search grid towing the proton magnetometer over the bottom when she motored into the bay at dawn. After anchoring, she'd crawled into her bunk for a few precious hours of shut-eye. When Riley finally pulled alongside in her dinghy four hours later, the guys had agreed to reel in the magnetometer's fish and drop the hook so Cole could accompany her to shore.

"Come on, Cole. One hour, OK? That's all I'm asking." The man was exasperating. He'd been fighting her on this issue ever since she'd picked him up in her dinghy.

"Dammit, Riley, this is the closest I've been. I feel it. I know this is where my father sent us." He pointed to the cone-shaped island to the south. "Scott's Head is a tombolo. He wanted us to come right here to this bay. It's plenty deep enough for a sub out there."

"I know all that, Cole, but what's the likelihood a submarine sank right off the beach out there in Soufriere Bay and nobody on shore saw a thing? Besides, what would she have been doing here?"

He threw his hands into the air. "How the hell do I know? Something happened when they left Bermuda, maybe. I don't know what. Mutiny? Hell, this is more than five hundred miles away from where she was supposed to be. I don't know *why* she was here, but if James Thatcher is telling me she's here, I believe him."

Yeah, Riley thought, your dead father is telling you what to do, and now my dead brother is telling me to go visit somebody in the village—and to make sure Cole comes along. "Cole," she said. "This is one of the hottest dive spots on the island. If there was a three-hundred-and-sixty-foot submarine out there with a hold full of gold, trust me, somebody would have found it by now—even way out there where it's over six hundred feet deep." She turned away and climbed up the soft sand embankment that led to the paved road. At the road, she turned. Cole still stood on the beach, his feet planted far apart, his fists clenched at his sides.

"I know for damn sure we're not going to find a submarine in the village."

She stood her ground, her hands on her hips. "Cole Thatcher, you are the most stubborn man I have ever met. *One hour.* That's all I ask."

He crossed his arms high on his chest and glared at her. "Stubborn? Riley, look in the mirror."

"Fine," she said. "Do whatever you want. *I'm* going to ask around." She turned and started walking. Before long, she heard his footfalls coming up behind her. She started to smile just before his hand grabbed her shoulder and spun her around. She opened her mouth to protest, but he wrapped his arms around her and held her face in the hollow of his neck.

Chin resting on her head, he said, "Oh, Miss Maggie Magee." She could feel his chest bounce as he laughed.

"What's so funny?"

"Us. I might be stubborn, but I'm not foolish enough to let you walk out on me. Come on. Let's get this excursion over with. There's one thing I know for certain. We work better as a team than we do when we're knocking heads, to quote Theo."

She leaned back and looked up at him. "You do have a way of making teamwork very pleasurable, Dr. Thatcher."

Cole framed her face with his hands. "OK, *this time,* we do it your way. One hour. But you'll owe me, Magee. And I have some very specific ideas on how to make you pay up."

"Hmmm," she said. "I might have to tap my savings account. After all, I've been saving it for a couple of years."

"I think I'll put you on a regular installment plan," he said as he ran his hands down her arms and then up under her T-shirt. "But frequent unscheduled payments will help—"

She swatted his hand away. "Town?" she said. "Submarine? Remember?"

He whirled on his heels and took off down the road, his hands in the pockets of his cargo shorts, whistling the tune, "We're Off to See the Wizard."

CHAPTER SEVENTY-FIVE

Scott's Head Bay, Dominica

March 30, 2008

When the colorful clapboard houses gave way to a few sundry shops, Riley knew they were in the "downtown" of Scott's Head village. Another ten minutes of walking and they'd be through it. Ahead, a couple of wood tables stood on the front porch of a house. When they got closer, she saw the sign *Ma Bert's Restaurant*. She climbed the steps and knocked on the doorframe.

"Hello?" she called out.

Cole stood in the street, his back to her, one hand on his hip. He was staring out at his boat.

From inside a voice sang out. "I be right with you."

Seconds later a large woman emerged from the back of the house. As she passed down the hall, she filled the space with her bulk. Riley stood aside as she stepped through the doorway. She was wearing an orange plaid jumper over a bright-yellow blouse, and in the midmorning sunlight, Riley squinted against the glare.

"Good afternoon," the woman said. There was something off about her island accent. "Would you like to eat?" She waved a hand with a flourish in the direction of the two empty wood tables.

"I was wondering if you could answer a couple of questions for me."

"All right." The singsong quality of the woman's voice sounded forced.

"Have you lived here long?"

Little lines appeared between the woman's eyebrows when she noticed the marks on Riley's neck, but then she pasted the smile back on her face. "Yes," she said drawing the word out. "Why do you ask?"

"We're looking to talk to someone about something that happened here during the Second World War. In 1942."

The woman reached for one of the laminated menus that rested on the table, and she began to fan herself. "Do you mind if I sit down?" The singsong voice was gone. It now sounded more Deep South than island-like. She eased herself into the chair.

Riley pulled out the other chair and sat across from her. She heard Cole cough several times out in the street.

"That's better," the woman said. "Whew! Nineteen forty-two. That's a long time ago." She stuck out her hand. "Eugenia Bert."

Riley introduced herself and they shook. "It's for this research project we're doing," she said.

The woman leaned across the table and lowered her voice. "Did he do that to your face?"

Riley smiled. "No, not him."

"Well, that's good, then. As you can tell," Eugenia continued, "I didn't grow up here. My daddy was from Dominica, but I grew up in St. Mary's, Georgia. Inherited this place. Tourists want the real thing, so I try, but this island life is getting to me." She fanned herself harder. "What I wouldn't give for a Big Mac."

Riley heard a sigh from out in the street, and the woman sitting across from her glanced out at Cole's back.

"Hmm. Not on island time, is he?"

Riley shrugged as if to say, *You know men.* "We are in a hurry, though. If you don't know anyone—"

"Now, hold on. I didn't say that. Everybody knows everybody round here."

"So you can help me?"

"Sure. Hmm. Old-timers. Start with the Charles family. They live up King Street here in the blue house with a plumeria tree out front. Name of the house is Parrot Perch. You'll see the sign. Old Mr. Charles is in his eighties. Then, let's see, there's Mr. Jules, he's the oldest, I believe. Lives right across the street from Mr. Charles. The two of them been friends a long time. No wait, I think I heard Mr. Jules married into that family after the war. His wife died just last year."

Riley stood. "I'll start with Mr. Charles. Thanks." She backed her way off the porch while Eugenia kept throwing names her way.

"Then there's the Shillingford family that lives up in the valley. Now don't rush off. I don't get many folks coming to visit."

Riley said, "Sorry, we've got to go," as she went down the steps.

"Come on," Cole said when her feet hit the street. He took her hand and started off at a trot.

Over her shoulder Riley called out, "Thanks Ms. Bert. You've been a big help."

After they had gone about fifty yards, she grabbed Cole's arm and pointed to a sign. It read King Street. "Look. Turn up there." On the side street, the incline increased. They slowed to a fast walk up the steep hill.

The houses were all painted bright colors, and next to the doorframes, some of the houses had signs with names. She read them out loud as they passed.

The electric-blue house would have been difficult to miss. Again, the door stood open, and Riley bounded up the stairs and knocked on the doorframe. This time the man who came to the door had very dark black skin that contrasted with his close-cut gray hair. There was no doubt about the origin of his lilting voice. He nodded.

"How d'you do," he said.

"Mr. Charles?"

"Yes, how may I help you?"

She felt Cole's eyes on her back, so she jumped right in this time. "My partner and I are here on the island doing some research on a submarine that may have sunk in this area in the Second World War. Did you live here at that time?"

"Ah. You must be looking for my father. I'm sorry. He's in hospital in Roseau at the moment."

"I'm sorry to hear that."

"Thank you. I was born here during the war, but I don't remember it. Still, I've never heard about any submarines going down near Dominica, and I've lived here for sixty-five years. I wish I could be of more help to you."

"Thanks for your time."

When she reached the street, Cole crossed his arms across his chest and said, "Is that it?"

She looked across the street at the yellow house, then up the street with houses that stretched for another quarter mile before giving way to the jungle on the side of the mountain. She understood his urgency, but she couldn't explain why she felt they were so close. James Thatcher had been so precise, he would not have sent them to search a five-square-mile area for a submarine. He wanted them in here Scott's Head, and Mikey did, too.

"Riley," he said. "Priest has got access to satellites, for Pete's sake. He will find us. *Come on.*" He turned and started walking back down the hill.

Riley was about to follow him when she could have sworn she heard her brother's voice. *Look*, he said.

Across the street, a cat stood up and stretched on the porch of the tidy yellow house with a red tin roof. The house looked more like those in the Saintes with the neat, whitewashed railing around the porch and the lacy gingerbread cornices. Next to the open door was a hand-painted sign. It said *Le p'tit coco* in bright-green letters.

"Cole!" she called out. "Come here."

He must have heard something in her voice. He stopped and retraced his steps. She pointed up the porch steps at the sign. "Look. What do you think?"

"What?"

"The song in your dad's journal. *Le p'tit coco.*"

"I don't know, Riley." He pointed to the dark-blue waters of the bay. "My gut's telling me the answer's out there."

And my brother is telling me to keep looking here, she thought. Riley climbed the steps. No one responded to her knock, but she heard voices around back. She descended the steps and waved at Cole to follow her on the dirt driveway that led alongside the house. As she neared the back, she heard a woman's voice speaking in Dominica's unique Creole patois.

"Hello?" she said.

The voices stopped.

When she came around the corner, she saw an old man sitting in a plastic chair just outside the back door of the cottage. He had a towel wrapped around his shoulders and a full head of straight, white hair. The old man's features were Caucasian, but his skin was so dark and wrinkled from decades in the sun, his eyes were mere slits in the folds of skin. On his right cheek, a mottled red shape looked as though it might be melanoma. Next to him stood a lovely coffee-colored woman, a pair of scissors poised above the old man's head.

"Excuse me," Riley said. "I'm sorry to interrupt you. I'm looking for Mr. Jules?"

The young woman lowered her scissors and stared. When the old man tried to stand, she placed one hand on his shoulder, restraining him. She spoke to him so softly Riley couldn't hear the words, then she said, "How may I help you?"

Riley heard Cole come up behind her. The old man's eyes grew wider. They were a very pale shade of blue, perhaps made even lighter by cataracts. "This is my friend Cole, and I'm Riley. We wondered," she said, "if we could ask you a few questions about the history of Scott's Head."

The woman rested one hand on the old man's shoulder. "My great-grandfather's health is not good. It distresses him to speak with strangers."

The old man pulled the towel off his shoulders and leaned forward to stand. This time when she tried to restrain him, he shook her off. Once on his feet, he stood hunched forward, teetering a bit. The woman grabbed a cane that rested against the back of the house and put it in his hand. She leaned down, and he whispered in her ear. She nodded, collected the towel and scissors, and went into the house without another word. The old man indicated some chairs in the center of the yard.

"Please sit," he said, then he stepped across the grass to the wooden chairs. Riley was surprised to hear his French accent.

When Cole approached, the man reached out and motioned for him to come closer. The old man pointed to the coin on the chain round Cole's neck and said, "May I see it?"

Cole surprised Riley when he lifted the chain over his head. The old man turned the gold piece over, held it close to his eyes, and carefully examined both sides. When he looked up, he was smiling. He handed the coin back to Cole.

"Welcome," the old man said. "I've been waiting for you. Your father said you would come." He stretched out his thin, boney hand. "My real name is Henri Michaut."

CHAPTER SEVENTY-SIX

Îles des Saintes

March 30, 2008

It was another bitch of a hot day, and Spyder's fucking head was killing him. He'd managed to swipe a wallet out of a tourist's beach bag yesterday, and he'd used the hundred euros he'd found inside to score some weed from the French wannabe Rastas with their blond dreads who hung out on the town beach. They'd passed around their jug of rum, too. It was some kind of island-made shit. Even the last doobie he smoked when he got up this morning hadn't made the steel spikes in his brain go away. The Polaroid glasses he'd found on the boat were too big, and they did a lousy job of keeping out the sun's glare.

Spyder was getting sick and tired of hauling his ass up this hill and over to Marigot Bay to check on the fucking boats. They had the GPS tracker inside the bitch's oars, but that asshole Thor wanted a phoned-in visual report on all three boats twice a day. He lit a cigarette, drew in a lungful of smoke, and blew it out through his nostrils. He woke up late this morning and dashed ashore to try to make his midday report. Didn't matter. Nothing never changed.

Spyder reached the small dock and walked out to the end where he could see beyond the fishermen's boats that were moored close in to shore. He saw the big white yacht that had entered the bay the day before—but the two boats he was supposed to be watching were gone.

"Shit," he said, throwing the smoldering butt of his cigarette into the water. He ran off the dock and hurried farther down the beach for a better look into all the coves around the bay, but the change in vantage point did not change the facts. The doc and the bitch had got back to the island somehow, and now they were gone.

Spyder turned around and started to run.

* * *

The inflatable dinghy was where Spyder had left it tied up at the town dock. He stepped into the boat, untied the painter, and yanked the cord to start the engine. He revved the engine and turned to round the big ferryboat at the end of the dock. That was when he saw the sleek, black Donzi tied alongside *Fish n' Chicks*.

"Fuck," he said aloud as he throttled back on the outboard. An ocean racing boat like that could only mean one thing. That asshole Thor or one of his goons was here. If it was Thor, he'd like to see what his face looked like after docking that sucker. Boat's name was *Fast Eddie*, and he could believe that baby was fast with her twin Merc sterndrives. Whoever came on that boat was already aboard *Fish n' Chicks*, and Pinky was in there, too. Much as Spyder wanted to turn around and wait 'til somebody left, he figured he couldn't do that to his brother.

Spyder cut the engine and glided alongside the swim step. After tying up the dinghy, he climbed up to the aft deck. When he slid open the door to the main salon, he was already thinking that whoever it was should have money, and maybe he could get a cold beer.

Thor was sitting on the couch with his arms spread on either side atop the cushions. His hair was messed up and his face looked a little white, so Spyder figured he'd driven the boat over from the big island on his own. He was lucky he made it. The dude was dressed like one of those guys in the ads for fancy watches that cost as much as a good boat. Thor lifted his left wrist and glanced at his own fancy watch.

Pinky stood in the galley holding a towel to the side of his face. Towel looked like it was full of ice cubes, and the skin under the towel was bright pink. His brother wouldn't meet his eyes.

On the low glass coffee table in front of Thor, he saw the black GPS box. The screen glowed blue, but Thor's eyes were on him, not the screen.

"Nice boat you got out there," Spyder said. "That your boat or a charter? You drive that here all by yourself?"

Thor crossed his legs, and there wasn't but one wrinkle on his pants—the crease straight down the front. For a minute Spyder wondered what Thor had looked like driving that black Donzi across the channel. Bet he almost crapped his fancy fuckin' pants.

"Were you born a complete moron or did your mother drop you on your head?"

"What the—"

"Shut up. Rhetorical question. One only need look at your brother to know there are issues with your gene pool. So, both boats are gone?" Thor asked.

Spyder nodded. He wanted more than anything to smash his fist into the asshole's face, but this asshole owed him money, and Spyder knew from experience that men had a tendency not to pay after you hit them.

"I assumed as much. Half the day is gone, and you are just now returning with this news. You have no idea when they left, I assume."

"Hey, you didn't say we had to sit up all fucking night watching 'em. We checked yesterday before dark, and they was both there."

Thor leaned forward and adjusted the screen on his GPS tracker. "We know she's down at the south end of Dominica. Odds are he is, too." He snapped the lid of the box closed and stood. "Let's get moving."

Spyder stood his ground in the middle of the salon. "We ain't going nowhere 'til we see some money," he said.

Thor stepped out from behind the table and faced Spyder. "You are going to do what I tell you to do."

"Hey, man, it's been four days since we bought that last food. It's gone. We got no food, no beer, and none of your fancy wine neither. Boat's gonna need both fuel and water. Me and my brother been working for you and your friends for more than a week now, and we ain't been paid nothing. 'Fore you go telling us what to do, you got to pony up, man."

"Working?" Thor looked around the salon. A pair of jeans lay across the glass coffee table next to the GPS tracker, the ashtrays overflowed, and the galley countertops were invisible beneath the double layer of dirty dishes. "This boat looks like a garbage dump, and judging from the smell in here, you've spent all your money on illegal drugs. I don't pay for that kind of stupidity."

"Fuck you," Spyder yelled. "I ain't stupid, and I ain't your boat nigger." Asshole could do his own work. Spyder headed for the sliding glass door.

He had no warning before something slammed into the back of his head. His knees buckled. He sprawled face-first onto the carpet. Before he really understood what was happening, Thor's fancy loafer slammed into his kidney. Spyder tried to yell *fuck you* again, but all that came out was another "ugh" as air was forced from his mouth by another kick. Spittle slid down his chin, dripping onto the carpet. He started to push himself up onto his knees and felt hands come from behind and close around his neck. The hands yanked him up, straightening his back, though he was still on his knees.

Spyder had a perfect view out the glass door, blue water and white yachts, dark birds circling the sky. He had no air in him, and those hands had cut off any hope of getting more. He struggled at first, flailing his arms, trying to strike at the body attached to the hands that now held his life in their steely grip. As he grew weaker, he focused on those birds, vultures probably, circling over some dead thing. Flying away like he wished...

Then, he heard a thunderous *bang*, and the hands released his throat as Thor was flung sideways. He heard the crash when Thor hit the glass coffee table, knocking it off the stand and shattering the glass. Then it was quiet except for the sound Spyder made as he gasped for air, leaning forward, his elbows on his knees. Over and above the noise of his own breathing, he heard a *click*. Followed by another *click*.

Spyder turned around. From the stairs that led down to the forward staterooms, Pinky came walking past the galley holding the stainless steel pistol in both hands, continuing to pull the trigger on the empty chambers. When he came within reach, Spyder stretched out his arm and took the weapon from his brother's hands. He'd never checked to see if the magazine carried a full load.

Thor lay still on his right side next to the broken glass, and a pool of blood darkened the rug under his shoulder. The side of his face that had struck the table was covered with blood. The man's eyes were closed, and Spyder hoped the fucker was dead.

Pinky got an arm under Spyder's elbow and helped him to his feet. Spyder shrugged off Pinky's assistance. His whole body hurt like a son of a bitch, but he'd had the shit kicked out of him before. It wasn't the first time. And they needed to get the hell out of there. He knew that cops weren't far off after the sound of a gunshot.

"I can walk. Let's go," he said, his voice little more than a hoarse whisper. Spyder stepped over Thor's legs and headed for the sliding door. He turned to look for his brother. Pinky had stopped in the middle of the main salon, and he was staring down at Thor. Spyder watched as Pinky pulled out another magazine from his pocket. He offered it to his brother.

Spyder shook his head. No more noise. The dude wasn't going anywhere. If he wasn't dead already, he was gonna bleed out. It was time to get moving before the fucking French cops arrived. His brother reached down then and pulled the wallet from Thor's back pocket. Then Pinky picked up the GPS black box off the glass-covered carpet.

"Hey, bro," Spyder said as he slid open the glass door. "Come on. I always wanted to drive one of these fucking cigarette boats."

CHAPTER SEVENTY-SEVEN

Scott's Head Bay, Dominica

March 30, 2008

"You knew my father?" Cole asked as he shook the man's small hand. The firm grip surprised him.

"Yes," Michaut said. "He was a very persistent man. Typical English."

Cole laughed. "I guess you did know him."

"Please, sit down." The old man dragged the chairs closer together. As he eased himself into the chair, he said, "We have much to talk about. I asked Julliette to bring us coffee."

Cole looked at Riley, then back at the old man. "Mr. Michaut, we don't have much time. There's a man looking for us. Not a nice guy. I don't want him to find you or your family."

The old man nodded. "Mademoiselle," he said, looking at Riley's face and neck. "He did this to you?"

Riley nodded.

"I understand. This will not take long. And please, call me Henri. It has been a long time since anyone called me by that name. Except your father. Like you, he wandered into my garden one day asking questions about the war. I did not know at the time that he would become a very dear friend."

The back door to the house opened, and the young woman came out carrying a tray with three glasses of ice water, mini cups of coffee, a bowl of sugar cubes, and a small silver pitcher.

"That smells so good," Riley said as she took a cup.

"My father didn't make it easy to find you, Henri," Cole said. He, too, took a cup and sat on the edge of a chair.

"Yes, that was to protect me." Henri shook his head. "But when a man is ninety-two years old, there is not so much to fear. It is only for my family that I am afraid. I spent most of my life hiding here on this island, afraid they would find out that I knew their secrets. It was only when I met your father that I realized there was something I needed to do before I die. Something I needed to share. Your father said he would help me."

"And now I will if I can."

Michaut nodded. "As he said you would. Your father suspected something might happen to him after he wrote about the *Surcouf*. And he told me if that happened, then I was to expect you."

Cole glanced at Riley and smiled. "For someone I only met once in my life, he knew me pretty well, I guess."

"Your father said you are a good man. That you would do the right thing with all this. He said you are a scuba diver, and I need someone to dive down and retrieve what went down with *Surcouf* more than sixty years ago."

"Are you saying you saw the *Surcouf* sink?" Riley asked.

"Oh yes," the old man said with a broad smile that revealed several gaps where teeth should have been. The colored patch of skin on his cheek darkened. "I nearly went down with her."

At first, Cole wasn't sure he had heard the man right. He set his coffee cup down on the small table. "You mean you were supposed to be on board?"

"No, I *was* on board. I was the signalman on *Surcouf*'s last voyage, and I saw her go down." He chuckled, then added, "From very close range."

Cole started to speak, but he didn't know what to say. He felt Riley's hand slip into his.

The old man continued to laugh. "You are very much like your father. He had the same reaction. He did not believe me at first." Henri pointed to the coin hanging at Cole's neck. "It was only when I produced that coin that he changed his mind."

Cole reached for the coin and rubbed it with his thumb. "You gave him this?"

The old man nodded.

Cole struggled to wrap his brain around the idea that the man sitting before him had served aboard *Surcouf*. There was so much he wanted to know. But Diggory Priest was out there using every asset available to him to locate them. They didn't have time for pleasantries. "Henri, this man who is looking for us right now. He wants something that is on *Surcouf*. We're running out of time."

"It will be easier if I tell you the story of that last day at sea. Then you will understand. I will make it as brief as I can."

Cole saw Riley glance at her watch. But from his many years of diving on wrecks, he knew how valuable it could be to know the events of that last day when he entered the wreck on the seafloor. Henri might be able to tell him exactly where to find what he was looking for.

"It was in February of 1942, and we had been at sea for five days. The men mutinied when we left Bermuda." The old man told them the story of the bomb on board.

"*Bomb?*" Cole said.

"Cole," Riley said, "let him tell it."

"Yes," the old man continued, "you see, they didn't trust us. The Allies, that is. France had surrendered to the Nazis, and there were always rumors that *Surcouf* was refueling German U-boats and crewed by Nazi sympathizers. But the crew were not traitors; we were simply a bunch of French boys who were rounded up in London to crew the big sub. We had little training. There were three English on *Surcouf* when we left Bermuda, but on that last day, only one remained."

"What happened?" Cole asked.

"That is a story for another day. Lieutenant Gerald Woolsey was the one who set the bomb. Woolsey told me the Allies no longer wanted to pay for the upkeep on this submarine with the Pacific war opening up. They wanted the world to think she was the victim of a Nazi U-Boat. He said he was only following orders. Woolsey was to set the bomb before we sailed and then leave with his secret documents. But the mutiny changed all that."

The old man coughed a chest-rattling, phlegmy cough, then reached for a glass of water and took a long drink. He set the water glass back down on the little table. "It was my job to bring food and drink to our English prisoner. During that last day, Woolsey told me about going to university in America and becoming a part of a secret organization. He said these men like war—not to fight, but to make money. He told me there were very secret papers in a diplomatic pouch in the safe in the radio room, and the Allies would sink *Surcouf* before letting them go to the Vichy government. Woolsey said these men had so much money and power, we could not hide *Surcouf* from them. They would come for us, and he was right. I took Woolsey to the captain, then retrieved the pouch. On the papers, I read the words *Operation Magic*. They were top-secret decoded messages. When he read them, it was clear even Woolsey was shocked."

The old man was trying to speak fast, but his voice was growing hoarse. Henri took another drink. "A sailor came in then and told us that planes were coming."

"What happened?"

"Everyone ran topsides. The captain told me to secure the documents. I took the waterproof bag from the lieutenant. He had already resealed it. I put it in the steel strongbox and placed the box in the bottom drawer of the captain's desk.

"On the bridge, the lieutenant explained the signals to me. We tried to signal the planes, but it was no good. They started shooting. I was resending my signals when I heard Woolsey call my name. I turned and saw I was alone on the bridge. Water was rising. Woolsey closed the hatch. I ran to it, screamed, and pounded. In my pocket, I had my knife, and I used it to beat on the metal hatch. I begged him to let me in." The old man licked his lips before he continued. "The water came up around me, rushed up over me. Even underwater, I heard the planes roar overhead. I held on. The pressure of the water threatened to force my mouth open. I felt myself being dragged deeper."

Henri took a deep breath. "So I let go. The turbulence spun me around, and I nearly drowned. Then I saw the sunlight shining down through the water, and I swam toward the light."

"They left you to drown?" Riley asked.

"Yes."

"That's awful, Henri."

"In reality, they saved my life. When I surfaced, I saw the planes tilting up in a wide turn. They came back over the path where *Surcouf* ran beneath the surface. I saw the small black shapes falling. They were one kilometer away when I heard the first explosion, saw the great upwelling of water and the fuel slick. Debris erupted at the surface along with many bodies, some men still moving, trying to swim. They waved their arms in the air, and I could hear their voices pleading for help.

"The American planes turned in another slow arc. They came back, their machine guns firing into the water, into the survivors.

After that, nothing moved. I kept very still, and they never spotted me. If I'd made it inside that hatch, I would have died with them.

"Once the planes were gone, I swam to the wreck site. The water was full of sharks tearing into the bodies. I expected to be eaten at any second. I do not know why not. Perhaps because there was so much food. I found a piece of wood and began swimming north toward the closest island, which I now know is one of a group called Îles de la Petite Terre."

Cole shook his head. "So that's where she went down. I was never even close."

"Yes, these islands are uninhabited. It was night when I arrived, and I was exhausted and cold. I spent three days there. I was near death when a fisherman found me. He was from Dominica. He knew I was a sailor, but he kept my identity secret. Later, I married his daughter, and we told everyone my name was Jules and I came from Guadeloupe." Henri's body shook again as he struggled to cough up the fluid in his chest.

The young woman came out the back door and brought a wood box to Henri. Then she turned to Cole. "If you please, my great-grandfather is tiring."

Cole nodded and stood. "Thank you so much, Henri."

Henri raised a hand like a traffic cop. "The papers are most important. It is possible they are still in the captain's cabin. But there is something else." He pointed to the coin Cole wore. A mischievous smile played around his wet lips. "I took five of those from the hold the last time I visited Woolsey. There is more, much more. Through the years, I melted down four of them and sold the gold. The gold from those four fed my family for many years." Cole saw the old man's body tense as he struggled to quell another cough. His voice was barely a whisper when he said, "I wanted more, but I was always too frightened to search for it. Didn't want anyone to come searching for me. I spent my whole life in hiding. Then I told your father my story, and then when I did not hear from him, I read on the Internet what happened."

Henri's pale eyes looked at him, and Cole felt him asking for understanding.

"You had a family to think about, Henri."

The old man nodded, then opened the box and withdrew a sheet of paper. He handed it to Cole. "This is a sketch of what I could see on Îles de la Petite Terre and the other island Marie-Galante. I went back on my father-in-law's fishing boat after the war and came up with this best guess as to the position where *Surcouf* went down." He pointed to an X on the sketched chart. "The water is thirty to fifty meters deep and then…" The old man lowered his hand to indicate the drop-off. He reached out and grasped Cole's forearm. "Do what I should have done years ago. Find her. Find *Surcouf* and Operation Magic for me and for your father."

Cole knelt down in front of the old man's chair and looked into his pale blue eyes, now red-rimmed and shiny with tears.

"I will, Henri. I promise. And when I do, I'll come back to tell you all about it."

CHAPTER SEVENTY-EIGHT

Aboard the Bonefish
Scott's Head Bay, Dominica

March 30, 2008

Riley screwed the cap on the diesel jerry jug she had just emptied into her tank, and she looked up at Cole. "We've got to get moving."

Bonefish was rafted up alongside the *Shadow Chaser* in the Scott's Head Bay anchorage. Earlier, as they had hurried back from Michaut's house, Riley mentioned she was concerned about how much fuel she had left on board after motor sailing nearly the whole way from the Saintes to Dominica. Cole insisted she bring her boat alongside the big trawler to top off her tanks.

Theo's face appeared at the rail. "Hey, Cap, I've got the radar running, and we've got a suspicious target out there." He hoisted another yellow plastic jug over the cap rail and handed it down to Cole. "This is the last one, right?"

"Yeah," Cole said.

Riley checked her watch. "Cole, it's almost three thirty. Theo, what do you see on radar?"

"We've got an AIS receiver, you know the Automatic Identification System, so I can see names on some of the targets.

There's a cruise ship and a smaller cargo ship up off Roseau. There are a couple of boats that aren't broadcasting any AIS data. Or they're too far off. We don't know who they are. And one is headed south along the coast, coming fast. Faster than that boat the Brewsters had in the Saintes—racing boat fast. It might be a pleasure boat, but it worries me."

Riley poured the last of the diesel into her fuel tank deck fill. She didn't like that news much either. They'd tarried too long here already. "Theo, have you thought about going along the windward coast east of the island?" she asked. "It would mean a bumpy ride, but it would put the island between us and anybody who might be heading south looking for us."

Theo slapped his hand on the cap rail. "I like the way you think, Captain Riley. I'll go check the mileage on that route."

She screwed the cap on the last jug and stood. Her legs were stiff from kneeling on the deck.

Cole slipped his arms around her. "I wish you'd come with us on *Shadow Chaser*. Leave *Bonefish* here. We could set a second anchor."

"I can't, Cole. She's my home. God only knows what that maniac would do to her if he found her unattended. I know your boat is faster, but I'll be right behind you."

"And if that maniac finds you alone on your boat in the middle of the channel? I'm having a hard time putting that picture out of my head."

"If he's going to find anybody, it's going to be you. You're bigger, more visible from satellites, and it's possible there is some sort of tracking device on there." She nodded toward his boat.

"Right. You know I'll be searching for that damn thing all night," he said. "Do you have a weapon aboard?"

"No, most of these islands impound your weapons while you're visiting. And I never wanted to lie on my customs declarations. Of course, now I'm wishing I had. What about you?"

He shook his head. "No guns. Same reasons."

"Cole, listen, if we're all together on your boat and we don't have any weapons, what makes you think I'd be safer with you? He's already tracked your boat to Dominica once. They're on one boat. It's standard operating procedure not to put all your eggs in one basket. It makes more sense to split up."

Theo leaned over the rail above their heads. He coughed, and they moved apart. "Riley, I think you've hit on a great idea. It's only a few miles more for us to go out and around the southern tip of the island. After that, it's a straight shot to the area your man has marked on his chart. It will be rough though. The forecast is for winds a little north of east at eighteen to twenty knots, stronger in gusts."

Riley grabbed one of her shrouds and shook it. "She's a tough old girl. She'll be fine. It will slow us down, but we'll get there by morning."

"And what about you?" Cole asked, his arm around her waist again.

"I know how to take care of myself."

He swung around to face her, wrapped both arms around her waist, and lifted her feet off the ground. Nose to nose, he said, "You know, you are one stubborn lady."

"Right back at ya, Mister."

"You be safe, Magee," he said and then closed his mouth over hers.

* * *

It did not take long for *Shadow Chaser* to disappear over the horizon once they'd rounded the southern tip of the island. That had happened even before it got dark. Now, she and *Bonefish* were alone, pounding into the wind under a double-reefed main and partially rolled-up headsail, making no more than five knots over the bottom. The sea was confused with a large north swell, and the smaller wind chop from north of east. The combination made the ocean here feel like a popcorn patch.

Riley adjusted the lines on her safety harness and pulled up the hood of her foul weather jacket. She sat tucked under the dodger, thankful her autopilot was handling the steering for her so she didn't have to sit behind the wheel where spume filled the air most of the time. The air temperature was warm enough, but with all the spray flying across the boat, she was shivering. Her T-shirt beneath the jacket was already damp from a wave that had caught her without her hood up and doused cold seawater down her neck. She was still only wearing shorts, and her feet were cold and puckered from the constant wet.

"Ah, the joys of sailing, eh, Mikey?" Her brother hadn't ever cared much for foul weather.

Riley remembered that time when they'd sailed with their father back to Antigua and they had been caught in a squall with full sails up. Her father had ordered Michael to take down the main, and Riley had shouldered her brother aside and lowered the sail herself. She knew her brother could do many things in math or science that she would never be able to do. They each had their strengths.

Her father had called her brother a weakling who'd let a girl do his job. His disdain for his son had always been there.

"Oh, Dad," she said aloud. *It appears you were the weak one— unable to protect your own son.* And yet, he was her father too, and in spite of his weakness, he had not deserved to die like that. All last night as she'd traveled south, she had gone over and over it in her mind. The real blame lay with a man she had once slept with, maybe even loved—and the organization.

Riley shuddered and pulled her rain jacket closed under her chin. *Concentrate on the task at hand, marine.*

She'd had to take a negative tack, motor sailing to hold tighter to the wind so that she could get clear of the reefs off the eastern side of Dominica. She'd tack again somewhere in the middle of the Dominica Channel to get around the island of Marie-Galante. It was going to be a very long night.

The airport was somewhere along this shore, but Riley didn't see any planes taking off or landing. She stuck her face outside the dodger and scanned the shoreline, but the boat reared up and then slammed down into another trough, and more spray splattered across the canvas, sounding like buckshot.

Once she was a good five miles beyond Jenny Point, Riley stood up, stretched, and made her way below, moving from handhold to handhold on the heaving boat. She wanted to check her radar again. Even on the twenty-four-mile range, aside from *Shadow Chaser*, she hadn't seen a thing. So far, so good. Maybe this idea of going up the ocean side of the island had thrown them off her tail. Or maybe Cole and Theo were dealing with them about now. She had tried contacting the guys on the other boat by radio earlier, but they were out of VHF range and they weren't reading her on the SSB channel they had chosen to monitor, either.

She slid into the chart table seat, turned on the radar at the panel, and waited for the image to appear. With her autopilot, chart plotter, and refrigeration all running, she needed to conserve her battery power now that the engine was off. She considered making another cup of coffee while she waited for the radar to warm up, but decided against it. She was already jittery enough. Solo night sailing did that to her.

She pushed the power button to start up the antenna. She watched as the green line made the sweep around the black screen. A large green blob emerged from the sea clutter off the northeast end of Dominica. It looked like a big rain shower. The blob changed shape with each sweep round the screen, but a small bit in the lower left-hand corner stayed solid. As she watched, she decided that hard blob might be moving.

Riley changed the range on the radar from twenty-four miles down to twelve. Using the buttons on the front of the screen, she moved the crosshair symbol over the radar target and marked the spot. The green target moved away from the X she had drawn. Yes, it was definitely moving. And fast. Too fast for a freighter. She judged the distance between her and the target to be something around ten miles. And shrinking. Maybe a cruise ship would move that fast.

She stood up and pulled herself up the companionway ladder until she could see through the dodger's windows to the sea ahead. Scanning the horizon as the boat crested a wave, she thought, no way a cruise ship could be that close and still not be visible. After assuring herself that she couldn't yet see anything off her bow, she climbed down and slid back into the seat.

Riley stared at the radar. They were only about eight miles off now and closing at a speed close to fifteen knots. That meant they were less than thirty minutes away even in this confused sea. And they were on a collision course.

CHAPTER SEVENTY-NINE

Aboard the Fast Eddie

March 30, 2008

"Christ, Pinky," Spyder said. "Can't you do that over the leeward side for Pete's sake? The fucking wind is blowing your chum all over my jacket."

He watched his brother clutching the gunnel of the boat, his head dangling over the side like a bar of soap on a rope. Spyder buried his nose in the crook of his own elbow. God, the smell was enough to make him get sick even though he'd never been seasick a day in his life. Didn't matter whether he was on a swordfish boat or a shrimper, Spyder could take the smells of rotten fish, diesel, you name it. But puke? Shit, no.

"Listen, bro," Spyder yelled toward the back of the red racing jumpsuit his brother wore. They had found a pair of these all-weather suits on board the big Donzi race boat, and they had both climbed into them when it had started to rain earlier. "The boat rolls a hell of a lot worse when we slow her down. She don't pound so bad, but she rolls like a bitch," he yelled. "That's what's making you sick, man." He had no idea if that was true or not, but Spyder loved opening up those big throaty engines and letting the *Fast*

Eddie show off her stuff. When the boat flew over flat water and he flexed his knees with the motion, it almost felt as good as sex. Almost.

Even with all the noise, Spyder heard the sound of his brother's retching one more time. He turned away lest the wind carry the vomit into his face.

Here we go again, Spyder thought. When they first took off in the *Fast Eddie*, his brother had started puking as soon as they'd got out into the channel. Spyder had slowed down, but once they got in the lee of the island, he'd opened her up again. Pinky was OK on the flat water. Still, by the time they got down to the south end of Dominica, it was almost dark and there was no sign of the doc or the bitch. Pissed him off.

That was when Pinky got out the GPS machine again. They seen she was on the other side of the island headed north. Pinky wanted to know how the hell he knew it was her boat and not the doc's. He told the freak that ain't no way they'd be going no five knots in that big trawler. So Pinky says, then let's follow her. Spyder knew for damn sure what would happen if they tried to take that route in the open ocean. Back to the vomiteria.

Then Pinky suggested they could cut her off just as easy at the north end. So they'd headed up the flat, sheltered water on the leeward side of the island. Since he was feeling better, Pinky went below and found some cold beer and packages of crackers and chips. Only once they rounded the point, they'd run into that squall, and here they were with Pinky spewing his guts over the side again. Those vinegar potato chips had smelled bad enough the first time around.

Spyder turned the wheel to point the boat into the swells and tilted his head off to one side so the windshield no longer blocked the rain-scented wind from his face. The beaded braids that dangled down either side of his face flew back and fluttered against the side of his head. God he loved how this boat made him feel. He pictured what he'd do to the bitch once he pulled up in this black bomber and got his hands on her. He was gonna tear her wide open. Show her not to mess with him.

"Damn," Pinky said as he pushed himself up and collapsed into the padded passenger seat.

"'Bout time," Spyder said. "You ready to go now?" He was ready to open that sucker up and start pounding those seas.

Pinky's hand flew out and grabbed Spyder's forearm. Shit! He had no idea the little freak could squeeze that tight. His long fingernails seemed to be cutting right through the rain jacket.

"Fuck, Pinky. You're hurting me!"

"Listen," his brother hissed.

Spyder had to lean in close to that puke face to hear.

"There's no way we both gonna jump from this boat to hers out here in this ocean."

Spyder started to interrupt, but his brother dug those fingernails into him again.

"Jesus, cut it out!" Spyder wailed.

"I said listen. You might be able to do it, but you ain't leaving me alone on this boat. What we gonna do is, we gonna follow her. Keep far enough back she can't see us. She either gonna lead us to the doc, or if she stops somewhere, we take her. Once she tells us where the doc is, you can do whatever the hell you want with her, bro."

CHAPTER EIGHTY

Aboard the Bonefish

March 30, 2008

The target on her radar screen was moving again after stopping for about ten minutes right off her beam. Now they were heading for her boat but no longer making much speed. They were about five miles off. She should be able to spot their lights by now.

Leaving the radar on, Riley pulled herself back up the companionway stairs, timing every step so that the boat's extreme motion worked with her instead of against her. The bow lifted again on an extra-large wave and then crashed down into the trough, flinging buckets of cold spray across the cockpit and making the hull, mast, and rigging all shudder at impact. She bent her knees and ducked her chin down into her rain gear. Rivulets of water streamed off the bill of the baseball cap she wore under her hood, and she shivered. The boat always handled this pounding better than she could.

She crouched under the dodger and scanned the horizon off her port bow through the dodger's spray-splattered plastic windows. She reached inside the cabin and pulled the binoculars from the teak holder. Standing and risking a dousing, she took a peek over the top of the dodger. She found that even through the glasses, there was no sign of a light or shadow on the horizon.

The boat had to be running dark. No lights.

She sat down on the cockpit seat on the low side of the companionway and leaned her head back against the dodger's stainless tubing frame. Closing her eyes for a minute felt so good. She was bone tired. Riley hadn't eaten a regular meal since that sumptuous feast on Niko's yacht over twenty-four hours ago. Surviving off granola bars, trail mix, and coffee was taking a toll. Her stomach was protesting with an acid burn. To make matters worse, this was her second night at sea, and she'd had only four hours bunk time that morning. The body was like a machine, and she knew she'd been treating hers badly. Too little sleep, too little decent food.

Riley snapped her eyes open. No falling asleep. Routine. Discipline. That was what she needed. She checked her watch. Nearly midnight. Soon it would be time to enter her position in the log. She stood and checked all around the horizon once more. The coast of Dominica was falling away. Her course was taking her into the channel between Dominica and Marie-Galante. But she still saw no lights or signs of other boats. The moon should rise in about an hour. It would only be a little bit of a thing, but it would still provide more light than these few billion stars.

When Riley climbed back below to check her radar again, she discovered the other boat was only four miles off—dead astern. She set about heating herself a can of beef-and-barley soup on the gimballed stove. She kept checking the radar every couple of minutes. They weren't closing. In fact, they were matching her speed, staying exactly four miles astern. There was no question about it. That boat was following her. Or perhaps stalking was a better word.

She poured the soup into a large mug and climbed the ladder back into the cockpit. She still saw nothing aft. No lights. The hot, thick liquid felt good in her belly. She set down the spoon and drank the rest of it down. Stepping back from the dodger, she looked up at the top of her mast. Her masthead tricolor light was showing a bright white light aft.

OK, she thought when she'd finished her soup. Two can play at this game. She ducked below and dropped the mug into the galley sink. At the nav station, she glanced at the radar again. Nothing had changed, so she flipped the switch to douse all her running lights.

That won't do much good, though, if they have radar, she thought, so she climbed back into the cockpit. First, she clipped the line from her safety harness to one of the jack lines running along the lee deck, and then she climbed out of the cockpit onto the side deck. As she crawled her way forward to the shrouds, the deck was rising and falling under her, the black water rushing past her hull like water from a fireman's hose. With her boat on autopilot, if she went overboard, she'd never be able to pull herself back aboard at this speed.

When she reached the shrouds, she pulled herself to a stand and wrapped one leg and one arm around the wire rigging for support. Spray from the bow waves splattered across her back. After several minutes' effort to untie the knot, she lowered the halyard that supported her radar reflector. Back on her knees again, she carried the bulky thing back to the cockpit and stowed it below.

Seated once again on the high side of the cockpit, Riley found she was sweating inside her foul weather gear from the exertion of moving around on the heaving boat. She unzipped the top of her jacket to let the breeze in and wondered how on earth they had found her and how they knew which boat out here was hers. Her decision to go up the outside of Dominica put her on a piece of water that very few sailboats would choose to be on—beating up a lee shore in the middle of the night. How did they know she was here?

She thought back to the first day she had seen that ponytailed Brewster character, the day after she had met up with Dig in Pointe-à-Pitre. That morning, she had departed from the Pointe-à-Pitre anchorage to sail to the Saintes. She had awakened early because she wanted to put some miles between her and Dig. When she went on deck, she found that someone had returned her oars. She knew that Dig wasn't much good with boats, so she assumed he had hired someone else to do it.

Of course, she thought. Her oars. As the realization hit her, she felt so stupid. It was so obvious. Why hadn't she seen it before? When they'd gone to Dominica on Cole's boat, they had taken *her* dinghy along. Her dinghy with the set of oars inside it. They'd made it so easy for Dig to find them. There never was a tracker on *Shadow Chaser*. It had to be in one of her oars.

Riley slid aft, knelt on the seat at the back of the cockpit, and reached into her inflatable dinghy that hung in davits above her transom. She pulled out an oar and shook it. It didn't feel as if there was anything inside the aluminum tubing. Shaking the other one gave the same result. She depressed the button that held the two halves together and pulled the oar apart. She grabbed the flashlight from her pocket and shone it into the tubes. Nothing. She fitted the two halves back together and stowed them in the dinghy. She repeated the process with the other oar, only the second time, she found something that looked like paper in one of the halves. She shook the oar, and the wad of paper dropped to the cockpit floor. When she picked it up, a clear plastic bag fell out onto the cockpit seat. Inside was a small, silver stick or tube that looked about the size of a AA battery.

"Goddammit," she shouted, flinging the device out into the black waves. "How stupid could I be?"

Then she felt her stomach jump, and the soup nearly backed up her throat. Was that a light? To the east, off her beam.

The stalker was behind her—not off her starboard side. From the glimpse she'd had of the bright white light, it looked like the masthead navigation light of a commercial ship. Again, it appeared for a moment before it slipped behind a wave. She waited, searching the horizon. There it was again, brighter this time. And here she was running with no navigation lights at all. That was all she needed now—to get run down by a freighter.

Riley grabbed the binoculars off the low seat and climbed back up to the high side of the cockpit. She couldn't see a thing because the binoculars' lenses were covered with spray. She slid back down off the seat, reached around into the cabin, and pulled a paper towel off the roll that hung on the bulkhead. She climbed back up and hooked one elbow around the winch to hang on to the heeling boat. The light was growing bigger. She rubbed harder at the glass, but she was just smearing salt water on the lenses in a greasy-looking mess. She looked up again.

And she froze.

Oh no, she thought. She felt some of the tension release as her shoulders sagged. Then Riley started laughing as she made out the curving top half of the scimitar moon that was climbing up out of the sea. Already, the sea to the east looked brighter as the bottom of the moon cleared the horizon and began to climb higher in the sky. She looked up at her sails and the laughter died on her lips. Her white main and jib seemed to glow with an inner light, as though they sucked in the moonlight, collecting every last ray.

Riley looked aft. Still no sign of her stalkers, but one thing was clear now. All her efforts of the last hour had been for nothing. They wouldn't need lights or radar or a GPS tracker to follow her now. But if she were to lower her sails and motor, her speed would be cut in half.

Down at the chart table, Riley made her decision. She knew that she wasn't Dig's only target. If she was all he wanted, he could have come alongside hours ago. He and his crew of half-wits were following her to stop Cole, and she was not about to lead them to the *Shadow Chaser* and hence to *Surcouf.*

The closest port on the chart was Grand Bourg on Marie-Galante, now about fourteen miles distant, which was half the distance to the *Surcouf* dive location where Cole and Theo were headed. Given her current rate of speed and the need to feel her way into what looked like a very tricky night entrance, she figured she might make it by four or five in the morning. There was a good-sized village there. She'd go ashore, find people, knock on doors, get herself out of the picture so Cole and Theo would have time to find what they were looking for by morning. She had a plan.

* * *

Four hours later, with the sky starting to lighten in the east, Riley dropped her anchor inside the sea wall off the village of Grand Bourg. Her GPS had brought her through the narrow entrance into this quiet little harbor, and once her anchor was well set, she stood on deck and glanced around the waterfront. No sign of any new boats yet. She figured she had time to try Cole one last time before lowering her dinghy and heading in to the village. She ducked down the companionway and slid onto the chart table seat.

She grabbed the single sideband radio mike and pushed the button to transmit. "*Shadow Chaser, Shadow Chaser,* this is *Bonefish.*"

She heard pops and crackles through the radio's speaker, but nothing more. She twisted her fingers in the coiled microphone cord. There were many different frequencies to choose from, and some worked better than others, depending on the location. They had chosen a frequency that was rarely used by sailors because they had wanted to be able to speak without fear of being overheard. Maybe there was a good reason nobody much used this frequency.

She brought the microphone to her mouth, pressed the transmit button, and tried them again. "*Shadow Chaser, Shadow Chaser,* this is *Bonefish.*"

In the distance, she heard the low rumble of a high performance engine running at idle. The noise grew louder.

Riley jumped up from the navigation station and grabbed the dive knife from the scabbard inside the companionway. Just as she reached the top step, she stumbled against the side of the hatch when a large black racing boat came hard alongside, slamming into her hull with a loud crunch. She saw a man on the foredeck of the racer get half thrown onto the deck of her boat. In her bulky foul weather gear, she struggled to climb out of the cockpit. The man on her boat was shouting.

"Goddammit, Pinky," he said, "turn off the engines and tie her up. Can't you do nothing right?"

Standing on the foredeck of her boat wearing a one-piece, full-body, red racing suit was Spyder Brewster. He was pointing a gun at her midsection.

"Hey, bitch," he shouted over the deep rumbling of the racing boat's engines. "Wassup?"

At the moment, the breeze had pinned the racing boat to the side of her boat. She knew they would soon swing apart. "Get off my boat!" She gestured with the knife toward the other boat.

"You ain't happy to see me? Drop that knife for your boy here. You and me, we gonna party."

The strangest-looking man Riley had ever seen emerged from the powerboat's cockpit in a matching red suit carrying a coil of black line. His hair looked like a cumulus cloud, and though he had a broad nose and African features, his face was white aside from freckles across his nose and a few patches of darker skin. He wobbled and held on to the windshield for support, and since he was upwind of her, she got a strong whiff of vomit as he steadied himself.

"Dammit, Pinky," Spyder shouted. "Gimme that line. I told you to shut down the fuckin' engines."

The odd man ignored Spyder, then knelt on the deck of the racing powerboat and cinched the two boats together.

Spyder waggled the gun in her direction. "Hey, bitch, the knife. I said, drop it."

"I'm not dropping anything, you idiot."

The man jumped a step toward her and thrust the gun forward, holding it sideways like the gangsters in the movies and aiming it at the center of her forehead. "Don't call me an idiot, or I will fucking blow your head off," he shouted.

From where she was standing next to the cockpit dodger, she heard radio static, then a faint voice. "*Bonefish*, this is *Shadow Chaser*, do you read me?"

Riley erupted with noise, and Spyder staggered back a step. Waving the knife, she began shouting at both men to get the hell off her foredeck. She kept shouting even as Spyder grew red in the face. He screamed at her, "Drop the knife or I'll shoot you, bitch!"

At least they couldn't hear the radio.

CHAPTER EIGHTY-ONE

Aboard the Shadow Chaser

March 31, 2008

"We've been at this three hours now, Cap," Theo said, his arms leaning on the bulwark at the stern of *Shadow Chaser*. The big trawler was operating on autopilot while the two men paced the deck. "We've covered more than a square mile with the magnetometer, and we haven't even had any false readings. Maybe your man's information wasn't so good after all."

"This is the spot all right. I can feel it. It's not like the guy had a hand-bearing compass when the sub sank under him. He was treading water and sighting positions off landmarks miles away on shore."

Theo looked up at the sky. Most of the stars had disappeared—only the planet Venus remained visible below the moon. "Gonna be light, soon," he said.

"Yup," Cole said. A thin band of gray had appeared on the eastern horizon. "I wish we'd hear something from Riley though. I'm worried that the reason she's not calling is because she *can't*."

"That's my captain—seeing trouble whether it's there or not."

"This guy, this Diggory. Theo, he scares the shit out of me—you weren't there in DC. This is real, Theo. Too real."

"Yeah, mon, I know. I saw the look on the man's face when he took Riley at the Indian River. Man must have a heart of ice to lie to her like that."

"I never should have left her alone out there."

"Her choice, not yours, mon. Besides, you know how unreliable single sideband radio is when you're this close. She could be calling but we can't pick her up. With cloud cover like this, who knows what kind of skip we're getting. Riley knows how to take care of herself. And we've got a submarine to locate."

Cole walked to the stern of the vessel and tested the tension on the tow cable that connected the sensor to the boat's network of electronics. "Feels like the darn thing is fouled again," he said. Cole began to haul in the cable hand over hand.

They had great equipment, thanks to Theo. He had designed the proton sensor casing with sleek, dolphin-like hydrodynamic fins, but the blasted thing still got fouled by this Sargasso weed. Cole had nicknamed the silver fish-shaped object "Flipper."

Floodlights lit the water behind the boat, and Flipper broke the surface skipping between two waves, its nose trailing a beard of yellow-green seaweed. Cole pulled it to the boat and shook off the debris. Then, he tossed the long silver magnetometer back into the water. "OK, Flipper." He waved both hands back over his shoulders, then pointed out to sea mimicking the motions of a dolphin trainer. "Go get me a submarine, boy!"

Theo fed out cable until the coil at his feet was gone. Then he walked over and picked up his tablet off the hatch cover that led down to the engine room. He tapped the screen a couple of times, and the RPMs increased on *Shadow Chaser*'s engine.

"We're back in business," he said.

"The alarm's set?"

"You bet. We float over an old tuna fish can and this baby will chirp a little. But if we pass over a hunk of iron the size of a submarine, this little magnet's going to sing for papa."

Cole knew he should feel tired, but he was running on pure adrenaline. For more than half the night, they'd pounded their way through the heavy seas and thunderstorms off the east coast of Dominica, and he hadn't slept. But at least he had been able to rest when Theo was on watch. Once they had arrived here at the coordinates that Henri had given them, they had set up their search grid, launched the towed proton magnetometer, and started the long, slow, tedious business of searching the seafloor. The swells rocked and rolled *Shadow Chaser* even with the stabilizers. He thought of Riley out in those same seas in her much smaller boat, and once again he had to push down the fear that crawled up the back of his neck. He wished they'd hear from her.

The best way to get his mind off his worries was to stay busy. Cole opened the deck box on the starboard side and lifted out a pair of scuba tanks, a buoyancy compensator, regulator, and mask and fins. He began prepping and testing his gear; he screwed the regulator onto the tanks, checked his gauges, and strapped the dual tanks to the BC.

Theo crossed to another of the many large spools of thick black cable on the aft deck. He uncoiled enough to reach the center of the deck. Right after they arrived on site and started their search grid, he and Theo had used the big boat's crane to hoist the *Enigma* out of the hold. The ROV rested in a cradle on its own pallet that they had strapped to the floor of the hold. Theo attached the cable ends to the little submersible and picked up his tablet again. He began a systems check.

When both men were satisfied that their gear was ready, they leaned against the deck box, arms crossed, and watched the roiling water in their wake.

Cole checked his watch. It read 6:40. The sun should be up, would be up if it weren't for the huge thunderstorm rolling in from the east. The wind had gone light and shifted to westerly. The noise of the seas and wind subsided for a moment, and he heard her.

"*Shadow Chaser, Shadow Chaser,* this is the *Bonefish.*"

"Thank God," Cole said, and he started across the deck to the wheelhouse. He'd only traveled two steps when the alarm squealed.

Theo whooped, and Cole heard the engines idle down, then rumble in reverse as Theo tried to slow their forward motion.

"You bring in Flipper," Cole shouted. "I'll drop the marker."

Cole ran to the starboard aft corner and lifted the coil of light line with a small anchor attached to one end and a white buoy on the other. "What's our depth?" he yelled over the high-pitched squeal from the magnetometer's alarm.

Theo was at the rail on the opposite side of the vessel, pulling in the cable for the Flipper, careful to keep it clear of the vessel's propeller. "Fifty meters," he said, breathless from the effort of hauling in the cable as fast as he could.

Cole stood up on the deck box and swung the grappling anchor back and heaved it out away from the big boat.

Theo got the big silver cylinder over the bulwark, dried his hands on his pants, and lifted his laptop. Cole heard the engine shift into neutral as he fed the line out, and the anchor sank toward the bottom. The line was one hundred meters long, but a tangle in it could put their marker underwater. When he'd fed out all the line, he tossed the buoy into the water.

"Hey, Cap," Theo shouted. "Go answer Riley and tell her the news. That was no soda can!"

"Right!" Cole said. He ran to the wheelhouse and grabbed the mike for the SSB radio. Before he pushed the button on the side of the mike, he glanced up at the color sonar screen. He saw a deeply angled ledge, and along the bottom of the screen he watched the number indicating their depth change with every flash—sixty-two meters, then sixty-six meters, seventy-one meters, seventy-nine meters, eighty-two meters, and then the readings went blank as it moved past the one-hundred-meter depth. Damn thing must be sitting on the edge of a cliff, Cole thought.

"*Bonefish, Bonefish*, this is *Shadow Chaser*." He bounced his right deck shoe on the wood floorboards. Come on, Riley. Wait until you hear this. OK, OK, where was she? She was just calling them a few minutes ago. But oh, how things had changed in those few minutes. He couldn't wait to give her the news. "*Bonefish, Bonefish*, this is *Shadow Chaser*," he called again. I know you're there, Riley. Answer me. He called a third time, but the only answer he got was silence.

CHAPTER EIGHTY-TWO

Aboard the Bonefish

March 31, 2008

Riley could see Spyder didn't really want to shoot. He wanted her to stop making noise. He had to know that the gun would wake up people in the village, including any gendarmes, and he sure as hell wouldn't want that. She felt confident she could handle the Brewster brothers alone—even if it was two against one.

"I said drop the knife, bitch!" Spyder yelled.

Riley hadn't heard Cole's voice on the radio for several long seconds. She hoped he had abandoned his attempt to reach her.

"OK, OK," she said. She rested one hand for balance on the canvas dodger next to her and crouched. She set the knife down on the fiberglass deck and then stood up again.

"Now, turn around and git your ass into that cockpit. But remember, I'm right here with this gun pointed at your back. Don't try nothing stupid."

Riley turned, her mind whirring. She would wait until they were inside the cabin below. It would muffle the noise, and she would have more options in that confined space she knew so well. She heard the two men talking in hushed voices behind her as she climbed down into the aft cockpit and sat on the far seat near the steering wheel.

"Come on. I know you like to watch, Pinky."

She saw the black boot scrape across the teak-topped coaming as Spyder climbed into the cockpit. Then he sat and swung the gun toward her.

"We ain't got time for this, Spyder," the chubby one said from outside the cockpit. He rocked from one foot to the other as he struggled with how to climb over the coaming and duck under the canvas dodger and bimini that shaded the cockpit from the rising sun.

While he was dawdling, Riley took a closer look at the gun. It looked like a Ruger Mark II target pistol. Twenty-two caliber. One of her buddies used to bring one to the range at Quantico. She knew it well.

"Fuck we ain't." Spyder slid across the seat opposite to make room for his brother, and he smiled his brown, gap-tooth smile at her. "Git into the cockpit here, bro. We gonna make this bitch tell us where the doc is. That's all."

The chubby guy swung a leg into the cockpit, then hit his head on the stainless tubing as he tried to duck under the canvas. "Ow! Shit." His other foot tripped on the winch, and he collapsed on the cockpit seat.

Now she understood why Spyder had slid so far out of the way.

The strange man acted as though nothing had happened. He sat up and ran his fingers through his white Afro. "I know you, Spyder. Talkin' ain't all you got in mind. Don't screw this up."

Spyder laughed. "I'm gonna be screwing all right, bro." He looked at her with eyes that shone and pulled down the zipper on the front of his jumpsuit, revealing a café-au-lait-colored concave chest with a small, scraggly patch of hair between his nipples. "We gonna have us a good time, eh, bitch?"

She let her eyes wander ever so slowly down the length of his body, then back up to his face. She held his gaze.

He nodded, his eyes growing brighter. "You like what you see, don't you? Pinky, get down there inside the cabin. I'll send her down right behind you. Keep an eye on her. I don't trust her. You let me know if she tries to grab anything down there. She's tricky."

The man called Pinky climbed down the steps into the main cabin and walked forward to the mast before he turned around.

"Now it's your turn," Spyder said. He waved the gun toward the companionway. "I don't want to shoot you before we had a chance to party, so you don't try nothing, hear? I'm right here with this gun."

Even though it sickened her, Riley was prepared to use whatever tools were at her disposal to get rid of these two. "If you don't mind, I'll just take off this rain jacket," she said. "It's getting so hot." She mirrored his action when she pulled down the zipper on her foul weather gear, then she pulled off the sleeves behind her back, thrusting her breasts toward him. She was braless under the damp T-shirt, and Spyder wasn't missing a minute of the show she was putting on for his benefit.

"Hurry up," he said, his voice growing hoarse. "Git down in the cabin."

She gave him time to watch her as she rose and stepped up into the companionway. Her khaki shorts weren't all that short, but there was still plenty of leg showing. The more she could arouse him, the less his brain would function. Because men always had a size advantage over her, she had learned to lull them into thinking her small stature meant she presented no threat.

She bent over and peered down into the cabin, then looked back at Spyder over her shoulder. "You're not going to hurt me, are you?" she asked in a small voice.

He sat up straighter and moved his torso toward her as he spoke. "I said git down there."

She hopped down to the top step, then held the edge of the hatch and swung down into the cabin.

Pinky jumped back as if he were afraid she was going to kick him in the nuts, and he almost tripped over the threshold of the doorway to her forward stateroom.

She turned to face Spyder as he came down the steps. He had stripped out of the jumpsuit, and he was wearing threadbare jeans cut off at the knees.

"I've been alone on this boat for a long time," she said, her eyes wandering over his skinny bare chest. "I almost forgot what it was like to have men aboard." She glanced over her shoulder at Pinky. He was standing directly behind her, watching.

"Don't pay him no mind," Spyder said. "Pretend he ain't there. It's just you and me."

"And your gun," she said.

"What's that line? You know, from that old movie?"

She leaned back, inclined her head, and studied the bulge in his jeans. "I can tell that's not a gun in *your* pocket." He smiled, and she took a step toward him.

"Hey, watch that," Spyder said, lifting the gun and extending his arm. "Stay back."

She drew in her breath and froze. "It's OK," she said raising her hands in the air. "I'll do whatever you tell me to do," she said, but she had closed the gap between them by one step.

"OK, then, take off them shorts."

She breathed in, held her breath for a few seconds, and ran the tip of her tongue around her lips. Then, looking down, she popped the button and eased the zipper down, revealing her suntanned belly and the dark-purple nylon of her bikini panties. She eased the khaki shorts past her thighs and all the way down to her calves.

She stepped out of them by stepping forward and then tossed the shorts through the starboard doorway into the aft stateroom. The gap between her and Spyder had closed by a few more inches.

"I've never undressed with someone pointing a gun at me before," she said, trying to smile at him. "It's kind of exciting."

He waved the gun at her chest. "Now take off your shirt."

She looked down at his crotch. "I think I should take *your* shorts off first." She took another step toward him, and now the barrel of the gun was no more than ten inches from her breastbone.

"Bitch, you gonna git naked and do everything I tell you to do—but don't do nothin' stupid," he said.

She kept her eyes on his and thought that this whole idea might turn out to be one of the stupidest things she'd ever done, but she knew she had to get close enough to get control of the gun. "You're the one with his finger on the trigger. Seems to me I should be the one worrying." She took another step forward and brushed the fingers of her right hand across the front of his jeans.

He moaned, and his eyes rolled out of focus.

She raised her left hand and let it rest on his right shoulder at the same time her fingers danced up and unbuttoned the top button of his jeans. As she lowered the zipper with her right hand, her left hand slid down his right arm. Riley could tell from his breathing which hand he was focusing on. When her right hand reached his wrist, she made her move.

It was only a matter of seconds, but to Riley, it seemed that the world had slowed and the three of them moved like dancers through that small space in her cabin. Riley thrust her left hand down over his gun hand at the exact same instant she pivoted her right shoulder backward, around and away from the front of the barrel so that in an instant she was standing next to him, no longer between the two men.

Spyder's surprise at her movement caused his reflexes to pull the trigger, but because his reactions were slowed by her distractions, she was out of the way when the gun went off. It sounded as though the pop of the gunshot and Pinky's high-pitched scream occurred at exactly the same moment. The pudgy man, who had been standing behind her, crumpled to the floor, both hands gripping his left knee, a red stain growing on his white pants. She heard Spyder cry out his brother's name, but without stopping the movement she had started, Riley guided the forward momentum of Spyder's gun hand down, then she bent his wrist around in an upward curve until the barrel pointed at the man's own chin. He was still screaming and struggling to get the gun away from his head when it went off. Riley let go of his hand and jumped back in surprise.

There was a second of silence after the shot, then Pinky screamed *"Spyder!"* when his brother toppled sideways against the door to the aft head. The man's eyes were open but unseeing. His mouth continued to open and close like that of a gaffed fish gasping for air on deck. Blood seeped from the ragged hole in the soft tissue under his chin and trickled from the corner of his mouth, but she saw no evidence of an exit wound. In straining to get his hand free, Spyder had pulled the trigger himself.

She stood in the galley, backed up against the stove, and she felt her body trembling. Spyder's sprawled legs twitched and blocked the bottom of the stairs. Though it would be easy enough to step over the legs, it meant she would have to approach him, and she was certain that if she had to get closer to that gasping *thing* on the floor right now, she would be sick.

She wished the other one would stop his wailing. She craned her neck to see past the galley counter. Pinky had crabbed his way across the cabin sole by pulling his useless leg with one hand while he pushed his hefty body forward with his good leg. She looked at Spyder. His mouth had stopped moving. Pinky got a hand on his brother's shoe and pulled. Both men slid across the floor toward each other.

The gun. Where was it? It had to be under Spyder. That was what Pinky was after: the gun.

Pinky rolled Spyder's body over, and she spotted the gun at the same time he did. Riley placed her right foot on the bottom step and pushed her body straight up into the air. She came down putting all her weight on her heel that landed on the back of Pinky's left hand. She felt the bones of his hand crack. Pinky screamed even louder, a high-pitched inhuman sound now. He grabbed her leg with his right hand and pulled her down on top of him. She fell away from the gun, but when she turned around and got to her feet, the screaming had fallen to a moaning whimper and Pinky was lying on the cabin sole propped up on one elbow, his right hand pointing the Ruger at her.

Beads of sweat covered his face, and where there had been splotches of pink color, now his skin was a uniform pale gray. "You're gonna get me to a doctor," he said. He spoke in a hiss through gritted teeth. With his good leg, he pushed himself up until his rump rested on the lowest step. She saw the pain on his face, and she didn't know how he was doing it. His left hand hung limp and useless. One at a time, he pulled himself up the three steps and dragged himself out into the cockpit.

"Get a dish towel and throw it to me." Pinky was breathing hard, and the pain was making it difficult for him to speak.

She followed his orders, grabbing the towel that was hanging on her oven door and tossing it up to him. He tried to rip the towel by holding one end with his gun hand and the other in his teeth, but he was too weak. He tried folding the towel on the diagonal with his broken hand, but the fingers flapped loose and lifeless. She saw how his good hand shook. He was losing a lot of blood from the wound in his knee.

"You—come up here." She could barely make out his slurred words. "Get your dinghy. Take me t'a doctor."

At that moment, the radio burst to life again. "*Bonefish, Bonefish*, this is *Shadow Chaser*, do you read me, Riley?"

The gun in his hand jerked up and his eyes widened. "Get away from there," he said.

"It's OK," she said. "I'm not going to answer it." She had to shout so he could hear her over the sound of Cole's voice. "I'm going to come out into the cockpit now and help you."

She could see how weak he was, but something inside her told her that this one was even more dangerous than Spyder. He wouldn't hesitate to pull the trigger. She had to make sure it wasn't pointed at her.

Pinky was sitting on the starboard seat, and she came up under his gun hand, her elbows locked, pushing it straight up. He fired one shot that pierced her canvas dodger. He wouldn't let go. She was using both of her good hands against his one arm, and yet she was struggling to hold her own. Her scarred shoulder burned as her muscles strained. He was trying to push the gun down, toward her head, and she knew she couldn't hold out against him much longer.

She moved before she was aware of any decision. In her training, she'd always been taught to use her opponent's momentum against him. She twisted her body and slid right, out from under the gun. With no force counteracting him, Pinky's hand and the gun came slamming down on the teak combing. His fingers loosened, and the pistol bounced onto the deck outside the cockpit. Riley scrambled out after it. She had one leg on the deck when the gun hit one of the stainless stanchions and tumbled off the side of the boat into the pale-blue water.

And then she screamed when she felt teeth clamp down on her calf. Her right leg hadn't cleared the cockpit coaming, and the idiot was biting her! She tried to kick her leg free, but she was off balance, and she came down hard on her hip, the nylon panties not providing any cushion. Warm blood flowed across her skin, and as she struggled, she slipped in the wet red liquid on the deck.

Then she saw it. The knife Spyder had made her drop on the deck earlier. The razor-sharp, saw-toothed blade glinted in the morning sunlight. Just beyond her fingertips. Riley grabbed the frame of one of the cabin windows and pulled herself forward just enough to touch it with her fingernail. The first time, she only managed to push it farther away. Damn, her leg hurt. His teeth were ripping her flesh the more she pulled away. She tried again, and with her second effort, she slid the knife closer and wrapped her fingers around the hefty handle.

She glanced over her shoulder, located Pinky's head, and with her other foot, she planted a kick with her heel right down on his nose. She grunted through clenched teeth as she felt her own flesh tear. But his jaw loosened, and she pulled her leg free.

Scrambling to get her legs under her, she saw him plant his good hand on the flat surface of the teak coaming to steady himself. His broad nose streamed blood, and as she breathed hard through his mouth, blood spume splattered the deck. Riley raised the knife over her head and brought it down with all her strength right into the back of that good hand. The blade plunged through the skin and bone and dug deep into the teak. Pinky screamed one last time and collapsed, the pain at last becoming too much for his mind to bear.

Riley got up and looked down at the unconscious figure. Then she extended her leg to examine the wound on her calf. A flap of skin hung loose, and her leg and foot were covered in blood.

"In spite of the blood, you look very fetching in that T-shirt and those panties, my dear."

Riley whirled around. A white sportfishing boat was tied to the far side of the sleek black powerboat. Diggory was standing on the foredeck, one arm in a white sling, the other hand holding a gun.

CHAPTER EIGHTY-THREE

Aboard the Shadow Chaser

March 31, 2008

Cole stood with his elbows resting on the wheelhouse dash just below the radio. He stared out through the windshield glass while holding the radio's microphone in one hand and tapping it against his chin.

Where was she? She had called them from her boat less than an hour ago, so why wasn't Riley answering her radio now? This was the second time he'd tried to raise her, and still nothing. If anyone had told him that once he got this close to finding *Surcouf* he would want to slow it all down, he would have called that person insane. But now, he knew the find wouldn't be the same without Riley here to share it. They'd only gotten this far because of her.

Theo shifted into reverse to slow them down. He began to chuckle. "Come look," he said.

Cole hung the microphone on the side of the radio and stepped behind his first mate so he could get a better look at the big monitor. Theo was running it split screen; the down imaging sonar offered a side view of the bottom; they could see the water at the top of the screen, and then the various striations of sand and the more dense rock of the seafloor at the bottom. They were beginning to see the hard outline of a large object on top of the sand. In a corner of the screen, Cole noted the depth scale; they were looking at a picture of the seafloor thirty-nine meters below, too deep to be visible to a plane flying over.

Neither man spoke as *Shadow Chaser* drifted forward and unbelievably clear details filled in on the screen. They saw the outline of a rudder canted upward at an angle. *Surcouf* was lying on her starboard side, and both men stopped breathing when the bulbous deck structure that had once served as a hangar for the seaplane came into view.

"Oh my God," Cole whispered as they saw, just forward of the conning tower, where the bow of the sub had been ripped open.

"Would you look at that," Theo said.

"I can't believe it," Cole said. "After all this time, there she is."

"Or what's left of her."

"After more than sixty years," Cole said.

"No question why she sank."

"No," Cole said, and he thought about the story Michaut had told them, about all the men who had died when the American bombers came in for that final run.

Theo said, "Can't even see the forward deck guns."

"They may have blown clear. Looks like she got hit by a depth charge right on top of the two big guns." The forward bow section was bent off to starboard, exposing a gaping hole into the sub's interior. As more of the bottom contour flowed into view, they saw how the forward section seemed to hang, floating, as the bottom disappeared off the screen. The wreck rested on a seafloor that angled downward forty-five degrees—in essence, the *Surcouf* was sitting on the slope of an undersea cliff.

Cole jumped when Riley's loud voice erupted out of the radio. "*Shadow Chaser, Shadow Chaser*, this is the *Bonefish*."

He grabbed the microphone, and catching Theo's eyes, he pressed the button with a big grin on his face. "Riley, this is *Shadow*

Chaser here. Thank God. You'll never guess what we're looking at on the sonar screen. Now get your little sailboat over here to celebrate with us!"

Cole stopped speaking, but Riley didn't answer him. He looked up at the SSB radio as if it could tell him why.

He lifted the mike. "*Bonefish,* this is *Shadow Chaser.* Did you copy that? Over."

Again, there was only silence.

"What the hell is going on?" Cole said. "Why can't she hear us?" He turned back to look at Theo, his raised eyebrows accenting his question. "Do you think it's the radio?"

Theo shook his head. "Don't know, Cap'n."

Cole raised the mike to his mouth again, but before he had a chance to push the transmit button, he heard a voice—and it was not Riley's.

"*Shadow Chaser,* this is the sailing vessel *Bonefish.* I'm very sorry to say so, but it appears the captain refuses to speak to you at the moment."

Cole's knuckles whitened as he squeezed the microphone. "Who is this?" he said. "Where's Riley?"

"I think you know very well who I am, Dr. Thatcher. And our Captain Riley is right here with me. Very close to me. You do know how close we are, don't you, Dr. Thatcher?"

"Riley," Cole said, hoping Priest was telling the truth and that she was there within earshot of his voice. "Talk to me. What can I do to help?"

"Ah, how very good of you—since Riley here won't cooperate. You see, Dr. Thatcher, I asked her to call you and get your location." He chuckled, and the airwaves went dead for a several seconds. Cole was about to respond when Priest came back on. "We want ever so much to come pay you a visit, but Riley here says she doesn't know where you are. And she refuses to get back on the radio to ask you. Do you see how that could be a dangerous position for her to take?"

"Priest. Don't hurt her, you hear me?"

Cole released the button on his mike, and he heard the sound of Priest's laughter from the radio.

"Or you'll do what? Kill me?"

Cole slammed the palm of his hand down on the boat's dash. "Listen, Priest, I'll soon have something you want. You can have it in exchange for her. You don't deliver her to me unharmed, and I'll destroy it all. The submarine is resting deep down on a ledge in the middle of the ocean, four miles from the nearest island. You'd never find it without my help. You hurt her and with one blast, I could send the wreck, the documents, and all the gold down into the trench."

"Now, now, Dr. Thatcher. There's no need for that. I think we can come to an amicable agreement. Why don't you tell us where you are so we can get started sailing. We're in Grand Bourg on Marie-Galante. I assume it will take us awhile to get to you."

In the background, Cole heard Riley's voice shout, "Cole, don't!"

"Priest, we're four miles east-southeast of Petite Terre. I assume you'll recognize my boat once you get close. We'll be ready to trade whatever we find down there by the time you get here."

"Roger, *Shadow Chaser.* We'll see you soon. We're over and out." The radio went silent.

Cole glanced at Theo and then turned his face toward the monitor that showed the blue outline of the wreck. Staring at the familiar shape, he whispered, "Shit."

Then he clapped his hands together, turned back to Theo, and said, "What time is it?"

"Just past eight."

"OK, given the speed of her sailboat, I reckon we've got four to five hours to figure out what the hell we're going to do."

CHAPTER EIGHTY-FOUR

From Bonefish to Fast Eddie

March 31, 2008

Riley followed orders. She climbed over Spyder's corpse and out into the cockpit. She stepped around Pinky's still form and then swung her injured leg over the lifelines. She stepped from her own boat onto the foredeck of the racing powerboat *Fast Eddie*. Dig followed.

"Get behind the wheel and start the engines. I'll untie the lines."

She needed to stall him any way she could. If Theo and Cole were convinced that Dig was coming on the slower *Bonefish*, they would think they had time. They didn't. This ocean racer could cover the miles in less than an hour.

"No, wait. I'll deal with the lines once I start the engine. Besides, the Bertram you came on hasn't got an anchor down."

"Don't argue with me. Set it adrift. We need to get moving."

"But it will be bound to attract attention."

Dig glanced around the waterfront. "I suspect the authorities are already on their way. Given it's the islands, the gendarmes may have had to finish their croissants first, but we need to go. Now."

Riley shrugged but didn't move.

She was half turned away from him when he hit the side of her jaw so hard, he knocked her off balance and she fell to the deck. Dazed, she raised herself to a sitting position and put her hand to her cheek. He must have used the butt of the gun. She made no effort to stand. Probing around inside her mouth with her index finger, she didn't find any loose teeth, but her hand came away bloodied.

"Don't fuck with me, Riley. You've seen what I can do."

That she had. She had no idea how hard she could push him. But she was also certain that as soon as he got what he wanted, he wouldn't leave anyone alive to tell about it.

Riley got up and slid into the driver's seat. She gripped the compact steering wheel and looked at the array of instruments on the dashboard. She had never driven a high-performance power-boat before. She was sorting out the fuel, oil pressure, and tempera-ture gauges when Dig kicked at the back of her seat.

"Let's go," he said.

She flipped the switch that started the bilge blowers. She hated boats with gasoline engines. Unlike diesel, the fumes from gas could turn a boat into a bomb, so you always had to make sure that no fumes had settled into the bilge. She turned the ignition keys. Both engines growled to life. She climbed out of the padded seat and saw Dig perched on the edge of the stern bench seat. He was staring down at his arm in the sling. His face looked pale, and the tendons in his neck were taut.

"The engines need to warm up," she said.

He lifted the gun, aiming it at her midsection.

"For real," she said, raising her hands in the air. "You don't want engine trouble when we're heading through the cut in the reef. Anyway, it looks like you're hurt. I'll take care of the lines."

He didn't answer her. She could see he was gritting his teeth.

The bowline on the *Fish n' Chicks* was long enough to reach across the deck of the racing machine, and she tied it to a forward cleat on her sailboat. She couldn't stand the idea of letting any boat get carried onto the rocks—even a powerboat.

As she untied the last line, Pinky's eyes fluttered. The black racer began to drift away from the sailboat. She looked up as Dig slid into the padded passenger seat and twisted his body sideways. He hadn't noticed Pinky. He swung the gun from her to the driver's seat, pointing. She sat down, put the engines in gear, and headed for the harbor entrance.

"I've never driven one of these before," she shouted when they'd made it through the narrow cut and the boat started to rock and roll. The motion was very different from a sailboat.

"I drove it myself from Trois Rivières to the Saintes. It's not that complicated. Shove those things forward." He pointed the gun at the throttles.

She pushed them forward until they were doing about ten knots, rising and falling into the troughs between the waves.

"Faster," he said.

"I'm afraid I'll lose control." She had to shout over the roar of the engines.

"Stop stalling, Riley."

She increased the speed a little more, but they were still doing less than half of what the boat could do. The boat would start to pound if she speeded it up.

"You're hurt," she said. "The pounding won't do you any good."

"More," he yelled.

Maybe she could take him in the wrong direction. Did Dig know where the Îles de la Petite Terre were located?

"Turn on the charts." He pointed the gun at the dark screen of the GPS chart plotter. "The guy who rented me the boat showed me how to use that."

So much for trying to take them off course.

As the chart plotter was going through its warm-up sequence, she turned to look at his face. She saw that the lines on either side of his mouth were etched deeper now, and there were strands of gray hair around his temples.

"What happened to you, Diggory?" Her voice was barely loud enough to be heard over the engines.

He reared his head back then spoke into the wind. "Some idiot shot me."

"That's not what I meant. How did you get to be like this?"

He looked at her. "Like what?"

"A monster."

He leaned back and barked a single laugh at the sky. "Monster?" he shouted. "If that's what I am, then that's what your father was too, Riley."

I don't doubt that, she thought. But I have found your favorite topic: you.

"Your father molded me into who and what I am. We're just men. Men who were born to rule other men."

"Amoral men, you mean."

"And women. You've played your part in this, Riley."

"What are you talking about?"

"Riley, the good soldier. The dutiful marine. That's still how you see yourself, isn't it?"

She turned away from him and looked across the tops of the waves that marched to the horizon. The sun was shining and the sea breeze smelled clean and pure, but she felt the menace in the air. It was how you felt when you were diving a lush coral reef and from the corner of your eye, you saw the dark shadow of a cruising shark.

"You're talking about Lima, aren't you?"

"Ah, well done. You always were good. Even when it was against regulations."

"Everything about our affair was against regulations, Diggory."
She spoke more for herself than him.

"Ha! Touché. More than you know—or will allow yourself to
know."

She turned around, and those dazzling blue eyes were so close,
watching her with amusement. She didn't look away this time.
"Dig, I'm sick of playing these games. Tell me."

"You've already figured it out, Riley. You simply can't admit it."

"That's not true," she said, but she felt the twisting blackness
in her growing.

"Of course, it's true. It was you. You remember. That morning,
you came by my apartment. We had sex, and you were all moony
eyed. What the fuck were you thinking? That what we had was
true love?"

"You said it was," she said. *And I believed you.*

The corner of his mouth lifted in a half smile, and he gave that
half cough, half laugh again. "I wanted to get laid."

The boat rose up on a large swell, then dropped with a jarring
slam into the trough.

"There were others you could have chosen for that. It was my father
you wanted to fuck with. Killing Michael wasn't enough for you."

She felt the sourness trying to crawl up her throat. She'd never
been seasick in her life, but this time, she wasn't sure she could
swallow it down.

Dig laughed. "I can't argue with that. It was time to add you to
the list of Yorick paybacks. But that morning, I also needed a bit of
a favor. I gave you a package to deliver to Hutchinson at the Marine
House. I knew you could get it through security. I told you it was a
radio. It wasn't, of course."

"You're lying."

"You keep telling yourself that, but inside, you know this is the
truth, Riley." He leaned his head back against his seat and looked

up at the sky again, as though he were struggling to remember one of hundreds of similar missions. "We had a problem with the Peruvians concerning a free-trade agreement and certain mining rights. We believed that the Peruvians would see things our way if they feared a reemergence of Shining Path and felt indebted to the Americans for their sacrifice. And I was finished with you—in fact, you were becoming a liability. I couldn't resist the delicious irony of taking out Yorick's daughter among the marines. I had everything worked out until you had to screw it all up by delivering the package, then leaving the Marine House. I wasn't rid of you after all."

She remembered again standing in the little bodega, buying a bottle of wine for that night after her shift. Then she felt the concussion as the old man placed her change in her palm, and she was running toward the smoke. Later, when they'd told her the blast had originated in Hutch's room, she kept pushing back at the blackness.

But she couldn't push it back any longer. Riley throttled back, pulled herself up out of the seat, hung her body over the rail, and vomited until her body was wracked with dry heaves.

"So I watched you," Dig continued as if nothing had happened. As if he couldn't hear her retching. "Granted, from a distance. You kept your mouth shut. It was remarkable, really. I knew a part of you suspected, but I suppose another part refused to believe that you could have been responsible for all that death and destruction."

Her mind hung like a broken record, repeating over and over, *Oh, Danny, sweet, funny Danny. I'm so sorry.*

"You've been a loose end for many years now, and I've never been certain you wouldn't find Jesus and decide to confess."

No, she hadn't known. Had she? In her nightmares when the flames burned around her and she carried Danny on her shoulder, she'd felt the guilt. And told herself it was survivor's guilt.

She was spent, empty. Still hanging over the side, she stared down into the white foam sliding by the black hull. She could kick with her legs and slide over the side into the dark, cool water. Deny him this pleasure. Put out the flames for good.

A long silver object streaked out from under the hull, startling her, and then it disappeared out into the dark water. She heard a splash in the distance. Then another silver torpedo shape raced by right under her face, a long jagged scar visible on her back. In a few seconds, the dolphin returned and swam alongside in the shadow of the boat, swinging her course from side to side with effortless pumps of her flukes, keeping perfect pace with the big black powerboat.

Riley was aware that Diggory was still speaking, but she couldn't hear him any longer. She reached her arm toward the water, her fingertips inches from the surface. She remembered Cole and his crazy talk of luck and dolphins. And again, she felt that vibration of connecting to another being. Was it a shark that had inflicted the wound that stretched from the dolphin's head to past the dorsal fin?

The sleek animal twisted her body round so that she was swimming on her side, her dark eye staring up, her mouth curving up into that natural smile. Then she rolled back over, and when her fin broke through the surface, Riley's fingers touched the rough white scar. In the next instant, with one mighty thrust of her flukes, she was gone.

Seconds later, the dolphin shot out of the water off the bow and arced up in a high leap, streaming water.

"Shit," Dig said. "Did you see that? Get back up here and drive. You almost hit a dolphin."

Riley pushed her belly up off the rail, and she slid back into her seat. She wiped her mouth on her sleeve. "I didn't kill them," she said.

"You delivered the bomb."

She shook her head. "It was you, Dig. I was just a tool you used. *You* killed them."

The corner of his mouth turned up again. She wanted to smash her fist into that mouth. But more than that. She had to stop him.

"You're not some kind of better breed of human being. Far from it. And lost as my father was, he was never like you. He hurt over the things he'd done. Not you. You're a malignancy. A bad seed. Something went wrong inside you, and you can't even recognize that you're a *freak*."

"Shut up, you stupid cunt."

It was her turn to laugh. "Now you sound like Spyder. You're no different than him. I bet he never knew his father either."

He hit her. Again. She'd known he would, but she was willing to take a beating to buy even a few seconds more time. She wiped the blood from her mouth.

"Just keep your mouth shut and drive the boat," he shouted.

She jammed the throttles forward. The boat leaped onto a plane and began bouncing from wave top to wave top. Get ready, Cole. It's time to stop this lunatic.

CHAPTER EIGHTY-FIVE

Off Îles de la Petite Terre

March 31, 2008

Cole treaded water as Theo swung the crane around and out over the water, then lowered the ROV *Enigma* over the side. The underwater vehicle's three-foot-square boxy frame and buoyancy tanks were made of PVC pipe painted bright yellow. *Enigma* was propelled and steered by a series of four blue bilge pumps that turned small red propellers. The forward-facing lights at the two top corners looked more like bug eyes than headlamps. The thing looked like a giant toy made out of Legos.

Neither man knew whether Theo's design would survive at the depths they would now attempt, but he had built her for just this kind of work. All the wires for the lights, video camera, manipulator arm, and propulsion system were bundled together in a thick, snakelike tether that was 150 feet in length. That had better be long enough, Cole thought as he caught the lower end of the ROV's frame and steered it away from *Shadow Chaser*'s steel hull. He opened the snap shackle that connected *Enigma* to the crane.

"Clear!" he shouted, and the crane's electric motor whirred as the line retracted and the arm swung back aboard.

Once he had secured the crane, Theo appeared at the rail with the joystick box that controlled *Enigma*. "Ready to test?" he said.

"Roger that."

The four little propellers began to spin all at once, and the ROV surged forward through the water. Cole had to pump his fins to keep up. "Forward thrust, check," he called out. The headlamps flashed. "Lights, check." A metal arm rose from the water, and the pincer claw snapped shut. "Nutcracker, check."

Theo said, "Swim around front and smile for the camera."

Cole lowered his face mask into place, put the scuba regulator in his mouth, and swam around to the front of the vehicle. He released some air from his buoyancy compensator so he could float a few feet below the surface in front of the video camera mounted on the *Enigma*'s frame. He waved, then kicked for the surface.

"Very photogenic, Dr. Thatcher." Theo was holding up his tablet PC to show the video feed when Cole surfaced.

Cole pulled the regulator out of his mouth. "Just like Lloyd Bridges. I get to star in my own episode of *Sea Hunt*." He removed his face mask, spit in it, and washed the saliva around to prevent the glass from fogging. "Listen, Theo, if Priest shows up while I'm below, blink *Enigma*'s lights twice. I'll know he's there and waiting for me. If you think you or Riley are in immediate danger, flash three times, and I'll know to get to the surface as fast as I can."

"What about decompressing?"

"Let me worry about that." Cole situated his mask back on his face. "And let me know what's going on topsides. You watch my hands on the video screen. I'll use sign language to communicate." During their trials of the *Enigma* back in North Carolina, they had both learned to sign the alphabet along with a few basic words.

"According to my computer, it's nine forty-seven," Theo said. "Remember, you've got the steel mesh cargo net and the air bag if you want to send anything topsides."

Cole checked his gauges, readjusted his backpack for comfort, and took hold of his regulator.

"And, Cap, also remember, you've got no backup. You be careful down there."

Cole attempted a grin for his friend. "Roger that. See ya in a few." He gave Theo a thumbs-up and popped the regulator into his mouth.

As he descended, Cole kept checking back over his shoulder to make sure the *Enigma* was right behind him. The little ROV was pretty fast once Theo got the ballast tanks flooded right so she descended at the correct angle. Cole shivered as he swam into a new thermal patch where the water was a good ten degrees cooler than the surface. He listened to his breathing—inhale hiss, exhale bubble. In the background, he both heard and felt his own heart pounding. He concentrated on calming his breathing in order to preserve his air. He'd made hundreds of dives in his life, but he hadn't felt nervous like this since he was a kid.

After the night of strong winds and rain, the visibility was not great. At forty-five feet down now, he could begin to make out the dark-blue shadow on the seafloor. The sunlight was starting to dim, and the *Enigma*'s headlamps made him feel as though he were swimming in a bright bubble of color while the sea around him turned a dusky shade of blue. The occasional fish darted off in surprise as he swam into its territory, but the most abundant life was evident in the thousands of tiny brine shrimp and microscopic creatures that made the seawater look like a thick biological soup.

Cole reached for his own light that hung by a tether from his backpack. He switched it on as he continued to pump his fins and pop his ears. At first, the concentrated beam reflected back off the matter floating in the water, but then he saw, far off in the column of light, a distinct dark shape. It was the rudder, sticking up into the water in such a way that he had a hard time believing what he was looking at. Then he saw the hull stretching out and down ahead of the rudder. He squinted. *Surcouf* was resting on her starboard side, the whole wreck pointing downward into the trench.

A long and thin line, not quite horizontal, caught his attention forward. As he swam deeper, it began to look like a crooked, arthritic finger pointing toward the surface. When he made out the larger shape attached to it, Cole recognized it as one of the pair of thirty-seven-millimeter cannons *Surcouf* carried aft of the conning tower and atop the seaplane hangar—the long barrel now covered with marine growth.

My God, she's enormous. He could not see where the dark hull ended in the gloom in either direction. As he swam closer, he saw the film of coral and barnacle growth on the lifelines surrounding the hangar deck, but there was less growth than he had imagined. It had to be the depth. Even in these clear Caribbean waters, one didn't find the lush coral down here where so little sunlight penetrated. It was amazing how intact she was. He reached out and grabbed the lifeline, and a small cloud of matter mushroomed around his gloved hand.

Cole looked over his shoulder at the bright headlamps of the ROV. He couldn't see the video camera, but he knew it was there and Theo was watching him. He gave another thumbs-up. He'd made it. He was touching *Surcouf*—the first human to do so in sixty-seven years. Just ahead of him was the round shape of the opening for the seaplane hangar. On top of it was the deck with the pair of deck cannons, and above that, the conning tower. All of it was tilted at such an extreme angle nose downward, it looked as though she were ready to slide down into the trench at any moment.

He kicked his fins and swam alongside the hull, heading forward and descending deeper. The wreck rested on a sandy slope that fell away into blue-black water. There was no grass or coral on the seafloor, but from under the wreck, small schools of fish flashed past him in their panic at having a visitor after all these years.

The forward gun turret had been ripped open. The gun barrels that once protruded there were now long gone, and the upper deck revealed a huge gaping hole. Cole wondered if it had been the sub's own ammunition that had caused the damage. Forward of the hole, the deck ran intact for several more feet before the entire forward section of the submarine had been ripped open. The bow section now hung by what looked like a combination of steel cables and thin pieces of twisted metal. The incline increased so rapidly there, the bottom fell away and the forward piece hung unsupported over the crevasse.

Much as he wanted to swim around the bow opening and look into the interior where that section had been cut away, Cole had little time to explore. If he didn't have something to bargain with by the time they arrived, Priest would kill them all. In fact, he probably planned to do that anyway. But if Cole had proof of Operation Magic in his hands, they might have a chance.

There were two options for entering the sub. Either down the hole in the deck where the rest of the gun turret had once stood, or through the gaping opening of the fractured hull forward. Both options could be deadly traps. The greatest danger in wreck diving was the possibility of getting hung up inside the wreck, with a piece of equipment or a foot or hand snagged or pinched in a too-narrow opening. And he had no buddy diver to free him.

Cole thought back to the plans of the sub he had studied for months. The captain's cabin was located two decks below the conning tower. He would need to get down here, through this black hole in the deck. He shone his dive light down, but the jagged metal sections were all uneven and they cast shadows, making it difficult to make out what was below. He turned to *Enigma* and signed to the video camera that he was going to enter the wreck there.

He knew that beneath the gun turret there had once been a walk-in refrigeration locker for food and beneath that, a storage area for artillery shells. He swam down into the hole with his dim dive light. A large compartment opened up, and judging from the debris scattered about, rusted metal pails and rotting wood boxes, he guessed it was the walk-in fridge. The deck beneath that was intact, and at the forward end of the compartment, he could make out a dark hole that went deeper into the hull. That would have been the elevator for transferring the shells from the ammo compartment below up to the big guns on deck. It appeared the ammo belowdecks had not exploded. Maybe the explosion had come only from the shells that were already in the gun turret. Thinking back to Michaut's story of the French captain watching the planes approach, Cole thought it likely he had told his men to arm all the deck guns.

Cole needed to get to the next deck down, but he wasn't going to try to pass through that elevator shaft.

He shone his light around the gloomy compartment. With each stroke of his fins, he was disturbing the organic matter that formed a thick layer over the top of the debris. Thick clouds floated up, obscuring his visibility. Soon, he would be able to see nothing. He stopped pumping his legs and floated, turning himself with small hand movements.

Behind him, *Enigma* sank down into the hole. When she was low enough, her lights lit the compartment much better than his hand light, and on the far side, he saw an opening. He slowly paddled in that direction. As he neared, he saw that the explosion had blown the door off the opposite side of the refrigeration compartment.

He reached the doorframe, but he was blocking the ROV's lights. Cole moved aside, reached back, and grabbed the PVC frame, pulling *Enigma* closer so the lights could shine into the opening. The compartment lit up like a museum diorama. A goliath grouper floated above the heavy refrigerator door that rested on the floor of the compartment at skewed angle. The big fish stared at him unafraid. The steel door half covered the black opening in the deck. Cole could see the ladder that descended to the officers' quarters below. Next to the opening, lying on the deck half under the thick steel door, were bones: the arm and skull of a human skeleton.

At that moment, the compartment went black. The lights blinked on again, then off, and then back on.

They're here.

CHAPTER EIGHTY-SIX

From Fast Eddie to Shadow Chaser

March 31, 2008

Riley slowed the racing powerboat and brought her alongside *Shadow Chaser*. Dig grabbed the rope ladder that hung on the side of the trawler. The gas engines were so loud, there was no way Cole and Theo hadn't heard them coming, but no one appeared on deck. When she shut the engines down, *Shadow Chaser* seemed eerily quiet, aside from creaking as she rolled in the swell.

"You go up first," Dig said. "And don't ever make the mistake of thinking you're faster or smarter than I am."

She said nothing to that. She would show him when the time came. On the foredeck, she pulled out the bowline that she had tucked into the forward locker earlier and threw a couple of hitches around the foredeck cleat. Her head was pounding, and her leg ached when she swung it over the bulwark and stepped onto the steel deck. Time was what she needed. Time to recoup some of her strength. To let him think she believed him when he said he was smarter and faster. She tied off the powerboat so it would drift back off the stern of the trawler. Dig wasn't going anywhere until he had what he'd come for.

"Cole? Theo!" she called out.

"In here." The mate's voice came from the wheelhouse.

Behind her, Dig climbed over the bulwark, his gun pointed at her back. "Go on," he said.

Before they arrived at the wheelhouse, Dig grabbed her elbow with his injured arm and pulled her close. He pressed the gun barrel into her ribs. They rounded the corner together, and Dig stopped her outside the doorway.

Theo was standing in front of his array of screens, a small box with a joystick in his hands. He didn't turn to look at them when he spoke. "Cole's inside the sub."

At Dig's prodding, Riley stepped over the doorsill and entered the wheelhouse with Dig attached to her side like an unwanted appendage. She looked at all the screens and could not make out which one was broadcasting video. "Where?"

Theo pointed. "That one."

The screen showed a murky gray scene that she had mistaken for what on a television people call snow.

"Can't see much, can you?"

"We could a few minutes ago, but Cole just went down the ladder from the mess deck."

"Geez," she said. "He's *deep* inside, then."

Theo nodded. "*Enigma* hasn't caught up with him yet. There's so much silt and biological matter down there that every time Cole moves, he stirs up what looks like a dust cloud."

"How did he get in?"

"One of the bombs from the American planes had blasted a hole in her. Took out the forward gun turret."

Dig shifted back and forth from foot to foot, his grip on her arm growing tighter. "What's this *Enigma*? Explain."

Theo turned and looked at him as though realizing for the first time that he was there. Then he turned his gaze to Riley. "You're bleeding," he said.

She rubbed her free hand across her mouth and wiped it on her shorts. "I'm OK."

Theo glanced down at the gun Dig held pressed against her side. "Is that necessary?"

"Answer my question. What's going on down there?" Dig lifted his head to indicate the monitor.

Theo turned back to face the monitor, and Riley looked, too. They could now see what looked like rungs of a ladder scrolling up the screen.

"Cole is already inside the *Surcouf.* The lights and video camera are on an underwater robot we call *Enigma.* It has a steel cargo net, so we can use it to transport delicate artifacts to the surface. Our information indicates that the documents, if they still exist, are inside the captain's cabin. That's where he's headed."

The camera swung away from the ladder and panned around. It looked like a narrow hall or companionway. Several rounded doorways in the bulkhead looked as though they were built crooked—they were tilted at an angle. The camera jostled and revealed the overhead where pipes and wires ran fore and aft, and silvery bubbles from Cole's scuba tank rolled around collecting into bigger bubbles like bits of mercury. The camera panned down, and a small school of pale, colorless fish hovered in the second open door. Moments after the light hit them, they darted off in panic. A new saying, Riley thought: caught like fish in the headlights.

"Cole must be hand carrying *Enigma,*" Theo said, "using it as his light source."

The camera glided through another doorway, and this time a gloved hand appeared on the monitor, and it pointed toward a pile of debris coated with pale-brown fur. Then they saw his backpack with the pair of air cylinders very close to the camera. His body glided across the compartment and hovered over the top of the debris, his fins not moving.

She knew the man on the screen was Cole, but she could not see his face. Silently, she pleaded with him. *Turn around. I need to see you. To know you're OK.*

Theo pointed to another screen above the helm that showed the sonar image of the bottom and the clear outline of a portion of the submarine. "You can see that the sub is on her side on a steep slope. It looks as though whatever was inside the cabin has collected on the low side."

That explained why everything looked askew. Why it looked as if the depth perception was off and it was so difficult to make out what they were looking at.

Moving slowly, so as not to disturb the film of growth and debris any more than was necessary, Cole lifted objects from the pile.

"He said he put the strongbox inside the captain's desk," Riley said.

"Who said this? What are you talking about?"

"James Thatcher," she said. She did not want Diggory to know about Henri Michaut. "He interviewed an old sailor who had once served on the *Surcouf.* He said that was where the captain kept important documents.

"That doesn't look much like a desk."

On the screen, Cole lifted a brown blob of growth and brushed away the feathery tendrils. Though several barnacles remained, she could make out the shape of a once-white ceramic mug. She remembered Michaut saying that he and Woolsey had interrupted the captain's dinner. Now, all these years later, Cole pushed the mug inside a string bag he had attached to his weight belt.

Every move Cole made caused the water to grow more cloudy. They saw all sorts of tiny sea creatures and particles float by close to the lens, reflecting the light, obscuring the view of the far side of the compartment.

Theo said, "I assume all furniture on a sub is bolted to the deck. There might be a desk under there, or we may be looking at the remains of clothing, bedclothes, a mattress. Or the wood might have rotted away or been eaten by worms."

"It's there," Dig said.

"The desk? Or do you mean the strongbox?" she asked.

"Shut up," Dig said. "You're in no position to be asking questions."

He jammed the gun harder against her ribs, and she winced at the pain.

"I think he's found something," Theo said.

Dig pushed her, and she stepped forward until her midriff was pressing against the wheelhouse dash. On the screen, it was difficult to make out what Cole was doing in the cloudy water.

Theo said, "I don't dare try to move *Enigma* any closer. If I start up her little props, it will make the visibility worse."

Cole lifted a long, flat plank. On top of it was a mass of some material, maybe the remains of clothing, maybe marine growth; it was difficult to tell on the small monitor. The piece he was lifting looked as if it might have once been the desktop. Either it had broken in the explosion or the wood had rotted and the whole thing collapsed during the years it had spent on the seabed. Cole got his head under the plank, and using both hands, he withdrew something. His back was to the camera, and they could not see what he held in the shadow of his body.

Cole slid his head out from under the plank of wood and turned. In his gloved hands, he held a box.

"Oh my God," she said, her voice a mere whisper.

The plank drifted back down onto the pile of debris. Cole floated there holding the thing in front of his face mask, turning it over and examining it. There was almost no growth on the box, and though it was rusted, the metal deteriorated, it looked intact.

Cole swam closer to the camera, and then, at last, his eyes appeared through the glass of his mask. He was looking at her, she was sure of it. Somehow, through the lens and camera and the more than a hundred feet of cable, he knew he was looking right into her eyes. She saw his lips curl up around the regulator as he held up the box with one hand. With his other hand, he made a big circle before pointing all his fingers at the box.

"What's he doing?" Dig asked.

Theo sighed. "I think he's playing Vanna White. It's his way of saying you win."

Cole reached forward and jostled the ROV.

"What's he doing now?"

"He's putting the strongbox into *Enigma*'s steel cargo net. It's the safest way to get it to the surface."

Cole backed away from the camera and pointed toward the surface. She recognized what his hands were doing, but she couldn't read it. He was signing letters.

"Theo?" she said. "What's he saying?"

Theo glanced at Dig. "He said I'm supposed to tell the asshole he's coming for him."

Dig snorted. "Just get that box to the surface."

Cole again disappeared from view, and they watched as the screen showed only the bluish, cloudy water. Then the rungs of the ladder flashed past in the light again as Cole swam up, pushing *Enigma* through the opening to the next deck.

The water was not quite as murky there. Once again, he appeared in front of the camera and began to sign.

"He's saying that it's OK now to use the *Enigma*'s own propulsion system."

On the screen they saw Cole's eyes widen. It looked as though someone were shaking the camera, and the image of Cole wavered from side to side. He looked up and then to both sides. Debris lifted up and floated around him, and a human skull floated past in the cloudy water. Cole pulled the camera close to his face. They saw the bubbles from his regulator stream past the lens. His fingers started flashing.

"What's happening?" she said.

"I don't know," Theo said, "but he's signing your name."

Cole's body jerked as if he'd been hit with something. The last image they saw on the screen was his hand, his pinkie and forefinger up, his thumb off to the side. It was the only sign Riley knew. It meant "I love you."

"Cole?" she said.

The screen showed more water and debris rushing past, then one of the lights went out on the ROV, and the image grew even darker. For a moment, it looked as if the video camera was showing a metal part of the submarine; then the screen went black when they lost the feed.

"If this is some kind of trick," Dig said.

Riley ignored him. "Theo?" She looked at the young man's face. He was staring at the screen. His horrified expression was no act. "What's going on? What's happening?"

Theo continued to stare, and she followed his gaze to the big monitor hanging over the helm.

It was the sonar screen, and it now showed only the sloping seafloor. The *Surcouf* was gone.

CHAPTER EIGHTY-SEVEN

Aboard the Shadow Chaser

March 31, 2008

She could not breathe. How? Was it possible for a submarine to disappear? Where had it gone? Maybe it was another of Cole's pranks, or better yet, part of Cole's plan. Theo was good with electronics. It *must* be one of his tricks.

Riley turned to look at him, and Theo's eyes told her it was no trick.

"I don't understand," she said.

Theo opened his mouth, then raised his hands and shook his head. "I don't either. It's a steep incline. Maybe when he moved that stuff inside, it was enough to shift the wreck—"

"You know the layout better than I do," she said. "The exit—how close was he? He could have gotten out, right?"

Theo kept staring at the screen. "It's possible. It will take him ten to fifteen minutes to get to the surface."

Dig yanked her arm and pulled her toward the wheelhouse door. "Bring up that robot. I've got to get that box."

She struggled against Diggory's grip. "Don't do it, Theo."

Dig shoved her through the door.

That was when she saw it. The gray, cauliflower-shaped cloud was visible in the distance beyond the island of Guadeloupe. It was the shape of it that stopped her. Unlike any cloud she had ever seen before. Riley grabbed the rail and blocked the way aft. "Theo," she called. "Come look."

The young man appeared behind Dig, and the three of them stood there watching the cloud grow. Theo was the first to say it. "Montserrat. The volcano."

Riley saw smoke from several fires on the island of Guadeloupe. She swung her head back and forth. "What's happening there?" She pointed to the smoke.

"It could have been a major seismic event," Theo said. "We wouldn't feel it on the water."

Dig said, "I don't give a damn about what's happening on the island. Bring up that box."

The VHF radio back in the wheelhouse erupted with voices speaking in rapid French.

"What are they saying?" Theo asked.

Riley listened. People were talking at once, stepping on one another's transmissions. One woman was screaming in incomprehensible Creole.

"Someone just said several buildings have collapsed in Pointe-à-Pitre," she said. "My God, Theo. If he's trapped…" She could not finish the sentence.

Theo turned on the FM radio. There was only static. "Power must be down on the island. That's why everyone is on the VHF."

Riley said, "Now they're asking for all emergency personnel to report for duty, and any people with medical training to go to the city to treat the injured."

Theo tapped the scan button. "I think I can pick up a Dominica station here."

A British-accented voice began speaking through the static. "The Soufrière Hills volcano on the island of Montserrat has erupted with an unprecedented explosion, causing more than half of the lava dome to collapse. The ash and steam plume is visible for miles. While here on Dominica, we felt a morning tremor, reports are coming in of a more severe earthquake—"

Dig smashed the butt of his gun into the front of the radio, silencing it. "Get me that box," he said.

Theo tucked his tablet computer under his arm and pushed past them. He trotted back to the big spool on the after deck and hit a switch with the palm of his hand. An electric motor hummed, and the cable began to reel in.

Dig pushed Riley ahead, and they followed. When they got to the rail on the afterdeck, she searched the surface for signs of bubbles. *Cole, tell me you're OK. You're going to surface in a minute, and we'll laugh, right?* Each time she saw something that looked as if it might be a diver's bubbles, hope rose in her chest, but then the water would turn smooth again, the disturbance nothing more than a wind wave.

She would know it if he were dead, wouldn't she? She'd known something was wrong when Michael died, and he had been across an ocean. Not under one. *Mikey, help me. Help me find him. Tell me he's all right.*

Theo stopped the winch.

"Why are you stopping?" Dig asked.

"It's a long shot, but Cole might have attached himself to the ROV. We bring him up too fast, and he'll get the bends."

Dig raised the gun and pressed the barrel against the side of Riley's head. "You reel that in right now, or I'll shoot her."

"Theo, don't—"

"Riley, look, so far, the cable's intact. If *Enigma* made it out, there's hope Cole did, too. He may be down there decompressing right now."

Then where are his bubbles, she wanted to ask.

"Stop talking and bring it up." Dig twisted away from her and trained the gun downward. She jumped at the *boom* when it went off.

Theo howled, his voice rising at the end as though in a question. He hopped a couple of times on one foot, his back arched, his face twisted in pain. He lifted his foot and examined the shoe. Blood dripped from a hole on the little toe side of his sneaker.

"Don't argue with me, boy."

Theo stared at Dig, the whites of his eyes huge behind his glasses, his lips pressed together as though he were forcing his mouth to stay shut.

Far across the water, Riley saw a sportfishing boat headed toward them. *Stay away,* she wanted to say. There is a crazy man here, and he will shoot all of us before this day is done.

After that first cry, Theo didn't make another sound. He hit the button, and the crane started up again. The three of them stood silent at the rail watching the black, snakelike cable emerge dripping and glistening in the sunlight. To the northwest, over the island, the ash cloud grew like a brain coral recorded on time-lapse photography. It spread toward them, coating the blue dome overhead with its gray pall.

Finally, the bright yellow of the PVC pipe appeared a few feet below the surface. There was no diver, either alive or dead, attached to the ROV. *Where are you, Cole? Please tell me you're hanging onto the anchor chain hatching some crazy plan.*

The *Enigma* no longer looked like a cute little toy. The yellow pipes were broken, mangled. Riley remembered how proud Cole had been when he had shown it to her during their first passage down to Dominica and the Indian River. The device now looked as if it had been hit by a truck, or more precisely, dragged out of a wreck.

Theo hit the button to stop the crane before the device was halfway out of the water. "There's something in the cargo net," he said.

"Bring it up on deck," Dig said.

"I can't. The cable can't support the weight of it. It breaks, and it will all sink. Somebody needs to get in the water to attach the line from the crane."

"I think I can do it from the *Fast Eddie*," Riley said. She wanted to get down closer to the water to look for Cole.

Theo nodded. "Good idea."

"You're not going anywhere without me," Dig said.

She gave him a curt nod. "Let me untie the boat so we can move it closer to the ladder." He released his grip on her arm, and she stepped back to the cleat. She handed the line to Theo, and he pulled the black speedboat alongside the rope ladder. Riley climbed down and Dig followed, struggling to hold the ladder with his injured arm. When he stepped onto the deck, he pulled the sling off over his head. Blood had stained the left side of his shirt.

Meanwhile, Theo swung the crane out over the water. Out on the boat's foredeck, she scanned the *Shadow Chaser*'s waterline. No sign of him. She reached up and grabbed the shackle dangling from the crane.

"Got it," she called. She pulled on the line and walked aft, then jumped down into the cockpit so she would be able to reach the *Enigma* where it bobbed at the surface. Once the shackle was secure, she gave Theo a thumbs-up, and the crane motor hummed.

Dig pushed her aside as the mangled ROV rose dripping out of the water. He swung it over the powerboat's afterdeck, and Theo reversed the crane. Over Dig's shoulder, she saw a flash of white. The ceramic mug. She smelled the sharp, acrid odor she always associated with low tide. Dig reached into the steel mesh bag that was slung beneath the ballast tanks, and he withdrew the white mug. She saw his hand go up into the air, and she held her breath. Two other men had touched that artifact before Dig—Cole and the captain of the *Surcouf.* She saw his hand fly past as he threw the mug to the deck, where it exploded into sharp white shards.

She felt as if something in her broke, too. She looked at Dig's back. He had tucked the gun into his front waistband, and he was using both hands to tug at whatever was still in the cargo net. She looked around for a weapon. Most sailboats or fishing boats at least had a winch handle or a gaff or a dive knife—but on this ocean racer, she saw nothing. As she searched every inch of the deck, desperate for something she could pull loose to hit him with, she spotted the fire extinguisher in a bracket next to the helm.

Dig swore, and she turned back to look at him. The box was in the net, but he couldn't get it out. The clasp had snagged on the steel mesh.

Riley popped the latch and pulled the white cylinder free from the bracket. Her attention was drawn back to the sportfishing boat that was still heading straight for them. The boat rode a huge creamy bow wave as it churned through the water, closing on them.

Dig uttered a high-pitched cry, and the box broke free. He staggered backward, clutching the box to his chest.

In a flash, Riley saw Michael and her father and Hutch and the box she had carried to the Marine House years ago. She raised the fire extinguisher and swung it straight for Dig's head. At the last second, his eyes flicked her way, and he pushed forward into her. The extinguisher bounced off his back and clattered to the deck. She heard him grunt with pain before his head rammed into her midsection, and they both went down on the deck. Riley cracked her head on the support post for the driver's seat, and she lay stunned for several seconds.

Diggory rolled off her and kept his body curled around the box, shielding it from her. No, not after everything he had taken from her. He could not take that box, too.

He pulled the gun from his belt, and as he swung it toward her, she kicked hard at his elbow. The gun flew from his hand and clattered across the fiberglass deck. It lodged in a scupper where seawater flowed in and drained back out as the boat rolled.

Over the top of the speedboat's gunnel, she saw the flybridge of the sportfisherman and the small figure of a man wearing a white shirt. Maybe he was coming over to tell them about the earthquake and the eruption. Maybe he wanted to warn them.

Diggory staggered to his feet. The powerboat beneath them was rocking in the waves, and he lurched after the gun, still clutching the box.

The sportfish boat was close enough now she could see the man's white hair blowing back in the wind. She turned to look for Theo. His back was turned. He was bent over the cabin top, but he had untied their painter and thrown it into the water. The *Fast Eddie* was starting to drift away. That was why the chop was throwing them around so much.

Standing over the scupper so she couldn't get the gun, Dig grabbed the top of the box and tried to pull the rusty old latch free. He groaned when it fell apart in his hands. He raised the lid.

Riley heard the deep guttural growl of the electric motors that powered the *Shadow Chaser*'s bow thrusters.

Behind her, Dig roared and threw the box to the deck. He strode over to it and kicked it once, and then again. The box was empty.

Then Dig looked up and faced the sportfish boat bearing down on them. He stepped back, his eyes wide with recognition, and he fell on top of the engine cowling. The whole front of his shirt was soaked with blood now.

The gun was on the other side of the boat, but the fire extinguisher lay only three feet from her.

Theo held his tablet computer as he steered *Shadow Chaser* away from the *Fast Eddie*. The gap between the boats was more than thirty feet and growing. Theo yelled, "Riley! Jump!"

Riley could see Pinky's face now. His mouth was opening and closing as he shouted, but the wind carried his words away. He pointed at them with one twisted hand while holding the helm steady with the wrist of his other injured hand.

Diggory struggled to his feet atop the engine compartment, his back to her, making ready to dive overboard. No, she thought. He was not going to get away this time. She grabbed the extinguisher as she bolted across the cockpit. She swung the cylinder in a wide arc. Even with all the engine noise, she heard the crunch when the metal hit Diggory's knee. She jumped aside as he collapsed back into the cockpit. Then she leaped onto the powerboat's rail and filled her lungs. As she dove, Riley caught one last glimpse of the *Fish n' Chicks* bearing down on the *Fast Eddie,* riding high on that creamy bow wave. Pinky was smiling.

She kicked harder and pulled wider than she ever had before as she reached for the deep blue depths. She reached for Cole. *Please, let him be down here, hiding under the boat. Dear Universe, God, Neptune, anyone who's listening. Please. Bring him back to me.* Her lungs burned, ears ached, and she thought she couldn't go any longer without air when she felt the impact of the explosion. She heard the boom a second later.

Riley surfaced on the far side of *Shadow Chaser* and sucked in the sweet air in great gulps. Clouds of smoke rose from the opposite side of the trawler.

Theo's face appeared over the rail. "Riley, here!" he shouted. He threw down the rope ladder. While he secured it to the bulwark, she saw that the heavy hemp rope was singed.

When she got up to the deck, Theo draped an arm over her shoulder and led her back to the stern. He had only one sneaker on, the other foot wrapped in a rag. Neither of them spoke. When they rounded the cabin, she felt the heat on her face. All the cabin and superstructure on *Fish n' Chicks* was gone. She was little more than a hull filled with flames. There was nothing at all left of the black-hulled ocean racer *Fast Eddie*. With the engines still hot and gasoline vapors in the bilge, the boat had gone off like a bomb.

From the direction of St. Francois on Guadeloupe, a self-important-looking little boat charged toward them, red and blue lights flashing. The French Coast Guard.

Gray clouds now covered most of the sky overhead. A thin strip of blue remained visible far off to the east. Through the gray film, the sun looked like a pale, sickly orb. A speck of something flew into her eye. She rubbed at it and felt the dried salt on her skin. Then she noticed other particles drifting through the air. So many tiny white flakes. In her mind, Riley saw the silt swirling around Cole moments before the camera died. She saw the white mug shattering into a thousand shards. Her legs buckled, and she collapsed. Her wet feet had left a single trail of footprints in the fine film covering the deck. Cole was gone, and the sky was raining ash.

EPILOGUE

Six months later
Cherbourg, France

November 19, 2008

"You look like you're a couple of thousand miles away."

Riley spun around at the sound of his voice. "Theo!" She wrapped her hands around his high narrow shoulders and held him tight to her. So he'd surprised her after all. "It's so good to see you," she said, her face pressed against the wool of his sweater.

The hug he gave her was short but fierce. Then he grasped her shoulders and stepped back, straightening his arms.

"You look great, Riley." The eyes behind the wire-rimmed spectacles twinkled with genuine pleasure.

She knew he was being kind, but she expected nothing less of him. That was Theo through and through. While she *was* back to work and living her life, she was neither eating nor sleeping enough to "look great."

"I was surprised when I got your e-mail," she said.

He took her elbow and led her to the bulkhead that ran along the seaward side of the jetty. He gestured for her to sit. Like her, he wore a yellow foul weather jacket. His was open at the front, and he tucked it under him as he settled his long frame on the stonework next to her. He slid the backpack off his shoulder and rested it on the stones at his feet. "Surprised?" he said. "Why?"

She scooted over closer to him until their arms touched. She felt something dig into her hip, and she remembered the bag of chestnuts she'd stuffed in her pocket earlier. She readjusted her rain jacket, then rested her head against his shoulder. "I owe you an apology. I ran out on you in Guadeloupe. I wouldn't blame you if you're mad at me. I should have stuck around longer."

She had neglected him in the weeks following the eruption and earthquake. She'd neglected everyone, living and dead, including herself. Dozens had died on Montserrat, and though the casualty list was not great on Guadeloupe, the damage from the earthquake there had been significant. They'd had to shut down the power plants, and the whole island had been under a boil water order for over a week.

Theo slid his arm around her shoulders. "Those were tough days for all of us. I heard you went back to your boat and sailed down to Martinique."

After days of answering questions and watching from St. Francois as the French authorities sent divers out to the site of the fatal collision, she'd returned to her boat at Marie-Galante, pulled up her anchor, and left, without even a good-bye to Theo. Though remains of both Brewsters had been recovered, no evidence was found of either Diggory Priest or Cole Thatcher, both of whom they reported as lost in the explosion.

"Yeah. I had to get away. I sailed south until I found this little bay. It was called Case-Pilote. Nobody knew me there, and I wanted to stay on the boat and wallow in my misery."

Theo rested his hand on her shoulder. "I'm sorry I wasn't able to help you."

"I'm sure you had your hands full."

"You're right there."

"I stayed in my bunk at first. For days. Didn't even go to my father's funeral. But after I had been twisting in my sheets for weeks, one of the local fishermen knocked on my hull. I tried to ignore him, but he wouldn't go away. When I finally went topsides, he said the people in the village were worried about me. They wanted to know if I was OK."

She had wanted to tell the man no, that she never would be OK, that the ash was still clogging her eyes and ears and mouth and lungs.

"Island people are like that," Theo said.

Riley nodded. "He gave me a gift of some fresh grouper," she said. "And I was surprised to discover I was hungry." She remembered grilling the fish on the little barbecue on her stern rail that night. She ate the entire filet, and for the first time in days, she threw no food overboard. Soon after, she contacted her employers at Mercury, and they offered her work on a project in Fort de France.

Theo smiled. "I understood why you left. But I still should have checked up on you."

Riley half-turned to face him. "Tell me about you. What happened to you afterward?"

"I managed all right. It took awhile though. At first, the French government made a stab at seizing *Shadow Chaser*, but I turned to my uncle for help. Cole had set me up as a partner of Full Fathom Five Maritime Exploration, and eventually, I was able to get away with the boat. I took her home to Dominica. I was based out of Portsmouth doing some local salvage work for most of the summer hurricane season. Went down and visited Henri Michaut several times. And I built the *Enigma II*. It's a new design for deep water work."

"And how is Henri?"

Theo smiled. "He's doing much better now."

"So where's *Shadow Chaser?*"

"Hauled out down in Puerto La Cruz, Venezuela. We're doing quite a bit of work on her—repairs, new paint, new electronics. You know."

She wondered where he was getting the money for all these repairs, but it wasn't any of her business anymore. "You've really grown up these past months, Theo. You were so boyish when I first met you, and now look at you. You're the captain of *Shadow Chaser* and head of Full Fathom Five."

Theo didn't say anything for over a minute. She felt him stiffen as he watched a tall, slender man in a green jogging outfit who strolled past them. The man wore sunglasses on this cloudy day, and black wires snaked from his ears down inside the collar of his jacket. When the man saw them watching, he began to sing and rock his head back and forth.

Theo patted her hand after the man had passed. They sat there next to the *Surcouf* memorial, both of them staring off to the southwest, lost in their thoughts.

"God, I miss him," she said.

Theo nodded, his lips pressed together in a half smile.

She sighed. "Cole Thatcher and his crazy theories. He sure had a way of getting to you, didn't he?"

Theo nodded.

"I mean, sometimes, I swear I'm suspicious of everything now. I get the feeling I'm being followed, but then the person I suspected just passes on by. I never have proof, but the feeling won't go away."

Theo turned his head to look at the man in the green jogging suit. "I know what you mean."

She took a deep breath and slapped her hands down on her thighs. "So, what does the future hold for Theo? What are your plans?"

"For one thing, I've been invited to your new president's inauguration."

"Theo! You're kidding! How marvelous for you. Are you going with your uncle? Part of some official delegation from Dominica?"

"Something like that. We worked a little magic."

"I guess. Those invitations aren't easy to come by."

Theo smiled at her but said nothing.

"I wish Cole had lived to see this," she said. "Maybe the world isn't as bleak a place as Cole thought. Maybe the Patriarchs..." Riley paused, then took a deep breath. "And my dad—weren't as bad as they seemed. Maybe it was just one crazy, evil man, Diggory Priest, who was responsible for all the killing."

She wanted to believe that.

Theo removed his arm from her shoulder and folded his hands in his lap. She looked at him and saw him suck his lips in over his teeth. Then he looked up at the sky and said, "Yeah."

"But Cole was so sure that the Patriarchs were going to take over the country and steal the election if he didn't get his hands on Operation Magic—and then look what happened. Maybe it was Priest's death. Maybe it was my father's. Or maybe those Bonesmen weren't as powerful as Cole's theories made them out to be. In the end, there were no Swift Boat politics, no hanging chads or dirty rumors that swayed the country, and the people's candidate won. God, I'd love to see Cole's face now."

Theo chuckled. Then he reached down and lifted his backpack. Setting it on his knees, he unzipped the top. He removed a tattered brown padded envelope. "Cole told me to give this to you."

He placed the envelope in her hands. She bit her lip. She wasn't going to cry.

"What's in it?" she asked.

"Just a couple of things he'd want you to have."

Theo stood and walked to the front of the monument. His eyes followed the list of names down the stones, then he looked away. "I have some research to do in the Maritime Museum here, so I'd better go. Investors want a constant feed of news, you know. We've got a new fellow from down in Venezuela pouring money our way. He's all hot about searching for another wreck, in the Pacific somewhere off Thailand, so when we get out of the yard, it'll be business as usual for *Shadow Chaser*." He bent down and kissed her on the cheek. "You take care, Riley. Be careful."

He turned then and strode off back down the jetty.

Her first impulse was to follow him. Why was he leaving so soon? What did he mean, be careful? She wanted to talk, take him out to dinner, hear more about what had happened after she left Guadeloupe.

She looked down at the envelope in her lap. The flap was not sealed. She lifted the folded edge and peered inside.

Riley recognized the book at once. It was the last volume of James Thatcher's journals, the one that ended with the poem. She went to pull it out of the bag, but it was tangled up with some sort of white cord. She yanked harder, and the book slid out along with a small metal square. It was one of those clip-on aluminum iPods. Attached to it was a set of ear buds.

She looked back down the pier and searched the waterfront for Theo's yellow jacket. He was gone.

Riley left the player and ear buds in her lap and raised the book to her face. She inhaled the familiar leather smell. She remained like that, sitting on the seawall, the wind whipping her skirt around her calves, the book pressed to her forehead and nose. If she lowered it, she was afraid someone would see her crying, and she had been so certain she wouldn't let that happen.

A couple of seagulls flew overhead, and the laughing caws startled her. She lowered the book and watched them riding the wind aloft. They were big birds. One of the two had a bit of carrion in his mouth, and the other bird was trying his darnedest to steal it away.

Riley untangled the cord and fit the buds into her ears. She pushed the button to play.

"Hey, Magee," he said, and she pressed the button to stop the player. It was him. She bent forward at the waist, hugging herself. She squeezed her eyes shut against the mounting pressure in her head.

How could she listen to his voice? But then again, how could she not.

She sat up, opened her eyes, and pushed the button again.

"So, you know, if you are listening to this, that things did not go according to plan. I'm sorry about that. Hurting you was the last thing I wanted to do. But I know you are one tough marine—uh, scratch that, one tough *former* marine. You'll survive this. Besides, a man's got to do—as the saying goes—and often he has to do it alone. Sometimes duty takes you far from your loved ones, but it's necessary to keep them safe.

"Speaking of which, did I ever tell you about the time that Theo and I took the *Shadow Chaser* down to a Venezuelan boat-yard for a haul-out? Yeah, we had loads of work to get done, and they have great skilled workers down there. And you know me, what I like best is the fact that their government is not friendly with ours. For the first time in a long time, I felt safe walking down the street. No bad guys hanging in the shadows. I knew that the fatherly American types wouldn't be able to get into the country to find me. So I slept soundly, and I even learned a Spanish lullaby.

"I love traveling abroad. Someday, I hope to visit Southeast Asia. They've got this place over there they call the Dragon's Triangle. It swallows up ships and makes them vanish just like the Bermuda Triangle swallowed up *Surcouf.*

"Listen, even if you believe I have left you alone, I know you will find some small kernel, some chestnut of wisdom that will point you on your way to finding future happiness.

"Good luck, Magee. And by the way, this iPod will self-destruct in five seconds."

The buds in her ears went silent, but Riley could still hear the gulls laughing in the distance. She was smiling, too.

She wiped under her eyes with the sides of her fingers. That last bit was so Cole. She laughed out loud. A shaft of sunlight broke though the dark clouds and bathed the wet stones in a golden glow.

It hurt, but it was a good hurt to hear his voice again. But what in the world was he talking about? Venezuela? He never mentioned that he'd been to Venezuela before. The Dragon's Triangle? Chestnut of wisdom?

"Oh my God," she said aloud. Riley yanked the earbuds out of her ears and clawed at the side of her foul weather jacket trying to find the pocket. She heard the ripping noise as she pulled the Velcro apart. She shoved her hand inside and drew out the bag of chestnuts.

"Southeast Asia," she said. She pictured the ragged man with the sign stating he was a veteran of *La guerre l'Indochine*.

Riley tore through the brown paper, and the chestnuts spilled onto the top of the leather journal, though several clattered to the pavement. Among the nuts, a gold coin shone bright in the momentary sunlight. Riley held up the coin and smiled at the familiar angel with his tablet and the word *Constitution*. Beneath it, there were no minuscule numbers engraved. This was a different coin. A new one. But there weren't supposed to be any others outside the sunken submarine. Henri Michaut had melted down his last remaining coins.

Clutching the French Angel, Riley swept the nuts and the paper off the book. She turned the journal over and started from the back. She found the last entry.

Only this time, the lullaby was in Spanish.

Dear Son,
You've won a battle, not the war. Stay ever vigilant. Jamais fais
do do.
   Arroz con leche me quiero casar
   con una señorita de la capital,
   que sepa coser,
   que sepa contar,
   que sepa abrir la puerta
   para ir a jugar.

The beggar with the black baseball cap and black slicker had been only two to three inches taller than she. That was Cole's height. The big, mirrored shades had covered most of his face, but when he'd touched her, she'd felt something she couldn't describe. It had frightened her, and she'd thought she was going crazy at the time. She'd only ever felt that kind of physical reaction once before.

She clutched the book and stood searching the docks, the waterfront, the faces of all who were near.

No, this was crazy. *But so was he.* It wasn't possible, was it? Why go through all this cloak-and-dagger stuff? Why not just come up to her and tell her if he was alive? Was someone playing a cruel trick on her? Or was there still some kind of real danger out there?

She swiveled her head around and looked at the few people out and about. Could one of them be watching her, hoping she would lead them to Cole?

Riley thought back to that day six months ago. She saw Dig pull the box out of the cargo net, saw the crushed hasp on the box. Could that have been Cole's work? Had he taken the diplomatic pouch out of the lockbox already?

She remembered Theo's invitation to the inauguration. What had he said when she'd asked if it was his uncle's work? *We worked a little magic?*

Operation Magic. Had Cole found it?

She looked at the coin in her hand. Theo said he'd been doing salvage work all summer, that he had visited Henri Michaut. He said he'd built a new *Enigma* that could go deeper. Like into that trench? Cole had promised to visit Michaut after he'd found the wreck.

Riley flipped the coin over. The familiar words, *Liberté, Égalité, Fraternité* were inscribed around the edge of the coin. In the center it read *50 Francs*, and between the number and the word, Riley saw something that looked liked etchings. A Spanish lullaby this time. Etchings on the coin. A new puzzle.

She would find him.

Riley took a deep breath, and the rain-washed air tasted fresh and clean. The ashy taste was gone. She started laughing, and though tears wet her cheeks, she didn't mind this time. The bookstore in town might carry a magnifying glass. And maps. She'd need maps.

She stuffed the iPod into her jacket pocket and started walking back down the quay toward the *centreville*. Her pace quickened until she was almost skipping.

Theo had told her to be careful, so she kept glancing back over her shoulder.

Cole was crazy.

But the next time she looked, the tall man in the green jogging suit had fallen in behind her.

The end

AUTHOR'S NOTE

The true story of the French submarine *Surcouf* is a fascinating and tragic chapter from World War II. When she was commissioned in 1934, she was the largest submarine in the world. In February of 1942, while serving under the Free French flag, she left Bermuda bound for Panama and disappeared. One hundred and thirty-one men died with her, making the *Surcouf* one of the deadliest submarine disasters on record. Though the wreck has never been found, many theories about her demise have been proposed by authors, archeologists, military specialists, and conspiracy buffs.

This book is a work of fiction, and I have taken a great many liberties with what is known and what is surmised about the fate of *Surcouf*. The characters in this book are not based on any of the real crew members of the *Surcouf*, and this imaginary tale does not reflect the great respect and admiration I have for the French and British naval men who sacrificed their lives for the Allies' cause.

It is my hope that my readers will become intrigued with *Surcouf* and spend a little time on the Internet reading about this marvelous chapter in naval history.

–Christine Kling

ACKNOWLEDGMENTS

I would like to thank the following people for their help, ideas, support, and encouragement: Kevin Foster for bringing me the idea of *Surcouf*; James Rusbridger, author of *Who Killed Surcouf*; my editors David Downing, Ramona DeFelice Long, and Mary Jastrzebski; my mentors Jim Hall and Lynne Barrett; friends Bruce Amlickc, Kathleen Ginestra, and Barbara Lichter; my Britishisms reader Judith Reiss; my brother and fight expert Stephen Gray; explosives expert Paul Laska; Intelligence community critics Michael John Smith and Ed Magno; readers Sheldon Nemeyer, M. Diane Vogt, Joyce Li, Kerry Fisher, Linda Lowe, Rochelle Stabb, Emily Adams, Hawkeye Sheene, P. J. Arnn, Lynn Hightower, and the muddlers from Writers in Paradise; members of the Bluewater writers group Mike Jastrzebski, Neil Plakcy, Sharon Potts, and Miriam Auerbach; my fellow contributors at writeonthewater.com; and Akinoluna of afemalemarine.com. Finally, thanks go to my son, Tim, for putting up with my passion for writing all these years.

ABOUT THE AUTHOR

Christine Kling was born in Missoula, Montana, but raised in Southern California, which meant she developed a love for beaches and boating at an early age. After writing for sailing magazines for many years, Christine turned to writing fiction, publishing several thrillers about sailing. She later became an English professor at Broward College in Fort Lauderdale, but retired in 2011; she now lives aboard her thirty-three-foot boat, *Talespinner*, and goes wherever the wind—and free Wi-Fi—may take her.